Cover Design: RBA Designs
Photographer: Wander Aguiar

Jenny Sims, Copy Editing at Editing4Indies
Kristen Johnson, Proofreader
Michele Ficht, Beta Reader,
Andrea Johnston, Beta Reader
Danielle Rairigh, Beta Reader

BEST I EVER HAD

S.L. SCOTT

S.L. SCOTT

THE BEST I EVER HAD

They came without warning—
the storm and the man.
One day, I'll look back and realize they were one and the
same.

PART I

THE FIRST TIME I SAW HER

No halo is hanging over her chestnut-colored hair, and she's paler than most of the sun-worshiping girls at the party. She blends into the background. Not much about her outfit stands out—corduroy miniskirt, sunset-orange tights, ankle boots, and a burgundy top caught at the waist. No one else seems to notice her.

Except me

...And Troy Hogan.

But seeing the way he wraps his arm around her neck, I'd say they're already well-acquainted. That's too bad.

For him.

She may be dating him tonight, but we haven't met yet.

1

Cooper Reed Haywood

Five Months Later

I'VE NEVER BELIEVED in omens or signs, but I've been given several in the past hour.

The lights of Bean There coffee shop shine like a beacon through the heavy pelts of rain. I make a mad dash for the door, swinging it open with more force than necessary in my rush to get inside. No one appears bothered when the bell above the door rings, but I get two quick glances from over the tops of laptops near the counter.

And then they carry on minding their own business.

"Seat yourself," chimes a voice from behind a swinging door. The porthole window gives me a glimpse of the brunette bustling in the back.

I score a table by the window and, as luck would have it, an outlet. My laptop doesn't have enough juice to last the hours needed to write my paper. When my building lost power and the generator didn't kick in, I went to the library. The horde of over-caffeinated and procrastinating students pouring out of the doors told me I'd have no luck in there.

After rubbing my hair dry with the hood of my jacket, I unpack my bag to prepare for the long night ahead. As this coffee shop is on the opposite side of town from where I live and farther from Atterton University's campus than I generally travel for a hot brew, this is my first visit. But it's decent in here, low key with a kind of old-school hideaway vibe to it —lamps instead of bright overhead lights, scuffed wood floors that have seen better days, and jazz playing in the background.

Apparently, I'm the only one not privy to this secret. Every table, though they're small, is occupied. Bags on the floor, laptops open, the unflattering glow of LED white lights reflecting across faces half-hidden by their screens.

Little plates with muffins and coffee cups fill the tables to the point I'm starting to think these people are taking up residency instead of just being here for the evening. That or the staff is slacking. Since I'm not seeing anyone other than the girl in the back, I'm thinking that might be more the case.

When I reach down to plug my laptop in, I hear, "The storm rolled in without warning."

I turn back to see golden-centered hazel eyes peering down at me and a smile that momentarily makes me think sunshine has broken through the rain. But those sunset-orange tights give the brunette beauty away as images of a party last summer come flashing back.

Not sure why I glance down at her ring finger. *Habit, I guess.*

I've been called a player a time or ten, but I've only ever set out to break apart one relationship.

Hers.

Wonder if it worked. "Hi," I say.

Her smile widens. "Hi." When she glances out the window, I'm given a quick chance to study her. *Again.*

It's not been a year since I last saw her, not even quite five months, but she looks a little different. Other than the telltale sign of a small green apron signifying that she works here, the strings are pulled tight around a curvy little waist I wouldn't mind exploring sometime, and her hair is longer with lighter-colored strands blended in.

High cheekbones highlight those pretty hazel eyes and long lashes, but I'm drawn to the natural pink pucker of her lips as she studies the weather outside. Most girls choose cherry gloss, but her mouth is matte. It makes me curious what she tastes like.

A black suede skirt instead of corduroy and the same boots she wore at my party. But that's not the difference I'm sensing. I can't quite put my finger on it.

She shifts to look back at me. "I was saying the storm came out of nowhere."

"The weather app predicted it, but no one expects a summer storm like this in December."

"Not without snow along with it, but the fifties won't get us there. And technically, that'd be a winter storm then."

"I hate snow."

Her smile remains as bright as her eyes. "I don't mind it so much."

"Yeah?" This time, I grin. "What is it about snow that you don't mind so much?"

She slips into the seat across from me without an invitation. I like that about her. Leaning forward as if she's revealing a secret, she replies, "I think it's more the images it conjures. A Baileys Irish Cream hot chocolate by a roaring fire. Curled up in a big, cushy chair reading a book while snow falls outside. Christmas morning and presents under the tree."

"Sounds perfect."

"To me, too." She stands. "Can I get you something to drink and eat?"

I look toward the display cabinet under the counter. Nothing appeals to me, so I eye the chalkboard menu on the wall. "What's your soup today?"

"Tomato basil. It's really good and even better with a grilled cheese." She pushes some hair behind her ear, revealing a name tag pinned to her green apron.

"You know how to upsell," I say, getting a good look at the name that I never got when I first saw her. "Story. That's a—"

"Unique. Weird. Strange name. I get that all the time." She shrugs and laughs to herself. "I could be describing my mom the same way."

Our eyes lock together, and I say, "Beautiful. I was going to say beautiful."

"Oh." Cringing, she seems to lose some of the composure she was holding on to seconds prior. *Ah, fuck.* She blushes, and I know I'm done for. "Um, that's very nice of you to say. Thank you."

"You're welcome, Story."

"Don't go wearing it out now."

God, I'd love to wear it out.

Her laughter dances around us, keeping smiles on both our faces. She's utterly breathtaking. "What's your name?" she asks.

"Story?" Some guy calls out to her from across the café, redirecting her attention to him.

"Be right there, Lou." She turns back to me but thumbs

over her shoulder. "Louis. He's a handful around finals." Snapping a pen and pad from her apron, she asks, "The soup and sandwich?"

"How can I resist?"

"Good choice." With a wink, she walks away but backs up and returns. "And to drink?"

"Coffee. Black is good."

I don't expect a smile in return for my order, but I get one anyway. She's easy to admire. *Pretty, like her name.* It's not one thing specifically, but how her features work together with the heart shape of her face that makes her so appealing. She taps my table with her pen. "I'll be back."

"Hope so."

She backs away, still looking at me, but then runs into the chair of another patron. "Oh, sorry."

The guy has no patience for her and grumbles something under his breath that makes me want to teach him some manners with a punch to the face. I let it go this time, though, and get back to why I'm here in the first place.

"I'm right here," Story says tableside.

"What?"

She drags her free hand under the mug for effect. "Your coffee."

"Oh, that." I rub the side of my neck. "Right. The coffee."

Setting it down, she says, "I didn't mean to sneak up on you."

"Sometimes life does that."

"When you least expect it," we say in unison and then break into laughter.

She rests a hand on the opposite chair and tilts her head like she plans to stay awhile. I can't say I'd be upset by it. I'd rather spend time with her than work on this fucking paper.

"I use that quote all the time, and no one ever knows what I'm talking about," she says.

"Maybe we were the only two who saw the film?"

"Could be." Her eyes widen and capture the shine from a nearby lamp. "There *was* only one other person in the theater when I watched it at the Pantheon."

"Two o'clock showing?"

"Yes," she replies, her smile growing by the second. "Did you know it only played for one day?"

Snapping my fingers, I then point. "The girl with the pickle?"

She bursts out laughing before she quietens and looks around. No one dares to give Story a dirty look. Me, on the other hand, I get three. They're just jealous.

"I feel like I'm owed a secret of yours since you know one of my dirty little ones."

"I have a strong suspicion you're not the only one who eats pickles during a movie."

"True. They do keep the jar right there on the counter. Oh, crap!" She dashes across the shop, pushing through to the back. "Dammit!" Her voice reaches all the way to my table in the front.

I start to wonder if I should offer assistance, but just as I stand, she pushes through the door and heads my way with a plate in her hands. "Everything okay?" I ask.

"It's all good. I burned one grilled cheese to smithereens because I left it too close to the fire on the grill." She sets the plate down with a bowl balanced on top. "Fortunately for you, that was my dinner and not yours."

Looking at the plate and then back at her, I offer, "We can share?" I gesture to the other chair again, my paper now on the back burner near the fire, ready to fail me for ignoring it.

"No, that's yours."

"I don't mind." Picking up one-half of the cut sandwich, I dunk it in the soup. "Chef recommended." I take a bite, letting the creamy soup meld with the cheesy bread. I haven't had a grilled cheese in a long time. I'd forgotten how good they are. The chill from the rain has worn off, but the soup and sandwich warm me on the inside. "It's really good."

Her hand covers her belly, and she looks around as if others are eavesdropping. "My stomach just growled."

I push the plate closer to her. "Take the other half."

"I—"

"I insist."

She bobbles her head in debate and then sits. "Well, since you insist." Picking up the other half, she dips a corner into the soup, then devours a big bite. "Little known fact about the coffee shop. We only make this meal on stormy days. I've pleaded to management to keep it on the menu, but the owner insists it tastes so good because we crave it."

"Absence makes the stomach grow fonder."

"Something like that." She takes another bite and monitors the other patrons. Everyone's too involved in their work to care about her taking a break with me.

When we finish our halves, she moves the bowl to my side of the table. "I appreciate the snack. Now eat your soup." Pushing up, she adds, "I need to get back to work."

Glancing at my laptop, I say, "I guess I should, too."

"I'll leave you to it." She backs away and adds, "Thanks for sharing. The food's on me."

I'm sure she means something entirely different than the images populating my brain. I finish the soup, then dig into my paper. The professor crossed a line when she threatened me with an F. So what if I skipped some classes and forgot about a few assignments? I aced the tests, and I'll be golden when I finish this paper.

If only something more interesting didn't hold my attention. It's when I'm watching her flutter around the shop that I realize that, unlike the party, she doesn't blend in here at all despite the dark-colored clothes.

No, Story is just the book I want to read.

But if memory serves me right, and it always does, she had a boyfriend back in August.

Fuck.

Troy Hogan.

He and I have had more than our fair share of encounters. None went well for him. The thing is, Story was never in attendance. *Did they break up?*

Catching her eyeing me, I grin. She smiles from behind the counter like I didn't just bust her and keeps staring at me. I don't mind those hazel eyes on me, but I can't figure her out.

When that Lou character calls her over again, I check her out. Five-three. Five-four max. Hair kissing the middle of her back. Even through the heavier material of the clothes, I can tell she's got a rockin' little body. She doesn't come off as the type of girl to hide her curves. She just has the confidence to wear what she likes.

Passing by, she drops off a glass of water and swipes the empty plate and bowl. I'd forgotten about the coffee since I only ordered it so I wouldn't get kicked out of the place. I take a sip of it even though it's cooled. I really need to focus, and maybe the caffeine can help.

I stick in my earbuds, turn on a white noise track, and start where I left off in my research. I'm not sure how long I've been working, but when I sit up to stretch, I notice half the place has emptied out.

Story hops off the counter and comes over with a water pitcher. As she tops off my glass, she says, "I never did get your name."

I've thought about this girl over the past five months, wondering what ever happened to her. I'd see Hogan and look for her to pop out of his beatdown truck. That never happened. But here she is as if something bigger just played their hand, and we've hit the jackpot. I hold my hand out. "Cooper."

She slips her hand in mine, and when we shake, she says, "It's nice to meet you, Cooper."

"The pleasure's all mine." Our hands fall apart. Since I was never one to beat around the bush, I ask, "Are you seeing anyone?"

2

Story Salenger

Cooper is so handsome that my body warms under his golden boy glow.

What's not to love or lust when it comes to that razor-sharp jaw or the way his green eyes pierce their target even in the dim light of the coffee shop? Broad shoulders and tall enough to make me feel tiny in his shadow? I can't determine if his athletic build was crafted through workouts or living life to its fullest.

I can't even get started on that hair that's just shy of black to match the images I've already created of him, or I'll be weaving my fingers through the soft waves like he's been doing. It's a tic of his, just like the way his jaw tenses when he's trying to read my mind. With determination set in the pupils of his eyes, I think he might be thinking about more than my social life.

Strangely, I've never seen him around—not on this side of town per se but not even on campus. And although he's asking about my relationship status, I've also wondered about his and who the lucky girl in his life might be and what she looked like. By the clothes, I'm pretty sure a girl on his arm would be on the designer side of fashion instead of walking around in ripped tights and an old sweater.

I'm just not sure that I should get involved in a relationship with only one semester left before graduation. I'll be gone from this town as soon as I receive my diploma.

On the same token, telling him I'm single isn't the same thing as shacking up with the man. Man . . . that's the difference between Troy and Cooper. Troy was a child with too much jealousy coursing through his veins and wasted time on his hands. His troubles were never idle, and I was tired of being dragged into his messes.

Cooper's here doing schoolwork as though he cares about his future. It's refreshing. I reply, "I'm not dating anyone."

He looks down and smiles to himself, but when his eyes find mine again, there's such an honesty in his confidence. Not arrogance. He's just sure of who he is. I probably shouldn't find that trait so attractive.

From what I've learned, the brunt of arrogance and confidence are one and the same. So why would Cooper be different?

I used to be more carefree before . . . *Give him a chance.*

He angles himself toward me in his chair. "I probably shouldn't ask during finals week since I'm sure you have enough going on in your life, but what do you think about getting together over the holiday break? After the semester wraps up?"

"You don't even know if I'm a student."

He scans the room but then comes back to me. "Sure, I do. Everyone here is a student."

"Lou's not."

"Lou comes here because he likes you." His gaze deviates past my hip in Lou's direction. "He can't stand seeing me talk to you."

My head whips around to see Lou's eyes bolt back to his screen. When I look at Cooper, he cocks an eyebrow as if his point has been proven while a smug smirk sits firmly on his expression, giving me a sneak peek of the arrogance that proves my point. He sits back and crosses his arms over his chest. "Am I wrong?"

He's not. Lou comes here for the good coffee and to see me. He's never mustered the nerve to ask me out, but I know he wants to. "Lou is . . ." I roll my eyes. "It doesn't matter about him. We're talking about us."

"I like the sound of that."

Tilting my head to the side, I ask, "Of what?"

He leans forward and dips the tip of his finger in the pocket of my apron. Pulling me closer, he then stands and leans to whisper in my ear, "The possibility of us."

My heart beats quicker as his words race through my veins. The warmth of his breath breezing across my skin has goose bumps rising as if on command.

I lift my chin, causing our cheeks to brush together. "I'm starting to suspect that Zeus's storm raging outside isn't the only god messing with the fates today."

Leaning back, he catches my gaze and stares into my eyes. The smirk has gone and been replaced with a look that causes my breath to catch and lie heavy in my chest. "That only leaves two choices for us, Story. We fight the fates and walk away. Or—"

"We take a chance and follow their lead." With my heart still pounding, I realize that our fate is already sealed.

Although I'm filled with doubts about stepping into

another fire I might not be able to contain, at least his smile is reassuring. "I'll pick you up on Thursday. Seven o'clock."

An electrical surge startles me, taking the lights out, and the coffee shop goes dark. The glow of computer screens dims, but collectively, they shine bright enough for everyone to be seen. I catch my breath and rush to the counter. "It's okay. You can stay until we close or collect your bill if you're ready to go."

Cooper sits at the table, watching as others scramble to gather their things. As I weave through the tables to check on everyone, I start hearing how most don't have cash. We're in a world of technology and don't have a way to pay. Go figure.

I start taking IOUs from the regulars, and the others . . . guess it's an early present for them as they walk out the door.

Since the coffee is already brewed, I guess the rest of the coffee is on me tonight even though the pot is slowly cooling. I know I'll have to cover the disparity out of my paycheck, but I'd just be throwing it out anyway. Ross, the owner of *Bean There Coffee Cafe*, accepts no excuses, no matter how valid. And no electricity in a thunderstorm seems like a valid reason to keep the doors open and the customers happy.

I'm sure he'll see it differently, though.

Screens start to dim over the course of the next hour, and more customers disappear out the front door when I'm in the back cleaning dishes by flashlight. When I return to the front, only one person remains. Cooper's concentration on the screen is intense. He doesn't even hear me come in, though my steps echo in the quiet of the room.

Removing my apron, I place it behind the counter. I'm mentally and physically done for the night, so I sit on the other side of the table from him. He looks up and grins. Removing his earbuds, he asks, "What brings you around, Story?"

"Tossed in the towel. It's just you and me and the storm outside."

He looks around in surprise as if he hasn't noticed the empty room until now. He chuckles. "I fuck up a lot, but I refuse to let my professor be right. This paper is due on her desk by nine o'clock."

"How much power do you have left?"

"Forty-three minutes, apparently."

"Can you finish it in that time?"

"No. I have at least two hours of work left to do." He scrubs his hands over his face and sighs as if exhaustion is about to win the battle. "My apartment lost power. The library was dark, and the bookstore kicked me out when they closed early because of the storm. This coffee shop was a saving grace, but even it can't save my ass this time."

I push to my aching feet again and stare at him. The flirting was fun. It feels good to be looked at like I'm as tasty as our homemade cinnamon buns. Even better that I find myself drawn to him for more than just his looks. There's a vibe that I'm attracted to, one I'd like to explore a little more. *Take a chance, Story.* "Come on. We can go to my place."

He sits up, the right corner of his lips following suit. "Your place?"

I swerve my finger through the air. "We're talking about electricity—"

"I consider it more chemistry that we're sharing."

"Ha," I scoff with a quick roll of my eyes. He's right, but something is so satisfying about not giving him the upper hand. "Look, I texted a neighbor to check in on her, and it seems my rinky-dink building has managed to survive the outage so far. So, if this paper is as important as you say it is, the offer is out there." I leave him watching me walk away.

Who cares if it's dark in here? He gets the drift.

"Either way, I need to lock up, so you can't stay here," I add.

The zipper of his backpack, the sound of his laptop closing, the loose change in his pocket, and then the shuffle of his feet are heard as he slips on his wool coat. "Your place it is, but I have to warn you . . ."

Damn. Maybe I shouldn't have thrown that invitation out so fast. Just because he seems like a nice guy doesn't mean he's not a serial killer. I pull the pepper spray from my back pocket and turn back, holding it in the air. "About?"

His gaze volleys between the pepper spray and me before he chooses to stay on my eyes. "Don't get mixed up with me, okay, Story?" he asks, his decidedly somber tone putting me on edge. With his hands shoved deep inside the pockets of his jeans, I don't worry about my physical wellbeing. After having a good time with him, flirting or whatever we've been doing, I can't say the same about my mental state.

Taken aback by the question, I ask, "But you asked me out? Thursday at seven, remember?"

"I shouldn't have asked you out."

"Wow," I say through a sigh. "I don't think I've ever had someone revoke an invitation for a date before." I give him a thumbs-up and then move to put on my coat. "Thanks for the ego boost. It goes well with being stiffed, not only for the food and drinks tonight but also my tips." Turning around, I throw my arms out wide. "Basically, I was working for free tonight, so this is just the cherry on top."

He comes closer, each step tentative as the floor creaks under his feet. "I don't mean it that way. Sincerely, I find you

incredibly enticing and would love to take you out on a
date."

"Enticing?" I slip my arms into the sleeves of my coat,
then reach for my hat. I laugh, but I'm not humored by this
turnabout. "What are you, a vampire?" Flipping my hair to
one side, I expose my neck. "Should I call you Edward?"

This time, he chuckles. It's real and hardy and worth
making a fool of myself to hear. "No." He snatches my hat,
then pulls it onto the top of my head. Still holding the knit
by the sides away from my ears, he says, "Just a guy who
already knows I'm no good for you."

He returns to his bag and swings it onto his shoulders. I
say, "Lucky for you, I never did have a good sense about
men. Let's go."

"I was afraid you'd say that." As if he's resolved to our
fate, he walks to the door behind me.

After setting the alarm, I grab an umbrella from the
holder. "This one will fit both of us underneath."

We step outside, squeezing into the opening under the
awning as I turn to lock the shop. "How far do you live from
here?"

"Two blocks." It's not just pouring rain. The water flows
like a river down the street. One step down and my suede
ankle boots are ruined forever. I can't afford another pair.
These were a splurge, and they were majorly discounted last
summer.

"Quickest route?" Cooper asks. I lean down, deciding I'm
willing to sacrifice my tights with the new run in them over
my boots, and start slipping them off. "What are you doing?"

When I have the other off, I reply, "I don't want to ruin
my boots."

"We can't even see the sidewalk. There could be glass
and other debris. No way. Put your shoes on."

"I love these boots, and I can't afford to buy another pair." I start to tuck them into my bag, but he stops me.

"You're not going barefoot. Not even for two blocks." A heated beat passes between us, but the tension rolls off his shoulders, and he adds, "I'll buy you a new pair, any pair of shoes you want, but you need to wear those boots."

There's not a threat woven into his tone, but concern had tugged his eyebrows together and dampened the lights in his eyes. I know he's right, but it'll be painful to slip my boots back on, purposely setting out to destroy them. "They'll never be the same."

"Better them than you."

We glare at each other for a few seconds before the standoff ends. "Fine." Using his arm to hold me upright, I slip the boots back on. He may have layers on, but the muscle under it all is rock hard. When my boots are back on, I give him a little attitude. "Happy?"

His eyes dart to my hand that's still squeezing his bicep. "Are you?"

I lower my hand and step onto the flooding sidewalk. "No, but that doesn't matter now. Come on."

Cooper has no problem stepping into the water though his shoes look like leather. Maybe that kind of stuff doesn't matter to him. Maybe he has enough money not to have to worry about such luxuries. He opens his palm. "Hold on to me."

The water rushes against the back of my ankles, pushing me forward. One wrong step and I might be flowing along with it. "This is worse than I thought." I take his hand, and that chemistry he mentioned earlier kicks up my heartbeat along with my adrenaline. We start forward again, walking at a clip that keeps us in control but is also safe.

Cutting down an alley helps alleviate the flooding

waters. Deep puddles have formed, but there's no river running through it. We take a corner, continuing to hold hands as we cross another street that would typically be busy this time of night. The lights of my building ahead draw us in like bees to honey.

"Your block seems to be the only one spared tonight," he observes.

We're soaked up to our knees from splashing through the rainwater, but we've managed to stay dry up top under the umbrella. "Yeah, looks like the Mexican restaurant is still operating. Hungry?"

"Let's get inside, and we can place an order. I owe you for letting me come over anyway."

The three steps leading to the door of my building have managed to stay above the fray of the bad weather. We launch onto the steps and climb up. He tugs the door but whips to face me. "No code or security to get inside?"

"It's been broken for at least two years." I pop the umbrella open and closed a few times to shake the excess rain off. "The landlord doesn't care."

"I do."

"Well, then you can fix it because he's not going to." I dump the umbrella in the corner of the small entry.

A growl rumbles through his chest, and only the sound of the metal door clicking closed overwhelms it. "Tell me you're not on the first floor."

I laugh and start up the stairs. "I'm not on the first floor."

"Good."

Our soggy socks and shoes squish underfoot as we trudge upstairs. When we reach the second floor, and I veer down the short hall, he says, "Really? You're practically the first door someone will find if they enter the building."

I shrug. "What do you want me to say, Cooper?" Exasperated, I add, "I can't help if you don't approve."

Cooper starts working on removing his shoes in the hall. "It's not that I don't approve. My approval doesn't actually matter. It's a safety issue."

I unlock my door and open it, leaning in to set my bag just inside but stay in the hallway. Bending my leg, I reach down and start tugging off my soaked boots. The water did the suede no favors. I think it shrank around my ankle.

"I appreciate your concern, but I'm safe. If you're worried about your safety," I start teasing, "no need to worry. I'll protect you."

"Funny girl." He grins and sets his shoes next to mine beside my doormat.

We tug off our socks and bring them inside the apartment with us.

Holding my free hand out, I say, "Welcome home."

3

Cooper

Welcome home.

Those are the sweetest words spoken to me in a long time.

It's not like I don't have a home. I do, a quite large one where my parents live back in Haywood. I've even technically lived in my apartment long enough to call it home.

But I feel different standing in Story's studio apartment, more of something I'm struggling to pinpoint. I'm already so fucked over this girl. Why?

"This is my place," she says awkwardly and looks around. "There's not much to it, but yeah, it's home."

"I like it." My voice is gravelly, so I clear my throat. "It's nice. It's very . . ."

She looks at me with curiosity in her eyes. "It's what?"

"Very you."

A softer smile shapes her mouth. "I'll take that as a compliment."

"It was meant as one."

Her grin grows as she takes my wet socks from me and carries both pairs with her to the closet. When she opens the door, I see a stackable washer and dryer tucked inside. "Take off your jeans."

"A little forward, don't you think?" I give her a wink.

"Har. Har. You said you need two hours. I can have them washed and dried in that time, then send you into the cold, wet world all clean and warm."

"Well, when you put it like that . . ." I take off my backpack and set it down near the door. She mimics me as we take off our coats and hats. When I reach for the button of my jeans, she says, "I think I'll change in the bathroom. I have some baggy pajama bottoms that might fit you in the second drawer of the dresser. You can borrow them if you want."

When she disappears into the bathroom, I look around again, using the time to see what Story's life is all about. A collection of hats hangs above the front door, and a rickety bookcase leaning to one side just inside the door looks ready to retire. The dresser she mentioned is in the corner, and a flow of furniture leads to a wooden desk under the window.

Despite the small space, she went with a queen-sized bed. Her nightstand has a stack of hardback books under a tiny blue lamp and a charger hanging over the drawer in the front.

Three doors align the other wall, the farthest one she entered being the bathroom. I can assume a closet, maybe two. No table in the kitchen area eats up space, and another tall dresser anchors the left side of the door.

It's not much, but she's made the most of the available space.

Moving to the corner, I slowly open the drawer and see

everything neatly tucked inside—shirts, tiny shorts, and the pants she was referring to. I pull a plaid pair out and toss them on the bed. After stripping off my jeans, I slip the pants on. Why she's wearing a men's large, I have no idea. They must swallow her whole. As for me, they hang just a bit at the waist, but they're about six inches too short. I'll suffer through the embarrassment if it means I have clean and dry jeans by the time I finish this paper.

The door opens, and she comes out dressed in a fuzzy light blue robe with bare legs and feet. She's fucking adorable. Holding it together at the neck, she says, "I forgot to grab clothes to change into."

"I can close my eyes if it makes you more comfortable."

"It's fine. Make yourself at home." She comes around the bed, then stops, quickly covering her mouth to mute her laughter.

"Yeah, they're a little short."

"Sorry, I shouldn't laugh. But yeah, they're a lot too short." She continues to giggle and eye me as she passes. "They grow them big wherever you're from."

"My mom was a model. She's tall, like five-ten or so. Or used to be. She claims she's shrinking, but it's hard to tell. And my dad is six-three."

"My mom just cleared five feet, so I'm lucky I hit five-four. I'm like a giant compared to my family." She opens the second drawer and pilfers through the items until she finds something that appears to satisfy her and snatches them.

I'm still waiting for her to mention her dad and give me insight into her life, but that reference never comes. "A real giant," I joke when she passes in front of me again. She doesn't even notice how she could walk under my chin without a connection.

She disappears again, and I look around. I assume I can

set up on the desk, so I grab my bag and start pulling the cable and laptop out.

Story exits the bathroom, then starts our clothes in the washer. I'm still surprised she has the space for the units. "It's nice to have the washer and dryer."

"Comes in handy, but it's a total luxury."

"I don't have one in my apartment."

Disbelief colors her hazel eyes when she turns back to me. "That's a surprise. I thought most apartments came with them these days."

Not wanting to talk about laundry in the limited time we have together, I ask, "Is it okay to use your desk?"

"Yes, I can highlight my chapters from the bed."

I sit down and power my computer back up. "What are you studying?"

"History. I can code my way out of a prison cell, but my memory for world history is not the best. I put this class off as long as I could, and now it's catching up with me if I want to graduate."

Swiveling to face her as she settles on the bed, I ask, "When do you graduate?"

"Next spring if I stay on track. You?"

I nod. "Same."

Her sweet smile renders me speechless. I hate that I put the brakes on earlier when I could be spending time admiring her. But looking around, she's got a good thing going. She has her life together, was smart enough to drop the dead weight of Troy Hogan, has a job, and goes to school. She doesn't need me impeding her goals.

Why does she have to make it so hard to turn away from her?

I do anyway, forcing myself to leave her be.

I'm about five minutes into my research when she says, "I forgot to offer you something to drink."

Looking back, because yeah, I want to see her again, I say, "I'm okay."

"Hungry?"

Starved actually. Soup and half a sandwich aren't going to tide me over, but it's not her job to keep me fed. "I can order from the restaurant downstairs."

"I could eat a taco or two." Grabbing my phone, I pull up a delivery app. We find the restaurant and order. "How much do you think they'll hate us for ordering in this weather?" she asks.

"Don't worry. I'll make it worth the trip in tip."

Her expression sours, but she doesn't say anything. She slinks lower in the bed and returns her attention to the book, the highlighter poised in her hand and ready for battle in the chapter.

Reading women's minds has never been my forte, so I stopped. But this feels different. I want to know what Story is thinking, what turned her expression from smiling to seemingly upset. "Did I say something wrong?"

Her eyes are the only things that move in acknowledgment. She then closes the textbook and sits up. "I work in a service capacity, and you don't know how many times people think they can treat me how they please if they just tip."

Rummaging through what I said to make her so defensive, I hit the line and instantly regret saying it. "I didn't mean—"

"I know, Cooper. That's why I didn't say anything." She scoots off the bed and heads into the kitchenette, which takes up a large corner of the small space. Taking out two cups from the cabinet, she continues, "Not everyone can be bought and paid for." She fills the glasses with water from the tap.

I don't think I've had tap water since . . . well, since ever. When she hands me the glass, she sits on the end of the bed across from me. Concern nor worry lies on her face. Patience comes and goes before she finally says, "It's not worth any tip to brave the storm outside, so let's just call it as it is—us being too lazy to pick up our order."

"I'd need pants to go out, even if it's just downstairs. Since I currently have none, I wasn't saying it to offend the delivery person."

"As I said, I know you didn't. It just felt personal even though I know it wasn't."

I'd already included a hefty tip but go back into the app and double it. She crawls back onto the bed, and we let the conversation lie like a canyon between us. I'm not usually one to give in to the whims and moods of others, but I can't concentrate on my work knowing she's upset. I swivel back around and rest my forearms on my legs. "I've hurt your feelings. I'm sorry."

This time, she gets up and comes closer. Crossing her legs in front of her on the mattress, she toys with the hem at her ankle, tugging a thread free from her pants. "Thank you, Cooper. I appreciate that."

I don't think she's oversensitive about the subject, but how can I ignore the reason behind her emotions? People are assholes. And that they're assholes to her is unacceptable.

A knock on the door rattles the wood. Jumping up, she goes to answer it. "I've never ordered delivery before, but that was fast." When she opens the door, she smiles, her guard completely down, totally unaware of any potential danger.

She takes the bag and is thanking him profusely when he looks around her to find me. "You Cooper?"

"Yes." I'd stand, but the short pajama pants knock points off my clout.

"Thanks," he says, holding up his phone. "Biggest tip I've ever had."

I nod. "No worries."

Story says, "Stay safe." She closes the door and twists around toward me with a knowing grin glued to her face. "Thank you."

"He deserved it."

We sort through the bag and take our meals to our respective areas where we've each set up our stuff. The tacos are tasty, and I finish mine a lot faster than I would have expected.

"You were hungry."

"I was." No long story will get this paper finished, so I turn my full attention to the screen and get back to work.

Just shy of the two-hour guesstimate, I wrap up this son of a bitch. With my hands behind my head, I rock back in the chair as relief washes through me. I'm ready to celebrate, so I swivel around. "I just—"

Bundled in a mess of blankets and pillows, Story is curled onto her side and sound asleep. There's so much about her that I'm drawn to, but I still can't pinpoint what it is besides her obvious beauty. I've been with a lot of pretty girls. It's kind of standard fare for me.

Something deeper, buried in the treasure of her eyes, tightens the pull to her. A need to not just get to know her but also to protect the innocence that remains. She looks at me like I'm not the bad guy, like I'm not the person so many have already deemed me to be.

She has a weakness for trouble, and unfortunately for

her, I have a fondness for her. Maybe it's like what Story said and the gods have already plotted our fate. Are we just puppets who need to go along with it?

I rub my eyes that burn from staring at a screen for too long and then run my hands through my hair.

My family would love her. My friends would think she's cute. She's everything I could use for damage control with the Atterton University's professors to graduate on time. They'd think I turned over a new leaf.

I'm not above using someone to get what I want. But I won't take advantage of someone who has pure intentions. *Fuck.* I don't even know this girl's last name, and I've already decided she needs protecting. *From me.*

She may be good for my image, but I'm bad for hers.

I get up, needing to get back to my life and out of hers, and check on my pants. They're still damp, so I set the dryer for another thirty minutes, then return to the desk.

I quietly pack my bag but then sit to wait for my jeans, not sure what to do other than stare at Story while she sleeps, making the most of the opportunity. I lean into it, resting forward to get a better look. Her dark lashes cast a long shadow over her cheekbones, and her lips have a sweet bow at the top that I wouldn't mind tracing with my tongue.

As much as I want to act like our meeting tonight is a coincidence, more than one event has brought us together. What are the chances that we were in that film at the same time last October? Or that we were within twenty feet of meeting at my party last summer? Unlike what she thinks, I have a feeling fate is telling us we're not meant to be together.

Since when did I listen to authority?

Story's lids flutter open, and she stares at me as if she's still dreaming. When the edges of her lips roll upward, she says, "You're here." Her voice straddles the line of sleep and reality.

"I am. I just finished my paper."

"That's great news. Congratulations." Something in her voice and in her sweet expression is so honest, so genuine that I can't help but wish things could be different between us.

I can't be the good guy she deserves. Based on what I know about her past dating relationship, I already know she'd be willing to travel the path I'd drag her down if I let her.

No, I need to get out of here before she does my head in by making me doubt my decision. I stand, already packed and ready to go, except my jeans are still drying. I'll take them wet if it means saving both of us the trouble of what comes next.

But then she asks, "Do you want to stay?"

Fuck.

4

Story

Cooper is different.

I remind myself not to hold my past against him. I hope he can offer me the same favor in return. Some can't. If I can find out earlier, it's better for both of us to walk away unscathed.

My nerves kick in because, despite the offer, I don't normally invite strangers to my apartment, much less into my bed. *What am I doing?*

Rejection starts blooming in my chest as he stands in front of the door like he's ready to bolt. Where's the confidence from earlier? I'd even take a little arrogance right now.

Glancing down at *my rainy days are for reading* T-shirt and pink flannel pants, I realize they may not be a set or even sexy, but I wasn't going for either when I put them on. Then I remember he canceled our date for Thursday before I had a chance to accept the invitation. I've misjudged the situation and read him all wrong. Embarrassed, I sit up and pull the covers off, ready to send him on his way.

It doesn't matter that he's so handsome, and I was flattered he gave me the time of day. Or that talking to him has come easily and that neither of us feels the need to fill in any empty space.

Who cares if holding his hand in the rain made my heart quicken and sent butterflies fluttering wildly out of control in my tummy? I haven't had this feeling in forever. Keeping myself closed off has a lot to do with it. Not believing I deserve better plagues my psyche.

I have no idea why I'm suddenly feeling hopeful where a guy's concerned. My mom always said never to trust a man.

Cooper came out of nowhere, needing Wi-Fi and a power source, so I shouldn't start tripping over myself, thinking it's more. It's not like the universe planted him in my path or anything.

"I'll stay," he says with a look that can be read as nothing less than genuine.

"Really?" I look at him, the way he scratches the back of his neck, not posturing like other guys do or putting on a front full of masculine pride. Trying to act casual and less desperate for his attention, I quickly add, "Only if you want. Don't do it for my sake."

Half a smirk appears like magic, and he chuckles. "Trust me, this is for me." He clicks the lamp off on the desk, then signals toward the kitchenette. "Light on or off?"

"I trust you, Cooper."

If I'd looked away, I would have missed the way his pupils narrowed before he moved to turn out the light in the kitchen area. His silence penetrates the darkness as he comes around the bed again. With the shade still open, the rain shines under the streetlamp just outside my building.

Sticking to the other side of the bed, he climbs in next to me, a total stranger, as if he's done it a million times. *Has he? Is this normal for him? Is he a player that I've not been warned about?*

I swear I can find a troubled soul in a haystack, but Cooper doesn't give off those vibes. Did I miss a red flag?

I'm lonely.

That's reality.

But letting just anyone fill the void won't get me to where I want to go in life. This isn't sex. It's kindness. I can't send him out in this weather, so this is nothing more than two people getting some shut-eye during a torrential rainstorm. *That's all.*

Your instincts are wiser than your head. Remembering one of my mom's favorite phrases, I smile to myself.

"No funny business," I say, trying to lighten the mood as I crawl back under the covers to settle in for the remainder of the night.

His hands go up in surrender. "Nothing funny going on here."

"I'm thinking there's a double entendre buried somewhere in that comment." I lie back and pull the covers up to my neck. "It's now or never."

"You seem tense." When he lies back, he tucks an arm under his head, then looks my way. "You sure about this, Story?"

I nod. "What am I supposed to do? Kick you out into the flooding streets and downpouring rain?"

"Yeah, and you'd have every right to do so."

Resignation returns to his features, dragging down the smile that I prefer on his face. I say, "Like I said, I trust you."

"You shouldn't trust guys around beautiful women. They're usually using lines to get you into bed."

"Well, looks like we skipped a step because I'm already here."

He grins again, but it's short-lived. "I think it's best if we go to sleep."

I didn't realize there were other options on the table, but now I can't help but wonder what they were.

Cooper closes his eyes with a sigh, his hand running from the back of his head over his face where he stops to rub his brow. The whole world appears to weigh him down.

"Finals suck," I say, breaking the quiet that had fallen between us.

His laughter rocks the mattress, and he looks at me. "I needed that."

"A good laugh? Yeah, feels good to—"

"Feel good." The lightness disappears again, and the earlier tension returns. "Where'd you come from, Story?"

I can just make out his eyes in the light that sneaks in from outside. There's an intensity that warms me, a depth to them that makes me feel like I'm important. If he can make me feel so much with a look in his eyes, it makes me curious what else he can do. I reply, "I've been here all along."

The brush of his fingers against the back of my hand sends goose bumps rippling across my skin, a simple touch that has me silently pleading for more. It's been so long since I've been touched, appreciated in a way that reminds me I'm one among humanity, that I'm not an island left to drift out to sea alone.

"Cooper?" I whisper.

"Yes?" The tension I feel inside has scratched his throat, making his smooth voice rough around the edges.

"Why did you cancel our date?" I roll to my side to face him, but his gaze stretches out the window into the rain. The pause becomes more as it lengthens, causing me to fill with doubt again. I hate that I don't do this better, that I don't understand the dynamics of a relationship. "Be honest," I say. Good or bad, I need him to be straightforward with me.

When his eyes return to mine, he searches my face as if he's mesmerized by the prisms in my eyes—fascinated and in awe.

His hand finds mine under the covers, his heat pressing to my skin. "Because I like you."

"You don't know me. That's what the date was for."

Pulling my hand to his mouth, he whispers against my fingers. "I know enough to know I should stay away from you."

"Here we go with that again. This isn't *Twilight*, and I don't believe in vampires."

His smile shines in the low light. "No, but you asked me to be honest. I asked you out because I find you incredibly attractive. I called it off because I enjoyed our encounter enough to know that I'm not the guy for you."

"That doesn't make sense, Cooper."

"Hmm," he hums but doesn't feel the need to go into it deeper. He kisses my fingers instead, one by one until all five are done, then our fingers fold together. "When's the last time you laid in bed with someone you just met?"

"Never."

He chuckles, though I didn't mean my answer to be funny. It's just the truth. Still grinning, he says, "We should sleep. Our finals tomorrow won't ace themselves." My hand is released, and he closes his eyes again. "It's been a long fucking day."

I shouldn't want him here or like his touch so much. I shouldn't want him to kiss me or wonder if he'll be gentle or rough. There's so much I shouldn't want or do with Cooper, but my better senses flew out the window the moment I invited him home. The more deviant ones took over when I asked him to stay in my bed. "It has," I reply, slightly breathless as I build up the courage to take advantage of this man beside me.

He looks at me like something's wrong. "Are you okay?"

"I'm okay."

The back of his hand presses to my cheek. I don't move away but lean in, wanting his heat all over. "You're warm. You might have a fever."

I can't hide my physical need for touch . . . for his touch specifically. Embarrassed by my ridiculous reaction to a gorgeous man in bed with me, I turn away and lie on my back. "I don't have a fever."

The tip of his finger taps my chin to angle me toward him again. "Are you turned on, Story?" His dulcet tone reaches into my chest, breaching my inhibitions and making me want to confess my sins.

Each beat of my heart now thunders as nerves kick in. "I just . . ." I start but take a hard breath to swallow down the profession that lumps in my throat. "I don't know what I'm doing."

"It's okay, sweet girl. We'll take it one step at a time." He leans in and kisses my forehead. "We'll do what feels right or nothing at all."

Loosen up.

Go off instinct.

Go by what feels right.

I exhale in a feeble attempt to stop my heart from racing.

"There was no expectation other than getting my paper done. Now we're just two people spending time together while this storm blows through."

Nodding, I'm unable to think clearly under his appreciative gaze. Though my mind is scrambling, I'm starting to think we're on two totally different pages. I was thinking this was leading somewhere.

He turns to face me. "What were you thinking?"

"Nothing. My mind is a blank canvas." He cocks his eyebrow, and I shrivel in humiliation. "I mean, sure, yeah, we're two people passing time in the same bed, but . . ."

"But?"

I gulp . . . loud enough for him to hear, and my nervousness threatens to drag me under.

A wry grin spreads like wildfire, and he leans in. My breath catches, and I close my eyes just as he's about to kiss me. And then I stay completely still . . . waiting for the moment, for a kiss I never saw coming but welcome wholeheartedly without the usual foreplay of flirting, banter, and first dates. Wait, I got two out of three.

Rejection begins licking the wounds of my battered heart the longer I wait with no contact. My eyes fly open to find Cooper staring at me. He's so close that his breath warms me when he says, "I thought it wise to give you one last chance."

"Chance for what?"

"To change our fate."

Our eyes are fixed on each other's long enough for me to gather the courage to touch his cheek. The scruff from a day or more since he had a good shave is coarse against my palm, but I press into it, the thrill of being so close to someone so masculine, so hard in all the good ways and gentle in how he treats me, taking over. Maybe I'm making a big mistake, but it's one that Cooper has me craving.

I lift on my elbow and lean closer, so close that I tilt my head just slightly to taste his breath. "I think it's too late."

I'm going to kiss this man. I'll blame it on the hour and feeling confident.

But his hands cup my face before I can, holding me while his gaze volleys between my eyes. Then he whispers, "I really wish you wouldn't have said that."

His mouth crashes into mine, and when I part my lips and our tongues touch for the first time, I know it won't be the last.

5

Cooper

Untethered from her inhibitions, Story moans into my mouth as her hands slide over my shoulders. Her grip tightens over my muscles as she rocks against me.

This is not something I could have predicted. Not with her. I can get laid any day of the week, but that's not what tonight was about. *At least not how it started.*

Is this how I want it to end?

Fuck yeah, I'd like a good time with her.

And by how she's kissing me, I'm not alone.

But . . . why is there an ounce of doubt lingering in the back of my mind?

I move to hold her by the waist and pull her close, our bodies finding purchase against each other and evoking another delicious moan from her. *Fuck.* Why'd she have to tempt me? Didn't her daddy teach her that playing with the devil never ends well?

Slipping a leg between hers, I run one hand over her hip while keeping the other in place around her waist. The pajamas she's wearing don't do her body justice, but I like that she chose comfort over anything else, including me.

What's the fun if dinner is served on a silver platter?

I'd much rather work for dessert.

She grinds against my thigh, and my head fucking spins from the thought of seeing her get off on me. Story has me feeling like a teenager making out in my Jaguar back in high school. Something about kissing her feels like the first time all over again. I don't remember my first kiss, much less who it was with, but I know I won't forget this, not with her.

Despite how hard she's made my dick, I never planned for this to happen, but the way our tongues tangle and our bodies move together, this feels too good. If I'm leaving, I know this is my last chance. I rip my mouth from hers, leaving both of us panting.

Her lashes flutter open, and a smile follows right after. "What is it?"

I push a section of hair behind her ear and look at her. God, she's beautiful, like the first time I saw her. It didn't matter that it was across a crowded room. This girl stood out to me, and now I realize why. She's an angel, her eyes peering at me like she knows who I am inside but doesn't hold it against me. I caress her cheek just to feel her again. "How are you real?" I whisper.

Her cheeks flame red, growing hot to the touch. "I don't understand."

I kiss her, her lips fire against mine. Resting my forehead to hers, I inhale her, weakening with each taste I get. "I have a confession." Still conflicted if we should even be doing this, I decide it might be too late to change our minds. I don't want to keep any secrets from her. Our bodies are still entwined, and I kiss each of her heated cheeks. When I lean back, I add, "I saw you once."

"I know. I was making a fool of myself by eating a large pickle in a movie theater."

This girl makes me smile so effortlessly that I'd thought I'd forgotten how. "No. I mean, *yes*, you were eating a pickle, but no, you weren't making a fool of yourself. I enjoyed watching you devour it if you want to know the truth."

She giggles and readjusts, keeping her hands on my shoulders as her middle stays pinned to mine.

Gripping her hip, I like that she's soft without bones sticking out, and has curves that could be considered dangerous when wet. And just like that, my imagination goes wild. I add, "You and I were together another time."

Intrigued, she wrangles her brows together when she asks, "We were?"

"Once at a party on Rainer Street."

"Last summer?" She digs her head into the pillow, smiling. "The one on top of the hill? Mirrored building?"

"Yeah."

"That place was amazing. The view of the city, the bartender, the fancy furniture. It looked like it was straight out of *Architectural Digest*. Pure money. Didn't you love it?"

"The place is great, but—"

"How did you end up there? Do you know who lives there?" She rolls onto her back with a dreamy look in her eyes. When she glances back at me, she asks, "What do you think it's like living somewhere so nice, so expens—?"

"Story." She looks at me with innocence tainting her eyes.

"It's okay, but I don't want to talk about the apartment or the party."

"Okay," she says, smiling gently. Reaching over and running her hand over my chest, she rests it on my shoulder. "What do you want to talk about?"

"I was there when you walked into the party." I don't know if I'll worry her by sounding like a stalker or if she'll appreciate the admission, but it's too late to turn back now.

Her eyes stay steady on me, and I'm grateful her smile doesn't falter. "I didn't see you."

"No, you were with someone else."

"My ex," she says, lowering her eyes to my chest. "We actually had a terrible fight that night in the bathroom." She peeks up at me again.

"I wish I would have known." I'm not innocent in this, but a failed attempt at a coup for her attention doesn't mean I should take the blame for their relationship.

"There was nothing you could have done. He has a terrible temper. It's one of the reasons I broke up with him."

"You broke up with him?" I want to grin but hold it in, though the hope in my question is unmistakable. She nods. Thinking of Hogan losing her brings more joy than I'd be able to explain if she busts me for laughing, though, so I clear my throat, trying to temper my tone. "What were you fighting about?"

"We fought all the time, but that night it was about a girl he wanted to hook up with." She shakes her head as if the memory itself annoys her all over again.

"I don't understand. He was with the prettiest girl there."

Her body eases, the wall she was starting to build falling as she looks at me like I just hung the moon for her. "That's so sweet, Cooper."

"I mean it, Story. I couldn't take my eyes off you." My gaze lowers to her chest as it rises and falls heavier under my confession. "I went to get a drink, and when I turned back, you were gone. When I saw you at the coffee shop, I didn't say anything, but I recognized you."

"Why are you telling me this?"

"Because I don't want any secrets between us." One I never expected to haunt me still does, but I'll bury it so deep that light can never find it.

Without saying a word, she stares at me, making me feel unlike myself. I'm not someone who doubts himself, but I start rubbing my chest like I can make this knot go away. "Cooper?"

"Yes?"

"I know we're kissing and stuff, but are you thinking that . . .?" She looks down again and smiles to herself. God, I wish I knew her secret.

"That what?"

"You're telling me because you think we'll see each other again?"

"I'm telling you that I didn't know who you were at the party, but when I saw you again tonight, I wasn't going to waste a second chance."

She tugs me closer by fisting my shirt. "I think you succeeded, considering you're in my bed." Her lips press to mine, and when our lips part, our tongues tango together again.

It doesn't matter that the universe gave me the perfect setup and created an opening through a torrential storm. I'm kissing this girl not because she's stunning or because it's raining outside. I'm kissing her because . . . *Why am I kissing her?*

Because we're here with nothing else to do? I call bullshit. I needed electricity, and she gave me access to that. Nothing else was on the table until she asked me to stay. Then our mouths became opposite electrical charges attracted to each other.

There are a million reasons I should have walked out that door.

But I only needed one to stay. *Her.*

I can kiss anyone. *Oh, shit.*

Story is gorgeous, even her heart is filled with beauty, but that look in her eyes makes me believe that maybe I'm not such a bad guy and has me leaning in and giving her another kiss.

Her hands press against my chest until our eyes meet again. She sees through me. "Hey, Cooper," she whispers, "let's not overthink this. It's just . . ." Her eyes leave mine but only momentarily. "It's just what we want to make of it."

Feeling my heartbeat pick up and the lightness escaping the room, I cup her face. "What do you want to make of it, Story?"

"I don't need much to be content. I'm easy like that." She starts laughing. "Well, not easy. I'm actually quite difficult in *that way* despite the offer to not only stay the night but spend it in bed with me."

Running a finger down the bridge of her nose, I lean and kiss the tip before going lower and kissing her quick on the lips. "Easy or hard, I'm glad I stayed." I'm about to kiss her again when the room brightens without the rain siphoning the light from the streetlamp. The rain has slowed, and maybe we have as well, but then Story gets to her knees and decides to straddle me, making me realize I've been so stuck in my head that I almost missed this moment.

"Bold and beautiful." *Damn, she's sexy.*

When she draws figure eights over my shirt, I'm tempted to strip it off just to feel her touching my skin. "I don't know if we have tonight or more, but I don't want to think about that and plan it all out. I just want you. You think you can handle that, Coop?" she asks.

When she punctuates her question with a wriggle of her hips, I give her a once-over. She wiggles again, this time with a lot more pressure against my hardness. *Fuck me.* The first time I try to be an upstanding guy and she's determined to be the death of me. Reaching up, I run my hands under the hem of her shirt. "Guess we'll find out."

I roll over and hover on top of her, balancing on my elbows as I kiss her until she's breathless and squirming for more. She starts tugging at my shirt and then going lower to run the tips of her fingers under the top of the pajama pants.

Kissing lower, I lay a trail down her neck as I run a hand over the ebb and flow of her waist to her hip. But then I back up and slide my hand under the top of her fleece pants. Damn, I'm such a sucker for her soft skin. I press my cock against her leg, and when she sucks in a breath, I return to those kiss-swollen lips to steal one again.

Sliding my hand around to her stomach, I start to go lower when the elastic starts giving way for me. Against her lips, I whisper, "You are so incredibly sexy."

The words spur her on, and she presses her fingertips into the top of my ass. "You are so hard."

I chuckle. "Have you not noticed another part of me? Kind of hard to miss."

"I've noticed," she says with a smile. "I just like all of your body."

"I like that, and you, and your killer body." I kiss her again because although it's fun to laugh, I'd rather keep my mouth busy on her. As if we didn't miss a beat, she moves her hands around to my front and dips under my boxer briefs, and I slide mine lower into her silk panties.

Still balancing on one forearm, I feel my muscles tensing until I wedge my knee between hers to even the load of my weight. Placing a trail of kisses to her ear, I whisper, "What are you thinking about?"

"How close your fingers are to where I want them, but how they still seem so far away."

I reach the softness between her legs and dip my middle finger between her lips. "Still too far?" Before she answers, I circle her bud, making her buck in pleasure.

I didn't want to fuck her because she's not like other girls I hang out with, but man, she makes it hard. *Literally.* I go lower and tease her entrance just as she teases the tip of my dick.

"Fuck," I growl as she takes hold of my erection.

When she squeezes and starts sliding, I finger-fuck her because damn, she feels amazing. The sound of our connection drags me under until I move by need and want, urge and craving. I thrust into her hand as we kiss erratically.

Dark brown hair, those eyes that stole my soul. Sunset tights and a smile that could compete with her halo. This girl has me caught in some memory and blown away that I'm with her now. What are the chances that I'd ever see this girl again? But here she is in her captivating beauty getting me off. Fuck. My stomach clenches, trying to stave off from coming.

The buildup isn't long before I'm tempted again, though, so I pump in and out of her, tease her clit, and deepen the kiss until she's pushing onto me, our bodies moving together and against each other. Her release strikes, sending her head back and her mouth wide open as her body tremors around my finger.

I let go, not able to hold on any longer. I can't with her. I come hard and fast, pumping into her hand until every drop of my pleasure is released . . . into my pants.

Fuck.

Rolling off her, I fall onto my back and drape my arm

over my head. Our heavy breaths are all that's heard before I finally look over at her. "How was that?"

"I'm glad you stayed."

6

Cooper

Story is scorching hot.

Literally.

Restless but still sleeping, she has sweat rolling down her temples. Earlier in the night, she was hot, so much so that I suspected she might have a fever. I reach over to feel her head with the back of my hand.

Shit. She's sick.

I check my phone from the edge of the desk. It's just past six. I get out of bed, trying to figure out where she might keep cold or flu medicine while wondering how long I have until I get sick since my mouth has been all over her. Well . . . almost all over her. There was a territory I was hoping to explore with my mouth later today after turning in my paper. I guess that's off the table.

For now.

In the meantime, I head into the bathroom and do what I was always told not to—dig through her medicine cabinet. I don't snoop through the general stuff but narrow my search for certain containers. I grab the Tylenol, knowing I'll need to find a pharmacy open at this hour once I see what symptoms she has.

I get a cup of water, sit next to her on the bed, and have two pills ready on the nightstand before I wake her. "Story?" I whisper, stroking her cheek. She groans but doesn't wake up. I've already been exposed, so I lean in and kiss her cheek. "Story?"

Her eyes fly open, and she sucks in a harsh breath, scrambling away from me. My hands fly up in front of me. "It's me. Cooper."

Through jagged breathing, she loosens her grip on the sheet and pillow as she comes to. "Cooper," she says as if I'm a breath of fresh air. She smiles. "Oh my God, Cooper. It's you."

"Yeah." I smile and nod. "It's me." Leaning forward, I rub her leg over the blanket. "You have a fever, Story. How are you feeling?"

Raising her hand up, she asks, "I do?" When the back of her hand rests against her forehead, her eyes go wide. "I feel hot, and my head hurts."

I hand her the cup and the pills. "Take these. They can help with the pain and the fever. It was all I could find, but I'm thinking you need something stronger."

A look of disgust tightens her lips when she sees the pills. She pushes up to stand. "I'll be okay." But then she wobbles and ends up staying seated.

"You're sure about that?" When she looks at me out of the corner of her eyes, it's then that I see how bloodshot they are. Taking hold of her arm, I help her to lean back. "I think you should take the pills, drink the water, and lie back down."

"I think you're right." She swallows hard as if her throat

has dried. Waving me off, she says, "You should go. I don't want you to get sick."

"Hmm. I'm pretty sure it's too late for me, especially after what we did a few hours ago."

A satisfied grin tips her lips up. "I suppose you're right, but just in case."

"No. You need someone to take care of you." I help her lie down again after she takes the pills. Going to the desk, I grab my phone again and start looking for pharmacies that deliver. When I find one, I ask, "Runny nose?"

"Not yet."

"Congestion?"

She rolls to her side with her hands tucked under her head. "Coming on."

"Fever? Yes." I glance up from my phone. The woman is beautiful even when she's sick. "No itchy eyes, but are you fatigued?"

"Always."

I chuckle because I can relate. "More than usual?"

When she reaches for her phone, she tilts it from the nightstand and glances at it. "It's six in the morning, so I can honestly say I'm exhausted."

"Valid." I pick a few over-the-counter medicines to be delivered, but when I go to check out, a message pops up that it's unavailable for delivery. "Shit," I grumble. Glancing back at the window, I'd almost forgotten about the storm earlier. It's probably what made her sick—the way it swept in without warning, along with the cold air.

I look at her with her red cheeks and the cherry tip of her nose, and say, "No one's delivering, but you need meds. I'm going to head out and get some supplies."

Grabbing my hand, she says, "You don't have to go out. We'll sleep, and I'll go get stuff later."

"I think it's better."

She props up on her elbow. "We don't know if electricity has been restored. You could end up traveling miles, and you don't even have a car."

"I have a car. It's parked at my place." . . . in the garage. *Fuck.* If there's no electricity, the security gate won't rise. Rubbing my chin, I try to think of another solution. "What's around here? A grocery store, convenience store, or pharmacy?"

"There's a twenty-four-hour pharmacy one block over and a convenience store where the street dead-ends into Atterton Drive." She flops back down, seeming exhausted just from holding herself up. Cuddling under the covers, she adds, "But I don't want you going out just to find they're closed because of the storm."

I'm already up and heading to the dryer to retrieve my jeans. I'd dropped the pajama pants when I got too hot during the night. Now I know it was her who was heated. Checking my own forehead, I don't notice a fever, and I feel fine so far. "I don't mind."

"I don't want you to go, Cooper."

After opening the dryer, I stand and look at her, pausing to admire the concern in her eyes. "Why not?" I tug on my jeans, but with the flap still open, I bend down to put my socks on.

"I feel bad."

"I know. That's why I'm going." I wink and return to my bag while zipping up my fly. I shove my wallet and phone into my pockets.

"No, I feel guilty."

"Don't." After snagging my hat from the desk, I go around to kiss her on top of the head. "I want to go. Try to get some sleep, and I'll be back before you know it."

She grabs my sleeve before I get out of reach. "Cooper?" I stop and sit down again. Her mouth opens, but then she closes it again.

"What is it?"

"This is a lot in one night. You didn't sign up for this when you decided to come over."

"It's an unconventional first date, but we get what we get."

"And we don't throw a fit."

I chuckle. "Something like that." Taking her hand, I look at her fingers and delicate wrist. "What do you say I make it up to you . . .?" I raise my gaze to her. "When you're feeling better?" I lean in again because I just really want to kiss her.

She leans back. "I don't want you to get sick, but I don't want you to go either."

I take the hat and hand it to her. "Here. A little something of me to hold onto while I'm gone." I pull the blankets up and then stand.

Her fingers wrap around it and a small smile appears. "Thanks."

With her tucked in, I ask, "Keys?"

"By the door." I tug my coat from the back of the chair and put it on. When I snatch the keys from the ring, she adds, "Yes."

I unlock the door but stop to look back. "Yes?"

"I'll go out with you."

Nodding, I swing open the door. "Drink the water and then get some rest."

With a salute and a smile, she replies, "I'll see you later."

There's no question that she trusts that I'll return. My stomach clenches, and I look away. I'm not sure why her words knock the breath out of me, but they're like a punch to the gut. I turn back like it's the last time I might see her. I take a prolonged look at her—everything from the sweet smile to that trust that still lies in her eyes as she holds my gaze.

I smile and give her a little wave. "I'll see you later, Story." Closing the door behind me, I lock it and shove her keys deep into my coat's pocket, not wanting to lose them. After putting on my shoes, I head out in search of something to make her feel better.

It's on that walk, along the soaked streets where the water has mostly drained away, that I realize this might be the first time in years I've felt at peace. There's no reason to feel a calm washing through me.

I'm roaming the streets with daylight just starting while I look for a store to purchase something that will help Story feel better quicker. Nothing about the task itself is really relaxing. So I guess it's the girl who has me feeling unlike myself.

Cutting across two blocks, I find a store on the corner and sort through their limited selection. Just as I decide on the liquid cold-and-flu remedy, I hear, "Is that you, Mr. Haywood?"

I steel myself before turning around. "Professor Greene, what a coincidence running into you like this."

"You survived the storm, but what has you out and about at this hour?"

I hold up the medicine. "My . . ." I stop, not sure what to call Story. What is she to me? Stranger? Girl I hooked up with? Savior? I go with, "My friend is sick and needed something to help with her symptoms."

"That's too bad. I hope she feels better."

"Me too." I rock back on my feet. "Guess I'll be seeing you in a few hours."

Her brow furrows and eyes narrow. "Why will I be seeing you?"

"I need to turn in my paper. You said nine o'clock."

"Ah." She hums. "It's been a rough night. First the storm and then, well, this." She holds up stomach acid pills. "Did you finish the paper?"

"I worked until after two to finish it. I think it's my best work."

Her eyebrows rise. "I look forward to reading it, but it won't be today. Take care of your friend. I'm hearing it could be tomorrow before campus gets electricity again. Drop it off then."

This is the professor who gave me the hardest time all semester. Sure, it didn't help that I skipped half my classes, but I more than made up for it on the exams. An extra day would allow me to get some rest before tackling anything else. "You sure? I have it ready to turn in."

She starts backing toward the register. "I'm sure. You've done the work, so take the day to study for your other classes. Just don't forget to turn in your paper tomorrow."

"I won't. Thank you."

"Stay safe out there," she says before she turns to pay.

Knowing I have extra time on my hands, I shop the aisles, looking for soup and electrolyte drinks to fill her fridge. After paying for the groceries, I head back, taking a little more time to examine any damage the town sustained. Fortunately, it doesn't look like much more than debris and standing water remain.

When I reach Story's building again, I mess with the lock on the lobby door for a minute before discovering it just needs to be replaced. I go upstairs and pull the keys out of my pocket like I live here. Feeling too natural to be normal, this is dangerous for me.

I don't do this with girls for a reason. They're a dime a dozen. *Why does she feel different?* I'm determined to find out.

Sneaking in the door, I spy her sound asleep, snuggled up and wearing my hat with the blankets wrapped around her. A hat is probably the last thing she needs with her fever, but she looks cute in the dark blue beanie.

I unpack the bags, then try to figure out what I should be doing. I made the effort, so getting medicine in her is first on the priority list. But am I staying after that? I guess it depends on how long the invitation remains open.

I find a spoon and sit next to her on the bed again. "Story?" She doesn't wake after a few gentle nudges, so I decide her sleep is more valuable in healing than this orange stuff. I set it on her nightstand, then check her forehead. It's cooled some, which means the Tylenol is working. I'd hate to have to shove her in an ice bath. I have a feeling our date would be off again after that.

Since she's still warm, though, I undress down to my underwear, knowing the flannel will be too hot. Sure, I could go home to my cold apartment, but I'd much rather be in bed with Story, even sick, than alone.

When I climb into bed, she moves closer the moment I've settled next to her. Fuck it. I've already been around her and kissed her, so I suspect I'll be sick soon.

I stare up at the ceiling for a while and then out the window, but it's when I turn to face her that I finally relax. My eyes grow heavy, and soon enough, I'm losing the strength to stay awake.

7

Story

*Shamelessly pressing my chest to him, the feel of his erection hard against my softness, I push up and straddle this sexy man. As soon as I do, I'm tossed onto my back and mercilessly kissed until I'm begging for more of everything—the way his green eyes drink me in, how his hands squeezed my ass when I mounted him, and how he fills me so—*I exhale, the temperature under the covers too hot to be comfortable.

These dreams are getting out of hand. It's like I can feel him against me even now. After licking my lips, I try to take a deep breath but end up coughing instead. Opening my eyes, it's not my dry throat that has my eyes as wide as saucers.

It's Cooper.

I lie there still as can be, noticing even my breath is held in place. But I need to breathe, so I do it slowly and then turn to face him.

His hard jaw remains taut, but his features are at peace. Something about his expression is so gentle when he sleeps.

I still prefer when he's awake. He's gorgeous. But more than that, he helped me break free from some of the fears I'd been holding on to. I'm not sure what it was about him that had me wanting more than time with him, but after making out and getting off, I have no regrets.

Fortunately for me, his eyes begin to open, and as soon as he sees me, he grins. Reaching forward, he presses his hand to my head. "You're a little hot. How are you feeling?" he asks.

"Only a little hot?" I grin.

He chuckles. "A lot hot in the sexual department, but as for your temperature, we still need to bring it down." He sits up and drops his feet to the floor.

It's the first time I'm seeing his body . . . without clothes. Sure, he looked great clothed. I checked him out at the coffee shop before I even approached him. His style is a cross between J. Crew and rugged, dressed for the weather and season from head to toe. His hair is still holding a style despite the bad weather. But it was his profile, the slightest of bumps on the bridge of his nose that broke up the handsome perfection of his other features.

But this . . . this practically naked Adonis standing before me now beats anything he could ever wear dressed. I stare as he comes around the mattress. Sitting next to me, he picks up the medicine. "You need to take this along with another dose of Tylenol. You're starting to feel feverish again."

"What do you think is wrong with me?" Other than wanting this man like I've never wanted anyone in my life— sexually, sure. That would be a bonus. But his company is more than I could have asked for already. Now he's here taking care of me. I win. Maybe this is the universe making up for all the bad I've been subjected to.

I'll take it.

He battles a rogue smile as if it appeared without his permission. "Nothing. You are perfect just the way you are."

How can I not grin after that? "I was referring to me being sick."

"Ah. I think it's just a cold. It's freezing outside, and we hiked through so much water last night. I think you'll be okay by tomorrow."

"Oh, shit!" I sit up, ready to bolt out the door to get to my final on time. "I'm late."

He stands as I struggle to untangle my legs from the sheet. "It's probably canceled. Most of the university is still without power. I'd check your email." He walks back to the desk, where he picks his phone up. "I got an extension to turn in my paper." When he looks my way, he adds, "I ran into my professor at the store."

Glancing back and forth between him and the medicine, I have a vague memory of him getting dressed and leaving. "You left." Not a question, but my mind is still trying to piece things together. "And then you came back."

"I did. I got supplies. Medicine. That was the best I could find at the store two blocks over. Some snacks and drinks." He goes to the fridge and pulls out a bottle of Gatorade before returning to the bed. He undoes the cap and hands it to me. "Stay hydrated."

I take a sip and then another, not realizing how thirsty I was until now. I can easily acknowledge that Cooper has attributed to my thirst in other ways. Watching him walk around my apartment with his athletic physique on display has me taking a few extra gulps.

He returns his phone to the desk, then he looks back at me. "My finals were postponed a day. What about yours?"

"What about my what?"

Grinning, he chuckles. "Your exams. Have your professors canceled today?"

"Oh, right. That." I reach for my phone and check. Finding two emails, I get the news I want. Let's face it, I'd rather be here with Cooper, even sick, than taking a final. Holding the screen toward him, I say, "Canceled."

Dropping back onto the bed, he groans. "Good. I'm fucking exhausted."

Everything is so natural between us. It's as if we've forgotten to have a beginning of our relationship if that's what we can call what we're doing. I take another sip and then swallow down a dose of the medicine he ventured out to retrieve for me. "Thank you for risking your life so I could feel better."

"Anytime." He smirks with his hands tucked under his head.

I lie down and tug the covers under my chin. Staring up at the ceiling, I whisper, "I don't know your last name."

"Haywood."

"Haywood," I say, letting the word slip across my lips.

"What's yours?"

Looking at him, I roll to my side. "Salenger with an E, not an I."

He rolls to face me, not afraid to be close even though I'm sick. "Story Salenger." Reaching over, he tucks some hair behind my ear. "What's your story morning glory?"

Not sure if it's the fever, but I have a feeling it's the way he's looking at me that has my cheeks heating. Being in the spotlight of the intensity of his eyes, the smile that's so genuine, and the touch of his hand when he finds mine under the covers to caress has my head swimming, never wanting to catch my breath.

"Your name."

"Huh?"

"I was saying your name, Story, is a unique name."

"Ah. Yes," I reply with a sigh. "My mom was sort of a flower child born in the wrong decade." I roll my wrist until our hands are aligned, and then our fingers fold together. His hand is warm and comforting like that look in his eyes. "She was an avid reader of anything really. There were nature and travel books, romance novels, and memoirs of obscure people we'd never learn about in school. She looked at life like an expedition. I don't think she ever stayed still. Not for long if she did."

"She sounds fascinating."

I take a deep breath, bracing myself to talk about her. I think of my mom all the time, but I don't share her much with anyone. "She was."

"*Was?*" His hand tightens just enough for me to notice the difference. "I'm sorry. Did she pass?"

"Pass is such a nicer way of putting it. No, she didn't pass. She left this world the same way she lived her life. There was nothing quiet or nice about it." The silence catches between us, making me realize that my mind had drifted further into the details than I've allowed myself in a long time. I look at Cooper, and though my heart is racing from memories that I've exposed to daylight, I try to right my expression and feign indifference. For him. And for me.

I can't get sucked into this emotional mess anymore. Even my leg aches from the memory.

Cooper exhales, tempering his response. I've been here before, so I try to head it off. "Let's not make a big deal out of this."

"It is a big deal. You can't hide the pain in your eyes, Story." He kisses my hand, then looks back up at me. "I'm sorry. I'm so sorry."

Tears fill my eyes, making me hate that I'm so weak just from the memories. "Don't do this, okay? Let's just . . . I was the storybook ending she always dreamed of having."

"That's why she named you Story?"

I nod, but my chin is wobbling, so I tuck my head down and stare at our hands. As I trace the veins across his hand, his strength isn't just seen but felt as if I could fall from a cliff and our bond wouldn't waver. "I could have been named Fairy for fairy tale just as easily."

"I prefer Story." He tilts my chin up with his other hand, and I'm met with a smile that makes my knees weak. "I don't know where you've been all these years, but I'm glad we met." This time, it's not my hand he kisses. It's me.

My forehead. My cheek. My—I pull back before he can kiss me on the mouth. "I don't want to get you sick."

"I think it's probably too late for that."

"I'll feel so guilty if you get sick."

Slipping his arm under me, he pulls me close, so close that I'm tucked under his chin and against his chest. "Don't. Let's just blame the bad weather and get some rest."

"Probably best." My lids start feeling the weight of the medicine, and each blink becomes a task. I'm so grateful I don't have finals today. There'd be no way I'd make it to Haywood Hall. And if I did, I'd surely . . . "Haywood Hall," I mutter, working through the familiar name. "I have classes in—"

"Get some rest, Story. We both need it."

Closing my eyes again, I struggle to reopen them as the pull of sleep drags me under.

Light slips under my lids, too bright to ignore. I swallow. My throat is dry, but my head feels better than I remember it did before falling asleep.

Stretching my arms above my head, I yawn and open my

eyes. The afternoon sun drenches my apartment and Cooper next to me. I turn to wake him with a kiss, but I find the bed beside me empty instead.

My eyes dart around the room to the desk, the hook by the door, the clothes dropped on the floor at the foot of the bed. Every trace of him has gone missing.

Maybe he's gone to the store again or out for food. Maybe he's gone out for fresh air, or . . . I sit up, hoping his bag is still here. If that's here, he'll return. If it's gone, he is.

I find the spot on the floor as empty as the space next to me. Still looking for a sign, a clue, a note, a number, anything that would show tangible proof he was here other than a bottle of medicine. Did I have that in the cabinet? Did I retrieve it in my hazy feverish hours in the middle of the night?

Getting out of bed, I rummage through the few papers on my desk. I check the hook for a scarf left behind, the floor for a forgotten glove, and even the dryer for something discarded. I need to find something to prove to my runaway heart that Cooper isn't a figment of my imagination.

But I'm left empty-handed.

I fall back on the bed, arms wide, and close my eyes, trying to process my feelings. They feel bigger to manage than they should over one night with him.

"Tell me I dreamed him, that I made him up in my imagination." That would make sense to me, like the heat between our hands, the feel of his fingers entwined with mine, the kisses he placed across my neck, and why I felt comfortable with a man who is basically a stranger being in my bed.

Our conversations were light, but he had me opening little by little until I exposed my personal secrets. I don't talk about my mom with anyone, except I did with him.

Taking a deep breath, I slowly exhale, wondering why I let him in—into my life, my apartment, and even my Wi-Fi —when I know better.

But more so, why'd he leave without a trace when I thought we had such a great connection?

8

Story

Crackers and cheese.

Strawberry yogurt.

Applesauce.

Two bananas.

Totino's pizza and ice cream in the fridge.

Three bottles of water and a six-pack of Gatorade.

Despite the rest of my apartment, my fridge and freezer have all kinds of surprises left behind, courtesy of Cooper. I just don't understand why he bought all this stuff when he didn't intend to stay and enjoy it with me.

Grabbing a yogurt and a spoon, I retreat to my desk. I get the occasional waft of Cooper's cologne, a stark reminder of his absence. I would have preferred smelling it on him than in the air.

From the café to this apartment, no one has filled a space as quickly as he did. I still find it odd how natural it felt with him here. How I grappled to find any excuse to ask him to stay. Sure, it was raining outside, but did I ask for his sake or mine?

Letting my guard down was my first mistake. Allowing him to invade my sanctuary was my second. Why am I still allowing him to consume my thoughts like I have nothing better to do?

Loneliness won't win.

I refuse to let it.

Changing my habits and the lessons I learned growing up will serve me better. Don't cling to someone else's life. It's okay to be alone. I'm basically a pro. I've been doing it for years now.

Positive self-talk may not help me out of this mess with Cooper. I open my journal and grab a pen, ready to confess my weakness—green eyes, six-two give or take a mini Reese's Cup, and a nurturing side that has me swooning like a ridiculous schoolgirl. That's the problem right there. I'm just not used to being treated like a princess.

The worst part . . . I liked it.

I don't even wear pink, so none of this makes sense.

Shoving a large spoonful of yogurt into my mouth, I hope to fight this foolishness and recalibrate my thoughts. Last night is in the past. It's time for me to return to reality.

A text flashes onto my screen. Leaning over, I see the message is from my manager, Lila: *We need to talk asap. Can you come to the shop?*

She's never short with me, but that text feels like a first time.

Not good.

Rubbing my temple, I remember few people paid before they bailed during the storm. I've not had time to figure out how to recoup the money other than hoping most will return to square up with me. If not, I may take the fall, and I can't even blame them. There were a few regulars, but other than that, I didn't even get their names.

I don't want to lose my job. It doesn't pay a lot, but it covers my bills and has great hours. I can study during the slow times and eat for free. That's not something I can do at most places.

With my fingers hovering over the screen, I try to form some coherent response, a justification to not fire me, or any reason that will allow me to keep my job. Already bracing myself for her response, I type: *I'll be there shortly.*

I probably shouldn't be going out in my condition. I'm feeling better, but I can still feel a tightness in my chest. I eat the yogurt for energy while I get dressed.

Grabbing my scarf as the last article of clothing, I wrap it around my neck and then slip on my tall rain boots. Just outside my door, I spot my suede ankle boots—the leather is hard and ruined. Maybe I can salvage them, but I'll have to deal with those later. I lock my door and tuck my hands in my pockets.

It's in the forties today, so not too cold, but it's kind of eerie with streams of debris and dirt filling the streets. Trash is speckled across the usually clean streets under overcast skies.

Dread fills every step I take to the shop, but as soon as I get there, the smell of muffins and coffee fills me with premature relief, and my stomach growls. Guess I've gotten a little of my appetite back. I can't let the comforting scents fool me. I'm about to be fired for a hefty shortchange. I don't have the wherewithal to even fight back right now.

"Story?" Lila waves me to the back.

I push through the door. "What's wrong?"

Lila's taller than me by only a few inches, but it feels like a mountain staring down at me in this situation. She leans against the wall with her arms crossed over her chest. Her brown hair catches in the crossing. She never wears much makeup, no more than a little mascara and maybe lipstick, but today, her face is bare. She probably had a rough time getting out the door with her young son, Jake. That's what she tells me when she has less time to get ready. "Why didn't you tell me about last night?"

"Umm . . ." I look around for a saving grace but don't spot anything but a bag of flour I forgot to put up and a stack of dishes next to the sink. "I'm sorry. It all happened so fast." Her brow crinkles, so I start to ramble, "The storm hit, and we were fine until we lost power, but then I couldn't just kick people out when the street was flooding, so I let them stay, and most didn't have money." I shrug. "Who carries cash these days anyway?"

"One thousand dollars, Story? That's crazy money."

"I know. I'm so sorry. The electricity went out, and people bailed before I could collect the tabs."

She narrows her eyes in confusion. "What are you talking about?"

"Last night." Taking a step back, I feel my ass run into the metal counter, so I take hold, my grip firm against the rounded steel. "What are you talking about?"

"Last night. Your tip."

"My tip?" My eyes jerk back. "I didn't have any tips once the storm hit, and really, I only had about ten dollars prior because again, most people don't carry cash. They just leave it on the receipt."

She holds up a credit card receipt. "What's this?"

I lean in and squint because nothing on the piece of paper is making sense. "I don't know," I reply, leaning back on my heels again. "What is that?"

A huge smile splits her lips. "It's your tip, Story." Tapping the paper, she adds, "Someone left you a one-thousand-dollar tip."

"Huh?" I snatch the receipt from her and study the numbers, looking for errors in the zeros or a misplaced period. "This doesn't make sense, Lila."

"Well, I'm not going to argue with you. Not only did this person pay for everything last night that you marked down on the notepad that wasn't paid for but they also overpaid by four hundred dollars. On top of that, they matched it in a tip for you. A thousand dollars, Story. That is huge money. I can't say I'm not jealous. I'm so freaking jealous. Think of what you can do with all that money." She nudges me as she walks by. "You must have given some damn good service last night."

"Very funny."

"I'm serious. You showed that sweet smile to the right guy." She backs through the door, still grinning. "I'm going to need details about this C. Haywood."

I snatch the receipt and scan down to the signature. "C. Haywood?" *Cooper.*

Cooper Haywood. Besides this absurd amount of money that's fallen into my lap, Cooper's last name comes back like a faded dream. He's slippery every time I mention it, and now, I can't get the thought that my major in business administration is based in Haywood Hall. *Coincidence?*

Holding onto the receipt, I follow her into the main dining area, but stop when I see the devil himself standing at the counter. Cooper looks up and gives me a small wave. "Hey, Story."

"Coop—" My ass is spanked by the door as it slams into me, forcing my body to fly forward and stumble toward him. "Ack!" Arms solid in their strength catch me before I fall flat on my face. I struggle to get a hold of him, but when I do,

I'm righted to my feet again. "Thanks," I say breathlessly and start adjusting my coat back into place.

"You're welcome," he replies, pulling the beanie from his head.

Humiliated, I scramble to free my face from the hair that engulfed it by pushing it back and behind my shoulders. Nothing about that move was smooth, and there was no playing it off, so I lean into it and plant my hand with the receipt now crumpled in it on my hip.

Looking over my shoulder, he catches Lila staring at us. I tug him by the sleeve to the corner of the coffee shop. "What brings you by?" I ask, still a little wobbly on my feet as heat consumes my cheeks. This time from embarrassment instead of a fever, though that might be coming on as well.

"I went by the apartment—"

"You did?"

"Yes. I brought lunch." I look at his hands holding the hat. "I left it outside your door, just in case you were sleeping."

"Then how—?" The clearing of Lila's throat pulls my attention to her. Tight lips and wide eyes are accompanied by her blinking rapidly.

"Should I come back later?" Cooper asks, grabbing my gaze back.

"No. I'm sorry." Stepping closer, I whisper, "Did you pay for everyone and leave me that tip?"

"You said you'd be fired," he replies like that is reason enough for him to do something so insane.

"I was exaggerating." My eyes drift to my friend, who's now pretending to swoon behind Cooper's back. "Well, Lila wouldn't fire me, but . . ." I scan the shop and see Lou staring at us. I look at Cooper, and continue, "The owner might or make me repay what the register was short." I bite my lip, still in shock over this whole matter.

Tilting his head closer to me, he says, "Now you don't have to worry."

"I worry because you gave me, personally, a thousand-dollar tip. That's crazy, Cooper. You can't do that—"

"I already did, so we can just move on."

I search the front of his black wool peacoat for lint or fuzz—something to tell me this guy isn't as perfect as I think he is—but even his coat fails to give me the evidence I need to convict him of his sins and walk away a free woman.

He smells so good that I find myself leaning in. Latching onto the hem of his coat, I look up at him. "I was hoping you were a figment of my imagination."

His hands cradle the underside of my wrists, and I hate that my puffy coat is keeping him from touching me. "I'm real, Story." Lowering his voice, he adds, "Last night . . ."

I'm hanging on his every word. "Yes?" I sound like a hussy in heat. Not that there's anything wrong with someone who likes casual sex, but I'm just not an expert in that field. Cooper, on the other hand, has me wanting to master in his class.

"Last night was really great." He seems to catch himself and shakes his head. "Well, other than you getting sick. How are you feeling?" He reaches up but stops and tucks his hands in his coat pocket, straightens his back, and looks around for any witnesses.

Butterflies ravage my stomach as the intimacy from last night extends beyond my little apartment, made its way down the street, and surrounds us now. I lick my lips, feeling better just being close to him. "I'm thinking it was some twenty-four-hour thing. I think my fever is gone, and I've gotten my appetite back, so normal?"

"That's good." This time he doesn't hold back. The tips of his fingers graze across my forehead, and he runs them under my chin. "You have color back in your cheeks. Not from a fever or—"

"Or?"

He seems embarrassed by how he smiles but looks away from me and chuckles. "I don't know. I like to think you were blushing for me."

"Don't put it past me. I can't hide what I'm thinking to save my life."

"Well, let's hope it never comes to that."

I uncrumple the paper in my hand. "Why did you do this? How did you do this? It's so much money."

He glances at the paper and then shrugs. "I didn't want you to get into trouble. Haven't you ever had anyone help you out before? I have. Just consider it me paying it forward."

"But the tip . . ." I shake my head. "It's too much, Cooper. I can't accept this."

"The money's already gone from the account. So you don't have to keep it, but promise you won't give it back to me."

My head is spinning with some kind of quippy thing to say to make him smile again or even a justification of why he should absolutely take this money back. I just can't seem to land on anything that will change his mind based on his answers. "You're serious, aren't you?"

"Deadly."

A shiver runs up my spine, not because of the handsome man in front of me, but that word strikes a chord deep inside me. I shake it off and swallow, forcing myself to return to this moment instead. "Let's hope it doesn't come to that," I say, using his words against him.

Cooper chuckles. "Clever."

"Speaking of clever. It's quite the coincidence that you share a name with a building on campus." Not a question. Just putting it out there and studying how this guy who can afford to drop two K without a worry has a name in common with distinguished and wealthy alumni.

He doesn't even bat his eyes. "It's not what you think, Story."

"What do I think?"

"What if we get something to eat?"

There's no squirming or evasive body language. He remains right here as sure in his stance as he was yesterday. "Are you changing the subject?"

"I'm starving."

"Smooth but I'll let it go." I point right at his face, the same face I want to kiss again. "For now." I smirk and head to Lila. "Am I free to go?"

"You are, and pizza is on you next time."

Holding up my hand in Scout's Honor, I laugh. "Definitely." I turn to Cooper. "So lunch . . .?" I leave it open for discussion.

He shifts around, seeming to exhale a deep breath of relief. "What do you have in mind?"

"I hear there's food at my place." I move around and bump into him sideways. "What do you say? Want to come over?"

"Thought you'd never ask."

9

Cooper

I'm not myself with Story.

I'm not sure who I am when I'm with her, but it's been entertaining to do things differently. *Fun even.* Fun in the past few years usually has me walking on the wilder side—from girls to fights to drinking until I pass out. With Story, it means lying in bed holding her in my arms while listening to the rain mix with her soft breaths.

This must be how dating usually plays out—spending time with each other and getting to know one another. Even though it's slower than how things typically go for me, I don't mind with her.

I appreciate it more, in fact.

Turning over a new leaf?

My parents would be so proud. I roll my eyes just thinking about them.

Back to more important things, like the little brunette with a penchant for heavy blankets and flannel pajamas currently hogging a lot of the covers.

After we ate chicken noodle soup and sandwiches, the meal I delivered to her door for us earlier, Story managed to get me to strip down to my underwear and spend the day with her in bed with one simple request. "I want you to stay."

Miniature gold candy wrappers litter the bed, and her nightstand has a cup of Gatorade and cold medicine in some cocktail she created. With one hand waving in front of her and candy in the other, she says, "I don't think I've ever had so much money in my life, Cooper." She pops a small Reese's in her mouth and falls back on a pile of pillows.

I'm not sure what to think about what she says. It's nothing in the scheme of things, but she acts like she won the lottery. Remembering how she got upset about the delivery guy's tip, seeing the small apartment, and how empty her fridge is, the pieces click together. But hearing her tone and the excitement rattling through it has me glad I gave it to her.

She's not had it easy and probably had to work for anything she ever got. I should feel good that I could make such an impact. But I don't. Lying on the bed next to her, I turn to look out the window. I've never been uncomfortable when it comes to discussions involving money. It's just not anything I've ever had to worry about. So, thinking about it isn't something I do very often.

I feel good when I'm with her until I fuck it up in regard to money by flaunting it without a second thought, which then makes me feel like a bastard. Has my life been so sheltered that I never realized the impact I could make? Before I get too self-indulgent and start analyzing all my failures, I bring her hand to my mouth and steal the mini Reese's from it with my teeth.

Story smiles. *Fucking hell.* My chest tightens, and I know

I'm in trouble. If she can do me in with her smile, I worry what other magic this goddess possesses.

I slowly chew the chocolate, biding my time to regroup my thoughts. This is nothing. Just two people having some fun on an unexpected free day.

The lie sours on my tongue, and I close my eyes to rid the wave of guilt that rolls through me.

She props her chin under her hands on top of my chest. "Do I want to know where that money came from?"

I stroke her head and then caress her cheek. "Nothing illegal but talk of money is not what I want to do with you."

"*Ooooh*," she says, flirting and sitting up. "What *do* you want to do with me, Mr. Haywood?" Her gaze slides to the wall behind the bed, troubling her lip, and then she repeats, "Haywood. Let's talk about that instead."

"Let's not. I want to kiss you. That's what I want to do." Grabbing her waist, I roll her onto her back and kiss her until her breath deepens, hoping her thoughts turn to other things.

One full day. One day where I can be just me. Not a name on a building bought and paid for almost a hundred years ago. Not the inheritor of a town settled two hundred years ago. Not the one with a target on his back for bearing the name so many hate.

Just me and her and this bed. That's what I really want.

Pushing me away, she leans back with a smile on her face. "You're going to get sick, Cooper." The words don't match the come-and-get-me expression she's sporting.

"What if I tell you I don't care as long as I get to kiss you again?"

"You just want me to take care of you, don't you?"

I move over her, pressing my hips and a certain well-built organ of mine against her. Settling my arms on either side of her head, I lean down and steal a kiss before whispering, "I would love for you to take care of me."

Laughing, she taps me on the nose. "You are definitely not talking about being sick."

"No, I'm not." I lower and start kissing her again. Gentle at first and then when she wraps her arms around my neck, holding me to her, I run my tongue over her lower lip. Her lips part, and our tongues meet in the middle.

God, she makes me want to skip a few steps, but when I hear her moan, I just want to keep going. Each sound is like a little victory for my dick and inspires me to stay the course. If Story's this responsive from a few kisses, I can only imagine how wild I'll drive her when we have sex.

She caresses my face, looking into my eyes like I can do no wrong. "I'd take care of you."

"I know." *I do know, too.* She's that good, has that kind of heart, and is a girl I want more than today with if given a chance. I start wondering if maybe I'm not such a bad match for that kind heart that beats hard in her chest.

I can't let myself go there.

This is a moment. *Fun.* There's that fucking word again. I need to remember that we're nothing more than a connection made from necessity. Looking into the soul of her eyes, though, I'm starting to believe I might be wrong.

Needing to bury my thoughts and let my body rule over my head, I kiss her again and then whisper against the corner of her lips, "You're so incredibly sexy, Story." Running my hand over the waistband of her pants, I dip down to kiss her neck. The dip of her waist draws me to trace it with my palm and then go higher under her shirt. Her skin is hot, but this time, it's not from a fever. It's from being with me.

Me. *Me alone.*

Seeing her nipples peak under the cotton T-shirt is such

a turn-on. The sound of her breath hitching has me lifting my head to check on her. No flirty smirk or eyes that captivate. Instead, she's looking at me for something more. "You okay?"

"It's so embarrassing, but . . ." Shaking her head, she keeps her eyes focused on mine. "No, I'm not okay."

"What?" I push up with my eyes still locked on hers. "What's wrong?"

Tugging me by the shirt, she pulls me back down on top of her, and I land with a thud before she kisses me again. This time, she rolls us to the side and mounts me.

This girl is trouble.

Now straddling me, she sits up and rubs the apex of her thighs against me. I say, "I thought something was really wrong."

"There is, but it only happens when you stop kissing me." Cupping my face, she bends down and presses her lips to mine.

I chuckle. This time, I pull back while rubbing her hips. "Then I won't stop." Our mouths crash into each other's, and as if it's open season because our bodies become frenzied.

Hands.

Legs.

Tongues.

Hair.

Tangled thoughts lost in her.

I kiss her until her lips are swollen. I fucking love seeing my work on her. She's come twice and is ready for rest. When her eyes can barely stay open, I slip out of bed and clean up in the bathroom. She never leaves me to seek my own release, but I'm ready to take this to the next level. At this rate, I need to keep extra underwear here.

Dropping them to the floor, I decide to take a shower to

wash off. The water never gets above lukewarm, making me miss the hot water at my place. Story will love it. I wonder if she enjoys baths. I could set her up, give her a romantic night—wait, what am I thinking?

These thoughts plague me when I have no idea what's happening with the two of us. I need to shut my mind off when it comes to her and get my shit together so I can graduate next semester.

When I return to the bedroom, Story's already asleep. Soft slumbering sighs escape from her barely parted lips as she lies under the covers we had previously shed. I grab a pair of her baggy-for-her, too-short-for-me pajama pants from the drawer and pull them on.

Before settling in for a nap with her, I set us up. The cup on the nightstand is empty, the remains of her concoction coating the bottom, so I take it to the sink. I pull two fresh ones from the cabinet to fill with water—one for her and one for me—and place them on either side of the bed.

I'm not sure how she's feeling, but judging by what we just did, I'm thinking she's on the mend. She sure moves like it. Fuck, she's hot.

I climb in on the other side of her and lie there. I should have pulled the shade to block some of the daylight flooding the room, but I leave it. I can't sleep the day away. Though she makes me want to if she'd stay tucked in next to me.

Where are these thoughts coming from? It's too soon to be this into a girl. I've been attracted to girls before, fucked them, and we went on our own way. Is it that Story and I haven't gone all the way that has me panting around her like a damn teenager? Am I really that easily manipulated? Or have I really changed this much in the twenty-four hours after meeting her?

Story isn't a game I'm playing. That's what separates her

from other girls. That and a million other things. But I can't keep who I am hidden for long, especially considering she's already onto me.

I should try to enjoy whatever is happening here before it's too late. My name won't be a warning, but once she finds out about my reputation and other things I've done, that should do the trick.

Moving toward the center of the bed, I pull her close and hold her in my arms. While I'm wrapped around the back of her, she stirs, and whispers, "Thank you for the money."

"You're welcome."

"Will you be here when I wake up?"

There's a fissure felt deep in my chest from the question. I've already lost her trust. Already. I can't lose her before we have a chance to explore where this is going. "I swear I was coming back after getting clean clothes and lunch for us." Leaning over, I kiss her cheek. "But I promise I'll be here when you wake up."

Her eyes never open, but a smile graces her lips as she relishes the intimacy. "I'm holding you to that, Cooper Haywood."

I kiss her temple and then close my eyes. Leaning my forehead against hers, I savor every minute I have with her. "I hope you do, Story Salenger."

10

Cooper

"Mr. Haywood?"

I left Story's apartment last night, letting her get a night of studying in and returning to mine when the power was restored. She's been on my mind all morning during my first final. Fortunately, I knew the information inside and out. My memory serves me well sometimes.

I thought I'd drop my paper off and then take off, but apparently, my teacher has other plans. I stop and turn back. "Yes, Professor Greene?"

Other students pass me after turning in the hard copy of their final papers. It's odd to even turn in a paper with everything else sent electronically these days. She holds my paper up. "I'm looking forward to reading this over the break. I saw you were signed up for my advanced communications course. I know you consider my courses as hurdles in your pursuits, but have you considered steering your interests in another direction?"

Walking back to her desk, I block the other students,

becoming a divider between the professor and myself to keep eavesdroppers from intruding. "Is this an unsubtle hint to drop the class?"

"I don't understand what you'll gain. You've shown no interest in this course, so why would a more rigorous class be any different? It seems you're setting yourself up for failure. Or should I just forget how you disrespected me this semester and then pulled rank by using your name to garner a second chance that most students never have the ability to do?"

She sounds bitter. I get it, but that's not my issue. While she straightens her black jacket, she ignores me despite the question she threw out. Trying to temper my irritation, I reply, "This is the recommended path for pre-law. I don't make the rules."

"And you don't follow them." She taps the stack of papers on the top of the aged wood desk and then shoots me a glare. "I may not be a lawyer, but I understand that manipulating the system to work to your advantage will only do more harm than good once you leave this campus." Acknowledging a student when she drops her paper down on the desk, the professor silently dismisses me.

The thing is, I'm not done. "Sure, I fucked up this semester. I had a lot of shit going on that you're not privy to, but I worked hard on that paper. I did it to prove that I'm not just my name." Lowering my voice, I add, "For the record, I didn't ask anyone to call in any favors for me."

"Does it matter if you did? My job was threatened over a spoiled twenty-one-year-old who thinks we're all here to serve at his whim."

"What do you mean? I've never asked you for anything other than a fair shot. Are you saying you can't give me a grade based on what I've earned?"

She takes my paper from the pile and sets it aside. Grabbing a red pen from her desk drawer, she shoots me a glare, then scribbles an A across the top of my paper. Handing it back to me, she says, "Professor Daubry is teaching the same course next semester. Do me a favor and sign up for his instead."

When she stands, I step out of her way. She follows the last student out the door, leaving me there with my paper already graded after not reading one fucking word.

I leave pissed when I should be celebrating. This class has been a pain in my ass all semester. She made me feel like I couldn't do anything right by calling me out over the dumbest shit, making me give impromptu speeches from an informative on a topic that she knew I'd fail to a persuasive, which to her dismay, I excelled and had the class cheering. "Fuck her." I push through the auditorium door and start down the hall to go home.

Walking outside the building, I look across campus at Haywood Hall gleaming high on the hill. I should be in that building instead of pursuing philosophy, economics, communications, and whatever else my dad thinks makes a well-rounded attorney.

I trot down the steps but spy Eliza and veer right . . . into a little brunette with hazel eyes I've been lost in for two days. "Hey," I say.

"Hi," Story says with a big smile that's starting to feel a lot like one that's just for me.

Glancing behind me, Eliza is busy caught up in her coven of friends and hasn't spotted me yet. "Where are you headed? I need to go this way." I take Story by the wrist and start walking in the opposite direction.

She puts on her brakes. "I'm not going in this direction."

When she stops altogether, I put my back to the others. "What class do you have next?"

"None. I'm done."

Disbelief covers her expression. "For the day?"

"The semester," I reply, sounding short. Fuck.

Her eyes brighten. "Really? That's so awesome. I just finished for the day, but I still have two finals tomorrow."

"Why don't we head to your place?" I try to start walking again, but she stands and looks back at me.

"Cooper?"

Looking past her, I see Eliza's eyes homing in on me. Shit. I grab Story's hand and say, "Run with me."

"What?" I gotta give it to her. The girl takes off running with me. "Why are we running?"

We duck into an alcove at the psychology building. Story's laughing, and seeing her happy has me walking on cloud nine. Out of breath, she tugs on the straps of her backpack. "Why exactly are we running?"

Wrapping an arm around her waist, I hold her closer, our bodies melding together. I cup her face with my hand, and whisper, "Just wanted to be alone with you." I kiss her, stealing the breath she'd managed to catch.

She falls back against the stone wall, bringing me with her as our lips lock and our tongues greet each other again like the lovers we've become. I lean against her as she breathes life into me again. What I thought was an escape from one situation quickly turns heated, and suddenly, we're becoming another type altogether.

Fuck, she makes me hard. If I knew we wouldn't be interrupted, I might be willing to take a chance in the corner of this alcove. Story deserves better than the cold stone as a backdrop and an audience if anyone saw us.

Forcing myself away from her, I push off the wall, and

my back hits the other side of the doorway. We're left panting and staring at each other.

The door opens, and I stop it from hitting me. Some guy mumbles an apology as he looks at us but never stops and keeps walking.

Story licks her lips, then tilts her head against the stone and closes her eyes. Looking at me, she says, "I have to go to work."

"Can I see you tonight?" She's becoming a habit that's actually good for me.

We may be in the shadows of the building, but her smile brightens even the darkest corners. She takes a step closer, but the door swings open again. An older woman in a trench coat looks at Story and then me when I hold the door open for her. "Excuse me," she says as she carries on her way.

As soon as I push the door closed, Story flies into my arms and kisses me. Then she pushes off giggling and starts backing out of the alcove. "I'd be disappointed if you didn't. I get off at ten. Meet me at my apartment at ten fifteen?"

"Can't wait." I wink.

"Me either." A shiver of excitement takes hold of her, and she giggles again. "Bye, Cooper." Rushing up the steps, she turns back and gives me a little wave.

"Bye, babe." I fall back against the wall again. I don't know what's come over me, but it feels good.

Wait . . . I know exactly what has. *Story.* Somehow, she has managed to make my bad day so much better just from seeing her again. And kissing her. I really like to kiss that woman.

With a plan in place to see her again, I head to my apartment. I need to pack for the holiday break, something I've put off until the last minute. I've dreaded it since I parted on bad terms at Thanksgiving.

Like me, my dad is stubborn. Guess it's an inherited trait. "Cooper?"

Shit.

I keep walking, pretending I don't hear her. The clack of her heels against the sidewalk gets closer as she continues to call my name. Then she yells, "Cooper?"

I stop.

When I turn back, I say, "Hey, Eliza. What's up?" I keep it short for my benefit. Hooking up with her on Halloween was a mistake that I repeated two more times before I realized she wasn't sticking with the friends-with-benefits deal we made. She made. I stupidly fell for her game.

Saran Wrap has nothing on her. She clings like she's being paid for it. "You didn't hear me calling your name for like the last fifty yards or so?" she asks.

Dipping a hand in my pocket, I pull out an earbud. "I was wearing these earlier."

"Oh," she replies. "What about just now?"

I raise my arms out from my sides. "I'm here."

She huffs. "Okay, well, I wanted to see if you wanted to get together before we leave town for the holidays." Eliza's hot, tight pants look painted on, her thigh high-heeled boots are impractical for the weather and finals week, and a tightly fitted cream-colored sweater sells the package before you even notice her face. Her thick red hair is not fire, but more fading, like my interest in her has. Call me an asshole, but I was looking for a hookup, not a commitment.

Coming closer, she smiles, but it lacks the brightness of Story's, lacks that something special that comes from within. Maybe it's sincerity. "I can't. I need to pack. I'm heading home tomorrow."

"I could come over tonight and help you."

My stomach twists like a knife turning in my gut. Slowly, the pain shoots upward. I'm not familiar with guilt, but I think I'm experiencing it for the first time since all I can think about is Story. I take a few shallow breaths, trying to figure out what I'm feeling, but I keep coming up empty on the diagnosis. "No. I'm . . ." This is where I'd usually lie, nothing that could be seen through but probably something Eliza would question and then get mad at me for telling. An image of Story sleeping next to me pops into my head, easing the discomfort I'm feeling. "I'm seeing someone."

Stunned, she stares at me and starts laughing. "I'm sorry. I thought you just said you're seeing someone."

"I did."

Anger morphs across her face. "You told me you don't do relationships, and now you're in one?"

"I don't. *I didn't.* But I met someone."

A humorless laugh bursts from her throat as she looks around. When her eyes land on me again, she scoffs. "You met someone? Someone other than me who you've been 'meeting' with on a regular basis."

"That's not accurate, Eliza." Lying, cheating, and stealing aren't so far off from who I've been. Greene just called me out on it and now Eliza. I am who I am with them.

With Story, I get a new start.

"Okay, Cooper. Lie to my face," she says sarcastically, crossing her arms over her chest. Scorn cinches her features together as she shakes her head. "We all know it's only a matter of time, so don't call me when you fuck it up."

"Good to know you think so highly of me." She knows the truth as well as I do. I've seen her on dates with other guys, so I'm not sure why she's angry. "What exactly was it that you saw in me again?"

"Haywood." *One word.*

I'm starting to think that name hinders more than helps me these days.

She spins so fast on her heel that her hair flies over her shoulders, and she walks away without a goodbye. Though she does slap her ass, so I'm thinking it's a kiss-off instead.

My hand covers my heart. Not because Eliza hurt me in any way, but I just admitted not only to her but to myself that I might be in a relationship with Story.

And I'm not upset about that at all.

I start for my apartment again, feeling freer than I have in forever, the baggage of my life suddenly not so heavy.

Now that I've admitted Story might be more than a little fun, that there might be something more there than someone to spend a power outage with, how do I break the news to her that she came to *my* party and I'm the prick who tried to ruin her relationship?

Story

"A third cup, Lou? You usually stop after two coffees."

He rubs a temple, glaring at the screen like it's a mortal enemy. "Finals are killing me this semester." When he looks up at me, he adds, "Pulled two all-nighters. How are yours going?"

I fill the cup. "Good." I shrug. "Better than good actually. The extra day yesterday was helpful."

He starts dumping loads of sugar into the black brew, his attention seemingly focused on the singular task. But then he says, "That guy who's been hanging around the shop . . ." A quick peek up at me doesn't lessen his nerves. I might have even added to them.

Now I catch his anxiety.

"I've seen him before." He takes a sip, but by how it's shaking in his hands, the act isn't working to cover his curiosity.

"He was here the other night when we lost power." Lou's a sweet guy. A few years older than me, he transferred in two years ago and has been coming to Bean There ever since. He's never asked me out, but the relationship has been pleasant and a constant. We may not spend time together outside this coffee shop's walls, but I consider us friendly acquaintances.

"Around town and campus, I guess."

"Why does this sound like you're going somewhere with this? What is it, Lou? You can just tell me."

The bell chimes above the door, and I turn to look. "Hi, I'll be right—"

Cooper smiles. "Hey."

Giddiness shoots up my spine. "Hi." I can already feel my cheeks heating when I add, "Sit wherever you'd like. I'll be right with you."

When I turn back to Lou, I say, "Sorry. You were saying?"

"It's nothing." He shakes his head, his attention returning to his laptop. "Just be careful."

I question the warning in his eyes by holding his gaze before nodding once. "I will."

Setting the pot back on the coffee burner, I rush back around to Cooper's table. I'm tempted to throw my arms around him, so excited to see him that I can barely contain it. I don't, though. I'm at work and should probably act professionally, but he makes it hard when he looks so good.

He stands for me, his jacket hanging open in the front. No scarf or hat or gloves today, but the weather is unseasonably warm at fifty degrees. Unlike me, he doesn't hold back. One large and strong hand takes hold of my waist while the other slides around my neck, tilting me back so he can kiss me.

I'm not usually one for such displays. But maybe it's because I've never had anyone who made me want to break the rules. Until now.

I give in and kiss him, wrapping my arms around him while melting into him, our lips pressed together, rivaling any kiss I've ever read about in a romance novel.

I'm usually prepared for life to hit me sideways with surprises, but I can't say that I saw this coming with Cooper. He holds his emotional cards close to his chest. I can respect that because I do, too.

Neither of us was caught up in nonsense that could throw us off track, but over the past two days ... *two days ... How has it only been two days?* It's felt like so much more, from holding hands in the rain to inviting him to stay with me even though I didn't know his last name.

Cooper Haywood has my mind going haywire. I giggle to myself over my ridiculousness. Disregarding my usual more serious stance, it feels good to just have fun with someone, to laugh, and I will never stop craving his kisses.

I have a feeling I'm not the first girl to go a little nutty over him. We stand, and even though I'm tempted to swoon just to kiss him all over again, the shattering of a glass has me jumping instead.

Lou is out of his seat and scrambling to pick up the broken pieces of his coffee cup. I glance at Cooper, wishing I could stay with him a minute longer. Reading my conflict, he nods. "Go. I understand."

"Don't touch the glass, Lou. I'll get a broom." I'm in and out of the back and start sweeping the wet pieces into the dustpan.

"Sorry, Story. I was rearranging my laptop."

"It's okay. No worries. I'll be quick to clean it up and get you another cup. I know you're stressed, so keep working. Don't mind me." Squatting down, I try to get more of the liquid near the base of the table, but I bend too far and lose my balance. Porcelain shards pierce my knee through my jeans and cause me to fall back in pain.

A knife slicing through my skin hits like a tidal wave dragging me under the surface of memories I've tried to bury. An open wound the size of a canyon scores my chest. Images from a night I've tried hard to forget come back like relics of a past, too scarring for me to avoid revisiting.

The fear.

The agony.

The helplessness.

"Story."

The voice is firm but soothing as he calls to me, but I struggle to find purchase in it. "Story. It's me. Cooper."

Unbreaking in his insistence when he summons me back to him, I open my eyes to sink into the comfort of his arms and green-eyed gaze. A gentle smile lifts the corners of his lips, and he says, "Hey, babe."

"Hi," I reply, my breath still coming heavy.

"Are you okay?"

"I'm great." Trying for a smile, I attempt to act natural. "How are you?"

His smile grows. "I'm doing all right. How about we get you up, and I can take a look at your knees?"

Bending to see my knees, I ask, "What's wrong with my knees?" Then I realize I'm on the floor of the shop, and everyone is staring at me. "Oh, um . . ." My heart starts beating erratically again, and I scurry from Cooper's arms. "I need to get . . . yeah." Freeing myself, I run into the back room, leaving the door to sway behind me.

I plant my hands on the cold steel of the counter and close my eyes, taking deep breaths. "One. Two. Three—"

"Story?" Cooper asks barely above the breeze of the swinging door. His tone is still so even that my beating heart steadies from the sound of it and from him being close again. I push that calm away because I have to do this on my own.

"Give me a sec, okay?" When I don't hear the door squeal against the hinges, I look back to find him standing there. I turn around abruptly and grip the counter. I'm unsure what to say since I can see how much I've worried him.

A line creases between his brows, and the smile from before has been wiped clean. I watch as he slowly slides his hands into his pockets, and I'm starting to realize there's a pattern when he does that unrelated to the weather. I hate that I've caused any uncertainty when it comes to us.

I look down at his feet. He stands so securely that I try to convince myself I'm reading too much into the rest of his body language. "I . . ." I start and stop, not sure where to go with this. "We're new, if we're even a we," I ramble, peeking up through fallen bangs over my eyes, "and I hate that you've seen something that might make you leave—"

"I'm not going anywhere. I'm right here, Story. Right here with you." He is, too. When he doesn't make a move to leave, I start to wonder how I feel about it and how he feels about me.

Too many thoughts cloud my mind to think rationally through the other trauma. "You don't have to be so nice about what just happened."

"What just happened?"

I'm usually most vulnerable when I'm trying to fall asleep at night. Being at work changes things. I stare at him, annoyance rising in my chest from the question. I usually have time to work through these little attacks, but I've never had one at work before. With customers waiting and Cooper worried, I don't have the benefit of time on my side.

Not reading the room or choosing to ignore it, Cooper waits for an answer. "It's nothing." My temper is short, and my words clipped. I hate myself for being this way with him.

"Nothing, huh?" The peace I heard in his tone before remains despite the sting of my response.

Pointing at my legs, he says, "We should probably get your jeans off and clean up your knees."

I had forgotten about that pain until the mention of that again. I look down and see little spots of blood penetrating the denim. "I don't have anyone to cover the front."

"I'll cover it for you." He sets his hand against the door. "You'll take care of yourself, right?"

I nod. "Thanks."

His chin dips once before he pushes through the door.

My heart still beats heavy in my chest, but it's not racing anymore. Thanks to Cooper. Grabbing the first-aid kit from the top shelf, I head into the office. I undo my jeans and push them down past the scar on my thigh that never sees daylight and lower past my knees. I didn't even realize the glass cut me, but it got me good.

Nothing that time won't heal. That's a lesson I've learned well.

I clean myself up and then return the kit to the shelf. Taking a moment to finish collecting myself, I check my appearance in a mirror in the office, lick my lips before they get chapped, and try to fix the nest that my hair is the best I can. It's pointless, so I tighten the apron strap around my waist and return to the front.

I stop, covering my mouth with my hand to keep from laughing. Cooper's standing behind the counter with a muffin in his hand. Speaking to a girl, he says, "Trust me, it's better than the croissant."

"I wanted the chocolate croissant," she insists, whining,

reminding me of Veruca Salt in *Charlie and the Chocolate Factory*. I expect her to stamp her foot for emphasis. She doesn't, fortunately.

Cooper grins. "This blueberry muffin won't disappoint. I promise."

She stammers and then sighs, batting her eyelashes. I get it, girl. I totally get it. "Fine, blueberry it is. How much?"

Lou stands. "I don't think you should be behind the counter."

Rushing forward, I say, "It's okay, Lou. Thanks." I go to the register. Lou hesitates and then returns to his table. I eye the to-go cup on the counter in front of her. "Is that coffee or tea?"

"Americano and a muffin," Cooper replies.

My eyebrows rise in surprise. "I'm impressed." His talents extend further than his coffee skills.

There's no amusement in his eyes, but he smiles, putting on a front like there is. "People always underestimate me."

His words sink in, but it's the sadness clouding his usually bright eyes that have me feeling guilty as charged. I want to take it away while making sure his happiness returns.

Two days.

Impossible.

How could I feel so much for someone I met only two days ago?

I reach up and run the tips of my fingers along his jaw and then caress him like he touches me. He turns and kisses my palm. The light returns to his eyes, and a small grin along with it.

That's when I know.

I didn't underestimate him. I underestimated the storm.

12

Story

Tucking the keys into the bag at my hip, I step down to the sidewalk to join Cooper, who's been quietly waiting for me to lock up for the night. The night air is cool but bearable without all the winter accessories. "It turned out to be a pretty day," I say, making small talk.

"It did."

Still, a chill decides to run up my spine. Reaching between us, he takes my hand.

Our fingers wrap around each other's, and we walk without acknowledging the elephant, the third wheel in our relationship. *Relationship?* Is that what we're in now?

I don't think it's ever happened so easily. It just slipped on like a pair of favorite cozy slippers and felt so right from the beginning.

Granted, I've not had many, so I may not be the right one to judge these things. Nevertheless, I like this—his hand wrapped so reassuringly around mine like I didn't have a meltdown earlier inside the shop from a little glass. "You know, I think we should just talk about this and get it over with." I have other issues that will probably scare him away, so I'm hoping this won't be one of them.

"What's that?" he asks.

I'm tempted to roll my eyes, but I shouldn't when he's only being polite. He's not pushed me for answers or to explain. That means a lot to me when it comes to this . . . situation . . . incident? I'm not sure what to call it anymore. It's morphed from reality to a nightmare to a past I've tried to forget. The only issue is it tends to occasionally come back to haunt me. Not in a long time, but last summer didn't do me any service.

I take a deep breath, exhaling slowly, breathing out any fear of judgment that I think he might have. "I'm not trying to freak you out or anything—"

"With a starter like that, I'm kind of freaked out."

"I know." I chuckle, understanding more than he realizes. "This is why I try not to bring it up, but after what happened, I owe you an explanation."

He stops and moves in front of me. In the middle of the sidewalk, he takes my hands. "You actually don't owe me anything, Story. You don't owe anyone anything that you don't want to share. So if you want to tell me what that was about, I'm here. I'm listening. If you want to pretend it didn't happen, I'll respect that. But just know that anything you do share with me stays with me."

"I'm starting to believe you're too perfect. Understanding. A good listener." I shrug, rolling my hand in front of me, knowing this list goes on longer than the few traits I'm listing. "Hot and a great kisser." Taking hold of the front of his coat, I pull him closer and lift on my toes to kiss him. It doesn't matter the weather. My body heats the moment our lips touch.

When we part, I lick my lips and then rub them together, still craving the taste of him. Cooper says, "I will do everything in my power to keep my flaws hidden if I keep getting kisses like that from you."

I laugh. "Secrets don't stay hidden for long." Guess it's not funny, though, since I'm the only one laughing. Trying to lighten the mood again, I fist his coat. "I didn't mean anything by it. I'm just playing." I kiss his chin, and then we start walking again. "Unless you have some skeletons in your closet that come to light that I need to know about." I laugh but realize I'm laughing by myself again. "You don't, do you?"

His laughter is guttural, deep, and resounding. "Doesn't everyone?"

He's right. I have a studio apartment full of secrets that I'm not looking to pull out to display. At least not yet.

We cut down the alley since it's more direct to my apartment. This time, I hold his hand. Despite the distance between us, I feel closer to him than I have with anyone since my mom. The restaurant is busy, co-eds feeding onto the street in celebration of the semester coming to an end. After two more finals, I'll be celebrating.

Cooper stops in front of my door but looks down the block at the bright lights and revelers. "Are you hungry?"

"You bought plenty of food for me."

"I bought snacks, not proper meals."

"Are tacos a proper meal?"

"Better than a yogurt and crackers."

"I don't know. I feel like you nailed it when you bought the good stuff." I'm starting to wonder if he wants to eat with me or to go out and do some celebrating himself. Releasing his hand, I move toward the door. "I have to study tonight, but I don't want to hold you back. You should go out and meet your friends. You're done for the semester, and most people leave by the weekend. Go out and party." I thumb over my shoulder. "I'll just have a quiet night in bed."

Cooper moves in closer. "You're not getting rid of me that easily. I don't mind hanging out with you while you study unless you prefer that I go."

"I feel selfish."

He smirks and takes hold of my hips, wiggling them back and forth. "Be selfish, Story. Tell me what you want." His playfulness belies the words.

"I'm afraid I won't get much studying done with you here." Disappointment sinks his grin. I dip my hands under his coat and hook my fingers around his belt loops. Tugging him with me, I add, "Fortunately, I've studied enough."

"You're very good at teasing, Ms. Salenger."

"I promise not to tease tonight." *Am I ready for this?* He makes me feel so ready, so ready for the first time. "I know how that can get hard." I wink, and on that note, I turn in his arms and open the door. Dashing up the stairs, he's quick behind me. I don't have a chance against those long legs of his, so I let him "win" at the top and give him his grand prize. *Me.*

Kissing him, I forget the past that came back today and get lost in the possibility of us and a future. "Come on," I say, anxious to continue kissing him inside.

Once the door is locked, I'm tossed onto the bed. I laugh and flop backward, spreading my arms wide across the mattress. "And here I thought this was going to be more romantic."

With not enough room to join me, Cooper climbs over me instead and tickles me under my coat and up my ribs. He hovers on top of me, his hands going wide to cover mine and pin me to the bed. I've not known heavy with him, but we seem to have straddled a line. "Is that what you want, babe? Romance? I can give you romance." He dips down, moving the collar of my coat and shirt aside with his teeth and a playful growl before nibbling along my exposed shoulder and following up with sweet little kisses.

"Oh, yeah?" I might be teasing him again, but considering how good his mouth feels on my skin right now, I'm not in a hurry to stop.

Is this it?

Is he the one?

I hold him close, knowing this is around the time my thoughts keep me from moving forward and following through. I swallow, not realizing it's in his ear until his head bolts up, and he looks at me. "You okay there?"

Staring into his eyes, I don't feel fear, and not an ounce of anxiety trickles through me. But my heart races for different reasons.

This is it.

He's the one.

There's no rhyme or rationale to how fast we're moving, but something deep inside me tells me I can trust him. "Cooper?" I hate that my voice shakes when I feel good about the decision I've made.

His reassuring smile is boyishly charming as he waits for me to say more. But I just like seeing him like this—that happiness in his eyes, a smile so genuine that it can't be mistaken for anything less than contentment, and so devastatingly handsome. "Story?" he asks, smirking again.

I giggle but quieter as my nerves start slipping in. I should tell him but wouldn't that just ruin things? I want to be treated like he would naturally, make love to me like he means it instead of being careful and using kid gloves.

His fingers fold with mine while he keeps eye contact.

"Hey," he says, tilting his head down and kissing me gently. "What's on your mind?"

Exhaling slowly, I whisper, "I was thinking this is going so fast—"

"Do you want to slow down?"

"No." Heat spreads over my chest. "This feels right. How do you feel?"

"You're asking a guy who's lying above the hottest girl he's ever seen if being between her legs feels right?" He chuckles. "Trust me, babe. You feel more than right."

I try to relax. There's no reason not to. I want this. I want him. "I want you."

"I want you so badly." He kisses me so deeply that I feel the passion all the way to my toes. A wave of his hips presses his hardness to the center at the top of my thighs. He wants me. He wants me as much as I want him.

Our bodies begin gyrating together, slowly at first and then a little harder, firmer, faster. Deeper. All the laughs we've shared are forgotten as we give in to the sensations we crave. His desire for me isn't just felt in the physical. It's more than skin deep. I can feel the connection, the bond we're forming. But then I realize I'm hot for other reasons. "We should take off our coats."

He looks down. "Damn." Sliding off me, he gets to his feet. "I don't know where my head's at when I'm with you, but no wonder it was so hot in here." Cooper strips his coat off and tosses it over the top of the chair. He doesn't stop there, though.

Lord have mercy, it's not just the coat that has me hot and bothered. Fanning myself, I remain lying on the bed and watch as he undresses—kicking his shoes off to the side, his sweater yanked over his head, and then he tugs the

T-shirt off from the back of his neck. *God, I love how he does that. Why is it so hot?*

Six-pack abs of sculpted muscle to run my fingers down and biceps I can't wait to see flexing on either side of my head are revealed without great fanfare, though they're so glorious they deserve a ticker-tape parade.

But as Cooper stands there half-naked, taking the rest of his clothes off, I'm still lying here fully clothed and jacketed like an idiot. He's the first man to ever give me an orgasm, then he did it again the next day. I scramble to the floor and kick off my sneakers, not sure why I was wasting so much time when I could be orgasming again.

I throw my coat at the door, watching it slide down and hit the floor while tugging off my Atterton sweatshirt. Cooper's jeans and socks hit the floor by the desk, and he dives back onto my bed.

Rolling over, he wears a smug grin across his face as his hands go behind his head, and he says, "Did I tell you how sexy you are?"

I flirt by wiggling the hips he can't seem to keep his hands off. "Once or twice, but feel free—"

"You're so incredibly sexy, Story."

The snap of my jeans is heard as I stand there stunned by his certainty, his conviction, and how he so easily navigates between sweet, playful, and drop-dead sexy. I don't know why my body reacts when his tone turns firm, and my breath struggles to clear my throat under the intensity of his gaze. His pupils widen, taking me in as I start tugging my jeans down.

But then I stop . . .

For one moment in time, I forgot my past and the scars I carry to this day.

And I have Cooper to thank for that.

But now I remember . . .

My hands slow, and then still.

I look at the man on the bed in front of me, and the fears I've carried for so long come rushing back.

What if he doesn't want me?

What if I turn him off?

What if he sees the real me, the one I hide?

What if . . . ?

"Story?"

I look back up at him from where I sit on the edge of the bed. I hadn't realized how I'd curled down in shame right in front of him, letting my thoughts get away with me.

He cups my face, running his thumbs over my cheeks to dry my tears. "I don't know who hurt you, but with me, you never have to be afraid."

It's a bold promise I'm not sure he can keep. But just hearing him say that, feeling his warm touch on my face, and seeing the empathy in his eyes, I stand back up before him and pull my jeans down to my ankles. As I step out of them, the light seems blinding on my legs, but I stay, not running to the bathroom like I want to.

I close my eyes, letting the air touch the bare skin of my legs and allowing him to see the real me.

Just as I gather the strength to share my history, the nightmare I survived, Cooper's lips caress the ugliness as his hands heat either side of my right thigh.

When I look down, a tear escapes my eye before I swipe it away, and it lands on his head. He looks up at me, and with our eyes fixed on each other's, he kisses my leg again, and says, "So. Fucking. Sexy."

13

Cooper

It's a vicious scar.

Running a good eight inches down the front of her thigh, the scar has faded over the years from angry to something on the softer side of pink. It's then that I realize she's been hiding this from me. Wearing everything from flannel pajama pants to jeans . . . to tights in the heat of summer. "Why do you hide this?" I ask, running the tips of my fingers over it.

Goose bumps pebble the skin on her inner thigh, and I'm quick to warm it, not realizing until more rise that I'm the cause of them.

She covers my hand and then comes and sits next to me on the bed. "Many reasons, the first of which is that it's hideous."

"It's not. We all have scars."

"I know. Some we just can't see. Trust me, Cooper, I've heard every platitude out there. They don't make me feel better. They make me realize how revolting people think I am that they have to say things like that in the first place."

I didn't expect the shortness. "Okay, how about I don't placate you. I just speak the truth?"

She looks at me, contemplating the offer. "Whose truth?"

"Mine. The only one that matters."

Laughing, she says, "You say that without any doubts."

"I'm an expert in the field of my truth." I kiss her shoulder while running my hand over her scar. Not sure if it's my comment or my kiss that has her smiling, but I'll take it either way.

"Can I ask you something, Cooper?"

"Anything."

Her head is lowered again, which I hate. Her eyes watch my hand like she's ready to bolt if I give her the chance. "Does seeing this make you feel any differently about me?" she asks.

"Truthfully?"

Tapping her head gently to my shoulder, she stays there a moment before she sits up again. "Honesty. Always."

"Yes." Her shoulders sag under the confession until I add, "I find you even more gorgeous than before."

As if the words themselves ran up her back, she sits straighter and then looks into my eyes with tears glistening in hers. "Really?"

"Really."

"Why?" she asks, not as shy as before.

"Because it's uniquely yours. You were right. We all have scars in different places, inside and out. I have some on my back from when I grew six inches over one summer in high school and one on my ankle when a deep-sea fishing line wrapped around my ankle and tightened, leaving me bleeding. I have one on my temple from when I got tackled in my junior year in high school and my helmet got knocked off, leaving a bad cut behind. God, I'm covered with them, and you know what? When I imagine my face the moment before I look in the mirror, you know how you expect to see something familiar in your reflection?" She nods as I take her hand between mine, holding it captive. "I see that scar in my mind. That's who I am."

"I don't want to be this scar. I want it to go away. I want the memory of being dragged across that glass to be gone forever."

My stomach tightens from the imagery, but my heart sinks from the pain shaping her face. I wrap my arm around her and kiss the side of her head. "I can't fix this, but I'm going to try my damnedest to take your mind off of it for a while."

She reaches over and pulls me closer with two fingers under my chin. "I think that's just about the sweetest thing anyone's ever said to me, Cooper Haywood." She kisses me, slowly standing. Pulling away, she asks, "I think I lost track of where we left off. Maybe you remember?"

"I remember." I slide back to the top of the bed, settling on the pillow again with my hands underneath my head for support. "You were just getting naked for me."

Laughter fills the apartment, and this time, she crawls up my body in her bra and panties. "Nice try, playboy."

I shrug. "Can you blame me?"

"I'd be offended if you didn't make the effort." She settles on my dick with only our underwear between us and then fucking wriggles. The woman can't resist teasing me.

When her gaze lowers to the scar on her thigh, I see her hand follow right after. I catch it and hold her hand, putting it above my head, which is a great decision on my part since her fantastic tits land in my face. Tilting down to look at me, she laughs. "What are you doing?"

"If we're going to be together—"

Dipping down, she runs the tip of her nose against mine, still smiling. "Are we going to be together, Cooper?"

"We're together now."

"What about tomorrow?" If another chick pushed the issue of a relationship, I'd lift her off me and be out the door before I was fully dressed.

I stretch and take her hand a little higher until her tits are at my mouth. She giggles. "You're so bad."

"You haven't seen anything yet. I promise I'll be so good to you." I place a kiss on each of her blooming nipples over the thin fabric. "I need you to make me a promise, though."

"What?"

Releasing her hand, I stroke her cheeks. "Don't cover yourself up with me. You never have to. Not with me, Story. Promise me."

Her smile hangs on, only slipping momentarily. An answer doesn't come as fast as I'd like, but then she says, "I promise."

Moving down with her still anchored on top of me, I then catch her as I flip her back to the mattress. "Now, should I start here?" I ask, rubbing my index finger over one nipple and then the other, wanting to remove the barrier so badly. Patience is a virtue I struggle with. "Or down here?" I slide my hand down between her legs.

"Depends. Fingers?" She sucks on the tip of her finger and then runs the wetness over my bottom lip. "Or mouth?"

"Mouth."

She sets her hands on top of my head and starts pushing me downward. Guess I got my answer.

My hand has been in her pants a couple of times now,

but I've not been this intimate with her, this naked, with not only our bodies exposed but also our intentions.

She likes to tease, but I know she's not teasing tonight. This will be our first time together, and I want to make it special for her.

Something about seeing her fall apart is so satisfying, but this time, I want to taste her. But first, I want to inhale her. I lean forward, pushing my nose against the satin fabric. Her fingers flex and wrap around my hair each time I do it. When I settle against her, taking deep breaths and filling my lungs with her scent, her hand tightens and pulls my hair.

When I exhale, I hear her do the same, and a wanton moan rings in my ears. Hooking my fingers around the sides of her panties, I start sliding them over the flow of her hips. She lifts her ass just enough for me to slide the silky material down her legs, leaving them wrapped around one ankle.

I lift the other and kiss the gentle slope on the top of her foot before resting her leg over my shoulder. Our eyes connect over the mounds of her chest, each breath a pant in anticipation that I refuse to disappoint.

Her legs butterfly and stay open for me as she watches me go down to kiss the innocence on her lower lips. One taste is all it takes for me to know there's no going back. I lift my chin, brushing the scruff against her, and say, "However long that you'll have me—tonight, tomorrow, and any or every day after that—I'm yours, Story, and you're mine."

Closing my eyes, I drag my tongue through the valley of her sweet pussy and savor the taste of her on my tongue.

"Promise?" she asks, the question a soft whisper from above my head.

I look up once more, only to be met with the beauty of that heart-shaped face and those hazel eyes staring into mine as if her entire world hinges on my answer. "I promise." And at that moment, though we're tangled in a compromising position, I swear to God I'll hold up my end of the deal.

With her pussy bare before me, she lies like a goddess I'm ready to serve, to bow at her feet and entertain every one of her whims. With our promise sealed, I get back to working on making her lose control.

I press my mouth to the most private part of her body and start kissing her like I'd kiss her on the mouth. I tickle her bud by circling it with my tongue, and I tease her entrance with one finger and then another before sinking them deep inside her.

Pushing off the bed, she arches her back as her mouth falls open. I play it cool, going gentle at first but with two fingers inside her, she moans and grabs a handful of my hair to tug on as if I grew it for this occasion.

I'll offer myself up for her to sacrifice any day or night. Running my hand, palm flat over her belly, up the middle of her body to reach her breasts, I ask, "You like that, baby?"

"I like it. So much, Cooper," she says eagerly. I could read her body's reaction—the squirming, how she pushes into my mouth, the arching back—but I really like hearing not only her reply but also my name slip off her tongue like a prayer. "Don't stop."

I pump my hand and flatten my tongue, licking her until she can't stop moving beneath me. Gripping her hip with my other hand, I hold her down and take over thrusting and licking, sucking and flicking until her body begins trembling, slowly at first, the release blooming for me with every exhale of my breath and inhale of hers.

I spy a hand fisting the blanket beside her just as the other returns to my head and her fingers fist my hair. "Yes.

Yes. Oh, my God, Cooper." She clamps down on her bottom lip to hold back, but her pleasure rips free again.

"Fuck," I groan, my dick a fucking traitor. I can't wait for my turn when the taste of her nectar coats my mouth.

Pushing my hips against the mattress, I try to think of anything that will keep me from coming from the dent in my Jaguar last year to that fucker at the coffee shop who made her cut her knees.

But with her release rattling through her body and my name shouted from her lips again, I give up the fight and give in to the sensation, closing my eyes. The darkness ceases, and the stars align as my body releases the buildup of days spent with the scent of her on me, the unforgettable kisses she has me craving, and the moments in quiet contemplation lying next to her.

I look up to find her with a lazy smile on her face and no smugness, but appreciation, admiration . . . or something more, filling her irises, and my heart clenches.

Between coming in my pants and now against her mattress, this is not how I saw things going. But more so, I never expected to feel this protective over someone, this in tune with or connected to a woman.

That promise was easy to make because I meant it. What does this mean? Could it . . .?

No.

Is it . . .?

Holy fuck.

Is this what love feels like?

14

Story

"It's okay."

When he doesn't respond to me, I get off the bed and walk to the bathroom. I slip a tank top over a bra and sleep shorts quickly since it seems he'll be a while and lean against the doorframe. Knocking with the back of my knuckles, I say, "Cooper? It's okay. *Really.* I don't mind."

The door swings open. His head is slightly dipped in disbelief, and his brow practically to his hairline. *And he's not wearing anything.* "You don't mind?" he grumbles, rocking his head back. Closing his eyes, he scrubs his hands over his face. "What the fuck is wrong with me?"

"Nothing is wrong with you. It was—"

"You shouldn't have to mind, Story." His gaze lands hard on me before he cups my face. "You should be lying on that bed unable to move from how spectacularly amazing I've made you feel. Instead, you're here, reassuring me."

Grabbing his wrist, I hold tight as I stare him straight in the eyes. "It's not like you're impotent."

"No." He releases me and storms across the apartment. "You don't say that word to a guy, not ever. Never."

"Got it. Never." I giggle and roll my eyes, completely helpless from the amusement of this scene.

"It's like a jinx or a hex, a fucking doomsday spell put on my dick."

"I think your"—I force the word from my mouth, trying to keep my eyes above board—"*dick* is going to be okay."

Shaking his head as he paces the small space, he mumbles, "Fucking hell."

I cross my arms over my chest and grin. He's always so put together, from his clothes to his composure. It's fun to see Cooper like this, so how can I not enjoy the show with the theatrics right here in my very own living room? And naked no less? "And here I thought girls were always the dramatic ones."

"Look." I catch him before he does a U-turn in the kitchen, taking hold of his arms and blocking him. But why does he have his body on full display? Those magnificent abs are a little distracting. That ass is so hardened it's criminal. I'm not sure what his routine is for keeping in that kind of shape, but it's so hard to not stare.

"Story?" We both know he busted me. He says, "My eyes are up here."

A quick shrug bounces off my shoulders. "Sorry. As I was going to say before, I was . . ." I run my fingers over each set of muscles, causing them to dance under my fingertips. "They really are pretty fantastic."

"My muscles aren't pretty. Can we find better words to describe me? You've already used the i-word, and now . . ." He runs his own hand over the summits and valleys of his six-pack. "Something I work my ass off to maintain is relegated to pretty?"

"This has gone too far. You're the sexiest man I've ever seen, Cooper. Probably the sexiest man alive. Every part of you is hard, and I just want to say thanks for working out and reaching this peak physical perfection."

"All right," he says, chuckling. His arms slide around me and cup my ass. "I get it. I'm hot."

I burst out laughing. "Yes, you are. And so humble."

Bending down, he kisses my neck and then nibbles on my earlobe. "You are, too." When he rubs against me, I can feel he might be ready to prove that the i-word isn't in his body's vocabulary.

I open myself up to him by bending my neck to the side, and then ask, "I'm humble?"

He chuckles, a warm breath breezing across my skin. "You are and very hot."

"Hot and humble. I have absolutely no problem with those descriptors." Wrapping my arms around his neck in hopes of keeping him exactly where he is, I close my eyes and enjoy his lips on my skin. I even find myself rubbing against him because I wouldn't be upset if he wanted to go for round two.

Am I ready?

Physically—my body is.

Emotionally—my heart is ready for the journey.

Coming around to my mouth, he kisses me and quickly deepens it. Cooper is so sweet to me, kindness residing in his eyes every time he looks into mine, careful, cautious, caring about my feelings and taking care of me when I was sick.

Obviously handsome.

Thoughtful for bringing lunch.

But he's also here, has had no issue spending time in my space, and has never once demeaned it—or me.

The thousand-dollar tip still needs to be discussed, but this isn't *Indecent Proposal.* He didn't buy my time or my body. He appreciates every inch, including the ugly and damaged parts of me, and makes sure I'm taken care of in all ways before thinking of himself.

Holding him tighter, I push up against him, relishing the feel of his erection and savoring the tingling sensation zipping through my body. I've been numb for years, going through life with nothing more than my full attention on surviving and getting out of this town. With Cooper, I feel alive. My body reacts to his. It's been nice to stay in the present, to live the past few days without a grand plan in place, to wing the hours and do what feels good, what feels right.

I hadn't even realized what my days had become until Cooper showed up and flipped my life on its axis.

His kisses make me weak in the knees and horny for more. "I'm ready," I whisper against his mouth through shortened breaths.

Bending back just enough to catch my eyes on him, he smiles. No smirk is found, just that smile of his that puts me at ease. "You're sure?"

"Are you trying to talk me out of it?"

"Nope." Scooping me into his arms, he sits on the bed with me across his lap and caresses my cheek.

Before he has a chance to say anything, I feel my heart racing, but ask, "Do you have a condom?"

He dips his chin. "I have one."

I'm not sure how I feel about that. I should be grateful he has one since the box I bought in anticipation of this moment has probably expired. "You're prepared."

As if he can read my mind, he kisses my forehead, then leans back again. "I don't usually carry condoms around with me, but . . ." He glances toward the window and back to me. "After the past few times we spent here, I felt we were progressing in that direction."

His response settles me, easing my mind with his reasoning. "We are, and I'm ready." I lean forward, cupping his face and kissing him again. This time, I don't stop. I maneuver off his lap and move over him until he's on his back.

Gripping me by the hips, he slides us to the middle of the bed while staying on his back and keeping his lips connected with mine. His hands run under my top and straight to my chest as he cups my breasts over my beige bra. *Beige.* Why'd I have to grab the boring beige bra?

There's nothing sexy about it, but he makes me feel like it is, like I am. The kneading, the flick of his thumbs over my nipples, the feel of him between my legs have me closing my eyes and dropping my head back, taking in the pleasure as it swims through me and releases in a breathy sigh of bliss.

His image spins in my head, but then I look down to see the real thing. Cooper's gaze meets mine but only briefly. He sits up enough to pull my top over my head. He's quick to lie back, returning his hands to my boobs. They've always been big for my frame at a small C, but in his hands, they seem smaller.

"I like your tits," he says.

I don't think a guy has ever called them that so bluntly as if that's their name. Sort of crude yet so sexy in the context of what we're doing. Bending forward, I let his hands roll over my breasts while I wiggle on top of his erection. "I like your dick."

He stills his hands and stares up at me. "Story."

With a shrug, I start giggling. "Touché to you, sir."

He eyes my breasts, and they demand his attention, so

he begins kneading again. "It was the truth. You have great tits."

Trying to keep up, to stay bold, I say, "I'm only telling the truth, too."

He chuckles. "You're out of hand tonight." Sitting up just by using those impeccable ab muscles, he kisses me. "And I like that, too." He takes my hand and kisses my palm before lowering it between us. With a lift of his legs, I slip back enough to expose his erection. Placing my hand over him, he covers mine and starts rubbing. With his eyes set on mine, he asks, "You like that, babe?"

I nod, a knot lumped in my throat before I can swallow it down. Leaving me to feel the length and girth as he slides his hands over my biceps and shoulders. Then he moves up my neck and into my hair with his lips following right behind. The tip of his nose toys with my earlobe when he whispers, "I want to be inside you."

With a quickening pulse, I harness the power he's given me and roll my head to the side, causing our cheeks to brush against each other. "I want you inside me." I lift off and get to my knees on either side of him. Reaching around my back, I unclasp my bra, letting the elastic loosen around me.

Cooper slides the straps over my shoulders, his attention captivated as if he's unwrapping a precious gift. He kisses my collarbone, then each shoulder when my chest is revealed. But he doesn't stare at my chest. Instead, he warms me by pulling me close and kissing my neck, always thinking of me first from my comfort to my pleasure.

I feel emboldened in his presence, in the way he lets me lead or retrieves control when I need it. He didn't miss a beat with my ugly scar and treated it with the same care he handles the rest of me. He made it easy to forget my flaws and made me feel beautiful for the first time.

Resting back with my hands on the mattress, I sit with my breasts exposed, wanting his eyes to drink me in and approve.

Cooper Haywood doesn't disappoint.

His breath staggers when he takes me in but not from nerves. "You're beautiful, Story." Running the tip of his finger over the bud of one breast and then the other, he says, "Like seeing the sun set for the first time over the bay or catching a dewdrop clinging to a rose petal early in the morning." He looks up again. "I'm going to make you feel so good."

He shifts me to the side and gets up to go to his coat. "By leaving me here alone?" I joke.

Digging in the pocket, he comes back to bed and drops a condom in front of me. "Trust me, I have no intention of leaving you alone tonight. Get naked."

He's so comfortable in his skin that he makes me envious of that freedom. But with him, I can feel that freedom. I do because of how we are together. It's irrational to feel this good with someone you barely know, but we're different. We don't need years or months to feel the connection. We're tasting it now.

We're creating it, molding it, defining our own path.

He climbs in bed and holds the sheet up. "You coming?"

"Oh God, yes, I want to come again." I scramble to my feet, tasting that freedom he's given me, and start pulling my shorts down. He watches as his hand slips under the covers, and he adjusts his body. Licking his lips, he doesn't take his eyes off me. Even though the lights in the kitchen are on and flooding the apartment, I don't feel embarrassed. I love seeing him turned on from his pupils darkening to the way he slowly rubs himself unashamed in any way.

I want that. I want all of this with him morning, noon, and night—the talks in bed, the cuddling, the lunch and dinners together. The sex. The making love. Whatever we want this to be, I want all of it.

Totally bare, I climb back in bed and slip under the covers next to him. He leans over, already kissing along my jaw and a hand dipping under the covers to cup my vagina. His middle finger slides between my legs, and he drags it higher, bringing it to his lips. He sucks it in, then rubs it along my bottom lip. All I taste is him. Lying back, I let the flavor consume me. He makes me want to beg, to plead, so I say, "I want you to fill the emptiness."

Cooper dips down and kisses my head before grabbing the condom and rolling it down his length. Neither nerves nor anxiety slips into the silence, and for that, I know this is right.

Popping onto his forearms, he hovers over me, basking in the reflection of my eyes like he can see the sunshine in them. Lowering his hand between us, he positions himself at my entrance. This will be good. Just like every other time with him. "Do we go slow?" I hate that I even ask. *Just flow with my instincts*, I remind myself.

"I don't want slow with you, Story." Our mouths mold together as he pushes forward. The pressure strikes, and my body burns as I acclimate. But I'll burn in hell if it always feels this great.

Tipping my head back, I try to regulate my breathing and debate if I should try some technique. "Story?"

"Yes?" My eyes bolt open. I realize that he's staring at me. Cooper Haywood is inside me. I inhale deeply and calm my racing thoughts.

"All good?"

"Yes, so good."

Comfort warms the concern on his face, and he says, "You feel amazing." Dropping his head to my shoulder, he starts moving slowly at first, but like his promise, he speeds up, plunging deep within me. His breath is hot on my neck, and his hands are gliding over my skin. He's on top of me, in me, and everywhere all at once.

Spreading my legs wider, I rock my hips against each of his thrusts, meeting him hard in the middle. My body takes over, and as sweat starts to coat our bodies, sliding slick against each other, he whispers words of beauty and praise, sensual and naughty things. I should cling to each one in case I'm never privy to the inner workings of this man's mind, but one captures my attention, causing me to slow down—*orange tights*.

I have to smile from the obscure things Cooper remembers, but I'm also flattered he noticed. I begin to relax and enjoy the act of being together. Running my hand into his hair, I say, "I never want this to end." Spoken the moment before his fingers find my clit, lightning strikes, and I'm quick to fall apart.

While my body is suspended in crushing bliss, his thrusts become erratic. Pushing up with his hands, he stares into my eyes as he makes love to me. And then his own release seizes to the edges of his psyche. His breathing deepens, then accelerates as his body fucks mine—kissing me, fucking me, biting and licking my neck until he groans, "Fuck."

The weight of the universe fills his sated body as he lies on top of me, our bodies still bonded, our breathing still unsteady. When my own breathing is ragged, he rolls off me, one arm falling wide and half hanging off the bed. The other rests between us, and he holds my hand.

Bringing it to his mouth, he kisses the back of my hand and then waits until I look at him. I ask, "What?"

"Why didn't you tell me you're a virgin?"

15

Story

"Why didn't you tell me that Haywood Hall is the same Haywood as your family tree?"

I ask, holding the sheet up to my neck as we stare at each other.

The silent standoff extends until he rubs his eyes and sighs heavily. Nothing in his expression tells me he wants to broach this subject. Maybe it wasn't fair of me to toss that out of nowhere, but my defenses kicked into gear. He says, "Long story."

"A long history as well. I've walked through the doors of that building a thousand times over the years and seen the plaque proudly displayed beside them. It dates back to 1902."

Anger has never entered his eyes, but I see a heaviness clouding them. I start regretting bringing it up after we just had such an amazing time. "I wouldn't have known other than how much you avoided the subject every time it was brought up."

"And now I just confirmed it." Resolve fills in the line between his brows, and he looks at the ceiling.

I've lost the heat of his closeness and the touch of his hand. The cold air from outside starts to sneak in through the crevices of the old brick building, and a chill runs up my spine. Not wanting to lose what we just shared, I try to go back in time, and say, "I thought you could tell."

He looks at me again. "Tell what?"

"That I was a virgin."

His eyes widen. "By looking at you?" Turning his body toward me again, he strokes his temple. "It doesn't work like that."

"Or touching me down there."

"It was . . ." He struggles to find the words when he searches for them above my head. His mood softens his expression, and the right side of his mouth tilts up. "You felt amazing, but I don't know what tipped me off. I think just how you reacted when I first entered . . . you know." He closes his eyes. For a moment, he's so peaceful that I consider closing mine, seeking the same. "I promise we'll talk about Haywood Hall, but let's have this conversation first. Is that okay?"

"Okay." I move closer. His arm lifts like a parking garage gate, and I slide into place tucked into the nook of his body. Our bodies simmer together as I control the flames threatening to flare into a full-on blaze from the connection.

"Why didn't you tell me?" he asks.

"Because I thought you'd treat me differently, and truthfully, I like how things have been between us."

"I do, too."

"I like how you see me. I feel that deep down," I say, a hand pressing to my chest. "I didn't want to ruin that."

"I get that, and you're right. I would have treated tonight, and you, differently. I wouldn't have gone as fast, and I would have checked in on you more along the way."

"But I don't need that. I didn't." I kiss his chest. "What we just did was perfect to me. Isn't that what matters?" I drape my arm over him, holding him. "The rest is just fluff or icing on the top."

He kisses my head, then my cheek, and lingers on my lips. "You deserve fluff and icing." His arm tightens around me, and he kisses me again. When he lies back, he adds, "I'll make it up to you."

"You don't have to do anything for me. I'm serious, Cooper. I lov—" I stop the words from flowing from my mouth, worried that even though I loved the sex we had, using the l-word in any context might rock the boat even more.

"You don't have to be careful with me, Story. Say what's on your mind when you feel it. It's the only way things are going to work in a relationship." A growing grin lends itself to the lighter mood working its way across his face. "I loved it, too. You felt . . . it was amazing."

Although he called me amazing, and that has me floating on air, it's the other word that has my heart racing again. "Relationship?" I ask, no longer careful with my words.

"Yeah." He runs his hand over his head, his eyes suddenly fixed on the small overhead light that needs dusting. "But we need to talk about tomorrow—"

Mentally ticking through my schedule for tomorrow— no more classes, a day off work—I come up blank. "What's happening tomorrow?"

He sits up, leaning against the wall for support. "I'm leaving."

The somberness of his tone starts to concern me, my

mind suddenly spinning. "Like for the holidays or for good?"

"The holidays, but I was going home until school started back up."

Now I sit up, holding the sheet over my chest. "That's four weeks, Cooper."

Nodding, he says, "That's why we should talk about the holiday break. What are your plans?"

"I'll be here working."

"The whole time?"

The question has me pausing to consider my answer as if I have another option. I don't. "I was thinking about spending a weekend at the Cape—"

"I can meet you there."

Of course, he can meet me there. Doesn't seem like he has many cares in the world. My eyes narrow. Although it's a sweet gesture, I can't stop my scoff. "I was being sarcastic. I've never been to Cape Cod."

"Oh." He tugs at a loose thread on the blanket as if it has become the most interesting thing in the world.

"Why am I starting to feel like something's off between us?"

Holding out his hand, he waits until I place mine on his palm before sandwiching it with his other. "It's not you or us. It's me. I don't want to go home, but I have family shit to deal with. Once that's done, I'm free."

"Free for what?"

"For you." He drops that bomb like he doesn't know the impact it would make. And then he raises an eyebrow. The shake of his head is minute, but I catch it. "If you'd like to continue this. Not just the sex . . . Fuck." He runs his fingers through his hair. "This is coming out all wrong. I'd like to see you again, to hang out and stuff."

I give him a smile, and he pushes up on my knees to rotate to sit next to him. With my back against the wall, our hands clasped together, fingers entwined, I lean my head on his shoulder. "I like hanging out with you." I bring his hand to my lips and kiss each finger. "I like a lot with you, especially the time we've spent together."

His arm reaches over me, and his hand cups my cheek, bringing me to meet his eyes. "I never expected to meet you. The timing sucks with winter break. I don't know much about you, Story. Where you're from . . ." My stomach clenches. "What's your major? How do I not know any of this?"

"The avoidance thing when Haywood Hall is brought up."

He chuckles. "You have classes in Haywood Hall, but I never imagined you as an accounting major."

"How did you imagine me?"

The boyish charm has returned with a little waggle of his brow. "The truth? Naked. Many, many times."

"Confession: I've let my eyes *and* mind linger on you."

Swinging his arm behind, he tucks me under his shoulder and kisses the top of my head. I love how easy, how open he is with kissing—from the deeper French kisses to the soft ones he places just because he feels the need. Cooper makes me feel appreciated, valued, too soon to say cherished? I feel that through and through because of his actions. I say, "The words and stories, the background, the information, and facts, our biographies will be shared in time. But I feel a connection with you that I've never felt with anyone else."

Staring at our hands, I twist my wrist and watch how strong the bond is as they stay together. Looking up at him, I add, "I feel like I know your soul. I'm okay waiting on the rest . . . except for Haywood and the Hall. I'll need that story sooner."

"I'm thirsty. Water?"

"Yes, please." I watch as he climbs out of bed still naked, the muscles working so beautifully together as he moves across the room that I can't think of any sculpture that would compare.

As he grabs two of the bottles he bought and stocked in my fridge, he says, "You want to talk about it and get it out of the way?"

I look at him, batting my eyelashes. "Yes, please," I reply giddily and with a little bounce on the bed.

"The shorter version because I promise it's boring, predictable, and has fucked me over a few times." He untwists the cap and hands me a bottle. "I'm kind of bitter over it."

"Only share what you want, Cooper. We have time ahead of us for all the ugly stuff."

He downs half the water and then returns to bed, holding the bottle when he readjusts back on his side. *His side.* I smile, kind of loving that we already have sides.

After taking another long swig, he says, "My grandfather, Daxton Haywood, four generations back, got accepted here after his father, Archibald, offered to build Haywood Hall for Atterton University. The honor of naming the building after Archibald came as part of the bargain. Little known fact. It was called Archie Hall until the twenties when the school was actively trying to up its clout to compete with the Ivy League. Hence, Haywood Hall."

"You could give tours."

"*Yeahhh* . . . no." He laughs, then empties the bottle.

I could fixate on the fact that Cooper's apparently from very old money with his notable name, but the story cements the truth. More so, I'm fascinated by him. "You're legacy."

"Five generations, but I've not held up the Haywood name as much as my father would like."

"How so?"

He stalls this time with a roguish grin on his face. "Well . . . that might have to wait for another time." He glances over and taps me on the nose. "Happy now?"

"Happy that I'm sleeping with the fifth generation of the building that holds my major?" I grin wildly. I move on top of him and straddle his deliciously muscular legs. "That's not what got me into bed."

Taking the bait, he drops the bottle on the floor next to the bed and grabs my ass, squeezing my cheeks and causing pressure between us. My body slickens against his length, and I bite my lip.

"What got you into bed, babe?"

I lean down and kiss him with all the passion he's shown me, and then whisper, "Meeting the right guy."

16

Cooper

Dawn steals the night away from us, peeking in the crack where the shade doesn't fully close and the sheer curtains won't hide us away from the rest of the world.

Although I only got a few hours of sleep, Story is sleeping soundly wrapped over me. She doesn't realize that I'm completely wrapped up in her.

I never believed I deserved anything so good or pure, someone who looks at me not like I'm who they want me to be but for who I am. Or maybe it's just because I've never met anyone like her.

Generous to a fault.
Charitable heart.
Thoughtful.
And smart.

The first time she spoke to me, I understood why Lou had a crush on her because I felt the same. It was as if I was the only one in the room with her. That's who Story is—she makes you feel important as if you're the only one who matters.

I'm still not sure how I'm the lucky bastard holding her now. *And fuck.* I took her virginity. I look down at her in my arms and how perfectly she fits there and grin like a fucking fool. Taking a V-card has never been a goal of mine, though I've had a few given to me over the years.

I don't know. I keep coming back to the same thing. There's something different, deeper, the two of us are sharing. I just wished I'd earned hers and given her a night she'd never forget.

Stirring, she keeps her eyes closed as she licks her lips, and the smallest smile exists from her sweet dreams. I wonder if I've made any appearances. She's provided me plenty of material for dreams to jerk off to and get me through the next month.

What am I saying?

That I'm off the market?

A taken man?

Story's boyfriend?

The last one fits the best, but that's a big step in a direction I don't usually travel. So why am I even considering a relationship with her? I'll fuck it up somehow.

"Cooper?"

Looking down, I see her pretty hazels gazing up at me. "It's early. You should be sleeping."

"You should too, but here we are."

"Yeah," I say, adjusting on the bed so I'm at eye level with her. "Here we are."

Reaching out, she runs her fingertips along my hairline and around my ears. "You look like you have the weight of the world on your shoulders. Want to talk about it?"

"We only have a few more hours, so I'm not sure I want to open that baggage and waste the time we have left."

"How much time do we have left?" A yawn captures her despite a fight to stave it off.

"I'll hit the road around ten to make it home when I'm expected."

"I'm not sure what to think about your family. It sounds like they've put a lot of pressure on you for some reason. I'm not asking you for the details, but I wish it didn't weigh on you like this." With her hand resting on the curve of my neck, so comfortable lying together naked, she says, "You said you have an apartment, but if they're tied to the university and kicking you out, you can stay here with me. Heck, even if they're not kicking you out, you can stay if you want."

Her generosity is on display again, and I don't mind being on the receiving end of it. I just wish I could take her up on the offer. What if I lived like she did, willing to give more than I receive? What would I do? "Where are you spending Christmas?"

She crickets her legs, rubbing them together. "In this bed waiting for you to return."

"You're very enticing, Ms. Salenger."

"Only when I want something." Maybe it's the early morning voice that makes her sound so seductive, but she knows what she wants.

And I'm game to play. "Oh, yeah? What do you want?"

Pushing forward, she kisses my chin and then moves down to my neck. "How much time do you need to pack?"

"Thirty minutes. Tops."

"Good," she replies. "I'm going to need the other three hours before you leave." Shifting down, she starts to slip under the covers.

Catching her arms before she disappears, I say, "I want

that. So badly. I want to see your mouth wrapped around me. But—"

"But?" Her lips are just barely parted as she waits with bated breath.

"You said you're staying to work, but what about Christmas Day?" She barely has time to take a breath to answer before I add, "What if you came home with me? Or for a visit? You can spend Christmas with my family."

"I'll be honest, you haven't done a great job of selling your family to me."

"No, but you being there will keep them on their best behavior. Ultimately though, you'd be there with me."

"For you," she corrects, seeing right through my plan.

I eat some humble pie and give her the credit she deserves. "Okay, *for* me."

"Who's the enticing one now, Mr. Haywood?" *Fuck, that's hot.* This time, I lie back and let her slide under the covers. Rolling down the blanket, I watch her take me in—just a little at first and then deeper—before slipping my hand into her hair and closing my eyes to let the pleasure rip through me.

WAKING Story up seems cruel after the activities of the past twelve hours, so I let her sleep instead. But this debate is getting the best of me, so I stop to rub my brow and think through how to end this.

Best?

Always?

Is always true?

Love?

No. Too soon for that.

Sincerely?

That works.

I sign, *Sincerely, Cooper*, at the bottom of the letter and then set the pen down on the desk beside it. I look around once more before I head to the door and open it. Stopping, I take a deep breath, still not sure if I want to leave.

I know I have to, but it's not what I'd choose if given a choice.

"You're just going to sneak out like that?" I look back to see her propped up on her elbows. "I don't like going to bed with you, then finding it empty in the morning."

"I'm sorry." I fill her doorway, my shoes full of emotional cement keeping me here. "You looked peaceful. I didn't want to ruin it."

A small smile appears, hard-earned it seems. "For the past two years, I've spent it with Lila, my manager—my friend from work—and her son. But I have no plans for Christmas. It's just me since my mom died."

Leaning against the doorframe, I settle in because I want to hear anything she's willing to share. "Where's your dad?"

"I don't know," she replies as if I've asked her something mundane and matter of fact. "I don't even know who he is other than a one-night stand my mom once had."

"Men are assholes."

She laughs, rolling onto her side, head propped up on her hand, looking every bit as youthful as she is. "My mom liked to sleep around. It wasn't about the sex. It was about the attention. She'd drink it like a shot, getting drunk on the foreplay of a man's admiration."

I'm not sure what to say about that or what to think. I'm all for people owning their desires, but I don't think I'd want to know that about my mom, speaking as her kid. It sounds like Story had a front row seat to the show. Not wanting to inject my own theories, I decide that listening is best.

Our gazes stay locked on each other's until she looks down, plucking at an unraveled string. The smile I've gotten used to seeing on her face has slipped into a sadness that looks unnatural on her. The energy of the air shifts between us, and then she says, "I don't know where we stand or if I'm even going to see you again after the holiday break. I'd understand, Cooper, I would. With you being a Haywood, you might not want to slum it on the wrong side of the tracks with me. But . . ."

Is she about to end us prematurely? "It's only bad timing," I say, trying to redirect and get us back on track.

"I don't know about bad timing." Her smile puts me at ease. "I've started believing that people come into your life when they're supposed to and most needed." Realizing I'm still filling her doorway, I step back inside the apartment and close the door. She adds, "So I may be bad timing in your life, but you have been a good change in my day-to-day."

Coming around, I sit on the bed where I was sleeping an hour earlier. "I need to tell you something, Story."

"Okay, you sound serious. Is something wrong?"

"No, just the opposite. It's been really right with you. That's what I mean about bad timing. I like the time we've spent together, but here we'll have a month and many miles separating us."

"Where are you from? If you're driving, we can drive to see each other . . . well, I don't have a car, but Lila might let me borrow hers for a day or two if the invitation is still open."

"It is for you. And hey, I can come back at least once for a quick visit." Leaning forward, we kiss as if a plan has been conspiratorially hatched. Maybe it has. Either way, we're in this together. "Normally, we'd celebrate Christmas in the city, but my mom insisted on our home in—" I stop, cringing inside.

"Where? Where's your other home, Cooper?" She smirks, giving me a little shit. Somehow, she makes it funny, unlike some of the guys when I was growing up.

I learned to throw a punch and take my opponent down in one hit after getting my ass kicked for being a Haywood. Learning to not only defend myself but also make sure people are too afraid to start anything has gotten me in trouble over the years.

I'm not exactly the son my parents dreamed of.

"Haywood."

"What's Haywood?"

Internally, I brace myself for the usual reaction I receive. "The town my family founded."

"You're so fancy, Cooper," she says, laughing. "I don't think I can take much more. Next, you're going to tell me you live up on the hill." But when I don't laugh, hers fades away. "You're kidding me?"

I shake my head. "I'm afraid not." Holding tighter to her hand, I ask, "Is this going to be a hurdle for us?"

She brings me closer by tugging on my hand with hers, and with her other, she grabs my coat and then kisses me. "Only if we let it."

"I won't," I say as if I can control the world and how it treats us, as if I have the final say. *God, I wish I did.*

With our foreheads tipped together, our gazes fixed on the bond of our hands, she says, "I can't promise that I won't be surprised again, but I'm glad I got to know you without any of that interfering."

This time, I nod, but I'm cautious of breaking our

connection, more than just our foreheads, but what the past few days has created. "I am, too. I care about you, Story." I let the sentiment settle between us, waiting for her to reply, to say something that lets me know we're in the same place and heading in the same direction.

Which is?

I'm not sure I'm ready to put a voice to it, but it feels good with her no matter where we land, as long as we're together.

I need to get going, but I stay and lean back to look in the eyes that make me feel invincible, like I can be more than I've been, more than the past that tries so hard to hold me back.

Story's a powerful aphrodisiac for wanting to live a better life. Guess she's rubbing off on me.

Dipping her head back, she moves in as close as she can while holding eye contact. "You came into my life and swept me off my feet, going a hundred miles an hour." She kisses my chin. "And I've loved every minute of it. I'm going to miss you, Cooper Haywood."

I kiss the top of her nose and then her lips because damn, those lips are amazing. "I'm going to promise you something, Story Salenger." She smiles. "I'm not going to be out of your life long enough to be missed. I promise you that I'll be back before you know it."

We kiss once more. She lies back as I head for the door. When I open it again, I glance at the note. "I might have been sneaking out, but this time, I left a note."

She's quick to her feet. Seeing it, she snatches it off the desk, scans it, and holds it to her chest. "You gave me your number?"

I don't give my number to every girl I fuck, but Story's not just any girl. My feelings have grown even stronger overnight. Of course, I don't need to sound like a sap, so I keep it simple. "Figured it was time since we've gone to the next level with this relationship."

"Do you want mine?"

"Text me whenever you want to share something or call me day or night."

Climbing onto the bed, she stays on her knees, looking at me like she'll find some loophole to this plan. "Even if I just want to hear your voice?" She doesn't understand how deep I'm falling for her, and saying it before I walk out this door doesn't seem like the right thing to do. Especially not after fucking her like she wasn't a virgin.

Moving forward, Story will get the best of me. Not only does she deserve it but it's also what she brings out in me.

"Anytime, babe." I give her a wink and close the door behind me.

I'm not sure how long I stand in the hall tempted to run back in and break my own rule, but I remember who I am, and leave, already morphing back into the prodigal son returning home.

PART II

WE FELL TOO FAST TO TURN BACK

Not giving a fuck, and being an angry teenager, I signed away my rights to the family fortune at seventeen.

At twenty-two, I sit before the jury of my family as they offer me pieces of my inheritance back. Enough to get my attention, to crave the freedom the money could give me, but I'm not able to stomach the amendments.

Not after this week.

Not after meeting Story.

I look down at the screen of my phone and the photo Story sent before I reached the bottom step of her apartment building when I had to leave. Hair splayed across the cream-colored pillowcase. Not a stitch of makeup left on her pretty face after I spent the night kissing every inch of it. Bare shoulders and a hint of the top mounds of her breasts, the sheet refusing to stay put. I approve of that for what it's worth.

It's those eyes that captivate me every time—the green of the bay battling for priority over the henna-hued cliffs at sunset. Her eyes bring me back to the coastline of the sea where I used to wish I could go during the familial battles in my life. It was my solace, my haven away from the expectations I failed and the disappointments I achieved.

Staring at this girl, the woman who I've developed intense feelings for, I look up and push the contract back. "I can't sign this."

17

Cooper

"It's so wonderful to see you again."

The moment I hear *her* voice mingling with my mother's tone in lilted discussion traveling from the foyer to the bar cart in the living room, I brace myself. I drop the ice into a crystal glass, realizing that reinforcements, namely Camille Arden, have been brought in.

My mom invited her over as if the breakup didn't happen at all. *How thoughtful of her . . .* I pour the bourbon over the ice and prepare myself for the onslaught that is Camille and my mom together. They're two peas in a pod.

The clack of their heels against the marble entry sounds alarms like sirens in the middle of the night. Unsettling. I find myself looking for the closest escape route.

"Cooper, look who stopped by." My mom holds her expression—too smiley for the coincidence. It doesn't suit her.

Too late.

My mom slides her hand gracefully along the side of her

hair that's perfectly pinned up without a hair out of place. She has a softer green than the harshness of my eyes and not a flaw on her, not even a freckle daring to mark her face. The black-and-white-houndstooth skirt and white blouse under a striking yellow sweater complete her Haywood look —country clubs, charity events, and society parties. She fits right in when we're here. I prefer how she dresses—more black, sleeker styles, "casual" days as she calls them when she wears jeans with a designer jacket—in the city better.

"Camille," I say. Even I can hear the boredom in my voice, and we haven't even exchanged formal greetings. As for "stopping by," that's not Camille's style. From her expensive clothes to the jewelry she wears, from dates to daily life, she never does anything unplanned. There's not a wild bone in her body. It was one of our greatest conflicts, though our match didn't rival it. It surpassed all other issues to become the barrier I relied on when I broke up with her last July.

She was never a girlfriend. She wasn't even really a friend of mine. Camille Arden was brought in for damage control. I just wish I would have figured it out sooner.

The perfect agent to pull off the job, her hair was styled long with no curls, her eyes as blue as mine are green, startling if you're not used to them. Taller than average, she's done some modeling but prefers hosting conversational dinner parties for twelve instead. But that means landing a husband in Haywood or waiting for her wealthy parents to pass away.

Right before I broke it off, I found out that a deal was struck between our two families years prior to my high school graduation. My arrest for disorderly conduct that landed me in a drunk tank overnight made them skittish about the commitment.

I take a long pull from the glass before I—*fuck it*. I don't have the energy to play these games.

My mom sidesteps while adjusting the sweater draped around her shoulders. "I'll just leave you two lovebirds alone."

I glare at her as she disappears down the corridor to my parents' wing of the house before I can correct her. I'm sure that's another piece of the plan.

Camille says, "You look good, really good, Coop. School's going well?" She gets compliments on her blue eyes all the time, but she's hollow inside with no soul to be found beyond the coloring. I'd almost forgotten.

And though it's not fair to compare the two, Story's eyes hold a world of depth. The thing is, I don't hate Camille. She was another pawn in the game. She just hasn't realized it yet, not like I have. "It's going. How's Huntley College?"

"It's such a bore, and since the university is small, it doesn't offer much either." She comes over to me, takes the glass, and holds it under her nose. "Bourbon always made you do bad things if memory serves. Interesting you're drinking again, or did you never give it up?"

"I was never an alcoholic, Camille. I was on a mission to destroy this town one bar brawl at a time."

She pulls a bottle of Dom Pérignon and starts ripping the wrapping from around the cork. "I've traveled a lot, but not much compares to home. So, I never did understand why you hate this place so much."

"Because the Haywoods are *and were* awful people."

"You're a Haywood, so what does that say about you?" she asks, handing me the bottle to open like our old routine is still in play.

"I was born with all their terrible deeds running through my veins."

Popping the cork, I then set it on the counter, thinking this isn't the war I'm waging with her. She gives me a look, and though she tries to hide it, I see the slight roll of her eyes as she starts filling the champagne flute. "Your history is wasted on you."

"It's not wasted. I'm the product of it."

Pressing the 18k carat gold rim of the glass to her bottom lip, she stares at me over the crystal and the bubbly liquid inside. Camille always loved to pause for dramatic effect and the attention it allowed to flow in her direction. She sips, and then her gaze turns to linger over the furnishings. "Your mom's redecorated. I like the beachy vibe."

For her whole life, Camille has had dreams of a home full of valuable antiques and a baroque and depressing art collection. And she's not shy about putting that out there to any suitor who shows interest. I witnessed it for years before I thought I'd try stepping in line to please my parents and get a trust fund owed to me from my grandparents back in my name.

Like a tiger trying to hide its stripes, it's impossible. I would never fit into the mold just the way they wanted. Not interested in my mom's new couch, I finally ask, "What are you doing here?"

She gingerly sips her champagne. "I heard you were back and wanted to see you."

I raise my arms out from my sides. "Here I am. Are we done now?"

"Rude, Coop." She finishes her drink and begins to refill it.

Pouring just a finger more of the bourbon into my glass over the melted ice, I wonder how much I want to entertain her.

If I'm hiking or running in the snow, pushing my lungs

to open while I work through my life, that contract, and the deadline they've added of Christmas Day, I spend hours in my room where my patience has worn thin by the lack of human contact.

They've tried to tame me my entire life. Glancing at Camille, I know it worked for a short time. I just couldn't hack the confinement of the prison they'd constructed for my life before I figured out what they were doing.

I move to the window to stare outside at the sky that decided to dump snow like there's no end in sight. I grin, hearing Story's voice inside my head. *"I don't mind it so much . . . it's more the images it conjures."* She'd love this snow and sitting by the fireplace keeping the living room warm.

Six days of little ways of touching base keep us connected. I've gotten a photo every day of things that remind her of me. A photo of rain through the window of the coffee shop somehow brings me comfort. Another of the note I left her that looks like it's been read a thousand times from the rough edges and bends in the paper. My side of the bed because yes, I've already claimed that. And some others of the world we're building together—the empty bottle I left on the floor after we had sex for the first time, a glove that stayed behind. I tore my apartment up looking for that.

All these things have me smiling.

Story has me feeling different about myself, the man I am here versus when I'm with her. I miss it—all of it—her, that bed, the dim coffee shop that feels like a second home to so many.

A difference in our schedules has left us fumbling to bridge the gap in time. She works late, and I'm up early, so we find ourselves somewhere in between.

There's no sexting, but that's understandable since I just took her V-card. *Fuck.* Guilt riddles through me, and I shake my head. Until I make that right, it just feels wrong to have it play out the way it did. Not that it wasn't great, but just not what it should have been.

But yeah, sending photos on the illicit side or even getting off on a live connection seems like something she might not be ready to do. I'm craving her—touch, the taste of her lips, the feel of her silky hair running between my fingers, being inside her, and spending time together.

Is it witchcraft? Or sorcery that has me feeling empty without her? What kind of spell has Story cast on me?

"Christmas morning and presents under the tree."

I turn back to find Camille staring at me. "What?" I ask.

"The tree is beautiful." She studies the ten-foot noble fir in the corner. "I was asking if you're looking forward to Christmas."

Not really. "Sure. It should be better than the four days since our family meeting."

"Sounds serious. Do you want to talk about it?"

"Talk about how my family hinges their love on if I bend their way?"

"We can talk about that." She comes closer but appears to remember we're not together and veers a little right, keeping a few feet between us. "We broke up, but we're still friends. Are we still friends, Coop?"

I always hated that name. She knows that but thinks it keeps us on a friendlier term like we hang out all the time. I let the liquid coat my throat, my thoughts more morose around the fakeness that used to motivate me to push boundaries. I remind myself of Camille's situation again. She's still Thomas A. Anderson before he takes the red pill in *Matrix*, blind to the reality of this place.

Finding myself more distant from the people and this place, the idea of getting drunk isn't a bad one. I'm not striving to black out. I simply want to burn away the edges of my irritation that have flared. If nothing else, she will always remind me of who I refuse to be and the mold that will never quite fit.

After another sip of mine, I lean against the counter. "Why are you really here?"

"Your mother said you were lonely and acting depressed."

And they wonder why I used to drink heavily . . .

"My mom wouldn't know. I've been here for days, and the only contact we've had are a family meeting with the attorney, a lunch where she was mortified that I'd wear jeans to the Chez Cab, and then her telling me 'don't ruin my future' when I said I'm considering options outside of Haywood or New York." I take another drink to calm the wave of anxiety crashing in my chest. "So my mom isn't the best judge of what's going on with me."

"Don't be too hard on her. At least she cares. It could be worse."

"How so?"

"You could be poor." Unblinking, she stares at me, unable to break into my psyche despite the concerted effort. Failure sets in, and she turns her attention to the cut crystal glass, running her finger over the design.

I'm still staring at her. How does that phrase leave her lips without her own conscience judging? I think about it, though, and I was just like her. I'm not much different now other than I've had my eyes opened to a new perspective thanks to Story. It doesn't make me a changed man, but I think I've used the fallback of my family's wealth as an excuse for too long.

"Anyway, you know there's a dress code at Chez Cab. You wore jeans to upset her." She shrugs and then takes a sip.

"And it worked, so you can't be upset that she fell for your tricks. Christmas is tomorrow. Maybe Santa will bring you what you wished for and turn your sour-puss attitude around." She keeps going as if I'm participating in this conversation. "But only if you're nice and stay off the naughty list."

"What's the fun in that?"

"You never change." The snowfall catches her attention, and her gaze is stripped from me to find interest outside the large doors that lead to the expansive patio.

I don't mind the reprieve. "You mean, I never learn." Since she's in no hurry to leave, I move to the couch and sit, crossing my ankle across the other leg.

"Same thing." She looks back. "What's going on with you?"

Still not able to wrap my head around her thoughts or actions, I ask, "Why do you listen to them?" She's twenty-two and has looks, makes great grades, and comes from money. "Why do you follow the ridiculous rules of this town? Not laws. Rules that our parents not only made up but also forced us to follow?"

"I follow the rules to win." *Said like a Stepford wife.*

"You'll lose. I promise you, Camille. You can be more than a wife to some rich guy who puts you in Connecticut locked into that life by a white picket fence while he sleeps with his mistress in the city."

"You make it sound so bad when I'd be okay with that."

I can't get through to her. I don't know why I continue to try, but I'm not ready to quit just yet. "You'll get the husband, the kids, and a hefty bank account but lose the rest of your soul along with it."

Her jaw drops. "The rest of my soul?" She sighs, finally some semblance of a human reaction. "We always were so different, but a fight with a neighboring town kid who can't afford to take a swing at you was never a fair fight to begin with."

"What are you saying?"

"You're untouchable to most because of your last name. Even when it came to your teenage angst. You may not be using your fists on some guy who looked at you sideways, but who are you really fighting? Who's the enemy in this scenario? Your family who cares about your future? Or yourself?"

The words hit home, making me uncomfortable sitting here, but I stay knowing unless I'm willing to walk out that door and never come back, I'm a hypocrite. I have been given everything, and I've treated it like the privilege is nothing. Thinking about Story and her mom, learning about the situation and her dad. Her experiences have shaped who she is, but she's doing better than where she came from, and she leads by example. *I just need to follow.*

I put my foot on the floor and shift forward. "I'm trying to figure shit out on my own."

"Your life is good, Coop. Look around. I don't know what you want from this life, but you've been given everything you could ever want. This could *all* be yours one day." Coming closer, she sits on the couch next to me, too close for my liking. Lowering her voice, she says, "If you hate being here that much, one day you can sell everything and move away. But for now, play the game and get what you can. Just take what you want."

She's right.

I have everything I could ever want.

All I need to do is take it.

18

Story

"You really don't have to wait for me," I say, backing out of the door with the key inserted in the lock.

Lou shivers. "Brrr. It's okay. It's okay. I'd rather you be safe."

"I'm safe, Lou. I close up and walk home by myself all the time." I click the bolt closed, pull the key from the lock, and then turn the knob to make sure the coffee shop is actually locked.

"Maybe you shouldn't. There aren't many people around. A lot could happen."

Facing him, I shove the keys in the pocket of my coat. "I appreciate the concern." Rocking back on my heels, I'm not sure how to wrap up a goodbye when it's starting to feel like the end of a blind date. It's Lou. I don't owe him anything other than kindness, but I hate hurting his feelings. "Merry Christmas, Lou."

"Merry Christmas, Story."

I turn and start down the sidewalk with my head tucked

down. The snow's not been sticking, though I was dreaming of waking up to a white Christmas tomorrow.

My phone buzzes in my pocket, and I pull it out to check the text. Cooper. I smile, the action just a natural response every time I catch myself thinking about him. Thinking about him has become a pastime since school's out, and he left for the holidays. For some reason, the thought of his return and us picking up where we left off doesn't seem so out of reach anymore.

The photo of him sitting in a car makes me curious about where he's going and what he's doing. The text says: *Didn't mean to sneak up on you.*

Referencing the film we once both saw together without knowing each other at the time, my stomach flutters with butterflies, and I type: *Sometimes life does that.*

A shiny black Jaguar blocks the alley I usually cut through, the silver animal emblem in launching position off the front of the car. The windows are tinted to Secret Service protection levels. It's perfection that I don't think I've ever been this close to before. I can only imagine the price tag.

As I approach, I start to debate what's best to do. What's my safest option because Lou has me feeling paranoid? It's almost eleven. I closed later than I should have. But I had too many in the coffee shop needing a place to be on Christmas Eve to throw them out on the streets. I have nothing better to do at home anyway, so I appreciate the extra tips.

But do I walk to the end of the block or maneuver through the small gap left for me to pass? Do I want to cut through the alley at this hour?

My phone vibrates with another message: *When you least expect it.*

The passenger car window begins rolling down, causing

me to stop in caution and take a step back. Shoving my hand back in my pocket, I position the keys between my fingers. I'm not above scratching the car or someone's eyes out.

"Want a ride?" Cooper leans toward the open window, grinning wide.

I bounce on the balls of my feet, then run to the car. "What are you doing here?"

He pops the door open for me as the window rises back into place. I slip inside and shut the door quickly behind me. Throwing myself over the console, I practically squeeze the life from him. I'm so happy to see him. The best part—he hugs me just as tight. Peppering my head with kisses, he says, "I'd rather be with you than anywhere else in the world."

Tears spring to my eyes. I don't usually consider myself emotional, but he's struck a chord that leads from his heart to mine. I sit back, grinning like a fool. "What about your family?"

"Well," he starts, shifting the car into gear. "Let's just say I had a revelation today."

"Oh, yeah?" I pull my seat belt on. "What is that?"

Keeping his foot on the brake, he looks me in the eyes. "I'm taking a chance on telling you this, but it's how I feel. You're all that I want. I want to be with you, Story. I want to wake up next to you in the morning, have coffee in bed, and just spend the day with you." Reaching over, he takes my hand and kisses my frozen fingers. I slowly melt into a puddle of swoons when he adds, "Unless you have other plans?"

Laughter bursts my heavier emotions as the tears fall from my eyes. "I do now."

He releases the brake and slowly pulls out onto the street, hooking a left. I'm so overwhelmed that he wants to be with me that I almost failed to notice his car. While we hold hands over the console, I run my other fingers across the soft tan leather on the door. I've rarely seen a car this nice. Riding in one is a first.

He brings my hand to his lips again. "I missed you, babe." Kissing my hand, he then keeps it against his lips.

"I missed you, too." Taking another left, he cruises slowly as if savoring the world passing by, or maybe it's the time with me in his car. He just drove hours through bad weather to come see me, so I'm thinking it's the latter.

Glancing over, he asks, "Are you hungry?"

"I could eat, but it's late. Most places are already closed."

"I know of a place, but it's a little drive from here."

So much about Cooper surprises me, and the tradition continues with his visit. "You know of a place we can eat in at midnight on Christmas Eve?"

He nods, blowing the low expectations I had for tonight before he arrived right out of my mind. "I do," he replies. "You up for an adventure?"

With no doubt in my heart or my head, I'd go anywhere with him tonight, probably anytime, if I'm being honest. "Absolutely."

His smile grows again. Reaching down, he wiggles my buckle. I don't think I've ever had anyone make sure I'm secured. Not even the free spirit that was my mom most days. She always felt society put too many restrictions on kids. Her thinking on this was more the flower child side of her personality. That version of her was better suited for a commune than the small college town of Atterton.

Pulling onto my street, he slows the car as we approach my building. "Do you need anything?"

I think for a moment, but I think I'm set for dinner. "I'm all good."

He picks up speed again and drives to the end of the block before taking a right toward the highway. "Are you going to tell me where we're heading, or is it a big secret?" I ask.

"I guess that depends on if you like surprises or not? "

"Surprises aren't something I've had to think about since my mom's passing." His hand rubs my thigh over the scar. "She loved them. I came to loathe them, realizing the surprises she enjoyed took me out of school, out of my environment, and away from my friends and my life. But it's been three years, and I didn't realize until now how much I missed the excitement and anticipation of surprises."

His hand returns to the steering wheel. I don't mind for safety. "I'm glad I can do this for you then," he says.

I'm not sure what's come over me. Maybe I'm feeling sentimental now, but I don't feel afraid to share this with him. "Cooper?"

He glances over before focusing on the road and accelerating onto the highway. "Yeah?"

"I miss my mom." There's a heavy pause between us where his eyes find me in the dark of the car. Suddenly feeling embarrassed, I drop my head while shaking it. "I don't know why I just said that."

"It's okay, Story." This time, he reaches over and takes hold of my hand again. "We're here, just the two of us. You can tell me anything you're thinking or feeling without judgment." He kisses the back of my hand as the scruff on his chin scrapes across my skin.

I love the feeling. The prick and pain that follows makes me feel seated back in reality. I'm in the here and now instead of stuck in my memories.

"Do you mind sharing more with me? Or—"

I'm not even sure why this topic is weighing so heavy on

my mind, but now that I've opened the faucet, I might as well let some of these emotions flow. Maybe they'll pack themselves away right after I talk about her. "I don't mind."

Releasing my hand, he says, "It's starting to drizzle. I should probably keep both hands on the wheel. But if it wasn't, I'd still be holding yours."

"I know." Maybe I just want my hands on him, and I definitely like the connection, but this time, I reach over and rub his bicep down to his elbow. "I'm so happy to see you, but I feel sad talking about my mom." My mom's a tricky topic for me to navigate because of the ending. I pull back and settle in for what I suspect will be a long drive.

"That's understandable."

"Christmas was her favorite. We used to have the best time together during the holidays. It's my favorite too. What about you?"

"I used to love it, but I'm not sure anymore." His knuckles whiten as he grips the steering wheel and rolls his palm over the leather. "Do you mind if I ask some questions about your mom?"

"I'm not used to opening up about her, so maybe that will make it easier for me."

It's not like he rushes into an interrogation, but right away, he asks, "What was your mom's name?"

"Calliope. She was named after the muse of epic poetry, *the one with a beautiful voice*." I hate that I sound like I'm mocking it when I'm not. It's just weird to voice it to someone else, someone I care about what they think of me. "Rumor has it that it wasn't her real name. Neither was Salenger."

"Salenger might not be your name?"

I laugh softly. "No, it's my name. It's even on my birth certificate. But I wouldn't put it past my mom to make up her own rules as she went along." This is nice so far, better than I thought, freeing even in some small way. "I have a theory."

"Which is?" he asks, his tone tipping into intrigue.

"Calliope Salenger was a very complex woman. Some days, she wore flowers in her hair. Others, she dressed in all black like she was going to a funeral. Most days, she was caught somewhere between Holly Golightly and Holden Caulfield."

I hear him hum. "She had good taste in authors. I can't say I've read *Breakfast at Tiffany's*, but I can say that I read Salinger's book. " He nods as if he's uncovered treasured secrets. "So you were named after the author?"

"I never got a straight answer, but my mom thought the E made it more unique."

The lights from the dash reflect onto his face, giving me the advantage of seeing him over Cooper seeing me sitting in the dark of the passenger's seat. Call me selfish, but I like looking at his face. His handsome features are already so defined that I can only imagine he'll get better with age. Although it would be fun to zigzag my tongue over the days' worth of scruff or stare enviously over his lashes, it's his eyes that mesmerize, and I can't see those properly in the car at night.

"Believe it or not, I have to spell Haywood every time I make a dinner reservation."

I've never eaten somewhere that required a reservation, but I don't tell Cooper. I hate when he feels bad over our money situations. I return to the details of my mom. "I have her old copy of *Catcher in the Rye*. It's one of the few things I have left from her." Picturing it in my nightstand with its tattered pages and broken spine, I know that book was well-read and even more loved. "I think she had some Holden

Caulfield in her, some little aspect that made her always feel like an outcast in Atterton. She's from there, the town of Atterton. Grew up down the street from the bus station."

"I don't know where that is."

No, of course not. The guy drives a Jaguar.

"Yeah, she just never quite fit into society. But I'm not sure if she ever tried or if she tried and failed and then decided to do the exact opposite." I take a breath, hating that I'm starting to feel sad. When will the sadness around my mom's death end? "I spent so many years trying to fit in but realized I didn't want to after she died."

The sound of gravel grinds under the tires when he exits the freeway. The car slows to the speed limit as we pass a gas station with a cop car parked in the parking lot. He watches like he's doing something wrong.

He catches hold of my gaze, making him smile, and then redirects his attention back to the road. He takes a right. The tall pine trees are covered with inches of snow as we drive down a curvy road. Careful, he slows down even more, and I can imagine we're under the speed limit by now, but I don't mind because I'm with him.

Glancing at me once more, he says, "I can't tell if you had a good or bad childhood, Story. But I get the feeling that either way, it made you who you are today."

"Aren't we all the products of our childhood, of our parents' flaws and qualities—

good or bad?"

He seems to weigh the words, not rushing to say anything for my benefit, but I assume he's thinking about what fits his circumstances best. "Holden wasn't alone in *Catcher in the Rye*," Cooper starts. "He just felt like an outcast in his head, and maybe he was in life as well. That was his self-protection, though, his MO, and I get it. It was just the way he preferred to exist in life. Alone."

"So you think he chose that path?"

I see worry crossing his brow and digging small lines into his forehead as he mulls over the question. "Do any of us get to choose our path in life?" He glances over at me. "Or do we just continue following the one chosen for us?"

The conversation veers into a deeper ravine of reflection that I'm not sure we can dig ourselves out of at this juncture. But I'm fascinated, more than riveted by how this man thinks, what makes him tick, the way he expresses his emotions to me, opening up in a way that makes me feel special. My gut tells me he doesn't do this with many people.

His eyes narrow as the snow gets heavier. Peering through the windshield, I stare ahead at the road, thinking it must have been salted days ago since it's beginning to cover with snow again. "It's easier to do what others want. I did for a long time."

Grimacing, he replies, "I did for a time."

"You don't any longer?" I only ask because he went home to discuss family business. I have no idea what that could be, but I notice he hasn't offered it up for discussion either. That, I understand. I'll be patient for when he's ready.

"I did . . . I did everything that was asked of me. And then, I just stopped. I couldn't hold on to the façade forever. That's what it was, a façade. What about you?"

"There's no one to tell me anything anymore. I'm not sure what I want, not in the big picture scheme of things. I know what's three steps ahead of me. Graduation. Move to the city. Start my career. But I do know what I don't want."

Although this conversation started with me, the floodgates have opened for us both, revealing parts of ourselves that we've kept hidden from others.

A lot like my mom.

I don't think I really knew her like I should have, and I was the closest person to her in life.

Cooper reaches over again and slides his fingers into the hair at the back of my head. A gentle caress and then a little rub give comfort that I didn't realize I needed until now. "What do you *not* want, Story?"

My heart starts racing, and I doubt myself for a moment, my breathing picking up as panic sets in. I never thought I'd tell anyone this story after how horrible it went last time.

But I'm safe with Cooper, I remind myself two times over before recalling how he made me feel beautiful when he saw my scar. This will not be different. He'll see me through the ugliness of what happened.

And if we're really moving into a committed relationship, like how it feels we are, it's a secret that can't stay buried for long. It's come to shape my life in too many ways and sent me in the opposite direction of how I was raised. How he reacts will determine if I'm too much of what *he* doesn't want.

Just as I open my mouth to let the full truth come out, the pull to the left has me looking out my window as we start up a hill on a long driveway. My mouth falls open before I can confess anything more.

High on a snowy hill sits a fairy-tale castle and the most beautiful hotel I've ever seen. Decorated in warm white lights, the hotel with its spires has me imagining I'm Cinderella. My castle is dressed in her finest Christmas attire—wreaths with red bows and garland draped underneath the windows. There's even a red carpet lining the walk to the main entrance.

Whipping my gaze back to Cooper, I'm smiling so big that my cheeks hurt. "Where are we?"

"I booked us a room." He eyes me quickly as we pull up the driveway. "We can have dinner and then drive back to your apartment, or we can stay the night. It's up to you."

"Um, yeah. There's no debate. We're staying, moving in, and never leaving this place. I can't believe you did this, Cooper. It's a fairy tale come to life." I want to hug him, but he needs to drive.

He runs the palm of his hand over my leg. "I'll do anything for you, Story, especially if I get to spend time with you. It's a win for both of us." He pulls under the porte cochere and puts the car in park. The valet rushes over to open my door and offer assistance, but Cooper is already out of the car and jogging around to my side. He tosses the keys to the valet when he passes.

I squeal, not able to restrain my excitement. I feel like a princess. But if I'd known I was coming here, I could have dressed more appropriately. Not that I have clothes to wear in a castle, but my jeans and a T-shirt aren't likely the proper attire.

When I take his hand, he pulls me into his arms. "I've waited all night to do this." I'm dipped, and our lips come together on the downswing. His one hand supports the back of my head, and his other is at my waist. He holds me so securely that I know I'd fall without him.

With our lips locked in a kiss, that's when I realize I've already fallen for him.

19

Cooper

Story's been lying on the bed with her legs and arms spread like a snow angel . . . a bed angel. I smirk, not only from seeing her enjoy the king-sized bed covered in pillows but also that being in bed with her is one of my favorite places to be.

But my initial concern returns.

She's been on the bed, completely motionless, for minutes. *Did she fall asleep?* "Story?" I whisper, just in case she has, from the couch in the sitting area near the fireplace. Everything in the suite was done according to my specifications and pulled off down to the detail of what I hoped she would love—a fire roaring in the fireplace, chocolate-covered strawberries, and a bottle of champagne on ice. Judging by the big flakes of snow outside the window, the concierge even managed to bring that to life.

Story deserves the petals waiting tub side, for me to use in hot water full of bubbles, the chocolate truffles on the tray in the small fridge, someone going all out for her, to know how special she is, the romance and what she means to me—already, the whole nine yards. And I want to be the man to give it to her.

It's late, rounding midnight fifteen minutes ago, and she worked a long shift. It wouldn't be out of the ordinary if she fell asleep. But then she pops up and rests back on her hands. "Yeah?"

After driving from Haywood back to Atterton, waiting three hours for her to close the coffee shop, starving, and now here, I could eat and pass out. That's just not the night I had planned. "The food should be here any minute."

Pushing off the mattress, she scoots across the top until her feet land on the floor. She pads barefooted across the floor and does a little spin on the balls of her feet as if no one is watching. Her arms fly away from her hips, and her gaze dips to the jeans that don't do anything more than cover her. She looks up again to see me staring and then lowers her feet until they're flat on the floor again.

Story smiles. "What?" she asks. "Why are you looking at me like that?"

Rubbing my thumb over my bottom lip, I stare at this woman who lives with such an open heart. She gives all she has and can to everyone else yet doesn't understand how the world will take advantage of her.

She's beautiful in her naiveté. So fucking spectacular that I've started to wonder if it wasn't a coincidence that I met her when I did. Maybe my misdeeds last summer paid off, or maybe the universe just knew I needed this woman in my life.

I don't want to question it, but I can't help thinking that she's the payoff for the shit I've been through, the reward of heaven after walking through hell.

Licking my lips, I smile—*for her, for me*—and dance

around the overwhelming need to say three specific words too soon for logic to make sense of, and instead, I downplay my true feelings and say, "I just like watching you."

Her head tilts, long strands of brown and golden hair waterfalling over her shoulders. Even now, after a day that I know was tiring for her and a shift that was longer than it should have been, there are no signs of slowing down. She appears the opposite. In fact, she appears ready to take on the world. Where does she get her energy?

"You know you're getting laid when you say such sweet things."

"I know, but that's not why I said it."

She crosses the room, detouring from her original mission to come to me. Sitting on the arm of the couch, she caresses my face and then leans down to kiss me. "Then why'd you say it?"

"Because it's how I feel. It's what I like to do. Watch life through you."

"Watch me?"

"Yes, Story." When I pull her into my lap, laughter escapes her, but she relaxes with her arms loose around my neck. I rub her hip, already feeling the urge to skip to the good part and make use of the bed, maybe the couch, and definitely the window. I get harder imagining her nipples pressed to the cold glass as I fuck her from behind.

Fuck. The woman's innocently sitting on my lap while I'm having filthy fucking thoughts about her. I'm an asshole. But I already knew that. *She just hasn't found out yet.*

"I like watching you in my apartment."

Her confession makes me grin. "Why is that?"

"Because you're like a giant there. Your whole being exists in that small space filling the nooks and crannies where your body doesn't. No part of my home is left untouched before you leave, including me."

I feel the same about her. I'm the one who's touched by her mere presence in my life. Every nook and cranny has her fingerprints. "I'm changing. I've started seeing things differently because of you."

"You don't have to change for me, Cooper," she whispers.

Leaning back, she takes me in, the signs of her feelings so prevalent in her widening pupils. I don't want to just be admired for my physical attributes, which is something I never thought twice about with a girl. With Story, I want her to feel like I feel, to know that something in my soul is addicted to hers, and my heartbeats feel like they belong to her.

I kiss her, needing her breath to be mine, to feel her need for me like I know she can feel mine for her. But a knock on the door sadly interrupts what was starting to heat. Tapping my chin, she says, "I'm starving. How about you?"

"Famished." I don't tell her that I'd rather taste her than the burger I ordered, but disappointment has already settled in for losing the opportunity before she hops off my lap.

I stand and go to the door, and she detours to the window. I can't help but notice when I look back that she's like a kid staring into a candy shop, studying anything and everything that the glow of the Christmas lights around the outside of our window gives life to in the darkness beyond.

Opening the door, I greet the room service attendant, then step aside so he can push the cart into the room. He says, "Merry Christmas, sir."

"Merry Christmas."

My gaze travels across the room to look at the woman

who's making this holiday more special than I could've ever imagined just by being here.

When I turn back, though, the attendant has also noticed Story as well. I step between him and my girlfriend, crossing my arms over my chest and giving him a chance to redirect his attention to me. "You working all night?" I ask, irritation causing my tone to clip.

His eyes quickly return to setting up the table, adjusting the wings, and draping the cloth over the exposed sides. With his head down, he replies, "Working the overnight shift."

Story crosses the room, her eyes set on the food. "I'm so hungry." The guy lifts a silver dome. She steals a fry and giggles. "Thanks."

Yeah, thanks, fucker. That's my job. I open the door, ready for him to leave. "Thanks. I got it from here."

"Yes, sir." When he dares to glance up at her again, to give her body a shameless once-over and not bother to be covert about it, jealousy begins coursing through my veins. I shoot him a glare that could kill if it was a weapon. Alas, I haven't developed that superpower.

His eyes hold a challenge that I've seen my whole life. He can't be much older than I am, but we're on opposite sides of this situation. A little arrogance hardens his shoulders as he returns to the door. He stops in the hallway, and says, "Sign the tab and you can leave it on the cart to be picked up later."

"Yep. Got it."

Once again, he looks beyond me to catch sight of my girlfriend . . . *Girlfriend?* The word feels childish for what we are and what I'm starting to realize we'll be. The big picture stuff is coming in heavy today. But isn't that why I left Haywood on Christmas Eve to be with her? Yeah.

"Merry Christmas," he adds just as Story says the same. I let the door slam closed before the words have a chance to end.

With my adrenaline still pumping, I turn back to her, knowing exactly how I'm going to burn through it. I'm about to eye the bed and drop some stupid come-on line, but Story's staring at me like I might have just lost my chance.

Picking up another fry, she bites the end and studies me. I ask, "What?"

"What was that exactly?" Waggling the fry in my direction, she asks, "Was that jealousy I just witnessed, Mr. Haywood?"

I could lie, but I'm supposed to be turning over a new leaf . . . "It was."

"Do we need to talk about it?" She finishes the fry.

As I move back to the cart, my stomach growls from the smell of the food filling the air around us. "I think it was obvious." I start lifting dome lids to see what surprises are beneath. "The dude thought he'd flirt with you right in front of me."

She covers my hand, stopping me from lifting the last lid, and tilts her head down to look me in the eyes. "And if he weren't doing it right in front of you, how would you react?"

"Truthfully?"

"Of course."

"If I knew about it, I'd probably find him and have a talk." I grab one of the thick-cut fries.

She laughs, but the humor's lost in it. Standing straighter, she asks, "And by talk, you mean . . .?"

"I'd punch his fucking face." I bite off the top of the fry as if that somehow illustrates my voracity for her or the fries.

Surprise grips her—those pretty lips parting, eyes widening—and her head jars her neck. "You'd do that because he lifted a lid on my food and wished us a Merry Christmas?"

"No, for how he looked at you when you weren't watching."

The shock softens into a different form in her features. She's about to say something but closes her mouth. Redirected on the cart, she takes a deep breath, momentarily closing her eyes, and licks her lips before sucking in the bottom one.

She slowly exhales, then looks up at me again. Touching her forehead, she says, "I think I'm feeling a bit lightheaded. I should eat something."

I pick up the plate with her burger. "The couch or the bed? Where do you want to eat?"

"The chair by the fire."

Taking a glass of water from the cart, she also grabs a miniature ketchup bottle and leads me to the chair. When she's settled, I hand her the plate and a rolled napkin wrapped around silverware.

I start eating on the couch. I don't know why the silence is unnerving this time, but I can sense the change that's come over her. On the surface, she's curled up eating a burger by the fire. But her eyes give her away, and the distant gaze and measured blinks have me needing to find out what's going on. I wait, though. I think she needs to eat before we dive into something heavier.

Transfixed on the flickering flames, she gets lost in her head, and I let her, knowing I'll follow her anywhere, even into the recesses of her memories to protect her.

When I take my last bite and set the plate aside, I drink water to clear my throat, then set it on the coaster beside me. "Story?" I try to sound casual, but my own thoughts are spinning to fill in the answers I don't have yet.

Her eyes find me, and, at that moment, sadness has shrouded the gold centers. I fucking hate whoever caused this woman any pain. I ask, "What happened?"

I don't ask more. She knows. She knows exactly what I mean. Sitting with her food discarded after eating only half, she sets the plate on the coffee table, and says, "I've never told anyone before."

"Then we'll go slow and start from the beginning."

20

Cooper

"I've always had a bad picker," she says as if I'll know what she's talking about.

"A what?"

"A bad picker is my radar for attraction, like I always pick the wrong guy for me, a bad judge of character. There could be a lineup of nine kind, intelligent, and successful men, and I'd pick the tenth. The worse, the better in so many cases." She hunkers down in the large, cushioned chair, dragging a small pillow from her back to hold to her chest. "It was an inherited trait. My mom had the worst taste in men. I just didn't recognize the pattern until I was removed from the situation."

"Should I be offended?" I grin, and fortunately, so does she, the levity welcome. I want her to feel safe and protected, and for her past not to weigh her down. It's not something I can fix, but if I can help her get there, I'll do whatever I can.

"No," she says with a soft laugh. "You're the change I purposely made."

If she only knew about my past, she might not be saying that. But I can't pretend it's not music to my ears. *Who knew I'd be considered one of the good guys?*

She continues, "In high school, I never met a bad boy I didn't like. The funny thing is, I was such a good girl."

"Isn't that what bad boys want? The good girls."

"You're probably right." She smiles to herself while running her fingertips aimlessly over the top of the pillow and leaving designs in the velvet material. "I had straight A's and was treasurer of the photography club, if you can believe it."

"I can believe it. Well, I have no idea about the treasury part, but the pictures you sent me have a unique perspective on life."

She snuggles her legs to her chest with the pillow squashed between the two. "Thanks. I find the mundane, the overlooked, or abandoned so interesting through a lens. Even if it's just my phone lens."

"You don't have a camera?"

"It's not been something I considered a necessity." She perks up. "If I have any money left after buying books in a few weeks, maybe some of the tip you left can go toward saving for one."

Some might consider it strange that she's keeping the money, especially now that we're dating, but I love that she is. She would never take it directly but siphoned through as business has her seeing things differently. Anyway, I wouldn't have given it if I didn't want her to have it.

I nod, but then say, "The glove, the bottle, the bed, and the rain. They already make a great collection."

She stares, and then pink colors her cheeks. "You

remembered each one," she says in awe. Tucking her hair behind an ear, she lets out a peal of soft laughter that rattles her shoulders. "I think it would be amazing to be a professional photographer."

"You're already of that caliber."

"Thanks, Cooper, but you know me and don't want to hurt my feelings."

"So I can't have an honest opinion without it coming off as tainted because we're dating?"

Amused, she relaxes, releasing the tight hold on the pillow. "No, you can't have an honest opinion because you've been inside me."

"Whoa. Whoa. Whoa. Settle down there."

She starts laughing. "It's true. No one will believe you're being honest about my photos once they find out we've slept together."

"I have an idea." Her eyebrow rises in piqued interest. "What if we don't tell them? What if one day, when your photos are hanging in a gallery, we pretend we don't know each other? That way, I won't ruin the sale for you."

Her smile slowly fades away, and her gaze lowers, drifting to the fire. "Us not knowing each other . . . That sounds tragic."

"Don't all great love stories end in tragedy?"

"No, only the ones that were never meant to be." She gets up and stretches her arms above her head, revealing a sliver of skin in the middle. "Want to take a bath with me?"

"If you give me five minutes to set it up."

"Deal."

Shoving my hand in my pocket, I feel for the foil packet I shoved in there earlier. I enter the bathroom and start the water flowing in the tub. Grabbing the bag of petals, I toss them in and then grab a small bottle of bubble bath. I pop the cork and smell. It's a nice floral. I think Story will like it, so I empty it into the tub.

Setting two big, fluffy towels on the small wooden table next to it, I think I'm ready. I look around and realize, nope, I'm missing the champagne and strawberries. Operation Seduction is in full swing. If it happens to make up for the other night, even better.

In the suite, I grab the bottle from the ice bucket, but when I reach for the plate of strawberries, half are already eaten. I glance at Story, who's standing near the bed. She shrugs unapologetically, still chewing the evidence.

Taking one, I pop it in my mouth because fuck it, I don't need strawberries to make this night romantic when I have her. I grab the two flutes and start for the bathroom again. Stopping, I lean back and say, "Get that cute ass in here."

As playful as I'd like the rest of the night to be, I know we have heavier topics to discuss ahead. It's just going to take a while to get there. We have a pattern I discovered. We swerve through conversations, taking unexpected detours and hitting roadblocks, but we always manage to get to our destination.

We'll do it again and come out on the other side stronger as a couple. Who am I with this couple talk? I grin, unashamed of this change in me, and pop the champagne to fill the glasses.

A knock has me turning back and then doing a double take. Story, dressed in nothing but a smile, asks, "You ready for me?"

I set the bottle down beside the tub, then cross the tiled floor, taking hold of her hips. I can't keep my hands off those delectable hips. "I'm ready for you, babe."

We kiss, but she pulls back, too excited and wanting to

peek around me. "Cooper." She covers her mouth, her eyes volleying between me and the tub. "You did not."

"I did. I did this for you. Do you want to get in?"

"I definitely want to get in." Releasing her briefly, I turn the faucet knobs to shut off the water. It's filled more than it should, knowing that two of us in the tub means there's a strong chance the water will overflow.

She steps into the tub and dips into the water until it's just barely covering her nipples. There's no awkwardness in her body language, and she doesn't hide from me, not even the scar that she purposely hid before. Like me, she's changing. I can only hope it's because of me. Like I have because of her. To have that kind of effect, one that is filled with, *dare I say, hope* is exhilarating. *A different kind of high than I used to need.*

Her hazel eyes are set on me as she runs soapy water down one arm and across her chest. *The teasing vixen.*

Leaning against the counter, it feels almost illegal to watch this woman bathe.

She takes the glass of champagne and a small sip before looking me over from head to toe and back again. "Are you going to come in? The temperature of the water is perfect." Red rose petals dot her skin, and her hair is twisted up on her head. She takes another sip and sinks back against the tub.

I stand there and let a few heartbeats pass before I need to touch her again and start undressing. It's late, but we're both wide-awake. There is no point rushing into the new day, even if it is a holiday.

When I step in, the water's warm, and the suds are already vanishing, but the petals remain vibrant against her pale skin. I ease down, cramming my body to fit and stretching my legs on either side of her, and spread my arms wide on the sides of the large porcelain tub.

Doesn't take long before she says, "I'm coming over." She spins to maneuver between my legs and rest her back against my chest. When she stills, her hands rub down my thighs.

I like her softness, the bones on the inside where they belong instead of protruding, and wrap my arms around her. The comfort I've found in this woman started like a shot of adrenaline—making my heart race as my soul calmed—but I'm already getting used to it. It feels good not to feel chaotic inside.

Sliding my hands up her arms, I stop when I reach her shoulders and start massaging—gentle but with firm pressure to reach any pains built up from the long day. Her body begins to release the tension as it melts against me. I tilt my head to the side and whisper, "I want us to be together, Story."

She shifts around to look me in the eyes. "We are together, Cooper." It's said as if we've always been this way.

"Committed to each other."

Confusion cinches her brows together. "I was already committed to you."

Maybe that's what I got wrong. I've been so caught up in how she makes me feel that I wasn't seeing the effect I've had on her. Hearing her say the words I wanted in return is a balm to the angst I've been carrying around for years.

Twisting even more, she kisses me before caressing my cheek and taking a moment to stare, and then tucks her head under my chin. I cover her back with water carried in the palm of my hand, wanting to keep her warm when so much skin is exposed to the cooler air.

"We've moved fast," she whispers.

"Like the storm that brought us together."

Nodding, she lifts her chin, looking me in the eyes again. "Just like that." Another thought she keeps hidden from me flickers in her eyes, and she adds, "Don't hurt me, okay?"

I've seen her sick.

Exposing shame she feels over a scar on her body.

Hide the fact that she was a virgin before me.

I've seen Story at the most opportune times of vulnerability, but I never witnessed it until now.

My soul shifts when I hear the fear in her voice and see it written in her eyes like it's always lived there. I'll take it away. I'll spend my days making sure she never has to feel this way again.

Tracing the outline of her face with the tips of my fingers, I stop and hold her chin, making sure her eyes are set on mine. "I will never hurt you. I promise, Story." It's the easiest promise I've ever made, the only one I knew the answer to before the question existed in the universe. "Never."

Relief comes quickly along with her smile. "I know you're not asking, but I promise not to hurt you either." She kisses me before turning around and easing back against me again.

Once she's secured in my arms, she misses the smile that splits my cheeks. I'm sure I look like an idiot, but I don't think anyone has ever said that to me before. If they have, there's no one in my life I would have believed.

Until Story.

"My mom's boyfriend killed her."

My smile's gone, the good replaced with horror as tension fills my body and my hold on her involuntarily tightens. She pushes forward again to look at me. "You're not breathing."

"I didn't notice." I try to act like she didn't just drop the bomb of all bombs into the middle of our bath. I take a few breaths, but acting indifferent is impossible, especially with her now staring at me.

She rests her hand on my chest. "Are you all right?"

"I'm . . ." I run my wet fingers through my hair, glancing away from her. "A little shocked, and I don't know what to say to you."

A small smile graces her face. "It's okay. You don't have to say anything."

My shoulders fall, feeling helpless to do or say the right thing. I wrap my arms around her. "I do. I want to know how you're doing."

She turns all the way around, pushing back to rest against the other side of the tub and face me. Her eyes scan mine as if she's the one who's checking on how I'm doing. Appearing satisfied, she drops her hands under the water. "I survived."

"What do you mean you survived?"

Resting her head back, she closes her eyes. "I wore shorts that day." Her lids lift. "Really short shorts, like my ass hanging out the back short."

I shrug. "People wear what they want. I'm not seeing a problem with this."

"Neither did I. But my mom's boyfriend, Hank, sure did."

Hank . . .

"He always told me if he were my father, he'd be stricter with me. It was a double standard because even though he wasn't my father—*thank God*—he still smacked me when my mom wasn't around. Gave me a black eye once. Popped me right in the face when he found my boyfriend in my room."

Rubbing the bridge of my nose, I try to temper the anger

growing inside. "Fucking hell, Story." I've been in fights, too many to count, sometimes picking shit just to feel something other than the void I felt at home. Sometimes, in defense of friends or even girls I knew when guys crossed lines. But for a guy to hit a woman . . . I'd fucking lose it on them.

"It was hell." She laughs, but it's jaded in disbelief as her eyes fill with tears. "We were only listening to music. That's all. I swear." Breaking as if she's reliving it again, pain morphs her into a scared little girl with rivulets of tears running down her face and into the tub.

I wrap my hands around her calves to pull her close until I can lift her into my arms and tuck her against my chest. She's curled into the smallest ball possible, her sobs wracking her body as her head rests against my shoulder. "It's okay, Story. You didn't do anything wrong."

"He once told me he wanted to make sure that I didn't end up like my mom and date someone like him. Sometimes, I can still hear his voice in my head. He's the nightmare I can't escape."

"Fucking nightmare you survived," I say, reminding her. "But I'd kill him." I kiss her on the head. "I'd have spent the rest of my life in jail if I'd been there."

"You're too good, Cooper Haywood, to ever know anyone as bad as Hank."

I feel . . . conflicted.

She sees me now as a better man, but I'm not sure she'd feel the same if she'd known me back then. *A better man in a week?* Who am I kidding? Is it possible for me to transform into someone other than who I am just because I met Story?

I could tell her how I've been to jail a couple of times, just the overnight stuff for the fighting, a little weed back in high school, and stealing my mom's Bentley to go joyriding with friends when I was fifteen. But that's petty stuff. Not the same as how Hank was living his life. If she sees me as the opposite of him, I'll take that.

I hold her tight to get her past the pain of having to relive that night alone.

When she calms again, she says, "The night she . . ." She sniffles, but her voice steadies. She may have been waiting for enough time to pass, or . . . the right person to show up, but now she's finally opening up. "Sounds like such a cliché." She takes a deep breath, wiping her face with the back of her hands and dipping them in the water to wash the makeup away.

Leaning back, she shifts just enough to put a little distance between our faces. "My mom was working at a bar, but Hank was drunk in the kitchen, grumbling about rich kids hot-rodding in town, and mad about a ticket he'd gotten. I showed up in those short shorts at the wrong time." Her swallow is harsh, but she continues, "He got even madder and called me a whore . . . *like my mom*, and then he decided that he didn't give a shit that I wasn't his daughter." She's shaking her head. "He didn't care. That night, he just needed to take his anger out on someone. And I was the chosen one."

"He's a fucker. You know that, right?"

"I know." Her emotions waver with her voice—an ebb and flow to it. She's had years to start processing, but I'm beginning to think that surviving meant blocking it out entirely. I don't know if that's good or bad, but not dealing with shit eventually comes out one way or the other.

The water's cooled from hot to warm, but my temper remains heated.

She exhales and starts fidgeting with petals, ripping

them apart and letting the pieces float away. I say, "He did that to you? Ripped you apart."

"That's not as bad as what he did to my insides." Through the dissipated bubbles, I notice the tips of her fingers running along the scar on her leg. *Shit.* My stomach drops when the pieces connect. *The scar.* That fucker gave her that scar.

I cover her hand as she continues to touch the jagged line. "He slapped me so hard that I fell into a lamp that had seen better days. It fell and broke . . . and then I fell and broke right on top of it." Her eyes are set on her leg when she says, "The broken glass ripped my leg wide open, cut through the muscle, exposing the bone."

"Fucking hell." My thoughts blur, and when I close my eyes, all I see is red. Anger holds me hostage as a million images of her getting hurt flash through my mind. *How could he do that to her?*

The feel of my fingers being wedged open causes me to also open my eyes. Even when pain clouds her hazel eyes, her soul shines through.

She kisses the palm of my hand and then rests her cheek on it. Closing her eyes, she says, "The report states that my mom came home."

"The report?"

She lifts her head and nods. "I'd lost so much blood."

"And passed out?"

"I was dying, Cooper, and all I could think about was the smell of the carpet. Lavender. She used to sprinkle it on the carpet and then vacuum." She holds her head. "Sorry. Sometimes the memories come when I least expect them. Anyway, the doctors said I was lucky to have survived because my femoral artery was spared from damage. I don't consider myself lucky when I think back on that night."

She's breaking my heart, but I feel selfish for even having that thought. It's not fair to her, the real victim in all this. "I'm sorry. I'm so sorry."

Her hand flattens over the physical wound, but she's right. The internal pain is still fresh. "I survived, but my mom didn't. She fought, though," Story says, adamantly, looking up at me. "She fought for me. I was losing so much blood. There was so much blood . . . I remember watching him throw her like a rag doll, and I was helpless to save her. He threw her like she wasn't a person, like she wasn't a woman, like she wasn't *my* mom. He threw her like she didn't matter." A stifling breath is taken and then she adds, "She mattered to me."

"I know, babe. I know," I whisper. She's been eerily calm for the most part, but that last part had her voice shaken. She wraps her arms around herself and then leans against me as quiet sobs rock her body.

Holding her so tight, I whisper, "I'm sorry. I'm so sorry, Story."

"The neighbors called the police, but I passed out before they arrived." Her tone trembles, but she slowly pushes off me to stand. With the water lowering and her body dripping, the scar is on display in front of me—not for effect, but for her to breathe easier as she pulls herself together again.

"I survived." Her words come back as a haunted memory. She's doing more than surviving. She's changed the course of her life. *She's fucking amazing.*

Taking a towel, she wraps it around her frame. "I'm cold," she says, shivering.

I nod, taking her hand so she can get out without slipping. When I stand and cover myself with the other towel, I step out and start drying off. I need to pace, to think, to do anything but sit here doing nothing.

"I never saw my mom again. I woke up in a hospital bed with my leg wrapped after surgery. They pieced my leg back together again, but I'm told she was found with shards of glass from the front door in her back. Though somehow, she was on the couch when they arrived." Exhaling loudly, she tempers her expressions, trying so hard to hold herself together.

"What happened?"

The stiffness of her spine loosens, and she rocks back but catches herself against the counter. Her arms cover her stomach as she bends over. "I . . . I never saw her again—not alive or dead. She just vanished from the earth and my life that night." Sinking to her knees, she curls over, crying. "I never got to hug her again or tell her that I was sorry for borrowing her favorite pair of shorts or that . . ."

I cover her with my body, hugging her. "Story . . . God, Story, it's not your fault. You have to believe me."

She looks up at me. "I never got to tell her I love her again. She was messed up, but she was my mess of a mother, Cooper."

"I know. I know, babe." It could have been a minute or ten, for all I know. We've lost track of time in here.

When her tears subside again, she says, "He was found dead in his truck from a self-inflicted wound. The coward." Her strength strikes like lightning and then settles into the dust of the memory.

I've never felt more like an asshole than after hearing her story. I have trust fund issues at worst when she's lucky to be alive.

I'm not sure what to do but holding her again feels right. Her arms come around, and she starts crying again. "Let it go. You don't have to hold it in any longer," I whisper.

Pink streaks stain her cheeks, and a soft laugh escapes. "I

bet you wish you would have never come into that coffee shop that day." She smiles, but it's full of embarrassment. Her eyes leveled on my stomach like she's facing regret.

Tilting my head to the side, I wait until she peeks at me under wet eyelashes and say, "I am." Her smile falls until I add, "I wish I'd gone in sooner."

21

Story

Wrapped in flannel pajamas with reindeer on them that Cooper surprised me with, I feel light as air lying on this cloud of a bed. I'm just not sure if I owe it to the hotel mattress or the man currently doing push-ups beside it.

I know the answer and roll to my side to get a better look at him. Even with a pair of flannel pants on, I can spend days admiring his shirtless body, but it's his heart and the beats pumping in his chest, the soul that embodies him that have my pulse racing.

Cooper just did something that no one else has ever even tried. He freed me from my past.

He looks up but never breaks his stride. "Want to join me?" I scramble off the bed and lie on the floor next to him. He laughs. "What are you doing?"

"Joining you."

Grinning, he moves sideways until he's over me and keeps pushing up. I score a kiss every time he comes down. Resting my hands on his shoulders, I say, "Thank you."

"No thanks needed." He knows without me saying more. He just reads me so well. "I am sorry you had to go through that, and you lost your mom. I know it will be easy to just reply that it's okay, but I want you to know that it was never okay for that to happen."

I thought I'd cried enough for a year's worth of saved-up tears, but shockingly, more surface in the corner of my eyes. This time, I have a chance to wipe them away before they fall.

He stills, and only his eyes move when they search mine. "Why are you crying?"

Wrapping my arms completely around his neck, I pull him closer and kiss him again. "Because I'm so happy. It doesn't feel real, so if this is a dream, I don't want to ever wake up from it."

"If this is a dream, let's stay asleep together forever." Moving to the side of me, he says, "I got something for you." With his body weighted on his right hand and only the side of his right foot, he starts doing push-ups again. His grin beams in pride. "What do you think, babe?"

"I think your strength is incredible."

He stops and then gets up. Offering me his hands, I raise mine, and he takes hold, helping me to my feet and right into his arms. With my legs wrapped around his middle, he says, "I think your strength is incredible."

My heart be still, I don't think this man can make me swoon any more than he already has, and then bam! He does it again.

We kiss, but it's not frenzied like so many other times. It's slow and measured, taking our time and enjoying this one sweet moment. When our lips break apart and our eyes open again, he asks, "Do you want more champagne? I can get it from the bathroom or order another bottle?"

"I feel very uncultured saying this since I've not actually had real champagne until tonight, but is it bad of me to say that I don't like it?"

He chuckles. "I'm actually glad to hear you say that."

"Why?" I lower my feet to the floor, but his arm stays wrapped around my waist, holding me like he's not ever going to let me go. I don't mind. In fact, I've never felt more at peace than when I'm with him—protected, safe in his arms and in his heart.

"Because when it comes to alcohol or anything else, you shouldn't drink anything you don't like." His hands find my hips, and he sways me. "Can I order you anything else?"

"No. I'm tired and thinking about sleeping in that bed. It's the most comfortable thing I've ever been in." Dropping my head against his chest, I laugh. "You must think I'm so small town. I keep saying it's the best, prettiest, most comfortable . . . God, I sound silly."

"You don't sound silly. Hey, look at me, babe." He stops until I'm looking at him again. "You appreciate everything around you. It's enjoyable to see life through your eyes. You have every reason to be cynical or mad at the world. But you're not. You find joy and pleasure in things the rest of us will never be able to appreciate or find that same contentment."

"I do have a reason to be mad." I move to retrieve a bottle of water from the bar near the entry. This hotel room is amazing, just like Cooper. From the spacious layout to the separate sitting area to the little Christmas tree in the corner, it really is magical in here. So, when I say, "I was mad for years," it doesn't reflect my current state. It's the opposite actually. "But what I found is that I was the one suffering for that anger I carried around. Not the man who did it. Not the world. Not the universe. Not even this town. My mom made nothing more than a blip on page two of the *Atterton Gazette* as if it was always expected to end that way."

Returning to be near him, I sit on the edge of the bed and open the bottle to take a sip. When I look up at him, sympathy enters his eyes. "I'm sorry."

I don't want that to be how he always looks at me. "You don't have to be sorry, and you don't have to feel sorry for me, Cooper. You just need to find what makes you happy because isn't that the best revenge?"

"Happiness?"

"Happiness is something money can never buy." I tap his chin. "Even if your last name is Haywood. So you might as well seek the good fortunes of every day instead." I take another sip. "You ready for bed?"

With a nod of his chin, he says, "I'm ready all right."

Before I get cozy under the covers with him, I go to the bathroom and then find packages of toothbrushes and toothpaste on the counter. "Did you even order the toothbrushes?"

From the bedroom, he replies, "It's what a concierge does. I told her that when we checked in, you wouldn't have anything except the clothes on your back. She said she'd take care of it."

Okay, so he went out of his way to make sure I'd have everything I needed, but one thing doesn't make sense since he surely brought a bag with him from Haywood. "Why'd you leave your bags in the car?"

"Out of solidarity."

I stop, toothbrush in one hand, paste in the other, and stare into the mirror. His words . . . no, him. All of Cooper Haywood has me grinning. Happiness not only consumes my face but is bursting into my heart. It's been so long since

I've seen the girl reflected back at me. A giddy shiver runs through me, and I mouth, "How'd I get so lucky?"

"It's not luck." He startles me, the handsome jerk leaning against the doorframe.

With my hand still pressed to my chest, I ask, "How long have you been standing there?"

"Long enough to correct you." A wry grin doesn't stop my heart from beating so fast, but it does cause it to race for other reasons. "It's your heart that drew me in, babe."

"And here I thought it was my 'tits'?" I laugh like I'm funnier than I am.

His chuckle is lighter as he comes into the bathroom. Tough crowd tonight. Looking me square in the eyes, he says, "They're fucking fantastic, but that heart of yours is hard to beat. Pun intended."

"Look at you, bringing the funnies." Bumping my hip into him, I hand him his personal dental care package.

Hugging me from behind, he sweeps my hair to the other shoulder and kisses my neck. "I'll be bringing funnies tonight."

I spin in his arms and wrap my arms around him. "Guess Christmas is coming early."

"Not sure about Christmas, but we will be."

I gut chuckle because the joke lands just right on this night in particular. "You're a very naughty boy. Isn't sex forbidden on Christmas?" Call it my mood, just a stage in life, or that it's him that has me feeling this way lighter than sunshine and more optimistic than ever, but I soak it in. Reaching behind me, I hold his head just where he is, letting him love on me, and for the first time, I feel deserving of it. I bend my fingers and scrape my nails lightly over his scalp.

His lips press to mine, and then he kisses the corner of

my mouth. "It's just us, babe. We get to make our own rules." His words are the permission to let all the things go that I've held on to so tightly for the past three years.

Being strict with myself and my needs, denying myself pleasure, guilt-free happiness, or even being myself haven't led to what this man's managed to give me in the past week. I was getting by, surviving, but I wasn't thriving or really living at all.

He's a dream come true, a knight in shining armor who's come to save me from myself. I kiss him to satisfy the cravings he brings out in me, wanting to feel his fingers digging into my skin, to taste the first drop that leads to him coming, and have him consume my body physically like he does emotionally. Call me selfish, but he's right.

We make our own rules.

Leaning back far enough to catch my gaze, he asks, "How do you feel about marble?"

I look around at the bathroom with no idea why he's asking. "I love it."

A smirk nothing less than one the devil himself would wear crosses his lips. "Good. Get naked and turn around."

Cocking an eyebrow, I reply, "As long as you drop the reindeer pants and join me."

"Don't worry, sweetheart. I plan to join you all right."

His words are the starter gun we both needed. I skip the buttons and yank the shirt over my head. My pants are down just after his. Standing naked in the warmth of the bathroom with his erection already at attention and my nipples hard, I turn around.

Eye contact is made in the reflection of the mirror. I watch as his hands come around to cup my breasts, and his mouth covers the bend of my neck, licking me to my shoulders. Sucking and kissing, kneading and squeezing. My body is already turned on and ready.

His erection presses against the crease of my ass, unafraid of pushing forward to make me wonder if that's his intent. My thoughts start swirling, my pulse now speeding as I try to figure out if that's something I'm ready for or want.

That's the thing about Cooper, though. I want everything with him. And if that's something he desires, I'm not opposed to trying it for the first time.

But then his hand slides between the front of my legs, and his fingers rub my clit. Though I'm already wet and feeling the need for him to fill me, there's an ounce of relief that we're only switching things up by being in the bathroom.

When I move against his hand, the pressure feels too good for him to let up. My eyes are already dipping closed, my palms pressed to the cold stone. When I look up, his eyes are fixed on me—my body's reaction and my facial expressions. I don't know if I should be embarrassed, but I can't reason myself into the emotion. Not when he feels this good.

His hand slips away as he kneels to pull a condom from the pocket of the discarded pants, but he doesn't leave me without for long. Sliding his hand between my thighs, he caresses the apex of my legs before standing back up. Our eyes find each other in the mirror again, and he says, "Bend over and brace yourself, babe."

I slowly bend, keeping my eyes on him as he rolls the condom down his length. Bracing myself the best I can with my hands on the counter and my fingertips pressed to the bottom of the mirror, I look up once more when he positions himself behind me.

The prod of his erection comes with his hands running

over the roundness of my ass and then down between my thighs again. He's quick to dip into my entrance and then adds another finger just as fast. I'm already squirming, the buildup causing my stomach to tingle in the best of ways as I wait to feel his cock inside me again.

Sex, any form of it, is anticipation and excitement. I may have waited for the right guy to come along, but the way he makes me feel so good, I've been missing out all along.

My body is abandoned other than a hand gripping my hip. But I'm not left waiting or wanting long when not only the tip of his dick slips inside me, but the entirety of his length fills me right after.

I jerk forward, the hard thrust catching me off guard despite the warning. His hands skim my back, then he takes hold of my shoulders to follow with a relentless fucking that feels too good to control. I let my mind rest. My thoughts go blank, focusing on the physical and sensations, the here and now, moving on instinct with him, against him, anything that gets me to the release I'm chasing.

But then I slow, and so does he. "I don't want to race to the finish line."

He runs the length of my spine with one of his hands again and then dips down to kiss me three times. "Me either."

Things slow but are just as intense. The fullness that reaches deep in my belly, the steady rocking against my body, the scent of his cologne, and the feel of his hot breath against my skin entrances me until I'm begging for more. "Cooper," I say breathlessly. "I need you. I need you." I reach around just to have my hands on his body and feel the muscles in his ass as he moves inside me.

His moans are an aphrodisiac to the onslaught. His groans feed my need, making my body hungrier for the deeper pleasure. My own are forced from my chest with each hard push, and hair that's pulled from being tangled with his hand. He pulls my head back, our eyes meeting in the reflection, and he growls, "Tell me how much you want me. Tell me how bad you need me."

Thrusts become harder.

Our bodies move faster.

I brace myself on the counter again, then lick my lips. "I need you so badly, babe." The words come as a purr and a demand. Then he slams into me. Each measured thrust comes with a kiss to my shoulder until I see the moment he begins to lose control.

"I'm close," I say, the words hard to express when I never want this to end.

"I want to feel your orgasm cover me. Come for me, baby."

Despite the request, I desperately cling to the last inklings of this connection, but I'm overcome and dragged into the ecstasy of my release. The pounding doesn't stop, tipping me to come again before recovering from the first orgasm. Relentless, his body thrusts into me with no rhyme or reason, just raw need driving him until it gets the best of him as well. "Fuck!" My name leaves his mouth like a swear word calling to me, bringing me back to him. "Story." And then it becomes a chanted prayer on heavy breaths. *"Story . . . Story . . . Story."*

He drops down on top of me, and I lie under him with my body pressed to the cold stone and my eyes closed. My breath can't regulate, and my heart is still beating strong against my rib cage. Loving the feel of him covering me, I would never ask him to leave, to move off me.

With his chest resting on my back and his cheek pressed to my shoulders, the weight of this man matches my emotions, growing heavier by the minute. I'm so tempted to tell him how I feel, how fast I've fallen for him. The words hang on the tip of my tongue. I'm ready to taste the words I've never said to any man.

"I'm in love with you, Story."

But he beats me to the punch.

22

Cooper

I've never said those words to anyone.

I've never felt this way about anyone else either.

I always believed it would ruin everything. Like my parents. They used to say it occasionally, in a card or when they thought I wasn't listening, but it's been years since I've heard either one of them say it. Was it life that ruined their relationship, or did they just never find true love in each other?

Thinking about them specifically, it wouldn't surprise me if it was neither, nor if they married for convenience to carry on the good Haywood name. Even my thoughts are inflicted with sarcasm these days.

We all have our crosses to bear . . .

As for the feelings I blurted earlier to the woman sleeping next to me, I couldn't hold back. Not this time. *Not with Story.*

I didn't want to. I'd say it now if she was awake. Now that I've slept, I was foolish to believe that telling her my feelings would have kept me awake, restless, or tossing and turning with regret. In fact, sharing my heart with her had me sleeping like a baby.

Glancing at the time, I find it's just past ten o'clock.

With the drapes left open from last night, I can see it's a beautiful day. Soft white reflected off the snow brightens the room as it falls outside the window. If Story ever dreamed of magical holidays, I think I've got this one covered.

She's got my back as well. I can't think of anything better than Christmas morning with the only person I want to spend it with. *Even if she is slightly snoring.*

Sneaking out of bed, I grab my phone from the bedside and check for a certain text before getting the fire started in the fireplace. Hopefully, that can clear the slight bite in the air from the room before she wakes up.

I try to be quiet but glance back when she stirs. When she stays asleep, I do a silent fist pump, glad she doesn't wake before I'm ready. It's a surprise that I want to keep.

The text message I've been waiting for from the concierge hits my screen—the final piece of the surprise puzzle. Tiptoeing across the room like a damn elf, I open the door to find the room service delivery.

Using my foot to prop open the door, I stretch to reach the cart and drag it in, then start setting up the table. I check to make sure all the dishes and the special surprise are here.

"Now I understand why Mommy was kissing Santa under the mistletoe."

The sound of her sweet voice has me grinning before I even turn around to see her watching me. "Oh, yeah. Why's that?" I rub my hand over my abs just because I know she likes it.

"Come back to bed, and I'll show you." Story pats the

bed next to her, then flips the corner of the blanket back to welcome me in.

"You're about to be put on the naughty list, little girl."

She props up on her elbows. "I'm not seeing the problem."

I walk over and sit down beside her. Leaning closer, I say, "Neither am I. Merry Christmas, babe."

Her arms come around my neck, and she smiles like an angel on Christmas morning . . . Oh wait, she is. *Goddamn, she's beautiful.* "Merry Christmas."

We kiss, not with fire and frenzy but with passion and my whole fucking heart wrapped up in her. When our lips slowly part, she strokes the hair back from my eyes. "I love you, Cooper Haywood."

I'm left stunned.

Speechless.

As I stare into her eyes, mine get wet. What the fuck?

My heart isn't racing but calm instead.

It dawns on me by just looking at her—she means what she says. "You love me?"

"I do. I love you."

Just like that. She just puts her own heart on the line, this time for my benefit.

I drop my gaze to the bed sheet between us and shake my head, trying to comprehend what that really means.

She adds, "Last night, you said you were in love with me?" The question has me looking up again. The tremble in her voice has me taking her hand and holding it between mine.

"I do. I'm so in love with you, Story."

She runs her thumb over the side of mine. "Then what's wrong?"

Grabbing my neck, I try to force down the lump that's

formed, but it's the overwhelming feeling that I don't deserve this woman. Her heart is bigger than the universe. "Nothing, actually," I start, struggling to figure out why I'm so fucking emotional. "It's all right. I mean, this." I bounce a finger in the air between us. "Everything is so right."

She smiles with a tilt of her head. "It is. So right."

Locking down whatever's happening on the inside, I grin. "We should eat while it's hot."

Commanded by the suggestion, her stomach growls. "What did you order?" She waggles her eyebrows. You'd think we were still talking about sex. Nope. *Food.*

I chuckle as I push off the bed. "Let me serve you, ma'am."

Reading my mood, she lets me go without protest. It's not that I want to leave her side. It's that I need to clear the air to figure out why I was just sideswiped by her telling me she loves me.

With the back of her hand to her forehead, she puts on a good damsel-in-distress act when we both know she doesn't need a man. For me, it's a privilege to be a part of her life . . . and have her love. *Shit.* Now the l-word is casually being thrown around like we're okay with it. *Am I okay?*

I think I am.

With her, I know I am.

"Your kindness is much appreciated, kind sir." The dramatic flair is fun at the moment, but I sure am glad that's the opposite of who she is.

It sucks that Camille and my mom come to mind, but they're prime examples of women who use those tactics to get what they want.

I prefer being grounded in Story over the fake I grew up around. She sits on the couch, and although she's waiting silently, her wiggling gives her excitement away.

"Lap or table?" I ask, holding a domed plate for her.

"Lap but only if you're sitting next to me."

I hand her the breakfast plate, then pour us both a cup of coffee. She says, "Orange juice, water, coffee, breakfast? I might be mistaken, but you're either trying to fatten me up or hydrate me so when we spend the next twenty-four hours in bed, I have the energy."

"Not a bad idea, but I'm not sure that waffles and straw-berries will be that energizing. They might have you back asleep in an hour." Chuckling, I sit on the couch with the plate on my lap. Taking a bite of bacon, I start thinking about Christmases past, and although I wouldn't trade this one for any other, it's strange not being home for the holi-day. "At home, I never ate anywhere but at a formal dining table until I went to college. I'm talking silver, china . . ." Always the rebel, I cut my waffle with my fork instead of the knife. "Servers. The whole works. Every night. It was . . ." I chuckle again, thinking about how much I hated that we couldn't act like a normal family. "It was a lot. I used to—"

"Servers? You had ser*vants*?"

The questions and the accusation built into them draw my eyes to her. "No, we had staff. They didn't wait on us hand and foot." Feeling defensive, I add, "I couldn't just order what I wanted or demand someone to do something. They did a job, and that was it."

"Like me," she states, her tone flat.

"No." *Fuck.* Not sure how I even fucked this up or how to proceed, I run my hand through my hair.

"Not like me?" she prompts.

"Like you at work. Yes, Story. Not like you now."

Her head jerks back. "You mean eating with you in this fancy hotel? They weren't allowed to eat with you?" She sets her plate on the table in front of us. That can't be good. *Not that it has been so far.*

"Story—"

"Cooper."

"I'm not sure why this upsets you, but let me be clear. The staff is paid. Yes, like you are at the coffee shop, but they're given a salary. We don't tip them at the dinner table, though they get bonuses." I shake my head as I dig this hole deeper. "We're fucking awful people, Story. Is that what you need me to admit? I admit it. Openly. You've seen the red flags." I don't think she's even aware that she's running her hand over her scar. I sigh heavily, losing my appetite. "I'm really fucking this up. I'm sorry."

"Why are you apologizing, Cooper?" she asks, her eyes set on mine.

"Because I don't know what to say to make this better."

She scoots across the sofa and rests her hand on my knee. "You don't have to make this better. I . . ." She shakes her head and exhales while looking between us. When her eyes lift to mine again, she says, "I'm the one who's sorry. I'm standing here on higher moral ground that I have no right to be on. I think I'm just shocked . . ." Her eyes begin to plead with mine, matching her tone. "I'm shocked people live in such luxury, but . . ." She looks around. "I understand the appeal. I've felt like a princess here. You've spoiled me, Cooper. If you don't dump me for being so rude, I promise never to judge where you have the good fortune to live again."

She picks up my hand and brings it to her mouth, kissing the palm, then holding it tight between her hands.

"I don't need an apology. I'm good, but I can't change those things about me."

"I don't want you to. You wouldn't be the man you are right now if you'd lived a different life."

This time, I kiss her hand and the tips of each finger. Glancing at the food, I say, "It's definitely going to be cold."

She reaches for her plate. "I'm okay with that. I think this was a good conversation."

Although I knew the reality of my family's wealth would strike a nerve with her, this wasn't as unpleasant of a conversation as I expected. "I do, too." I take a bite, putting this behind us, but then stop before taking another to ask, "Is this how healthy relationships work?"

She balks. "How would I know?"

"We're a fucked-up pair."

Shrugging, she says, "At least we have each other." She takes a drink of her juice.

At least we have each other.

When we're finished eating, she gets up and rubs her hands together in front of the fire. "What time do we have to check out?"

"We have a late checkout and can stay until noon."

"It's going to be hard to leave here." Her tone softens. "Thank you for booking this for us. It's been really special."

"You're welcome." A bird landing on the stone ledge outside the window has both of us turning.

Doing a quick bare-footed spin on her way over, she bends down to get a better look, but it flies away. She was doing this last night, looking outside like she couldn't believe this was real. And each time, she smiled a little bigger.

Turning back to me, she says, "It snowed a lot last night. Do you know what that means?"

"No. What does that mean?" Joining her side, I look over her shoulder and out the window. Snow has covered every surface, and with the sun beginning to peek through the clouds, I need sunglasses.

"We might be stuck here for a few days." She giggles, her happiness too big to contain. I'll buy this hotel if it brings her this much joy.

"Do you want to stay?"

"Yes," she replies, nodding. "But we should go. Our real lives await." They do, and since I met her, I don't hate reality so much anymore.

Time is ticking, so I try to act casual when I get dressed in my other clothes. "There's one last dish on the tray."

I spy her reaction out of the corners of my eyes. Story looks over after setting her coffee cup back on the table. "What is it?"

"I don't know," I mumble.

She walks over and lifts the silver dome. Motionless, she stares in confusion. Still holding the lid in the air, she asks, "What is this, Cooper?"

Glancing between the box on the plate and her a few times, I reply, "Looks like a new camera to me." I slip a shoe on and then start on the other.

I give her a moment to digest what's happening while I continue putting my shoes on. When I'm dressed, I walk over and stand next to her. "Are you going to touch it?"

She sets the lid down and takes the box in her hands. Wrapping it in her arms, she holds it to her stomach and looks up at me. "You can't give this to me."

"I already did." Leaning down, I kiss her cheek. "Merry Christmas, baby."

Tears spring to her eyes. "Oh my God, Cooper." Holding the box with one arm, the other wraps around me. "This is the best present I've ever received. Thank you. Thank you.

Thank you so much." Then she lifts onto her toes and kisses me. "This means more to me than you'll ever know."

"I'll know because you're going to take amazing photos, and one day, you'll be in that gallery like we talked about."

"The one where we don't know each other?" She laughs.

"I don't think I could hide my pride if I saw your art on the walls."

She lifts again, and we kiss. When she lowers back down, she says, "I didn't buy you anything. I mean, I didn't know we would be spending Christmas together, but I made something for you at my apartment."

"You don't have to give me anything, Story."

"Just know, it's not much."

"I can't wait to see it. Come on." I place a kiss on her head when I pass to pick up my stuff and pack it to go. "Let's get on the road."

As she's getting undressed, her head appears to be swimming with happiness, judging by the smile on her face and that dreamy look in her eyes. "I'm going to be utterly unbearable after being spoiled like this," she says.

"I think I can handle you."

I'm hit with a pointed look. "You sure about that?"

"Abso-fucking-lutely." I wink.

When she walks by me, she pokes me in the chest. "I have no doubt whatsoever." She winks right back, the sass. I laugh, her lightness contagious. This trip has been quick but amazing for me too.

I'll never regret choosing her and leaving Haywood yesterday. And then I remember the promise I made to them.

Fuck.

23

Story

It's a hard adjustment coming back from a five-star hotel to my little rinky-dink studio apartment. There's not much food stocked in the fridge, but it's never felt more like home than it does with Cooper here.

Our matching Christmas pajamas are in the washer, and I have a pot of hot water beginning to boil for tea. Towel-drying my hair after taking a shower, I ask, "What do you want to do for dinner? I have some lunch meat and bread, some ramen noodle cups, or when I texted Lila to wish her and Jake a Merry Christmas, she said it was okay for us to go to the coffee shop and make something there. Any of those options sound appealing?"

I struggle to know what to do with him when it comes to things like meals. He has servers and Michelin star dining every night. I'm used to fending for myself on an extremely tight budget. If more places were open tonight, I'd use some of my tips to spoil him.

Spinning to face me from the desk, he asks, "Who's Jake?"

"Lila's son." I hang the towel on the hook inside the bathroom. "He's five and the sweetest kid. He loves his mama." When I come back out, I tighten the towel wrapped around my body, and add, "She's a single mom. The dad skipped town right after Jake was born."

"That's too bad."

"Yeah. There might be a restaurant open?" I ask, hoping he lands on something that sounds enticing because I'm starting to get hungry again. The waffle was good, but it's burned off four hours later.

He's been distracted for the past thirty minutes, staring at his phone like he's expecting something important or got something he's not sure how to deal with. "Whatever you want," he says, not looking up. "Find something you like on your app and let me know. I can order."

"I don't have a delivery app on my phone." I open the dresser drawer and grab a T-shirt and shorts, but I put the T-shirt back and opt for a sweatshirt instead. "Between the surcharges and cost of food plus tip, I just pop in somewhere if I'm treating myself or I eat at the coffee shop."

Finally looking at me, he smiles. There's the Cooper I know. "How about we keep it simple and have the ramen?"

"Good choice."

Before the noodles are prepared, I go to my desk and pick up the small present I have for him. Forcing it forward, I say, "It's not much. Just a token."

Holding it in his hands, he says, "I already love it."

A quick eye roll ends with me shaking my head. "Don't assume too much. You may hate it."

"Never." He rips the paper off the box and then lifts the lid. He gave me a camera . . . and I only have a stack of photographs for him. There aren't many times I've been ashamed to be poor. This time, I am.

Taking the photos out of the box, he flips through them, studying each one of the six I've given him. "I'm honored. They're Story Salenger originals." He holds them up. "You sure this is okay for me to take?"

My shoulders rise with a quick jump before falling. "They're just copies I had made."

"But no others exist in the world, right?"

Now I see where he's going with this. "No others."

He stands and hugs me. "This is an incredible gift. Thank you."

I slide my arms around him, not even understanding what just happened. He managed to take my shame and turn it like he just won the lottery. A kiss is placed on my head, and he adds, "I'll hold on to these forever." When he steps back, he flips to the last one—the one of us lying in bed tangled up in each other with lazy grins and love in our eyes. I can only wish for that euphoria to last forever. "This will always be my favorite."

WE'RE BACK in our reindeer pj's, curled up together on the bed after finishing our noodles earlier. It's not a tradition I particularly love, but watching *Breakfast at Tiffany's* has carried on from watching it with my mom. And Cooper was patient enough to sit through it with me.

Pushing up on my hand, I twist toward him. "It's glamorous in some ways and quirky in others, but ultimately, I've always felt the characters are so sad on the inside."

With his back against the wall, he says, "Maybe we're all a little sad, but some of us are better at hiding it than others." He looks at the laptop as the credits roll across the screen. "Moon River" adds to the somberness as it plays in the background. "I think there's this inflated view of the storyline because of Audrey Hepburn. A girl I once dated was obsessed with little black dresses instead of how the only joy the characters find is in the little moments in each other's company."

Listening to him talk, I didn't realize that my heart had crawled into my throat. Cooper's eyes were once so bright that I thought emeralds would pale in comparison, but as I've gotten to know him, I've started to realize that it's not the light in them that's mesmerizing. It's the dark. You just have to look a little harder.

He has so many layers to him that most will never have the privilege of knowing. I crawl onto his lap and don't find comfort until his hand rests on my hip and the other arm wraps around my middle. "I love you," I say, just us with no big fanfare.

"I love you, too, babe." He kisses my head, and then I rest it on his shoulder. I lose track of time lying in his arms, but that's the nice thing about holidays when everything is closed. Instead of days off when you have to run errands and finish to-do lists, we get to do what we want on Christmas.

Eventually, the silence is broken when he says, "I'm sorry about your mom and what you had to go through."

I lift to see if maybe the movie's sadness has carried over, or maybe my loss fits the mood we're in. Either way, my heart squeezes like he just gave it a kiss. "I know, Cooper. I feel the same."

I curl around him again, never feeling closer to anyone than him. I'm not sure words will be enough, so I kiss him. When it deepens, I know we're not going to get much sleep tonight, and I'm okay with that. Sad is the last thing I want to be with him.

Morning comes too soon. I yawn, my body becoming a traitor and forcing me to wake. I'd much rather stay tucked in Cooper's arms all day than work. Alas, his arms won't pay the bills.

I get out of bed and sneak around to get dressed. He's sleeping so heavily that he doesn't even move by the time I'm ready to leave. I decide to leave him a note like he left instead of waking him. I move to the desk where his phone is charging and shift it off the pad of paper. I write just a sweet nothing: *Went to work. I love you, Story.*

When his phone lights, I can't help but read the text on the screen.

Mom: *What time will you be here?*

Caught up in my own feelings yesterday, I hadn't thought about how his parents didn't contact him, not even to wish him a happy holiday. My chest tightens as I swivel to look at him. He's sleeping so peacefully, his expression and mind at rest.

Is it because he's here?

I'm not sure what made him leave Haywood to come spend the past two days with me, but I also won't question his motives. Whether he had a good reason or just wanted to see me, he came to be with me. For that alone, I just fell even harder for this man.

"WE ALREADY SAID I LOVE YOU."

"You're kidding me," Lila says, mimicking the kid from *Home Alone*. "You guys didn't waste time." Emotion fills her eyes and causes her lip to wobble. I'm worried tears will follow. "Story?" Pulling me into a hug, she strokes me like a mom and her baby. "My little girl is all grown up."

I laugh and push her off me. "You're ridiculous, you know that?"

"Yes, and you're ridiculously in love." She moves to the display case to restock the cookies. "He's handsome, seems smart." She glances at me as I lean against the counter. "Rich."

"What makes you say that?"

"First of all, the bill and the tip were dead giveaways. But also, look at how he dresses. Designer clothes for a college kid? He's from money, and you just struck oil, friend."

Having his family's wealth rank in the top three when describing Cooper seems like such a disservice. That's when it dawns on me—he didn't want to tell me his last name or that Haywood Hall is named after his family. He's used to these things mattering to people, whether it helps or hurts him, and he's trying to come out from under the Haywood shadow.

I smile to myself. I'm proud of him for wanting to be his own man.

She returns the glass cover and asks, "So where does he live?"

Taking the coffee pot from the burner, I say, "The mirrored tower on the other side of campus," and walk across the shop. Wonder when he's going to show me his apartment?

She shakes her head. "Of course, he does."

"All good today, Lou?" I go ahead and top off his coffee mug.

Smiling, he looks up at me, stopping everything he's doing as if my presence deserves more attention than the . . .

206   S.L. SCOTT

I bend to see the molecular model he's constructing. "Just peachy, Story. How's it going with you? Nice holiday?"

He's such a sweet guy. Not my type, but maybe he and Lila should talk. "The best, in fact."

"That's good to hear—"

Already detouring to the next table, I say, "I need to get back to work," over my shoulder.

He waves. "Yes, of course."

After I make a round, I return the empty pot to the burner again and get another pot brewing. During the past six hours of my shift, I've got three texts from Cooper, one specifically mentioning that he's going to his place to shower and change clothes. Another to say good morning, and the last asked what time I get off work so he can meet me at my apartment.

Why am I never invited to his place?

Does he have roommates I don't know about or magazines he doesn't want me to see lying around? I mean, really, what could a twenty-two-year-old male keep at his apartment that he would want to hide? I don't know, but I want to find out.

My curiosity getting the best of me, I ask Lila, "You don't need me to do anything else?"

"No, I'm good. The rush is over." She rests her elbow on the counter and then her chin in her hand. Grinning like a fool, she adds, "Go have fun with your boyfriend. At least one of us will be having a good time."

Wrapping my hand over hers, I say, "Your true love will come along. In the meantime, Lou's kind of cute, right?"

Her gaze flies over my shoulder, and her spine straightens. "Lou's too nice. Not my type at all."

I shrug. "I'm happy to say that I'm officially over the bad boys."

"The guys you dated weren't bad. They were awful."

I untie the apron and wad it in my hands. "Truer words were never spoken." I stuff it in my bag and then head for the door. "Good night."

The towering apartment building can't be seen from the street in daylight. And although it's not late at 8:17, it's been dark for a few hours. I decide to make the trek anyway and surprise him. I hope he's happy when he sees me, and I'm not opening Pandora's box instead.

As I stand in front of the building, it's bigger than I remember the last time I was here. But Troy had already been drinking and starting to make a scene, so we shuffled inside quickly. I didn't know he had rich friends, but he said he knew this guy and hadn't seen him in a while. I never did get to meet his friend.

Even though I'm looking up as far as I can see, the top of the building is hidden from view and engulfed by clouds. I go in. There's no doorman, but the building feels fancy enough to have one.

I don't know what floor Cooper lives on, so I look for a directory. It's not exactly safe to post people's names and apartment numbers these days, but I check the lobby anyway. When I don't see one, I plug his name and the street address into a search app on my phone and *bingo*.

The elevator door opens as soon as I approach. Stepping in, I push the button for the fifteenth floor. There are only sixteen, so that means Cooper lives under the penthouse. *No surprise.* The higher the floor, the higher the cost. The reality real estate shows have taught me a lot.

Checking my phone again, I find another text from him asking if it's going to be a late night. He's sweet to offer to help with any cravings. Hopefully, I can satisfy his craving for me instead. I'm getting more excited with each floor I pass.

The door slides open, and when I step out, I look around. Déjà vu strikes, but I can't put my finger on why it's familiar. Sure, it's nicely decorated with a calm blue on the walls and dark blue carpets lining the hall. Maybe every floor in this building is the same, so that can't be it.

I keep walking, checking numbers above the doors. When I reach his, something in my gut twists as a memory of following this same path hits.

My heart starts pounding in my chest as I stand there, the number 15B gleaming in gold letters above his door. I listen but don't immediately hear anything—no music or voices—but I'm suddenly nervous like I'm intruding.

Maybe I shouldn't have come, after all, and waited for an invitation.

Panic sets in. What do I do?

Stay or walk away?

Cooper loves me. He's said it. *He's shown me how he feels.* There's nothing behind that door he needs to worry about when it comes to me.

I'm being silly. I swallow down my nerves and knock.

And then the door opens . . .

24

Story

"Story?" Cooper's eyes leave me to look down the hall. "What are you doing here?"

Suspicious. I look behind me, just in case, but I feel sick to my stomach for doing it. Jealousy is something I've managed to escape in my relationships. *Until now.* "Expecting someone?"

"No," he replies with a nervous laugh. "Of course, not. Not even you."

My heart drops as a lump forms in my throat. I force the words to wedge around it, and ask, "Why does it feel like I just busted you doing something?"

"I'm not doing anything." Pulling his phone from his pocket, he holds it up. "I was literally waiting to hear from you." He kicks the door wide and then catches it with his palm on the return. "Come in."

"I'm not sure I'm welcome."

His shoulders and whatever guard he had falls as he enters the hallway. Taking my hands in his, he lets the door shut behind him. "You're welcome here anytime, Story. You don't need an invitation. You can give me a heads-up or show up unannounced. I was surprised to see you, but it wasn't a bad surprise. I'm sorry if I made you feel otherwise."

He leans down to kiss me. I could fight this and live with the distrust or jealousy causing my stomach to clench, or I could trust him.

We just started telling each other we're in love, so I choose to trust. "I was curious why you never invited me to your apartment and figured I'd find out what you're hiding over here." My eyes dart to the door but then return to his eyes. I hold up my phone. "I got your texts, but honestly, I didn't think twice about showing up here until I was standing in the lobby."

"I'm glad you're here. I just didn't expect you or anyone to be knocking on my door. I'm sorry if that freaked you out."

"It's okay, but can we go in?"

Holding my hand, he turns to open the door for me and then follows. "You walked all that way?"

Though I have the freedom to walk all the way inside, I don't go too far, thinking he should lead. "It wasn't too bad of a hike."

"Except that it's nine o'clock at night and freezing outside. I would have picked you up. I was ready to drive you home." Our hands fall apart, and he moves around me to take the lead. "I'll give you the quick tour. Living room. Kitchen and dining off to the right, hall on the left with two bedrooms."

The entry isn't as grand as I imagined, but I'm not sure why I imagined his place as a palace instead of a normal apartment. "That was a quick tour. Mine's quicker." I laugh, but when I look ahead, my gaze traveling across the living room, I see the balcony that extends the length of the living room. A memory of my ex and some redhead on a balcony flirting comes back as if it's happening before me.

I shake my head and steady my breathing. That night only went downhill after that.

Walking into the living room, I brush away the competing images and look around.

This apartment is not like any other college kids I've seen. Did I expect less from Cooper? Not really. Not anymore.

It's warmer than I expected it to be, not in temperature, though it does feel cozy, but the color palette. There's less white as it leans into warm greens on the sofa, probably leather. Everyone else I know has the imitation, but I'm pretty sure that's not Cooper's style. As if a designer came in and took charge, there's a blanket on one end of the couch, not draped but bundled like it's been used recently, and two throw pillows that match the chairs anchoring either end. "It's really nice, Cooper. I like the colors."

The man never needs anyone's approval, but when he hears mine, a genuine smile appears as pride lifts the corners. "Thanks."

There's a large TV hanging on the wall, and even a table in the dining area. It's contemporary, not formal. "Can I see your bedroom?"

"Happily." There's a cockiness to his tone that I don't hear much, but it doesn't bother me when I do.

Walking down the short hall, I look to the left, recalling a bathroom being there the night of that party. When I see it with the door propped open, my feet stop as if this time I can protect myself. I'd be wise not to go there again.

My hands start shaking, and my chest tightens, causing

my breathing to labor. I close my eyes and try to put the reality of the circumstance into perspective. That night, and Troy cheating, was never about me. It was always about him.

"Story?"

I open my eyes to see Cooper standing in the doorway of his bedroom. "Are you coming?"

Putting on a happy face for him, I refuse to hold that night against the man who's been nothing short of a knight in shining armor. I close the distance between us. "Yeah, can't wait to see where the magic happens. Wait . . ." I start laughing, though a twinge has stifled the usual butterflies I feel around him. "That didn't come out right. I don't want to think about you having magic with other people." I laugh, but even I can hear the hollowness, so I know he can.

"I can assure you that no magic has ever happened with anyone else."

"Look, I know you're not a virgin." But then his words sink deeper, what he means reaching the surface of my understanding. Instead of invading his bedroom, I wrap myself around his middle and just hold him, hug him, and savor how sweet he is to me, how lucky I am to have found him—for us to find each other.

We spin in the doorway, and I'm greeted by a bed that reminds me of the hotel—big with thick covers, fluffy sleeping pillows, and a wooden headboard. The same wood is used in the nightstands and a dresser. The room is a deep blue with a hint of green saturated into the paint. Without any knickknacks around, the room looks more temporary as if he's just passing through. My stomach knots.

We haven't talked about long-term plans. Hell, we haven't even talked about next week. I assume he's leaving for the rest of the break, but a little hope living in my heart prays he'll stay. Without the weight of school filling our days, we'd have those hours with each other. Am I being selfish for wanting all his time for myself?

Probably, but it's so fun being in a relationship with him that I'm okay with being called selfish.

I look up at him, a plot formulating. "Can I?"

He already knows what I'm asking. "Go for it."

I run and jump onto the bed, facedown, and then starfish my limbs to claim as much space as I can.

"How is it?" he asks. "Is it Story approved?"

Rolling over, I sigh, closing my eyes and sinking deeper into this cloud. "Exceeds the gold-star standard." Lifting my head, I ask, "Why have you been keeping this bed from me?"

He chuckles and comes over, sitting at the end of the mattress. His hand rests over my ankle so casually that I can't help but feel a jolt of happiness through me. I'm becoming a part of his every day. I love that.

Then he says, "I need to tell you something."

It's tempting to pull back, to tuck my legs under me and move toward the headboard to put space between us. But that's not what I'm going to do, not with Cooper. Instead, I say, "You can tell me anything."

He glances back, and that's when I see the concern in his eyes, the weight of something bigger tidal-waving and dimming the light.

I move down and sit next to him. Our hands find each other's, and our fingers fold together. When he doesn't say anything, I keep my gaze to the floor and whisper, "It's okay. We'll be okay." I'm not even sure why I say that other than the pit of my stomach is now cradling my heart. "I promise."

Looking at me out of the corner of his eye, he says, "You've been here before. That's why I haven't invited you over. I didn't want you to think poorly of me."

"Don't worry, poor never factors into the equation when

it comes to you." I laugh lightly, but I know there's more truth in that joke than I'm admitting.

"And I saw you. I saw you with... him."

"I don't understand. What do you mean you saw me? How would you even remember me? A packed party." I lean my head on his shoulder. His arm comes around to cover my back, his hand comforting me by rubbing my side. "It was not a good night."

"No. Not my finest hour, but I remember you. I remember the skirt and tights, how you wore your hair down with a wave in the front. I remember how he had his arm around your neck, not your back or shoulders, but your neck."

My heartbeat quickens, listening to the details that stood out to him—*me*. Shifting to see him better, I still feel confused. "I knew I recognized this place." The hall, the door, and that balcony. I would still like to forget the bathroom. "Why are you upset? It's quite the coincidence, right?" I smile. "Like the film and how we were the only two in there."

I get up, thinking there's more at play here. "Did you feel I would be mad that you knew, and I didn't?"

"Something like that. I wasn't sure how you would take it."

Wedging between his legs, I cup his face and angle him up to look at me. "It's like the universe keeps throwing us together, and we finally got the message." Leaning down, I kiss him, and then again for good measure and because I just like kissing him a whole lot. Resting my forehead against his, I add, "There's no denying it. You and I were destined to be together."

We kiss again, but this time he picks me up by my ass, and I'm flat on my back in less than two seconds. Now working his way between my legs, he kisses me again, and then says, "There's just one other thing I need to tell you."

"What is it?"

He kisses me once more and works his way to my neck. When I'm putty in his hands, he says, "I promised my parents I would be back for New Year's Eve."

"Oh." Not what I expected or what I wanted to hear.

Stroking my cheek, he says, "But I'm not going back without you."

Oh . . . that changes things. I grin because I'm so in love with him, and I feel his love so deeply. "So we're spending New Year's Eve in Haywood?"

"No. New York City."

Oh. *This should be interesting.*

25

Cooper

"I don't want to screw this up. Can we go over it one more time?"

"No one's going to quiz you, babe." I park the car in the garage of my parents' building and reach over. Covering her leg, I add, "They're going to love you. What's not to love?"

I thought she'd shake the nerves from her system on the drive from Atterton to the city. Two hours should have done the trick. But then they kicked back in as soon as she put on the dress—which is so fucking sexy that I almost took it off her and tried to convince her we should stay in and celebrate in bed.

"I'm not like you, Cooper. I don't remember ever having dinner at a table growing up unless it was inside a fast-food restaurant or on a picnic bench. I looked up which fork to use, but now all that information has gone out the window. Ask me about the new law that just went into effect in January regarding deductibles on financial gains—I got ya covered. Am I supposed to shake your mom's hand or hug her when we meet—I have no clue? I'm a hugger, but only when I want someone in my space." She flips the visor down and checks her face in the mirror. "Otherwise, I don't really do all that. Are they huggers? Or hand shakers? I'm so nervous I could puke. Help me, Coo—"

"It's going to be all right. You're going to be fine. You're going to be spectacular, actually. Like you always are. They're going to love you just like I do."

She's nodding, taking every word in like it will be on a test. Flipping the visor back up, she takes a deep breath, and then on the exhale, says, "Let's just get on with meeting the parents and get it over with, so we can enjoy the rest of the night."

Before she pops the door open, I grab her arm. "We don't have to do this, babe. We can buckle back up and do anything or go anywhere. The night is ours. Not theirs."

"You promised them you'd be here."

"I did, but you're more important than that promise."

"Not to your parents. It will be fun. I'm just overreacting because I'm anxious. I've never met a boyfriend's parents before."

"Trust me, it's not something I've done either, but I'll stay with you. You have nothing to be nervous about."

I run around the car and open her door before helping her out. She's gorgeous tonight. Her hair hangs down over her shoulders in soft waves. Her eyes are lined heavier than usual, making the green pop in the dim lights of the car. I've wanted to kiss her pink lipstick right off her mouth since she walked out of the bathroom back at the hotel. Story is gorgeous every day, but tonight, she's breathtaking.

Every guy is going to be staring at her. I just wish I could keep her to myself a little longer. *But duty calls . . .*

I bend down and kiss her cheek. "I know I told you before we left, but you really do look incredible."

"I hope so. This is the most I've ever spent on a dress, and even though I got it online, and it's secondhand, it cost a lot. Fortunately, I came into a little money recently." She gives me a wink. Kicking up a heel, she adds, "Lila let me borrow the shoes," as we walk to the elevator holding hands.

"I like them." They're sexy, but it feels weird to say that since they belong to her friend. "They look great on you."

"You look so sexy in black head to toe, Mr. Haywood. A little rebellious, cutting-edge style, handsome as always, but a little danger thrown in the mix tonight."

"That's what I'm going for—dangerous and sexy."

"Goal achieved." We step into the elevator, and she's taking another deep breath when I punch the button for the penthouse. She asks, "So Daxton was the father of Archibald Haywood, right?"

"No. It's the other way around, but seriously, no one's going to be talking about my family tree." We spend the ascent in silence, both of us bracing ourselves for different reasons. I regret not texting my mom prior to give her a heads-up. I give Story's hand a little squeeze just as the doors open. "Here we go."

"Why am I hearing Darth Vader's theme song in my head?"

I chuckle. "That would make us the bad guys."

She waffles her head back and forth. "True. And there's no way we're not the good guys in this scenario."

Bringing her hand to my chest, I say, "Us against them, babe."

"Us against them," she says, nodding. Upon entry to the vast apartment, her jaw isn't hitting the floor, but by how her eyes are taking things in—her lips are just parted and her steps slowing—I'm worried she'll never see me the same. "You grew up here?"

"Yes. This is the main residence. The Haywood House is used for the holidays, weekend getaways, and summer breaks."

"Okay."

That's it. That's all I get.

Not good.

I stop when I see Patrice. She hands a coat check ticket to Caffrey and Janet Williams of East Hampton—their son is an asshole who picked one fight with me before I taught him a lesson about fucking with me. He just did time down in Florida on a drug charge. They act like they don't have any children now and scurry away when they see me.

When Patrice sees me, she smiles like she's seeing her own son. "Cooper, I didn't know if we'd get to see you tonight." Her gaze flicks to Story, and her smile grows wider. "And you brought a date."

"I did." I give her a hug.

Patrice looks at Story when we part and holds out her hand. "Hi, I'm Patrice Fielder. This guy's former nanny."

Story smiles, instantly at ease as her shoulders soften. She shakes her hand, but then Patrice hugs her. I'm not sure if Story will like that based on her earlier commentary, but it doesn't matter because she hugs her right back.

Stepping apart, Patrice adds, "This is the first time he's brought home someone he—"

"Cooper!"

Fuck.

The high squeal burst the good moment we were having, which I'm sure was the intention. Camille throws her arms around me, blocking my view of Story, the connection lost as I try to pry Camille off me in a hurry.

I hear Patrice continue, "Cares about," her tone souring as she glares at the back of Camille's head. She's not telling a lie.

"Camille," I snap, untangling her arms from around me. Putting distance between us, I look at Story and then hold out my hand to her.

The ire of burning bronze licks in her eyes, but she raises her hand and joins with mine.

The jerk of Camille's head has her glaring in confusion at Story's and my hands. "What's going on, Coop?"

I catch the roll of Story's eyes before she starts to pull away. I hold her tighter. No way am I letting her slip away. I will make it very clear to everyone in this fucking party who I'm with and who I'm choosing.

More guests arrive, pulling Patrice away to take their coats and leaving the three of us standing there.

"This is my girlfriend, Story Salenger," I reply, glancing at Story beside me. "Story, this is Camille Arden."

Camille grins like the Cheshire cat from *Alice in Wonderland*. "How sweet," she says condescendingly as she looks from Story back to me. She pats my arm. "Is this the suit I bought you?"

Fuck.

Fuck.

Fuck.

Shaking her head like she's innocent to the pot she's stirring, she adds, "I always did like the cut of Tom Ford on you. Don't you agree, Story? That's such a unique name. Very . . . I'm not sure."

Fuck.

Fuck.

Waving her hand to brush the small talk away, she continues to blabber, "I had no idea you were dating anyone. Why didn't you mention her last week when we got together?"

Fuck.

I could stand here and do this, go a few verbal rounds with her . . . but I tuck Story under my arm and walk away instead. Letting me lead, I hold her hand as we weave through the crowd, the party well into the swing of things. "Drink?"

"A double," she replies.

Glad she's still holding my hand after that fiasco, I lean down and ask, "A double what?"

"Anything."

We reach the bar, and I order bourbon on the rocks. Looking at Story, I realize I've never seen her drink alcohol besides a few sips of champagne. "What do you normally drink?"

"I don't really."

I turn back to the bartender and look at the selection on display. If she doesn't drink, a double of anything will be the trouble neither of us needs. "A glass of rosé."

I hand her the glass and take a long drink of mine when he sets it on the bar in front of me. Since people are waiting to place their drink orders, I take Story by the crook of her arm and lead her toward the door that leads to the west-facing balcony. "It's cold outside, but do you need some fresh air?"

"I think it would be good for a minute."

I haven't seen my parents yet, but I'm okay with that after what just happened with Camille. Very few people are outside due to the low temperature, but it gives Story and me a moment alone. I take my jacket off and wrap it around her shoulders. "I'm sorry—"

"Cooper," she says, sighing. "I'm not naïve. Maybe I'm

not as classy as Camille, but if that means being catty to someone you don't know out of jealousy, I'd rather be me."

"You blow me away by how you handle everything with grace. So don't think for a minute that you're not sophisticated."

She sidles closer and leans against me. I slip my arm under the jacket and around her waist, holding her close and hoping I can keep her warm for just a few minutes more. I'm not sure what lies ahead when she meets my parents, but here right now, I'm happy and hope she is.

I take another drink to warm my insides. When she takes a sip of her wine, I ask, "How is it?"

"Spectacular."

I smile as the lights reflect in her eyes, mesmerized by this incredible woman. "I meant the wine, though you're right. The view is pretty spectacular."

Music invades our peace when the door opens. "I didn't realize you were here, Cooper," my mom observes.

I step away from Story like I'm sixteen and was just busted having sex on the couch or something. Since that happened, my reaction is now automatic. When I turn around, my dad is with her as they stare back and forth between Story and me.

Tempted to reach for her hand again but not sure if it's to comfort her or me, I stop myself when I see her free hand tucked behind her back and the wine held down by her side. The body language isn't hard to read. "Mom, hi. I'm here."

She leans in to kiss my cheek before I shake hands with my dad.

"Who's this?" he asks, his voice gruffer than usual. As he's much older than my mom, his aging seems to accelerate as visually while my mom hasn't changed in twenty years.

"Hello," my mom says to Story before I have a chance to introduce them. "Camille told me our Cooper brought someone with him." She holds out her hand. "I didn't see your name on the RSVP list, so this is quite a surprise."

I step closer, feeling protective of Story. "We're not staying long."

My mom levels me with a glare. "That wasn't the deal we made. Neither was bringing a date, dear." She smiles, but it's so fake that it struggles to turn the corners of her mouth north. "What is your name?"

Camille didn't rattle Story.

My mom does. When she replies, "Story Salenger," the tremble in her voice is heard. I fucking hate it, and I hate them more for causing it.

Why did I bring her here? It was never going to be different, despite how much I hoped it would change the temperament of our disagreements.

Not satisfied, my mom turns to me as if we're the only two in the conversation. "I'm not sure how I feel about this."

"Well, that's too bad because you're not the one in this relationship. I am, and I love Story."

My dad asks, "You love her?" His cynical side gets the better of him. "You're young. You know nothing about love."

"This is not the time for this conversation."

My mom rubs her temple and looks up at the sky as if relief will be found in the stars. I've tried to find it myself many times over the years and never lucked out. I found Story instead. That's when I realized I had been searching in the wrong place all along.

I take Story's hand and hold it between mine to warm it and to hopefully reassure her if that notion is even plausible at this time.

Narrowing her eyes back on Story, my mom says, "It's

nothing personal. Cooper should have known better than to surprise us like this." She references behind her toward the party. "Poor Camille has been waiting all night for his arrival, so you can imagine the mess I'll have to sort out inside."

Story squeezes my hand. "And you expect me not to take that personally?"

"It's not about you, dear. It's about Camille."

"Camille's a big girl. I think she knew he wasn't coming to see her, but my apologies for not RSVPing. I thought I was on the list."

"You are always on mine," I say. "I think it's best if we leave now."

My dad puts his hands in his pockets and raises his chin. "Probably best. We have guests to tend to, and most are aware of your problematic history, so let's not make a scene." He reaches into the interior pocket of his suit's jacket and pulls out an envelope. Handing it to me, he adds, "Just pick out what you like. It's taken care of."

The dealership's name is embossed across the front, so I know what it is. I stare at it between us before he puts it to my chest and pats. "Merry Christmas." Wrapping his arms around my mom's shoulders, he tells her, "It's cold out. Let's get you inside."

It's not anger, disappointment, or pain in her eyes when she looks back at me before returning to the party. *It's indifference.*

And that hurts even more.

I tuck the envelope in my pocket and look down at Story. If the interaction with Camille didn't make her want to dump me, I'm sure that encounter did. I exhale, the tension still there because I know Story and I have a heavy conversation ahead of us, but after I choke down what just happened with my parents.

"Ready to go?" I ask.

"Thought you'd never ask."

26

Story

"Why didn't you tell them I was coming, Cooper?"

"Because I didn't want the fight that would come right after." *If that doesn't tell me everything . . .*

Whipping my gaze from outside the window to where he sits across the suite, I see a fresh drink in front of him and a bag of chips that he took from the minibar. We'd discarded our unfinished drinks on a table before working our way toward the exit, but he doesn't see me pouring a cocktail as soon as we get back. I'm too mad to drink. "How'd that work out for you?"

"I'm thinking it didn't." The crunch of another chip as he chews grates on my nerves. How can he eat after what happened? I look at Cooper again with his expensive liquor and chips that will probably cost a fortune. He doesn't even care about money when I feel my whole world hinges on my next paycheck.

I can't hold that against him, or I'm no better than Camille. Ugh. I'm mad with every fiber of my being. I've been irritated since before we left. When I think about it, it was the moment *she* showed up to greet my boyfriend like I didn't even exist. Why do girls have to compete with each other?

Am I competing with her?

No.

Maybe.

Dammit, I don't know.

"What happened tonight?" I ask, remembering the sound of rain on the windshield as we drove back to the hotel. The sound is usually soothing, but the silence between Cooper and me kept me on edge.

I was hit by a semi-truck of emotions tonight but didn't realize it until we got to the lobby. And then it was over-whelming.

That question still lingers unanswered. I cross my arms over my chest and return my gaze out the window. "This is how we're ending the year and starting a new one."

"How?" he asks, the sound of the ice hitting the sides of the glass.

"Fighting." I glance back once more. "That's not a good sign, Cooper."

"I'm not superstitious."

"This has nothing to do with superstition. It's about the warning signs leading up to this."

That draws his gaze to travel the distance between us and land on me harder than before. "Fill me in. What warning signs?"

I move to sit on the sofa. The room is pretty—floral fabrics on the furniture and the bedspread, silk-like striped wallpaper in a pastel pink. I still prefer our winter wonder-land castle more, but that's hard to find in the middle of the city. Maybe I'm already spoiled like Camille and can't appreciate five-star luxury at the expense of spending time with people I despise like at that party. "I thought you left Haywood because you missed me?"

"I did."

"You left Haywood based on an agreement with your parents that didn't include me. So maybe I'm lost on how exactly I play into that scheme."

Keeping me waiting, he takes a long pull with his eyes still set on me. When he sets the glass down, his fingers spin it around. "It wasn't a scheme, Story. My parents and I have unfinished business. When I was leaving to spend the holiday with you, they made me promise I'd put on a good front at the party."

"What business? You're twenty-two, Cooper. You make it sound like you're in debt to the mafia."

With a shrug, he nods his head. "Kind of feels that way."

Feeling anxious, I sit forward. "Make this make sense to a layman."

The chair slides out from under him abruptly, and he stalks toward me. Kneeling before me, he pleads, "If I could, I would."

"You have to. I can't be in a relationship that has secrets." I hear my own plea in my tone, but I know my capabilities, and if we lose trust between us, we'll go up in flames. "I've never been able to trust anyone I've dated, Cooper. I trust you. I trust the promise you made me because I feel you meant it. I could see it in your eyes. But we're a team, or we're not. You tell me."

"We are. Us against them." Taking my hand, he moves to the sofa next to me. "You can trust me. I came back to Atterton to be with you, babe. It doesn't take away the strain that I have with them, but I chose you," he says, pain working through his irises. "More than you'll ever know."

My hand would shake from the anxiety, but he's holding the one so firmly between his that it can't. "I've been very careful about curating a life free from trauma. I've made a lot of missteps and lapses in judgment prior to you." I move closer so our legs are pressed together. "Cooper, I had stopped dating altogether to let myself heal, but then you came along. Maybe you think I was hitting on you by inviting you over, but I wasn't. I wasn't thinking that at all."

Tentatively, he reaches for my face and caresses my cheek. The roughness of the pad of his thumb scrapes as it rolls over my skin. I'll take the pain, the marks, the scars if it gets me to the truth. Those will heal. I'm not so sure about my heart.

Catching a tear that I didn't know had fallen, he wipes it away as if he can't bear it. "We're together in this. Whatever this is or will be, I want you, Story. I want everything we are together because I'm so fucking in love with you."

"How do you know in such a short time?"

"Because I'm going out of my mind trying to figure out how to deal with my feelings."

"How did you used to handle them?"

"Used to?" he asks, shaking his head. "I've never felt like this before. Do you not feel how my heart beats for you? Do you not see how I can't stop looking at you? Amazed you're mine?" He cradles my face in his hands and runs his nose along mine. With his lips pressed to the corner of my mouth, he whispers, "I don't deserve you, but my soul is tied to yours. You're my savior, and I'm your curse. This is what we are together. Each other's destiny."

My breath is knocked from my lungs as his admission becomes a prayer on his tongue. I kiss him. Selfishly, I kiss him for me. And then I kiss him to take away the pain that's filled his breath and body.

He's right about our hearts aligning and our purpose changing. I wasn't living before him. I was waiting.

We were either brought together or found each other. I'm not sure if it's the former or the latter, but he feels right in every way to me. So I won't argue against our fate when time doesn't matter when we're together. *Two weeks. Two months. Two years. Two lifetimes.* With him, it's easy to believe that we have time on our side without the threat of fate intervening.

I'll stick with destiny.

If he's willing to fight for me, I'll let him and come back twice as strong to fight for him.

I kiss him again because it's not just my body craving the bond this time. It's also my soul. *Cooper Haywood was mine before I knew he existed.*

That's how souls work. They find each other in every lifetime.

But when he pulls back, his eyes fall closed as his head drops. "I gave up my inheritance."

"What? What are you talking about? Look at me," I say, my heart pounding, my chest aching for him. "Look at me, Cooper."

When he does, there are no tears to be shed. Instead, rejection fills his features, a shame that shouldn't be there. Failure rounds his shoulders and has them caving forward. He lifts his eyes to meet mine. "I didn't expect it. I swear. I'd signed it away years ago just to piss off my parents. But then they came around." He stands and begins to pace. "I could be good."

"What do you mean you could be good?"

"I'd done everything prior." He stops in front of the large picture window where a different view of the city is framed from the balcony where we stood earlier. Laughter rumbles under his breath as he runs his hand through his hair. "I was so fucking self-destructive. Classic Psychology 101 case. Doing anything to get Mommy and Daddy's attention. When I had it, I tried to forget who I was, and then when that didn't happen, I wanted to disappear again."

Turning his back to me, he aims his focus out the window and keeps his voice low. "I used to go to bad neighborhoods and pick fights. I wanted to feel good about myself, powerful, to try to control something in my life. My friends were there with me. But it's a joke that we're all in college like we weren't left for dead a few times."

He looks back at me over his shoulder. "You fought to survive while I was fighting to die."

It's hard to swallow as I decipher between the man I know and the guy he speaks of. "I don't understand."

"I know, but one day, you'll see me for who I am. Our souls won't matter. We'll have to try again in the next lifetime."

I stand and go to him. "I'm not a scared little girl. I've been through hell. I'll go back if I can pull you from its bowels." Wrapping my arms around him, I lean against him, listening to his beating heart. It's as strong as he is.

The angst calms, and his arm comes around me. He kisses my head. I say, "Good thing I didn't fall for you because of your money."

He balks, then starts laughing. When he looks down at me, I say, "Richer or poorer—with lifetimes behind us, I'm sure we've said those vows before."

Taking my hand, he kisses my knuckles. "For better or worse."

I don't say the next lines because in this life or the next, death will always divide us. And I've never felt this strongly for anyone, so I can't handle those consequences.

But after seeing the pain of what his family is doing to him, their need for him to be what they want instead of who he is with me, I must be the bigger person in this scenario. Bringing his hand to my mouth, I kiss it, closing my eyes and savoring the feel of him against my lips.

The city comes to life as the countdown ends. He checks his watch and then looks at me like he wants me to decide. "I choose you always, Cooper Haywood."

We kiss, our mouths coming together on the stroke of midnight. "Happy New Year, Story Salenger."

It's then that I believe it. "Us against them."

We kiss again as fireworks shoot in the distance.

We might not always have explosions to celebrate our time together, but we'll always have this kiss to launch our future.

Our love will keep us strong, but with so much left for him to reconcile, I make him a promise that I'll keep forever. "I will never pit you against your parents. An ultimatum of you having to choose between your family or me will never be put into the universe. So you do what you need to feel whole, Cooper, and I'll be waiting."

27

Story

Three months later . . .

"I LOVE SILVER, but I'm still confused why you got a brand-new car in March."

"Because it was a Christmas gift, and it takes time to build. It's customized to my order." Cooper's arm is extended across the top of the passenger seat as we talk through the open window. "And how my other one wasn't just green; this one is not just silver. It's Indus Silver."

If I stare at him long enough, I'm hoping this will make sense. "Okay." I'm still lost how parents who seemingly hate their kid go out and spend whatever this car costs on them. And more importantly, why did he take it?

He revs the engine enough to cause me to look back at the coffee shop in embarrassment. Lila gives me two thumbs-up in approval. I just roll my eyes. Leaning over the passenger's seat, he pops the door open. "C'mon, get in."

Guess I need to, or everyone on the block will soon be staring. I slip into the car and buckle up. Inside the luxurious dark interior, I finally let him enjoy his present. "It is a very pretty car."

Eyeing the front through the windshield, I ask, "No leaping jaguar on the front?"

"I had that installed aftermarket. This time, since it's the sports car . . ." He beams as he shifts into gear. "The Jaguar F-type luxury sports car, to be exact. I'm going with the sleek design of the hood."

I laugh. His excitement, the joy that he's found in this car, is contagious. "Okay. Okay. Let's just get going."

"I need gas. Do you mind if we detour to the station?"

"Nope, as long as you treat me to a hot dog and a thirty-two ouncer." I used to be weirded out about him spending money on me, but after three months into our relationship, I know he truly doesn't mind. He enjoys doing it, and I win. So sometimes he treats me.

Chuckling, he replies, "Deal."

Gas stations aren't on every corner in Atterton. We have to drive to the outskirts, which he loves as he massages the steering wheel in appreciation. I don't mind because it gives me a few extra minutes to talk without the distraction of a show or movie, or other people being around.

"How was class?" I ask.

"I have a paper due for a mid-term grade in advanced psychology."

"You seem to really be enjoying that class. Have you ever considered going into psychology or becoming a therapist?"

"Sure, but although I like the class, that profession doesn't interest me." He glances from the road to me quickly before returning to the road ahead. "It's the first time a professor has treated me like my thoughts matter."

"That's amazing, babe. I'm happy for you."

There's a pause as I load the university's student portal on my phone to see if my advanced business course test has been graded. His hand covers my thigh, and he asks, "Is everything all right?"

"It's fine. I've been stressing about this test score for a week, and it's still not graded."

Pulling under the lights of the gas station, he parks at the pump. Not wanting him to rush around to open the door, I hop out. "What can I get you?"

"A soda."

"You got it." I drop my phone onto the seat and head inside. Making a beeline to the soda machine, I pull two large cups. But with all the choices, I debate whether I want to replenish my electrolytes or run off sugar for the rest of the night.

Sugar wins.

I fill one cup and then stick the other under the fountain. Holding the button, I look out the window at that incredible car and the man pumping gas into it.

Three months have flown fast. Cooper and I have settled into our relationship, generally stress-free. There's just something cozy about my place, so we still spend more time at my apartment, like before, but it's fun to visit his palace in the sky.

"Well, look what the cat dragged in."

That voice, the one that used to shoot fear through my bones, causes contempt to fill me instead. My body still tenses, the cup wobbling in my hand. I hate that I give my weaknesses away.

My gaze darts beside me to the man I hoped I'd never see again. Troy walks around me, checking out my lower half. "Girl, you're looking good. How've you been?"

I glance out the window once more to Cooper. The last thing I want him to do is see me talking to Troy. And that's the last thing I want to do. I keep my mouth shut and start for the door.

The attendant gripes, "You need to pay for those cups."

Digging into my pocket, I pull out a five-dollar bill that I earned in tips and return to set it on the counter with no intention of heading back to retrieve them next to where Troy is standing.

"What's the big rush, Story?" Troy asks.

I push through the door and head for the car. But I hear the bell behind me chime once more. I squeeze my eyes closed as dread chills my veins. *Just get in the car and go.*

Cooper finishes and sees me over the pump. "No hot dog or drinks?"

"Changed my mind. Let's try that new chicken place down the street."

"Hey, Story . . ." Troy says, "come hang out." My stomach does somersaults as Cooper's gaze travels over my shoulder. *Oh no.* "Like old times," Troy stupidly goes on. *Please shut up. Please shut up. Please shut up.*

Cooper hangs the handle on the pump. I move quicker, reaching him just as he shuts the fuel door on the car. "We need to go."

"What the fuck is going on?" Cooper comes around the pump, but then his feet stop.

Looking back, Troy has stopped in the middle of the next lane. I've only heard about Cooper's past, but I was fine with that. A vague memory resurfaces outside Cooper's building that night last summer of Troy saying he knew the guy having the party but hadn't seen him in a while.

A knife twists in my chest as I try to figure out the

connection between them. I hate lies . . . *How did I not piece this together sooner?*

Seeing them staring not only confirms that they know each other but also that there's bad blood between them. *So why did Troy want to go to Cooper's party if they hate each other?* I have a feeling Troy was instigating a fight that night. Just like he is now.

I begin to panic that I'm about to see both in action as well. "Let's go, Cooper."

Troy howls. "You're fucking kidding me, right? The two of you are together?" He goes to the back of his truck where his buddy Brian hops out. "Check this out, B. The rich kid from the city and the girl from the wrong side of the tracks. It's like Romeo and Juliet."

Cooper takes my hand and pulls me close. With his eyes fixed on Troy, he whispers in my ear, "I'll handle this. Go ahead and get in the car."

"I don't want you handling it. I want us to go." I tug his hand toward the car, but his body doesn't budge. "Come on, let's go together. Just walk away."

Troy props himself against his truck as if this is the most entertaining thing he's seen in a while. "You gonna listen to your old lady, Haywood?"

"Fuck off, Hogan." Cooper stands his ground, but he's not filled with tension. Adrenaline is not coursing through him, judging by his actions. Instead, he's calm.

He's eerily calm, like the storm that comes without warning.

I've never once been afraid of him, but right now, I'm afraid of the destruction he'll leave behind.

I move next to him and wrap myself around his middle. It's how we stand together, so close, all the time that it's unnatural when we don't. When his arm—hard muscle and formidable strength—comes around me, I know I've reached the Cooper I know.

Looking down at me, he says, "Don't worry, babe. I can handle him."

"I don't want you to." I try to smile, but it feels like I'm failing. "I want us to get chicken and go home."

"What's it going to be, Haywood?" Troy taunts. "You want to tango with me? Or eat *chicken* with your whore . . ."

I hit Troy with my own glare this time. "Whore? You never got close enough to know, unlike him." I shrug. "If having sex until we're sweaty, exhausted, and depleted of orgasms makes me a whore—I'm guilty as charged." The smile is wiped from Troy's face. "But again, you wouldn't know."

"Maybe cunt fits better."

Cooper jerks forward. My grip tightens, holding him back, but the storm is brewing, and I know I won't be able to control it for long. "Cooper?" His eyes connect with mine, and I whisper, "Choose me."

Without hesitation, he turns us around, and we walk to the car. He opens the door for me and then keeps his eye on Troy as he returns to the driver's side and gets inside.

Troy doesn't stop us, though we can hear him yelling as we pull away—name-calling and stupid stuff that we're insulated from inside the car.

A few blocks down from the gas station, Cooper asks, "So you're hungry for chicken?"

I don't know whether to laugh or cry, so I just nod. "I heard the spicy sandwich is good."

It's nice to hear him laugh. I'm already feeling lighter after that encounter. Then he asks, "Why me?"

"Why you what?"

"Why did you sleep with me? We'd only known each other for a short time. Why'd you choose me?"

Reaching over, I scrape my nails at the base of his hairline on the back of his neck. As I look at him, his gaze shifting between me and the road, I think back on those first few days when we were stuck together in my apartment. "I . . ." I start but stop, wanting to gather my thoughts. It wasn't his kindness, though that's what got him in the door. Nor was it his eyes that extended a mutual trust I needed to be reassured. "I think I knew you were the man I wanted to be with, in all ways, when you told me you had seen me at the party last summer and that you didn't want any secrets between us. I feel like every failed relationship I've had was buried in lies and omissions."

The smile I expect doesn't come, but then he says, "Oh, yeah? That's what did it?"

"Well, it's one of a thousand other things, but yeah, I'd never had anyone be so open and up front like that before. I was basically feral growing up, left in most ways to fend for myself." When our eyes meet again, even briefly, I smile. "Trust never came easy, but with you, it did. You might have been saying all that, though, because I gave you Wi-Fi."

"I told you that because I'd been in love with you since the moment I saw you." He reaches over and rests his hand on my leg and then smirks. "And because you gave me a Wi-Fi connection and didn't give it to Lou."

I scoff and chuckle, rolling my eyes. "You never have anything to worry about." Noticing we're not driving toward my place, I ask, "Where are we going?"

"I need to check my mail. I'm waiting on the law school admissions test registration."

Bringing my hand to rest on his, I watch as we approach the tower. "I was sort of afraid to broach the subject, not sure what you thought about it more recently. You're still wanting to go to law school?"

He pulls to the curb and shifts into park. "I'm taking the test because I'm not sure anymore, and I don't want to lose an opportunity if I decide I want to be an attorney."

"Will you join the family business?"

Licking his lips, he stares ahead through the windshield. When he turns back to me, he replies, "I'm not sure what I'm doing, Story. I guess that's a conversation for us both to have, considering how well this is going." He opens the door. "I'll be right back."

I watch as he enters the lobby—a man so sure of himself except when it comes to his family. I always thought I had it bad, never knowing what Calliope would do next, but I knew she loved me. Despite the bad decisions she made, she did the best she could. That allows me to forgive her now.

I can only imagine the pain Cooper endures daily, knowing his parents care more about their reputations and bank account than their only son. I'll make up for them. I'll love him so hard that he'll never know what he's missing.

As he jogs back with a stack of mail in hand, his hair appears darker, moodier even, the scruff covering his jaw matching the sky at midnight. He's changing for the better —inside and out. I'm lucky I get to witness it.

"Do you mind holding this?" he asks, settling into the driver's seat.

"Nope." I take the mail and set it on my lap. As soon as he pulls away from the curb, the top few letters slide onto the floor, leaving the LSAT mail on top of the stack. "You got it."

"Yeah." He glances over his shoulder before changing lanes. "The test is in three weeks. I need to study because my grades won't get me into law school. I fucked up for too long to get in on my grade point average."

"You can do it. I have no doubt." He rounds the campus and is approaching my street when I reach down to get the letters that fell. I eye the sender's address on the larger one. MCAT. "Did you register for the medical college admissions test as well?"

"Is that in there?"

"It's right here." I hold it up.

Pulling into a spot on my street, he parks and then shrugs. "Our conversation about pursuing psychology as a career got me thinking."

"About?"

"I don't have any interest in therapy, but if I'm considering the years ahead for law school, I figured I could put those into becoming a doctor."

"That's a lot more years of schooling."

Grabbing his phone from the console, he says, "It's four years versus three in law school, and then you enter residency from three to seven."

"I think that's amazing if it's something you want to pursue. I just didn't know the medical field interested you."

My non-question is answered with another shrug. "Guess I'm a late bloomer. I checked into it casually a month or so ago. Didn't feel it needed an announcement simply because it does feel more like a whim than a decision. But most of my classes apply toward medical school, so I thought I'd make up a few this summer if I decide to move in that direction. If I can't score well on the test, though, my decision will be made for me."

A mixture of love and pride blooms inside. "I'm proud of you, Cooper."

Grinning, he nods. "Thanks. You've been a big inspiration in finding what you want to do and going for it."

"I didn't dream of being an accountant, but I do enjoy the financial analyst side of things." When I get out of the car, I hand him his mail. Reaching back in, I retrieve the straggler from the floorboard that I couldn't reach before. This time when I see the sender's address, my heartbeat stills, and my breath clogs in my chest.

I slowly turn around, not wanting to ruin how good this feels with him right now. I do, though. His eyes follow the same pattern as mine had when he scans it. Swallowing down the lump in my throat, I ask, "What is it?"

"I don't know." He rips it open, his optimism already gone. Pulling out the cardstock, he reads it and then flips it around. "We've been cordially invited to my graduation party in May at the Haywood House."

"Did you know about this?"

"No, I had no idea."

Just when things were going so well, I couldn't help but think, *here we go again*.

28

Story

Two months later . . .

THE INVITATION HAS HAUNTED us for months.

I didn't mention it, and neither did he. Even hidden out of sight in a kitchen drawer at his place, though, its presence was always known. I think that's why he stopped going to his apartment more than a few times a week. We just needed to get our footing on solid ground and have a better understanding of what we wanted before involving others.

The warmer weather had brought a nice tan to Cooper's skin from spending more time outdoors. He'd gotten quieter since the invitation's arrival but also more attentive if that makes any sense. I was surprised with picnics and rides on rented boats down at the lake.

My romantic side loved every minute. But a thought had embedded itself into the back of my mind, whispering that our time was running out.

I wouldn't blame him for leaving because deep down, I know he'd never leave me if he had another choice. I'm still not sure what's involved with his inheritance, but how long is he expected to go through life without contact with his family? It's something I could never require of him, no matter how much they hate me.

With the end of the semester approaching in less than a month, the bell above the shop door rings, causing me to look up from a customer's order. Standing with his hands in his pockets, Cooper looks every bit the traitor with his somber expression.

I used to be an optimist, but that was before I had so much to lose.

"You can sit anywhere," I say, trying to hold my emotions in check and pretend he's not here to break my heart. "I'll be right over."

Forcing my attention back to ringing up the customer in front of me, I hand the bagged muffin to them, and say, "Thank you."

When they walk away, I tread across the floor, checking on the few customers here today. I stop at Cooper's table and bend to kiss him. His lips are cold instead of the warm embrace I'm used to. Sitting across the table from him, I ask, "How was your day?" and then tug at my bottom lip, waiting for him to answer.

"Story . . ." His voice is more somber than his expression. He runs his hand through his hair—that nervous tic getting the best of him.

"That's not a great."

He shifts in his chair, glancing at a couple passing by outside on the sidewalk. "I can't leave the business with my family unfinished any longer." I nod once, trying to read every thought crossing his eyes.

"You didn't leave it unfinished. You chose me. Remember?"

"I did." He doesn't reach across the table to hold my hand or bother trying to reassure me. "And I still do."

Oh, thank God.

I still can't manage to say anything over the blockage in my throat.

"But I've decided to go to the party."

"Your graduation party that they are hosting whether you show up or not?"

This time, he nods. "I can be mad that they're assholes, but—"

"But?"

"But I've never needed anything or been left to want—"

"Except their love, which they use to blackmail you."

Shaking his head, he replies, "I don't need their love because I have you."

I shouldn't have an argument against that. We designed our relationship to work that way. Guilt still tinges my heart, though, so I say, "If you can meet them in the middle and come to peace with them, you should."

He finally reaches across the table and holds his hand palm up for me. When I slide my hand in his, he says, "But I won't go without you."

"I'm not going." Just as I begin to pull back, his grasp on me tightens. Stuck in a deadlocked staring contest, I finally blink. Leaning forward, I whisper, "They hate me, Cooper."

"They do." His confirmation smacks me in the chest, but his hand still holds mine like he's never going to let go. "They hate you because of me, not because of you."

"How is that different?"

"Because this time we go back with nothing to lose. We

know where we stand with our relationship. I need to know where I stand with them."

I look around at the other customers. No one appears to need anything, so I stay, his reasoning making sense. Before I decide, he adds, "I won't go unless you go. I can promise you that."

Am I going to be the one to stand in their way on the path to making up? I promised I would never make him choose between them or me, and I can't start now.

"You can RSVP for both of us."

"I will." I get that golden boy smile that will always work to get his way. Fortunately for me, I received it after I'd already made my decision—what's best for us and for me personally.

This time, I won't be thrown into the lion's den unprepared.

IT'S A BEAUTIFUL DAY—BLUE skies, birds chirping, perfect temperature of seventy-five. I kind of wish I had someone here to see it. My phone vibrates in my hand, and I see a sneaky picture of Cooper as if he knew. Making a silly face, I giggle quietly, and then even more when I read the caption: *I'm thinking chicken tonight.*

It's become a running joke with us. Although we also like fried chicken.

I text: *Spicy chicken sandwich?*

Cooper: *Yes, and I have plans for you, but can't say now. Got to run. See you on the flipside.*

I look up just as they call his name. He crosses that stage with the confidence he always carries, but this time, he has a degree to back him up.

When he reaches the other side and walks down from the stage, he texts: *I'll work out the kinks with you tonight.*

Me: *I was hoping you'd say that. ;)*

It takes a while to get to the letter S alphabetically, but I'm one of the first when they do. So much crosses my mind as I wait to hear my name called—I have no family with me, no friends in the stands, but I do have Cooper, who's stuck with me today since he's graduating as well. When I cross the stage to shake hands, a breeze blows in, knocking the hat right off my head. *Calliope always did steal the attention.*

Closing my eyes, I let the wind blow through me.

A professor hands the hat back to me, and I readjust it on my head before moving toward the steps. As I walk through the grass back to my row, Cooper calls, "Hey Salenger?"

I stop at the end of his row, where he's seated five people deep, and smile with my hand on my hip. "Yeah, Haywood?"

The playfulness evaporates, and sincerity filters through his handsome features. "You did good, babe."

"Thanks. You did, too." There's no wiping the smile from my face as I return to my seat, sitting in the realization that I did do it. All on my own. Sure, I have a pile of debt, but I earned my college degree, and no one can ever take that away from me.

The last Z receives their degree. Finally, we get to move our tassels from right to left and toss our mortarboard hats in the air. I hug a few acquaintances around me before searching the ground for my cap.

"Looking for something?" I know that deep voice, enticing when he wants to be.

I look up to find Cooper standing with my hat in his hands. I step closer and take the hat when he hands it to me. "Seems I found it."

"Things that are yours won't stay lost forever."

"What about people?" I ask, staring into his vibrant green eyes.

A strong arm comes around my waist, and he rubs my side with his hand. "Same goes for them."

Lifting up on my toes, we meet in the middle and kiss. "Congratulations, Cooper."

"Congratulations to you." We stand together, taking in the hard-earned achievement.

His parents didn't come, not that I know of. The stands were full, so if they did, they're not here as the crowd disperses. And I'm not mentioning it. *That's on them.*

When my stomach growls, I finally ask, "What do you say we go get that chicken sandwich to celebrate?"

The sun is in his eyes, so he uses his hat as a visor. "I could have it delivered so we can start the celebration sooner?"

"Sounds like the perfect way to spend our first night as new graduates."

"Story? Cooper?" We both look forward at the same time to see Lila with her hand waving in the air and the other holding Jake's hand as they work their way toward us.

She rushes around a family, and then we scream in excitement as we run into each other's arms. "What are you doing here?" I ask, stepping back. "Who's watching the shop?"

"No one. I locked up for a few hours, but I wouldn't miss this for anything." She brings me in for another hug. It's comforting and strong like she's always been for me.

"Thank you." I hold her a little bit longer, knowing I may not get many more chances. When we part this time, she congratulates Cooper, and they hug. It's been nice to see them become friends over the last semester. I kneel and ask Jake, "What did you think of the ceremony?"

"It was long."

Laughing, I reply. "It was." He leans against me, wrapping his arms around my neck. "I want to be just like you and graduate, too, when I grow up."

I hug him so tight until I look at him and those sweet brown eyes that match his hair. Tapping him on the nose, I say, "I believe in you." That brings a big smile to his face. "I want you to meet my friend."

His bottom lip pops out as he pouts. "Your boyfriend. Mom told me you kiss him."

I shoot Lila a questioning look.

"That's not exactly what happened." She starts to stumble over her words. Looking down at him like he sold her out to secret agents, she says, "You said you were going to marry Story one day. I simply pointed out that she had a boyfriend. I didn't say anything about kissing."

Jake looks at Cooper with a slight scowl on his face. "Are you the boyfriend?" he asks with an air of protectiveness.

I try so hard not to laugh.

Cooper wraps his arm around my shoulder, and though he knows he has no competition, I appreciate that he's ready to fight for me, even when it comes to a five-year-old. "I am."

I can't contain my laughter and finally let it out. Cooper holds out his hand to Jake, and they shake. "Story has told me a lot about you, Jake."

"She has?" his eyes brighten.

"She has." Cooper kneels so he's eye level and engages with him. "She said you have a mean left arm when it comes to football."

"I do. My coach says so."

As a group, we start walking toward the parking lot. Lila

hooks her arm with mine as we follow the boys, who we can overhear talking about everything from football to who's the best character on *Phineas and Ferb*. Jake picks Doofenshmirtz. Cooper goes with Perry. Somehow, that works, and it's endearing to watch them together.

Lila asks, "So New York or bust?"

"Not sure yet. I need to work out a few details, and we have his graduation party in Haywood next weekend."

Her expression sours along with her tone. "Oh yeah, I'd forgotten." She knows all about what happened on New Year's Eve.

"Yet *I* can't stop thinking about it."

She rubs my arm. "It will be okay. You know what you're getting into this time."

I nod. When we reach the parking lot, I say, "Keep me on the schedule, okay?"

"No one's replacing you just yet." We hug once more, and then Cooper and I walk to his car.

"Cute kid," he says.

"Yeah, he's super sweet."

Our hands come together like they always do, and when we reach the car, he asks, "My place or yours?"

"Let's mix it up and celebrate at your apartment."

29

Story

The chicken was good but not as good as Cooper's mouth on my body. The tremors dwindle as I gasp until my breathing evens out.

His head pops up from between my legs, but his fingers still work their magic down there. "You're ready for me," he says, starting to crawl up my body.

"What makes you think that?" I tease and run my hands over the sweat glistening on his shoulders.

"I'll give you a clue." He kisses me, and though he wants me focusing on the taste of what we just did, the gentle prodding of his erection against my entrance has me leveraging his body for my own purposes—to feel him deeper inside me.

"Oh fuck, babe." He pulls out, disbelief cinching his expression together. "What are you doing?"

"You feel so good," I say, wanting to feel all of him with nothing between us. I'm a loose cannon, too turned on to think beyond this bed. I pull him closer, bobbing on the tip just ever so slightly. And he lets me, soaking in the sensation. I know he wants me just as badly, but he's restraining himself. I whisper in his ear. "I want you, Cooper. So bad that my body aches for you."

The five o'clock shadow has grown to a seven and scratches against my cheek when he slides his gaze to me. The dulcet, desperate groan reveals his struggle to fight between what we want and what's sensible. He moves his arm up and strokes my cheek. "We can't, Story. You're not on the pill."

"I just want to feel you. All of you."

He kisses me again, our mouths clashing as he steals every one of my breaths away. He sinks into me, just a little more with caution, and then pulls out again. "That's all you get for now." *And he calls* me *the tease.*

"Just once."

As he reaches for a condom, I lie here panting next to him while my body is left empty. Kissing each nipple upon his return, the energy sparks through me, and I try to wrap my legs around him. A smirk lies squarely on his face, but he still looks up and says, "Trust me, baby. Once won't be enough," he says pointedly. "But I promise to make you feel so good."

I know he's right, but I'm still fighting my traitorous intentions that have thrown caution to the wind. One feel of him bare and I could tell the difference. Is it wrong to crave that feeling? I push up on my elbows and face him again. "I'm getting on the pill next week. I have access to the university doctor until campus closes next Friday, and I'm going to do it." The words come out as if they're a threat.

"Okay. If that's what you want, I'm not going to object."

I lie back down as he returns to hover over me with his

erection sheathed in a condom. Sweet kisses aren't what I want, so I say, "I want on top."

Maneuvering, we swap positions until I'm straddling him and sliding my body against his hardness until we're both slick. With my weight balanced on my hands pushed against his chest, he lifts his cock so I can slide down. I sink down slowly, not wanting to rush the initial connection, my eyes closing as I savor every inch of him.

We've been together for five months, but every time we're together like this, it's like the first time all over again— the stretching, a mild burn, and the fullness . . . The overwhelming feeling of how he fills me so completely. But maybe that's also the emotions taking over.

I lift my hips and slide back down, and then again, rocking back and forth and watching how I affect him. The pinch of his brows, the lashes squeezed when it appears to be too much for him. The glory of his determination and the demise of his willpower. It's all on display for me to see.

That line between pain and pleasure vibrates between us, each kiss and push, thrust, and pull driving us for more. "So good," I say, taking what I need from him.

Holding my hips, he digs his fingertips into my skin, controlling them to take what he needs from me.

I lean forward and kiss him, kiss him so hard that we forget that there's another world outside this bedroom. But as I struggle to keep up, bouncing up and down to reach our peak, he flips me over, and commands, "Turn around."

I roll over and get to my knees, eagerness corrupting my veins. His hand slips between my thighs and lower, wedging my knees apart even farther. There's no kindness when he thrusts into me this time. I'm thinking there might not even be love. This is raw desire, us setting ourselves on fire just to feel the heat.

I've never felt such madness—my body craving and my thoughts going wild.

Though I'm braced on the bed with my hands fisting the blankets, I turn and look over my shoulder just to see him again. I expect rawness to add a cold tint to his eyes, but that's not what I find. I find love prevalent in the green like he always holds for me.

He scrapes his nails lightly up my spine as his fingers slide into the hair at the nape of my neck and then higher until he's cupping the crown of my head. With that hand pushing my head forward and his other pressing to my belly, I start to lose myself. Closing my eyes, I let my mind rest and my body take over, meeting him thrust for thrust. My chanted name becomes a swear to the siren who taunts and a praise to the muse who inspires him.

His erratic movements push all the right buttons until I scream his name in pleasure, then he returns the favor, and we release together.

In the aftermath of our downfall, my body is spent in the most delicious ways, and I fall to the mattress. He falls on top of me, kissing my cheek. The feel of his lips caresses my shoulder before he rolls to the side but keeps a leg draped over the back of me.

The sound of our breaths mingling is all that's heard in my ears. My neck is peppered with more sweet kisses before he collapses next to me, the weight causing the mattress to dip and the gravitational pull is too much to resist. At least, I'll blame gravity for me smothering this man with my body.

When I open my eyes, he says, "I want us to be together."

My smile is lazy and full of the pleasure we just experienced as one. "We just were."

He chuckles and finds my hand to hold it. "I feel like this is déjà vu of a conversation we've had before." He's right. It is the first time we committed to be exclusive, though I was already his long before he asked me.

Then the laughter lightens and eventually subsides altogether. Lying on our stomachs facing each other, I stare into his eyes as he stares into mine, our hearts entangled as much as our bodies. "We've done a great job of avoiding talking about what's going to happen after graduation."

"Stellar job," I say, hating that the future lies fully in the unknown. I'm a planner by nature.

"You've never mentioned New York to me directly, but I heard Lila ask you about it."

I can't answer why this was a topic I avoided with most people, specifically with him. What if my dream doesn't come true? I just don't want people to see me fail since it's expected of me. "I don't know what I'm doing or where I'm going. I have no money to move, so everything is based on if I get a job in the city."

"Have you sent your résumé anywhere?"

"No." Although I find relief when his brow is released from worry, we still have a lot to discuss. "What about you?"

"I haven't had my scores sent anywhere."

"Doctor? Lawyer? Bumming around for the summer and taking a break?" I lean forward and kiss his bicep simply because his muscles deserve more attention. "What's the great Cooper Haywood going to do with his life?"

He scrubs his free hand over his face. "Survive this party next weekend." Turning back to me, he says, "After that, be with you, and then *we* can decide what to do with the rest of our lives. We don't have to rush anything. We have time to make the right decision for us."

"I like this plan. Slow and steady, unlike everything else we've done together." I sit up. "Want to take a bath with me?"

"Absolutely, I do."

THE LAST TIME we were driving to a party with his family, I was worried about screwing up his family tree or accidentally insulting the Haywood legacy.

Not this time.

As the valet pulls away in Cooper's Jag, I'm more worried about if we'll make it to dinner before we leave. "They've turned me into a Debbie Downer." I used another small chunk of change on my sundress and shoes in a desperate attempt to fit in, but I'm not sure why since I already know they'll never accept me into this tight-knit society.

"Understandable. I've learned to expect the worst so you won't be disappointed."

I squeeze his hand. "That's such a sad way to live."

"Yeah. I was a sad kid for a reason. I've never been more than an heir to carry on our legacy."

"It's their loss. They've missed out on getting to know an incredible man."

"The right environment, water, food, and attention." Chuckling, he adds, "I'm basically a plant who's now thriving because I found my very own sunshine."

Pulling myself closer to him, I tap my head against his arm. "That's so sweet."

"You're sweet, and you look beautiful, so don't let anyone steal your sunshine or bring you down."

Stopping in front of the house, I finally have a moment to take it in—the long drive in from the entry gate to the slow roll up to the white-sided two-story with green shutters and a matching roof. It's cute how Cooper pretends this is some little farmhouse in the country when the house alone could fit five suburban houses inside it. It's a massive mansion in the style of a New England bed and breakfast. I just have to laugh at this point. "I can't with you Haywoods and all this money."

"It's not me. I chose love over money, and I'd do it again."

He says this after living off a bank account that appears to have a regular flow of money injected into it every week. I'm not knocking the guy, but it does make me wonder when they'll cut him off. More importantly, how he'll handle it.

Cooper says, "If you want to know the truth, I always loved being on this property. There was a lot of peace to be found here when my parents were in Manhattan."

The words "let's do this" aren't spoken but felt by both of us. The difference entering this party versus the last one is that he's the guest of honor tonight. That brings a whole new level of stress to the equation.

Seeing Patrice greeting guests and directing them to the backyard is comforting despite the chaos of what's to come swirling like a tornado in my stomach. She opens her arms to me first this time. "Story, I'm so glad to see you again." We embrace, and then she says, "Congratulations on graduating."

"Thank you."

Turning to Cooper, she gives him a quick hug and then eyes both of us. "You two have caused quite the stir around the house."

Cooper laughs. "I bet we have. Any words of wisdom?"

She glances toward the party that can be seen through the large windows. When she turns back, she says, "Be yourselves."

"That's all I know how to be," he replies, grinning. When the front door opens, we start for the living room. I know the décor and the beautiful style of the house. It reflects the peaceful feeling Cooper mentioned earlier.

"Do you wanna get a drink first before we head out back?" We're by the bar, and I think yeah, I do. "Definitely."

With a repeat of the drink I had at the last party, we walk out of the opening of large doors. I see Camille immediately and look at Cooper, who I'm pretty sure spotted her as well. Before we get knocked on our asses by her greeting us again, he leads me by the hand along the lap pool and around to the grounds near the tennis courts. And I try to pretend that this is normal when nothing is normal about this property. "You sure you're an only kid?"

"Why? Is there something I should know?"

Planters are overflowing with flowers and shaped topiaries, and the lawnmower has left perfect stripes in the grass. White cloths are draped over every table and blow gently in the breeze while flower arrangements are the centerpieces. With another bar out here and a huge buffet, this looks more like a wedding than a graduation party. "No. Nothing."

Cooper suddenly veers us off the sidewalk. "Did you see the Bougainvilla?"

"Cooperrrrrr," a male voice comes from behind us.

"Fuck," Cooper says under his breath. "Just smile and keep it short."

We turn around before I have a chance to ask questions. A handsome man, maybe early sixties, is already holding out his hand. "Congratulations," he says, his gaze darting to me every few seconds.

I should probably take it as a compliment that he's congratulating him on dating me . . . oh wait, he means from Atterton. I inwardly laugh.

"Thanks, Mr. Lambert."

Patting him on the shoulder, he says, "Professor, son."

"Right. I always forget that."

Salt and pepper haven't overcome the medium brown hair on his head, and he has unique coloring to his eyes. Especially visible is the gold in them out here in the sunshine. His smile is disarming, but judging from Cooper's annoyance underneath the smile, I stay on my toes.

The professor asks, "Who's your pretty date?"

"My apologies," Cooper's quick to say. "Story Salenger. Professor Lambert." I can hear the strain in calling him professor. Some beef or history lies there.

His piercing eyes slide down my body, giving me a once-over. "Well, aren't you just a sight to behold?"

Ew. I cling to my boyfriend's arm, hoping the creep gets the picture.

"Oh, look. There are my parents." Cooper takes my hand, and we hightail it away from that guy. Looking back over his shoulder, he leans down and whispers, "He's a professor at NYU. Married four times and divorced because he cheated on all of them with students. I heard he's a real asshole from a friend who goes there, treats the girls like shit after he gets what he wants from them, and does anything to protect his rep."

"How charming," I reply sarcastically. "Sounds like someone worth avoiding."

"I tried." He laughs.

His parents see us before we reach them and are quick to excuse themselves from the small circle they're entertaining. I'm shocked to see his mom's arms reaching out to greet us not only with a smile but also with hugs. First Cooper, who stands like he's being searched at the airport, and then she's coming for me.

Maybe she's turning over a new leaf, or she finally developed a conscience. I don't know, but I only have a few milliseconds to cut her off with a handshake or go for the full embrace. I go for the latter because my mom always said you attract more bees with honey.

"Congratulations, dear." She looks up at her son with the sunlight behind him making her squint.

She's pretty in a floral dress, so clearly, her model figure is still intact. I shouldn't feel less because of her, but I do feel a little squatty next to her.

Her hair is swept up in a chignon, and diamonds and pearls hang around her neck and decorate her ears.

His father, dressed in a sandy-colored linen suit that's already wrinkled, pulls an envelope from his pocket and hands it to Cooper. "Congratulations, son. I look forward to you joining the family business."

First off, if that's another freaking new car, I'm going to go ballistic.

Secondly, joining the family business sounds like Cooper's already made up his mind. So that leaves me confused, but I'll keep that to myself for now to get through this party.

While shaking hands, Cooper replies, "Thanks, but nothing's settled just yet."

Patting him on the back like a proud papa, he pulls two cigars from his jacket pocket and hands one to his son.

That pocket is more interesting than a clown car at this point. What's coming out of it next? Who knows? Not me.

Cooper tucks the envelope into his pants pocket since he's not wearing a jacket, but he declines the cigar. That makes me happy because I've always hated the smell of smoke, even before Troy tried to put out a cigarette on my scar, citing it wouldn't matter.

I try not to let my dirty past sully my time with my

boyfriend. I still love saying that. "It's a beautiful party, Mrs. Haywood."

"Thank you, Story. I hear congratulations are in order for you as well."

'Thank you. I worked very hard the past four years to be here."

Her head tilts as suspicion enters her eyes. "To be at Cooper's party?"

"What?" It takes me a moment before I catch on. "Oh, no. I meant to earn my degree. I didn't know Cooper until he came into the coffee shop one night drenched and needing Wi-Fi." I smile, loving our story.

"He needed your Wi-Fi?" she asks, clasping her hands in front of her. She laughs and taps Cooper on the shoulder. "Is that what the kids call it?"

"Mom," Cooper says, his voice stern.

I say, "It's okay. I think we're not quite ready to share pleasantries."

"Manners are always appreciated, Ms. Salenger."

"I'll remember that."

Standing in silence, I wait for someone else to make a move since I'm merely a distraction to their son in their view. If they only knew that we'd be moving in and starting our life together, maybe they'd sing a different tune.

Tired of the game, I break and drink half my glass of rosé. With all their eyes on me, I just go ahead and finish it. That's when Cooper steps in. "Story and I are going to mingle."

"If she's that thirsty," his mom starts. "You might want to take a stroll around the punch bowl and steer clear of the bar."

"Noted, *Mother*."

How he emphasizes mother cracks me up. "She's a

regular Mommy Dearest." I start giggling. He takes the glass and sets it on a tray when a server passes by, along with his drink that he barely took two sips from.

He stops near the tennis court and turns to me. Lowering his head, he looks me in the eyes. "You can't be drunk that fast."

"I'm not drunk. I'm just over it."

"Over what?"

Spreading my arms wide, I say, "This."

He sighs and straightens his spine. Looking around, he says, "I've been over it since I was ten. How they treat you, I got it five times over. So I get the frustration, babe. But we need to decide if we're staying or leaving then because this isn't how I want you to feel." He cups my face and caresses my cheek with his thumbs. "I think you're brilliant, beautiful, a heart bigger than the sun, and a soul with more depth than the ocean. You don't owe these people any part of yourself."

Cupping his face, I caress him the same way. "Neither do you."

Our hands fall to our sides again as he looks around. I feel the stares. Becoming self-conscious, I had forgotten myself. So I stand tall and raise my chin, which is still a lot shorter than Cooper. "I think I'll stick to water. That wine went straight to my head."

"Hopefully, it doesn't go to your stomach, or you'll be puking soon." We start walking toward the buffet. "Why don't you get something to eat, and I'm going to talk to my dad in private. I don't want anything left out on the table. It's time to deal with this and figure out where things stand."

I lift on my toes and kiss him. "I think that's a wise idea. It's information. Nothing more."

"Nothing more." He kisses me like he's about to go into

battle, and I, shamelessly, love it that he's making a statement.

He stalks off on a mission while I pick up a little white plate with gold edging on a mission of my own. Strawberries and mini quiches, brioche buns, and colorful macarons are already filling my plate. I'm debating the Havarti slices or the tiny brie cheese when I hear, "Cheese goes right to my hips."

I look up. Camille is standing on the other side of the table with only one strawberry on her plate. Her gaze darts to my lower body, and she adds, "I wish I didn't care."

The plate falters in my hands, and I lose a green macaron to the ground. "Let's not do this, Camille."

I set my plate down, ready to puke, though it has nothing to do with the wine. With my back turned as I start walking away, she says, "I would have never thought you were his type."

. . . Annnnnd I bite.

Crossing my arms over my chest, I spin back around. She's a stick who probably survives off cabbage juice, caffeine, and sucking the fun out of a room. "And what type is that, Camille? I know you're dying to say it, so just say it, and let's get your body-shaming out in the open."

She gasps, literally clutching her pearls. "Pointing out the truth is called constructive criticism."

"Okay," I say, rolling my eyes. "You're cruel, and you're desperate. That isn't ever going to attract Cooper. My thighs may touch in the middle, but he fucking loves them, especially when his face is buried down there."

Her necklace snaps, and the pearls fall to the ground. When tears fill the corners of her eyes, she bends to search for the pearls in the grass.

And now I hate myself for stooping to her level. She may

have been cruel, but that's not who I am or who I want to be. She brings out the worst in me, someone I don't even recognize who flagrantly used the love of my life to destroy her. "That was mean. I'm sorry, Camille."

She doesn't say anything, so I add, "We don't have to be enemies." The pearls are easy to spot against the kelly green of the grass. I pluck a handful out and then offer them to her like an olive branch.

She fills the pocket hidden in her skirt, but as she picks up the last few, she asks, "Do you know what the difference is between us?"

I don't think I want to bite the bait she's laid out. She says, "You'll never marry Cooper."

Still reeling from her earlier comment, my mind goes blank from the anger. I have no good comeback, and I refuse to play this disgustingly petty, rich person's game. So I stick to the truth, or what she'd like to call constructive criticism, and say, "No, Camille, the difference between us is that I don't need to marry him. I can stand on my own two feet."

"Good. That will carry you far in life without Cooper and his wealth performing the job."

The job? *I'm work he'll have to deal with?*

I want no part of this world or these horrible people. "I'm not sure who hurt you so badly, but believe me, Camille, attacking me, belittling me, or purposely hurting me won't heal you. It will only make that gaping wound where your heart used to be wider." I turn to leave again. In a cheery voice, she says, "Have a great day, Story."

I look back once more over my shoulder, and tell her, "Have the day you deserve."

30

Cooper

"Must we have this conversation in the middle of the party, Cooper?" My dad starts hacking and then clears his throat, blissfully unaware that his cough is caused by smoking. Listening to the sound that's grated on my nerves for years, I clench my jaw.

I got my penchant for swearing from Cooper Haywood, the second, but I've never been much on tobacco, probably because it directly reminds me of him.

Cigar smoke wafts, leaving a trail behind him as he crosses his home office. The stubby brown addiction is lodged between his fingers like one always was while growing up. He even has permanent stains on his skin to prove it.

"We're getting out of here as soon as we're done with this discussion, so yes," I reply, "now is a great time to wrap this up once and for all." I take the seat on the other side of the desk, knowing my dad will eventually take his burgundy wingback throne.

"Should we call your mother?" He settles in as if he's ready to be the judge, jury, and executioner. *Nothing new.*

While other kids played catch with their dads, I was always the criminal in my dad's prosecutorial mock trials and my mom the victim. Nothing has changed, except me, in this scenario. I reply, "If you feel it's necessary."

He tips his head to dig through a short stack of files in his desk drawer, then lays it on the desk mat in front of him and flips it open. Why does it feel like he's moving in slow motion? Purposeful tactic? Everything he does has a reason, even if it's not initially apparent.

Scanning the papers like he doesn't already know what's in them is insulting to both of our intelligence. He's been an attorney for over thirty-five years and wrote the contract himself, though he had the family lawyer execute it.

I know better than to interrupt. A few smacks across the face taught me that. Sitting here now, I'm not the same kid I once was although my past will be used against me. In some respects, I don't blame them. A year later, I'm a changed man?

The notion seems impossible.

I had no reason to change, though I put on a good show. That life was unsustainable for any length of time. I knew I would fail before I even tried to be with Camille like they wanted. After that, I precariously balanced between being the heir they wanted and living so hard that I might not wake up. *But I hadn't met Story yet.*

Closing the file again as if he's now caught up on the latest news, he sits back, his eyes becoming beady as he stares at me. "You're a good-looking kid. You take after your mother."

I chuckle, never predicting this would be the direction

the conversation would go. "You don't think the Haywoods are attractive?"

"Fuck, no. You think your mom would have married me if I didn't have money? I believe there's a side of her that loves me, but I might be confusing that with tolerance."

"Then why would you want me to marry Camille?" I ask, leaning forward. It's always been a part of their deal. I know the contract well. Some parts still shock me that they were even written down, much less there like it's normal.

Nothing about signing a contract regarding your partner and future personal life is normal. He says, "Because it's something your mother wants. She and Camille's mom are best friends. Arranged marriages are one of the oldest traditions—"

"Not in America. Your marriage wasn't arranged. No one in our goddamn history had an arranged marriage, Dad."

"No one needed one before." He puffs on the cigar, then rocks back in the leather wingchair.

"So you'd rather me spend my life with someone who tolerates me instead of loves me?"

Little billows of smoke are exhaled into the air as he mulls it over. For a second, one brief one, I see a man who cares. "It's a dilemma, son." Rocking forward again, he takes his fountain pen and centers it on the mat. "The time for debate is over. We gave you the year you asked for. You've graduated, but now it's time to grow up and be responsible. You're the sole heir to wealth that will continue to support our family for generations to come. Settle down and get married. Camille can pop out a few kids, and you can fuck whoever you want on the side. Work or sit back and enjoy your brood. We're giving you more than you could ever want, Cooper. But now it's time to make a decision using your brain and not your dick."

"What about my heart?" I ask with less anger, less of me altogether. The wiggle room I had to get out for good has closed in on me. He's going to get what he wants—a decision being made after I was pushed in a corner.

"It's always been a worthless organ. Don't fall into the traps, and there will be plenty more in the future."

Story has been relegated to a "trap" in their eyes. They don't know her at all, or her heart and intentions. They're judging her by other women who preceded her in my life, and it sounds like from his as well. "That sounds like you know from experience."

"Your mother was a wise decision. She's still beautiful, intelligent, and she's passionate about upholding the Haywood legacy. I couldn't have asked for a better wife."

I sit back in the chair and look out the window. "Is that all that matters? If she looks good on my arm and on paper?"

The question seems to stump the great legal mind of Cooper Haywood, *Esquire*. "Maybe you need to ask yourself why you're with someone that doesn't add to your standing in society."

"Society turned its back on me a long time ago. Why would I give a shit about my standing in it now?"

Resting his forearms on the desk, he clasps his hands together. The white knuckling has always been one of his tics that I've used to monitor how far I can push things. As it stands now, white knuckles leave no room for him to change his mind.

"You're in love with a girl who hasn't traveled fifty miles outside Atterton until you took her to New York City and then brought her to Haywood. You saw her eyes. They were as big as saucers when she saw this place. I'm sure her ears were ringing with the sound of the register. Scoring a Haywood would be a big windfall for Ms. Salenger."

"No," I say, slamming my fist on the desk. "Stop it. Now. Don't fucking talk about her like you're doing her or me a favor." My mind is still blown by how shortsighted he's being. "If you can give her any credit for what she's survived and achieved on her own, then look at me, your only son. I'm the healthiest I've ever been because of her. Doesn't that matter?"

He chuckles, then sucks on his cigar again. "Healthy, huh? We all saw how she handles alcohol. The girl drinks like a fish. If that's the standard you're working from, I guess she matches your drinking problem."

I stand, tired of this bullshit. "I should have known any conversation that I came to you in earnest would devolve into insults and inventing shit as a verbal knockdown." I stare at him. "The saddest part to me doesn't involve money. It's that I'm left wondering why I wasted so many years caring. Fuck you and your legacy."

"You don't care. Okay, I didn't want to go there."

Throwing my arms out, I ask, "Go where? To hell? Look around, Dad. We're already there." I'm done. I'm done with everything. I'll start over with Story. We'll make ends meet. I'll sell my cars. I'll sell everything if it means I get to be with her. I walk to the door and swing it open. "Give it all away for all I care."

Before I have time to walk through the doorway, he says, "Calliope Salenger."

With my back to him, I still, the name freezing me to the spot, even my breath refusing to escape. When he doesn't say anything, I shut the door and turn back around. "What about her?"

He reaches for a drawer again, but this time that particular one is locked. He jiggles it and then laughs to himself as if it's an inside joke. Pulling the key from his pocket, he mumbles, "I always forget I lock this one." The sound of the cylinders clicking free the drawer, and my dad slides it open. He sets a red file in front of him. "Pretty girl. Tragic death."

A depravity that has never been a part of our conversations has seeped into the room, smelling of desperation. "What are you doing?"

"I'm doing what any good father would. I'm making sure my son doesn't fuck up his life any more than he has."

"No, I don't want you to give me the answer you think is right. I want you to look me in the eyes and use the organ you claim is worthless to speak to me. It may be your last chance."

The time that passes—*seconds, maybe minutes*—severs another tie that binds us. There are very few left to be risking them so callously.

The creak of his chair when he shifts across the worn leather amps up the adrenaline inside me, causing me the anxiety I was always running to escape. He'll hold his cards to his chest all damn day, so I ask, "So this is blackmail?"

"Let's not throw words around that could get us all arrested."

"You can't touch me."

"No," he says, "but I can touch her." When he taps the file, ashes fall from the cigar, scorching the folder. He pushes it toward me. "Go on. Take a look. It will tell you everything your girlfriend doesn't know about her mother, including her real name."

I'd been staring at the file, tempted to study the information to give to Story until he said that. "What do you mean?"

"I think you're smart enough to figure it out. You're a college graduate, after all."

I thought my mom was bad, devious to the core, but I hate him. I fucking hate them both so much. I feel sickness growing in my stomach, the ultimatum they're threatening —arms and legs crawling from the ashes he discarded—and gaining strength. "This was never about me getting my inheritance back, was it?"

His body language eases from the battle he appeared to be armored for when he walked into the office. "It was." A calmer tone is frequenting his tone. Unlike the reputation he's built as a hard-ass in the courtroom, I'm wondering if it's finally dawned on him that he's treating me like the enemy he's trying to take down instead of the son he's supposed to love. "It's a package deal."

Guess I was wrong. Again. "Which includes Camille . . ."

"Your mother really has her heart set on Camille. It would be a shame to disappoint her."

"They can fuck themselves before I end up with Camille Arden again."

"You're talking about your mother."

"And you're talking about *my* life."

"You have no life without us, Cooper." His anger finally surges, his own patience unraveling. "We've given you everything you could ever want." The chair hits the wall behind him, and he jabs his cigar into the ashtray.

"Except the one thing you refused me?"

"What?"

"Your love."

"Our love?" He laughs humorlessly, unable to hide the disbelief in his eyes. "What the fuck is wrong with you, Cooper? Everything we have fucking done is because we care about you more than you have ever cared about yourself."

"I hated myself because I saw character traits of you in me."

"Get the fuck out of my office."

He will never understand that I'd rather be beaten than to endure their hatred of me. A black eye, broken ribs, physical pain that I purposely sought out to make me feel anything other than this torture would heal. The hatred they have for me lives on. Eyeing the paperwork in front of him, I can't leave now. It would expose Story to more pain she can't survive. She's warned me before. I'm not sure how I can protect her now.

I ask, "What are you going to do with that file?"

"Whatever I need to."

I stare at him through a suspicious lens flooding red with anger. I've lost this battle, and it may have been the war. I can't protect her any more than I can save myself.

He's won the case against me.

He knows it, and I know it.

Now I have to act from the standpoint of damage control. "What are my options?"

He pulls his chair back toward the desk and sits down again. "Can we have a civil conversation?"

Cornered like a wild animal, I shout, "What are my fucking options?" Anger shoots through my veins, blinding me with rage. I should have known that using my happiness against me isn't beneath them. It's my fault.

I should have never brought Story around them.

They see her as a weak link, a way to force me to cooperate. *How can they not see how good she is for me?* If they just gave her a chance, they'd get to feel the warmth of her sunshine as well.

Fuck them and this whole damn town.

I'm close to leaving again when he says, "Sit. Down. Cooper."

Tugging my hair, I finally give in to the demand and sit in the chair. For someone who thought I'd gotten rid of anxiety, my bouncing knee tells a different story. So does my anger.

He says, "The girl has a good thing going. She just graduated, a job at some coffee shop, and a mother who, let's just put it bluntly, would have held Story back in life."

I feel like a traitor for sitting here listening to those words coming from his mouth. He's made me an accomplice to his dirty deeds, willing to sacrifice the only thing that matters to me to get his way. *He's quite the role model.* "Get on with it."

"Give us a five-year commitment and a grandkid. Is that too much to ask for?"

"Yes, it fucking is. Camille aside because I know she's all in for this bullshit, but you're not only talking about my life but also another human's—a kid's life. You fucked me up, and now you want to fuck up my kid? Do you hear yourself?"

"That was a rhetorical question."

"Is it in the contract? If it's in the contract, it's not fucking rhetorical." Waving my hand to hurry this along, I say, "What's the blackmail portion of this scheme?"

Disapproval wraps around his brows, and he steeples his fingers. "Like I already said, let's not degrade this to some street hustle deal made in a back alley. We're gentlemen, Cooper."

"Just save me the lecture and tell me the catch? What's the trade?"

"You serve your time, and this file gets burned."

Serving time? That's the most honest thing he's said in a long time. "I think you're underestimating what Story can handle. What if she wants to know the information contained inside?"

"Let me ask you something, Cooper." He picks up the file again and taps it against the desk twice. "How's Story doing?"

"Why are you asking?"

"Emotionally?" Now he cares about the damage she's suffered? *I don't trust him.* "Well . . . I heard there was a glitch with grades, that some of the diplomas were mistakenly distributed. The system will be corrected, and the diplomas rescinded."

I'm not sure when my heart stopped beating, but I'm fairly certain it worked when I walked into the room.

"Hit 'em where it hurts, huh, Dad?" Outplayed and outsmarted. For what? Grandkids with Camille? It just doesn't make sense to me, but it never did. "Let me ask you something. What kind of relationship do you think we'll have under these circumstances?"

"Sometimes people can't see what's best for them, son. We're happy to support this healthier journey you're on along with offering our guidance—"

"Guidance," I balk. "Is that what you're calling it?" Something catches my eyes, and I glance out the window.

Story.

When she starts running, I push up from the chair so fast that it wobbles on its back legs. I know what I'm leaving behind, but they've forced my hand in the matter. I rush to the door, but this time, my dad says, "I'll let you think about it."

"I don't need to. The answer is go fuck yourself." I cut around the corner and run out the front door. "Story?" I call, dashing down the steps after her. She hasn't gotten far but just out of hearing range.

I pick up speed and call her once more. She turns back, which slows her, but then keeps running. Catching up, I jog beside her and even show her my moves by turning backward and keeping pace, hoping to make her smile. "I saw they opened a new chicken—"

Her tear-streaked face has me stopping in my tracks. "What's wrong?"

She only makes it a few more feet before she drops forward at the waist, huffing for air. I rub her back, but she angles out of my reach. "Don't touch me."

That heart that died in my dad's office has now revived in her presence, beating so hard that I'm not sure my ribs can contain it. I give her the distance she needs but plead with her for more. "Talk to me, Story."

Her breathing starts to even, but the tears are still in her eyes and falling. Pointing at the house, she screams, "They're awful people." She walks away and then stops and turns back, crossing her arms over her shoulders. "I love you. I love you so much, Cooper, but I can't have people like that in my life. They're hateful. They're evil."

"They are," I say, approaching slowly. "They're horrible and will destroy you if you let them." Her breathing is heavy in her chest, her hair as wild as her eyes from running, but she stays, even when I reach for her hand to hold it.

A soft sob shivers through her, and she shakes her head. "I'm not strong enough."

"We'll be strong together. We'll always have each other."

"Cooper?" *Fuck.*

Story's eyes leave mine and narrow on the owner of that voice—Camille. When I turn around, Camille has almost reached us. It's not her presence that has me tucking Story out from the line of fire. It's the folder she's tapping in her hands.

Fuck my life. And the next after this, for that matter.

I turn back to Story, knowing I have no time left to prepare her for the onslaught of what's about to happen. Grabbing her arms, I lean down and look into her eyes. "You have to listen to me. Whatever they say, you can't believe it, okay?"

"What? Why?"

"Please, just trust me. Trust. Me. Story. Only me." I hand her the claim check to my car. "Go home, and I'll be there later to explain."

"What's happening?" she asks, panic already set into her eyes.

"Go, babe. It's okay. I promise you. It will all work out how it's supposed to." I don't know why I say that other than I can feel the walls closing in and the cage ready to fall over my head.

Her gaze darts from Camille to me. "Cooper?"

"Go. It's okay. I'll be there later." I kiss her quickly.

She starts walking away, slowly at first, and then she says, "I love you."

"I love you, too."

Camille comes closer, and asks, "What are you doing, silly goose?" She watches Story rush across the lawn to the valet stand and then turns back to me with a fake smile on her face. "Aw, poor thing. Did you guys have a fight?" She touches my brow to brush my hair aside, but I duck away.

It was always best when I ignored her and removed myself from the situation, but I have a feeling that won't work this time. I start for the house anyway.

Camille says, "Your dad wanted me to give this to you. I think it's something about her mom?" The doe-eyed innocence she's aiming for is lost on me. I see her for who she is. *I always did.*

She starts rambling like this is just another day in paradise. When I reach the house again, I turn back to see Story driving away. Not sure if she can see me in her rearview mirror, but I wave just in case she can.

Camille reaches the bottom step, and asks, "When are you going to stop fighting against a system that's rigged in your favor?"

"I love her, but you'll never understand because you conflate happiness with a bank account. They're not the same thing."

"You're right, but you need to decide whose happiness is worth more to you—yours or Story's?"

"Story's. Always hers."

She comes up the steps and hands me the file. "If that's true, sign the contract, and let's start our life then."

Story can get a new degree. It's a glitch they've rigged. She'll take a class or two over, and I'll pay her way. She'll be disappointed, but we'll be together.

Maybe she'll want to know her mom's real name. We can overcome these threats together. We're enough. Our love will be enough for us.

I need to find a ride back to Atterton. I can hole up in my room, take anything that ever mattered, and get the hell out of here when the car arrives. I take the file, not naïve enough to believe it's the only copy, and start inside.

"She'll end up hating you, Cooper." I stop and look back, her voice sounding genuine. "You know as well as I do that she'll be gone when it becomes unbearable. And it will be . . . her life will be unbearable if you choose her. What's in that file will change everything."

"Tell me something, Camille, you're okay with marrying me and having a kid with me, knowing I despise everything about you? And all for money and the Haywood last name?"

"I'm jealous that you feel anything other than numbness. I'm envious of Story because you love her. I don't know what I want anymore. Everything you said before Christmas still plays on a loop in my head." She comes closer and looks around before whispering, "I'm not strong like she is, but I'll be a good wife to you."

My gaze volleys between her eyes, not an ounce of lie found in them. "But I can't be a good husband to you." I walk inside and take the stairs by two. As soon as I get inside my childhood bedroom, I lock the door and flip open the file.

The kinds of threats thrown out today will only work if they're backed in substance. I also believe my father has more tricks up his sleeve than a bomb with a faulty detonator. The degree aside, I don't think Story would mind knowing her mom's real name based on discussions we've had before.

Scanning each page rapidly, I search for the bombshell that must be hidden in here. There's nothing, though . . . until the last page.

And that seals our fate.

31

Story

Night had fallen before I got home.

The minutes matched the miles, every one of them feeling longer than the last and stretching between the heart I left back in Haywood and the home I was driving toward.

But wasn't Cooper one and the same—my heart and home. I couldn't distinguish between the two any longer. Each waking hour of this separation that passes brings a fresh surge of pain and leaves more questions unanswered.

Did he stay?

Party on like we'd never met?

Choose them over me?

Choose the money?

My mind's going wild, and he hasn't answered his phone. Did something happen to him? Was he in an accident? How was he even getting back to me when I have his car?

Curled up on top of my desk, I've wedged myself into the

frame of the window, not wanting to miss Cooper's arrival. I check my watch, convinced he would be right behind me, but now I'm not so sure. It's been hours since I arrived home.

I can't eat, and nothing can quench the loss of missing him. Except Cooper.

"Please, Cooper. Please choose me," I whisper like a prayer to the universe.

Ten o'clock passes.

Eleven forty-seven.

Twelve fifteen AM . . . I finally decide to give up hope and go to bed. But then I see headlights turn onto my street and sit upright. *Please. Please. Please. Please. Please.*

The car passes without so much as slowing down.

Deflated, I hop off the desk, my butt aching from being pressed to the hard wood, and climb into bed. My stomach growls, and I try to remember the last thing I ate. I know what it wasn't—a plate full of cheese, fruit, and macarons at the party. Come to think of it, I don't think I've eaten since breakfast yesterday.

Knowing I'm not going to be able to fall asleep with my hunger keeping me awake, I flip off the covers and pad into the kitchen. The bag of chips on the counter isn't appealing, and I always have the option to make popcorn in the microwave. *Eh.* I open the fridge and grab a yogurt, too tired to debate what will satisfy these pangs.

With no energy, I lean against the counter and start eating, but I only take a few bites before my stomach gets upset again. *Maybe it's gone bad?* I scoop another spoonful into my mouth, and with the utensil still there, I tilt the container sideways to look at the expiration date.

Fortunately, it's still good for two more weeks. I eat more, but then a cramp shoots across my belly, causing me to squeeze the spoon in one hand and the container in the other until it passes. Exhaling through pursed lips, I slow down, closing my eyes, and try to breathe through the pain.

A roll of my stomach surges again, and I throw the stuff into the sink and dash into the bathroom to throw up. I grip the seat, and wave after wave rips through me until I'm exhausted and sweat dots my forehead.

Food poisoning?

Resting against the side of the tub, I drop my head into my hands and start crying. I'm alone. I could die, and no one would even know.

Cooper left me with his car when I would have preferred a love note instead. I'm not surprised that my body's rejecting everything that would make it feel better right now. How could it when my heart and my head know the truth? It's not going to be better until Cooper comes home.

I clean up and brush my teeth before getting a cold glass of water to drink. Careful of my shaky stomach, I sip slowly. As the heat recedes from my cheeks, I sit on the edge of the bed, ready for sleep.

But I know that can't happen, not until I hear from him. I pick up my phone and text him once more before setting it on the nightstand and willing him to reply.

I'm left disappointed again . . .

I hate how dependent I've become, how desperate I feel, and how I've constructed my world to hinge on one man. This is how Calliope used to act when she met a new man—so worried he wouldn't love her she'd stay up and pace into the wee hours if she didn't hear from him. Eventually, I'd get her to lie down on the couch and fall asleep.

That was who she was.

That's not who I am. Closing my eyes, I repeat my mantra, "Break the cycle."

When the heaviness of night rises, everything looks better in the daylight. I roll to my side, facing the empty space next to me, and give in to sleep.

Morning comes, flooding the room with light because I forgot to close the blinds.

Just as I stretch, my body kicks into overdrive, and I run to the bathroom to expel the lining of my stomach since there's nothing else in there. This is miserable. I must have a virus. It's probably from being so close to Camille. She probably slipped something into my drink. I wouldn't put it past her.

My heated tears fill the bowl along with the water I had last night. Zapped of energy and my muscles aching for a reprieve, I sit on my knees, resting my hands on the toilet seat and my head on my wrists.

What the fresh hell is happening? Why is my body turning against me?

I wash up again, this time deciding to take a shower, but with no food in my stomach and a pounding headache, it's safer for me to sit in the bath. The water comes down, the warmth helping to wash away some of the sharper edges of my pain.

With the new day, I renew my hope to get answers today.

But then I realize I don't need answers. *I just need him.*

I grab my phone as soon as I return to the bedroom. The blank screen doesn't upset my stomach, but my chest aches with pain. I'm not sure what to do or how to feel. Who just ghosts someone they love like this? I don't understand.

The nuisance of tears fills my eyes again as I try to focus by digging out a pair of yoga pants and one of his T-shirts that stayed after the last wash. I get dressed and then check my phone again. He's had hours upon hours of chances to reach out to me. Nothing makes sense.

Desperation wins, and I call him again. When the rings lead into his voicemail message, and then it beeps, I say, "Hi. I . . . I love you."

Crazy ideas start populating in my head. I have his car. I could drive back to Haywood and pick him up. Maybe he couldn't find a ride. That's got to be it. *That has to be it.* One thing I do know is that I can't sit here any longer. I grab his keys, my phone, and my purse, and decide to leave. Should I go to his apartment to see if he's there, or should I go back to Haywood?

By the time I reach the bottom step, I'm out of breath, and my stomach is upset again. Is it possible to have food poisoning from something you ate two nights ago? I don't remember what that could be, but it doesn't feel like a cold or anything like that. Food poisoning is all that fits the symptoms.

I think I should visit the pharmacy before going anywhere else. I'll grab something to settle my stomach and drink ginger ale. That's what my mom always did when she had a bad hangover.

Worried the car ride will make me sicker, I cover the two blocks and cut down the next. After finding what I need on the shelves, I move to the check-out line at the counter. The cashier, a woman not much older than me, laughs as she scans the items before bagging. "Last time I needed this," she says, holding up the anti-nausea medicine, "I found out I was pregnant. Sure you don't need a pregnancy test?"

Her words amuse her until she looks up from the items, and her smile falls. "Honey, are you all right?"

"I . . ."

"Oh, no. Just because I said that's what *I* needed, and a baby came nine months later after I mistakenly thought it was indigestion, doesn't mean that you are . . . *or that you're not . . .*" She stumbles through her words, apologizing right after.

But the implanted thought triggers something inside me, causing my stomach to do somersaults. "Maybe I should take a test?"

I don't know why I'm even asking her other than I'm starting to freak out.

"If you think it's a possibility—"

"It's a possibility," I snap, not meaning to take it out on her.

"Let me get one for you." She adds it to the order, and then whispers, "I've always found this one very reliable."

"Thank you." I pay and take the bag, feeling like I'm doing a walk of shame at the door, as if I've done something wrong.

She says, "Good luck," just before the door closes.

The walk back to my apartment is much slower despite the frantic beating of my heart. I use the time in the fresh air to recall the times we've been together more recently. He was wearing protection. Every time.

But then the memory of him dipping the tip inside me comes back . . .

"You feel so good," I say, wanting to feel all of him with nothing between us. "I want you, Cooper. So bad that my body aches for you."

That memory leads to the guilt I feel for not going to the infirmary. I was supposed to get on the pill this past week but got so busy with work and then preparing for the party that it slipped my mind.

Though I feel I could throw up again, I walk up the stairs in a hurry, fighting the quicksand of my emotions. I open the box and kick the door closed, tossing the other stuff on the bed as I rush into the bathroom. My hands are shaking, but I scan the pamphlet and manage to take the test according to the directions.

I look at my watch and start the countdown, closing the door and pacing my apartment. It reminds me of how Cooper has paced this floor and makes me wonder if he's pacing now. Or is he too content in Camille's arms to worry about my heart?

My nerves are running hot, my body a live wire. I pour a glass of water and drink it down. As soon as the designated time has passed, I burst into the bathroom and stare at the test on the edge of the counter.

I'm not sure what to feel — happy or sad—when alone is the overwhelming emotion. I carry the stick with me, still staring at it, and realize I was never going to find relief no matter which way it turned out.

It won't change the fact that Cooper didn't choose me.

32

Cooper

Maybe I am an alcoholic . . .

The bourbon swirls around the bottle once more before I finish the rest of it. I'd stopped bothering to use a glass hours ago. Who's here to judge me in the back seat of my mom's Bentley? *No one.* No one because I chose to betray the woman I love to save her from a different fate.

Dropping the bottle to the floorboard, I angle down to get a clear view of her apartment. Story hasn't left the window, not once since she climbed into it. I know what she's doing and who she's waiting for, blowing up my phone with missed calls and unanswered texts.

A half-hearted smile comes over me seeing her hair pulled high on her head and the shape of her body swallowed by one of her many pairs of flannel pajamas she owns. I've learned she's in for the night once those come on. She's a woman of routine, of reliability. Accountability, which is something I never did until more recently.

Everyone has a clean slate when you meet her, including

me. There wasn't googling identities or checking out profiles on dating apps. No background checks or searching for police records. No one's past is held against them. She gives everyone the benefit of the doubt. She's still doing it now by keeping the faith in me even though she doesn't realize it.

So give me an answer if you're up there? Send me a sign or show me the light because I'm struggling to see how I survive this. I shouldn't.

I won't.

How do I break her heart?

How do I let her down?

How do I break every promise I made to her?

How will I walk away knowing how much I'm hurting her? I can't.

The file spilled open on the way back to Atterton, the papers out of order and spread all over the car from hitting the brakes too hard. *The fucking squirrel was saved.*

I can't say the same for Story's and my relationship.

Four hours on the road gave me time to think, to figure a way out of this mess and make sure we stay together. In the end, there is none. There's no saving us from the inevitable. She'll shoot the messenger if I tell her, or I'll lose her if I don't.

I'm fucked either way.

My family royally screwed me. And they knew it. They're probably celebrating.

Accountability . . . That fucking word creeps back into my psyche. It's another thing that she believes in. I've caused her more pain than anyone should ever experience. So calling myself just a messenger in this mess is downplaying the role I played. I'm the instigator that led to her mother's death. Now, Karma has come to collect her dues, and I'll pay the price, even years later, for the recklessness of my youth.

I watch Story, wishing I could be the one to comfort her, but that job will go to someone else, a candidate more qualified to be in her life. More deserving. *And I'll need to learn to live with it.*

———

THE SOUND of rain wakes me up.

But it doesn't make sense. It's loud, causing me to jerk open my eyes just as pain shoots across my back from being twisted in the back seat of the Bentley. "Fuck," I grumble.

"I could say the same." *Grief is heard in her somber tone.*

I sit up too quickly, my head aching from drinking too much. The car is shrouded in rain, but sitting in the driver's seat, Story stares out the windshield, refusing to look at me. Red blotches cover her cheek and what's exposed of her neck. Strands have escaped the tornado twisted on top of her head, and her face is tear-streaked. It doesn't look like she's fared much better than me since the party, and she still manages to be beautiful.

Looking down at her lap, she says, "You should lock your doors in this neighborhood. It's not the kind you're used to."

"Story—"

"I know, Cooper." Her voice has lost its vibrance and is almost unrecognizable. She turns back, giving me the gift of her eyes, that gaze that I fell so hard in love with. "I'm not sure an explanation is going to get us to the other side of this."

Putting pressure on the side of my head to stop it from aching, I ask, "Of what?"

When she holds up a piece of paper, my eyes scan the headline "Murder Suicide in Atterton," and my stomach drops. I rush to open the door to hang my head out just in time to throw up. *She knows . . .*

She knows my actions led to her mom's death. And I need to face her, to face the victim of my poor decision that night. My hair and the collar of my shirt get soaked, but I don't care. The cool rain revives me enough to sit back up. "Story—"

The front door slams shut, so I open mine again to get out, not caring if I get wet. "Story?" I run to catch her on the sidewalk, cutting off her path. I grab her arms and plant myself in front of her. "I need you to listen. I was young and—"

"Rich and bored and didn't give a fuck about anyone else. I know, Cooper. I read the police report and how you sideswiped his truck. I read how you were so high and drunk that you didn't realize you were alive until you sobered in a jail cell. I read Hank's account of the accident and how you came out of nowhere and hit him on Taylor Drive. And then I read your account. You didn't even bother to lie." She tries to step forward, but I hold her there.

"I wanted to die, but I didn't want to hurt anyone else."

"But you did," she screams, but the rain dampens the sound. "You hurt me, Cooper!" She looks away, denying me the window to her soul that gave me life. As long as I had that, I still believed we could find our way back.

That hope is gone when she says, "The crime wasn't you denting Hank's truck. The crime is that you set him on a mission to take his anger out on me. I told you that he had an ax to grind that night all because a 'rich kid' fucked up his truck. And since the police were already there, they gave him a ticket for out-of-date registration." She takes a breath and hits me with a glare. "Your parents' insurance would have covered the truck, so that means my mom died because of a hundred-dollar ticket. His mood and that money are why he broke me and killed her."

"I'm sorry. I'm so fucking sorry." The heat in my eyes isn't from the rain that remains cool on my skin. It's the tears that I've never cried and the reality of losing her.

"I was fucking stupid."

"You forgot high. Was it weed . . . or ecstasy? What were you on that made you feel invincible?"

"Everything," I reply too hurriedly, convicting myself before I even have my trial.

Last night, I was hell-bent on causing her to break up with me to keep the truth of my role in her mom's death a secret. If I went away, so would the truth. Living the lies would be better than torturing her a second time in life.

I would leave. I'd do that for her. I would make her hate me, so she'd have a chance to find someone new. Now, I would do anything to keep her for just one more day, even if it means she knows that truth. I'll confess every sin I ever committed if I just get to stand here with her. "Anything I could get my hands on."

Her arms are lifeless in my hands but never once has she pulled away. "To numb your pain?" she asks.

"To numb my life away."

"And instead, you destroyed mine." Wrangling free, she dips the umbrella, exposing her to the pouring rain. As her hair begins to drown and the pajamas she's wearing are drenched, she stares at me like she doesn't know me. She stares at me as if it's the last time she'll get the chance. Then walks around me.

I jog next to her, trying to stop to talk to her again because if she gets to her apartment, I may never get my second chance. "I didn't know."

"You didn't know," she repeats. "You didn't, but you also

didn't care. When you were speeding down a busy road, you didn't care that you might hit somebody. You didn't care that you were so high that you lost control of your car that Mommy and Daddy gave you. You didn't care, Cooper, that you could have killed an innocent victim. So yes, you didn't know, but you also didn't care."

"I was arrested and thought that was the end."

She holds up the drenched paper. "Because it was the end for you. Your daddy would come bail you out like he'd done before for your reckless behavior." Her tears fall with the rain, and I'm not sure what's louder, the sound or my blood rushing in my ears. "But the end of your story was only the beginning of my nightmare."

Although she had told me about that night and what happened, I didn't put the pieces together until I read the file. *How could I have known that my actions that night would have a domino effect?*

My friends and I were in town partying for the weekend. We'd gotten high and started some fights. My parents threatened to send me to a military boarding school. If I thought my life was bad then, it was about to get worse. I don't know what I took because it didn't matter anymore.

The umbrella falls to the ground as if she has no will to hold it with everything else weighing her down. "If I could take away your pain, I would. Let me try." I step closer in the pause between us. She stays, so I say, "I'm sorry."

A button is pushed, the words a trigger. Fire burns in her eyes, and she says, "You're sorry? Stop saying you're sorry." Her hands fist at her sides, the paper already falling apart from getting wet, and she yells, "Sorry doesn't bring back my mother. Sorry doesn't fix Hank's truck or take away the ticket that led to my scar and my mother's death." The tears she cries are no different than those from heaven above, but they still stream down filled with her pain.

She charges me and shoves me in the chest, and I let her direct her pain at me. I can handle it, but as she's said before, she might not survive it again. "It was the end—the end of your night, Cooper, led to the end of my mom's life."

Turning away, she drops her head into her hands, and the pain wreaks havoc on her body as it wins. This is it. This is when it all ends. There's no hope of a reconciliation. There's no getting past this, not when Story can't even look at me.

"If I could have died in her place, I would have."

Story sighs, and her spine straightens before she looks down the street one way and then the other. When her eyes find me again, calm has come over her. "Calliope was always meant to die young. A soul like hers was too fragile to survive. But you . . . a cloud will hang over your soul for decades to come. And every time you look up, you'll remember that you once lived in sunshine. Mine."

"I'm already burdened with that curse."

This goddess, my muse, and my savior. She gave me everything I had always been missing, and now I have nothing . . . Nothing more than wanting to die at her feet. But it's too late to spare her life from the atrocities of mine.

Her sniffling leads to a fleeing sob breaking free from her chest. Then she stops, and I'm pierced with another heartbreaking peek into her windows. I'm not sure what to say—damned if you do and damned if you don't. I can't bring her mom back, but I'll sacrifice myself in her place.

The calm is washed away, and she trembles like a leaf when she says, "Your actions set off a chain of events that led to someone's death." She starts walking but stops, too conflicted to make a decision on a direction. Thrashing the umbrella against the brick wall next to us, she takes her frustration out until it's bent and broken . . . like us.

After discarding the umbrella, she runs back to me, fisting my shirt and pulling me closer—a plea and a push— she begs, "If you ever loved me—"

"I love you, Story."

"Then tell me," she says, crying. "I need to hear the truth. Please tell me my mom's life wasn't taken because you were bored with yours."

Darkness has taken hold of her, though it's still morning. Cupping her face, I plead with her, "I can't lie to you—"

"That's all you've done."

"No. I've never been more honest than when I'm with you."

A stifled breath works through her, and she asks, "What does that say about your character?" She pushes off me, and the sudden movement has me stumbling backward. Searching my face for something I can't give her, her tears stop, and the life we lived, we loved, leaves her eyes for good. "Hank was the match, but you lit the fuse. My mom would still be alive if you had never been out joyriding."

And there it is—the truth.

I'm to blame for her mom's death. It only took me having a run-in with the wrong person to set him off on his own personal path of destruction. I may not have been the one to murder with my hands, but my actions led to her death.

That's not something I can take back or that my parents can bail me out of. They tried to protect me, but secrets always surface.

Stopping with at least ten feet between us, she adds, "You didn't just kill my mom that night. You broke me." The final blow lands right where it's intended—my heart—and knocks the breath from me.

This time, I let her go, unsure what to say anymore because she's right. If she carries that hate for me around with her for the rest of her life, I'd deserve no less.

I remain where she left me until she crosses the street and disappears inside her building. We're lost in a circumstance that's out of our control, pawns in a bigger game.

But the one thing I can control is not allowing my parents to win. *The truth will set us free.* Even if it's away from my eternity. My parents no longer have power over me.

Without Story, what's left in this world for me?

Getting in the car, I find the papers scattered across the front seat. She found Hank's statement from the accident that night, but my arrest record is still lying on the passenger's seat. She put the puzzle together just like I did. Until I saw the repercussions of my actions that night in this file, I didn't realize that the ties that bound Story and me together were the same ones that tore us apart.

I thought the lie that would destroy us would be how I got Eliza to hook up with Troy the night of the party. Because who does that? *Someone selfish. Someone evil. Someone sad.* Me. Now that's another secret that will remain buried inside me.

I can't be mad that we ended this way. Story Salenger deserves a good life, and that's something I would never be able to give her. I have to listen to the universe. It always has a master plan. I nod, starting the engine and knowing that I'll take the fall and pay my dues if it allows Story to sleep better at night.

As noble as that sounds to me, the pain of losing her is too much to bear.

I WAIT ALL DAY, ready for it to be night.

I'm not waiting for dusk but the hours before dawn. It doesn't take that long to be noticed and for them to take the bait just before midnight. No way would a two-hundred-and-fifty-thousand-dollar car be left alone all night. Not in Troy Hogan's neighborhood. He and his friends show up, ready for me as if they've been waiting for years.

I know they have because I did too for the longest time.

It may have been the car that got their attention first. *But I got it second.* Standing in front of his truck blocking a headlight, he's predictable with his hand pumping into the other. Something about crossing lines too many times is being yelled across the divide, but I don't need the foreplay. I just need this pain to be replaced by another.

The first blow takes me down.

The next has me gasping for air.

I'll take every punch, every hit and kick if it gets me closer to blacking out. Going to hell under his hands beats the purgatory of existing without Story in my life.

Death is sweeter than the bitter taste of my past. With no future to look forward to, I don't bother fighting back.

33

Story

I waited.

I don't know why.

For days, I waited to hear from him again.

No calls. Or texts.

No flowers or apologies.

He didn't even pick up his car as it sat parked outside my apartment for a week.

Instead of sleeping with him each night like I used to do, the pregnancy stick on his pillow keeps me company. There's something about those two little lines that make me feel less . . . *alone.*

The vomiting subsided after twenty-four hours. That's when I realized it wasn't being pregnant that made me sick, but the trauma of losing Cooper. But maybe it was the sign I needed to make me take the test, along with the cashier, of course.

After doing some research, since I had time on my hands, the positive test meant I'd been pregnant for weeks, if not a month or more, before graduation. And now I've started puking again. I just can't tell if it's from the horrendous pain of losing him, learning of his part in my mom's death, or because this baby wants my attention.

To overcome the heartbreak that has settled into my chest, I find comfort in rubbing my belly sometimes when I think of him. I'm not sure it's healthy or even matters, but the thought of this baby created from love is more appealing than from the end of our relationship.

And then a dose of reality and the role he's played in my life comes crashing in again. How can I forgive him? How do I show him grace for a mistake he made?

It was a mistake. My logical side knows this, but it doesn't change the outcome or the devastation. Cooper's actions led directly to her death and took my one constant, even if not always reliable, away from me. I was a parentless teenager with no one left to care about me.

I can't forgive him.

Surviving means protecting myself and now my baby. The complications are too vast to think rationally, so I put off dealing with it at all. I will . . . one day when I'm in a better place.

After calling in sick from work all week and lying in bed all day, Saturday rolls around. It's time to face life again. Cooper made it clear that he wants nothing to do with me. He could spy on me last Saturday night but couldn't come up to talk to me. I know he wasn't even planning to until I forced the issue and got in that car. What was he thinking drinking himself into oblivion and leaving the doors unlocked?

It's like he wanted to get robbed or worse.

But I can't make his problems mine. I have too many of my own. I can't let those problems skew my moral compass.

I grew up without a dad. It's not ideal for this baby to tie me to a man who has damaged me, but that can't keep me from doing the right thing and telling him.

I can do this alone. I may not make much money, but one day, I will. I'm a survivor, though, and my baby will never need Haywood money.

I pack supplies in a bowl for the day—snacks and bottles of water, fresh fruit, and a pair of flannel pajama pants for the drive home if I end up traveling to his parents' Haywood home. The bowl just in case I get sick.

Fingers crossed I won't need to make that long trip, but I'm not sure I'll feel much better if I find out he's been across campus from me this entire time either.

Plugging in my phone, I then shift into gear, still not used to driving a sports car or something this decked out. I'm still wondering why he hasn't come to retrieve his car —*his baby*. Okay, fine, he doesn't want to see me, but so much so that it comes at the expense of his car?

I take the long way around campus, doing breathing exercises to regulate my speeding heartbeat. It's not good for me to be in a constant state of distress. But if I think the baby making me ill when I eat is rough, it holds nothing on this elevator ascent.

The door opens, and I step out, the Darth Vader March kicking in. Cooper and I had a good laugh the first time, but the humor this time is lost in translation to what we've become, and my concern for my future overshadows the past laughs. With the distance from then to now, I look back, wondering if we were the bad guys all along. That's the only explanation I can come up with for not getting our happy ending.

Did I hold him too tightly?

Love him too hard?

He didn't even fight for me, or us, to be together. He let me leave, and then he left right after. What could I have done to Cooper Haywood to make him disappear without a trace from my life?

Standing in front of his door, I take one more breath and then knock. Just like the last time, I don't hear music or voices from inside the apartment. I don't hear anything at all, which brings a sense of dread for *where he could be* filling my chest.

Too impatient to wait, I knock again. *And again.* And then I'm banging on the door, begging him to open it.

A door down the hall clicks open, and a girl with octagon-shaped glasses pokes her head out. Giving me a dirty look, she says, "He's not home. He's not been there all week. I think he went home for the break." She rolls her eyes in annoyance and then pushes her glasses up the bridge of her nose.

"Are you sure?"

"Yes. Geez. I don't keep track of the man, but I can hear his music and TV all the way in my apartment because he plays it so loud." The door closes and, as if to make a point, slams.

It's probably not wise to spend my time riddling through our demise when he's already made up his mind. And I should follow his lead. But, at least, I now know he's not been here and that allows me to figure out my next step.

Another visit to Haywood. *Oh joy* . . . I start bracing myself now.

It's not until I've been in the car for two hours and see a detour sign to the city that I start to wonder if maybe he went there instead. Fool's gold to take that route. It would be an impossible mission to find him in a city of eight million. I couldn't tell someone what hotel we stayed in, much less where his parents lived. Staying the course to Haywood is the only option I've been given.

Clouds roll in midafternoon, and by the time I reach the town, I'm stuck in a downpour. Though it's only been a week since I've been here, my wounds are still fresh from Camille's attack. I need to get a hold of myself, use my mental strength and keep a clear head because I don't know what I'm going to encounter next, and it would be stupid not to prepare for the unexpected.

The rain ceases at the entrance as if the Haywoods have paid for their own personal sunshine. It wouldn't surprise me one bit. Everything in their world can be bought.

The driveway feels longer than before, but I'm assuming it's the same and just the dread that keeps me from going. I start to second-guess myself. What am I doing? What is my goal?

To tell Cooper goodbye or to see if he's even alive? Is the baby an excuse to see him again, or am I doing the right thing by opening this door?

I have no clue anymore. The only one who's ever disappeared without warning was my mother. Her murder taught me that we don't always get the goodbye we deserve. Sometimes, there's no closure and only pain left behind.

Somehow, I've managed to give Cooper the benefit of the doubt most of the week. Sure, it ebbed and flowed with my emotions, but it never sank in that he did this willingly. As I park the car in front of the house, his will or purpose becomes my prevailing thought. What if he just couldn't say the words to break up, he's too weak to talk to me, or worse, I tell him that I'm pregnant, and he still wants nothing to do with me or my baby?

I rub my stomach once more like Buddha, hoping it will bring me luck. All I can do is play it by ear. I raise my head, mustering my strength. If he wants nothing to do with us, he's going to have to say it, to taste those words and swallow them down. That way, I'll have something to remember him by.

Looking around gives me no clue whether Cooper is here or if his family has gone back to the city. I don't see any signifiers, not even other cars. But I didn't drive all this way to ask for him to take me back or to give my forgiveness for him running away. One goal. *I'm having his baby.*

Opening the door, I step out and shove the keys in the front pocket of my jeans.

Five steps up and I'm standing in front of the door. I can ring the bell, or I can knock, but it shouldn't be this big of a decision. *Why am I hesitating?*

I look back over my shoulder at the long walk just to leave the property. I need to prepare for that if they take the car away from me. I can't afford a ride app to get me back to Atterton. Suddenly, I'm not feeling so good about this plan. The door swings open, though, and I'm caught in it.

I was hoping for Patrice, though the buildup was so great that I almost expected Camille to be there flashing an engagement ring. So many different scenarios played out in my head that I'm thrown by this guy in ordinary clothes. He asks, "How may I help you?"

"I'm here to see Cooper."

His eyes volley between mine, and then a gentle smile appears. "I'm sorry. He's not available right now."

The door starts to close, so I shove my hand out to block it. "I've driven a long way. Can I please wait?"

He checks behind him, and uncertainty reaches his eyes. "I guess. Would you like to wait in the foyer?"

If that means I'm about to see Cooper, hell yes, I want to wait in the foyer. "Yes, thank you," I reply, thinking that's a more appropriate response.

He leads me inside and then directs me to sit on a bench. "I'll let the Haywoods know we have company."

"Thank you." It dawns on me too late when I realize he said Haywoods—plural. *Oh, shit.* Do I dart to the door and make a run for it? Or stay and hope Cooper finds me first?

I've never been much of an eavesdropper, but when I hear voices travel from the living room around the corner and off the marble floors to my ears, and the name Cooper is mentioned, I listen.

"He doesn't know what he wants . . ." *His mom.* Her voice trails into a whisper.

"He does." I'd know that voice anywhere. My blood pressure rises from the sound of Camille's high octave. *Why is she even here?* "We're not allowing him to have it." I perk up. That's the most sensible thing I've heard come from her mouth.

"Camille, dear, Cooper is too different from her. He's strong-willed and has all the connections in the world to make him successful. You'll plant the seed, water it, and watch him grow into the man we know he can be." I hate that she refers to him as a plant. He once made the same comparison because I was the sunlight he needed.

She goes on to say, "He will come around. I promise you." *Those Haywoods love to make promises.* They're just words to them with no meaning.

"In the meantime?" Camille asks.

"In the meantime, we continue to encourage him. It's been a rough week. *For all of us.* He needs time to heal, but we'll get through this as a family." Get through what? They won.

Oh, his heartbreak?

Is it wrong to hope?

The sound of the heels clicking across the floors has me standing and grasping my hands in front of me nervously. I want to see him, not them. I have nothing to say to either of them ever again.

The topic of their conversation turns into gardening advice as they round the corner. His mother says, "You must plant that double heirloom in your garden, Camille. It has the most fragrant—" Their eyes meet mine at the same time.

Camille gasps, so I feel like I'm one-love at this stage in the match. Stopped and staring at me with mouths gaping open, his mother yanks on the hem of her jacket and stands up straighter. "What are you doing here? Who let you in?"

I look behind them, but I haven't seen him since he left to supposedly tell them of my arrival. "Some man did. I'm here to see Cooper."

"Well, you can't," she snaps. "He's resting."

"I can wait. I drove all this—"

"I don't care how far you drove. We're not allowing any visitors." Camille is smart enough to make an exit.

I ask, "*You're* not allowing?"

"*You're* not allowed. He doesn't want to see you." She raises her chin, her snobbish air infiltrating the foyer and filling it with tension. "I don't blame him. He now understands the kind of person in which he commingled." His mom goes quiet, her lips as terse as her words.

"Commingled? Like mingling?" I ask stupidly when I know I shouldn't have. It just gives her the advantage.

"No, dear," she says condescendingly. "The legal term used in regard to money." She leans back and peeks out the window. "Have you been enjoying his car?"

Everything comes down to money with these people. "I'd rather have him."

"I'm sure you would, but as you'll *not* be getting him, maybe we can cut a deal for the vehicle. How about you hold it in exchange for never contacting my son again."

Stunned that anyone even thinks to make an offer like that . . . she's pure evil.

I start for the stairs, refusing to sit here and make a deal with the devil herself as she insults me every chance she gets. "Ms. Salenger?" I keep walking. I'll find his room in this mansion somehow. She says, "If you take one more step, Story, I'll have you arrested."

I stop because I believe her. What was I thinking? How did I imagine this playing out? Not going to jail would be a good start.

My head catches up to the moment, and swirls, making me feel light-headed. I'm quick to grab the railing, worried I'll take a fall if I don't. I rub my temple in an attempt to assuage the rush that keeps me off-balance and try to make this nightmare go away. But when I open my eyes, I'm still in the middle of it.

I turn back to his mother, and our eyes lock together. For a moment, I believe I see sympathy softening the faint lines beside her eyes and the darkness that hovers in her brow. It disappears just as my better senses return. I reply, "Cooper and I had become one. Commingling is when there's a breach of trust. That wasn't the case with us."

"Are you sure?"

I'm sensing there's a bigger picture I'm not privy to. I can only imagine the brainwashing they've performed this week with me not around. The file . . . I can assume it was provided by them since it was first seen in Camille's hand. They orchestrated everything. Cooper set it in motion, but they took advantage of the crisis. "Despite what you think you know, Cooper loves me." I know that. He does. We just aren't in a place to be like we were once before. "No matter how hard you try to deny it, we will always feel that love inside, even if we're not together."

The last thing I want is an arrest record, so feeling steady on my feet again, I carefully walk down the stairs.

When I reach the tiled floor, she's there to see me out. "I'm sorry you're disappointed. I imagine it's a great loss to lose Cooper. But did you really think it would work out?" She raises a finely plucked brow. "What could you possibly have in common? You, the girl from the wrong side of town with no mother to speak of and no clue who your father is. You've done better than expected by all standards of society. You'll continue that journey without my son because he deserves someone with the same pedigree standing by his side."

I could let her words sting, but they were expected. She's attacking because she knows there's truth in my words. I walk to the door. "I'm surprised you gave me the courtesy of stabbing me in the chest when it would've been so much easier in the back. But that's what arrogance does. It makes you feel superior to those you feel you're above. But it also reveals your weakness."

"My weakness is my child."

"Cooper's not a child, and trust me, he never belonged to you."

She opens the door and looks me over once more. "If you choose to become a mother one day, you'll understand why I'm doing this. As a mother, I will do anything to protect my child."

"One day" is not as far off as she believes, but I'll give her credit where it's due. I will do anything to protect my child . . . *from her*. Even if it means giving up the love of my life.

Six Years Later

PART III

WHEN YOU LEAST EXPECT IT

"That's quite the victory. You should be very pleased, Cooper."

I'm too busy staring at the settlement in my hands to focus on celebrations or participate in a round of back-patting.

All legal fees are paid.

Trust funds from relatives I never knew are now available to access.

No contact—the condition I added agreed upon.

But it's the amendment my parents added that I keep rereading. It's hush money at best. They'll do anything to save their reputation and re-stabilize their standing in society.

I've spent years fighting for what's rightfully mine, what was taken from me illegally, that I'll never get back . . . like other things, and people . . .

Specifically, Story.

But like my lawyer said, this is a victory in most ways. I

34

Story

New York City

"IT'S AN AMAZING TURNOUT, STORY." Lila one-arm hugs me since her other hand is busy holding Reed's hand. "You know how I feel about your photography already, but I'm blown away by this exhibit. I'm so proud of you."

"Thank you. That means so much to me. *Annnnd*," I say, booping Reed on the nose. "I wouldn't have been able to do this without your help."

I kneel, smiling while looking into those hazel eyes of his. "What do you think, buddy?"

"I'm proud of you, too, Mommy." Releasing Lila, his arms come around my neck in a tight squeeze. Wobbling on my heels, I balance by hugging him right back, forgetting that he's already too tall to do this anymore. Kneeling definitely gives him the advantage in this situation to his average height mom.

"Thank you, sweetie. That means even more to me."

When he smiles, getting that look in his eyes like I'm his whole world, I see so much of his dad in him. My heart beats a little faster as if he's near me again. Maybe because he never really left, still taking up time in my head and space in my heart.

Lila takes his hand again, and says, "We should get going and let the artiste do her thing. I also promised Jake we'd get Shake Shack on the way home. Bribery is about the only thing I can do to get him to leave his room and those computer games behind."

"Whatever works, right?"

"We do what we can." Understanding is exchanged in a look and a nod. We're both survivors in different ways, but single motherhood was an unexpected turn that continued to bond us together. Lila moved her son to the city five years ago after I had been in my new job for six months. Now she runs a donut shop in Brooklyn that she's turned into a word-of-mouth sensation. "I'm keeping Reed for the night since I'm off in the morning."

"You don't have to do that."

"I do. It's the only way I can force you to have some fun. Drink some wine, mingle," she says, laughing and bobbing her head. Raising an eyebrow, she mouths, "Get laid."

I roll my eyes. "That's what got me into this." I won't ever call my son a mess in this context because for him, I would go through everything all over again. But dating and sex, together or individually, are really the last thing I have time for between being a mommy to a five-year-old, my day as a financial analyst, and my photography that I'm trying my best to turn from a hobby into my profession.

Who has room for anything else? *Not me.*

After she retrieves Jake from the hors d'oeuvre buffet, I

walk them out after another warm embrace. Kissing my boy on top of his head, I can't help but notice how much darker his hair is getting as he grows older.

I wave goodbye through the window before getting dragged away to "talk up" my pieces to sell.

After a few hours, my heels start to kill my feet. I get a glass of wine, my first all evening, and head for a barstool hidden near the main desk to sit for a minute. Kathy, the gallery director, says, "You've sold five pieces with three options to sell the Haywood collection."

"At these price points?"

"I told you we weren't charging enough."

High four figures seemed like a lot for an unknown artist, but I'm not going to argue. She adds, "We're going to test the market on Tuesday with the remaining pieces. Fifteen to twenty-five thousand with a small discount for the collections."

"I want to act like that isn't blowing my mind, but it's impossible." I start to calculate my percentage, and it looks like Reed and I can take that Disney vacation, after all. I'll drink to that.

Kathy and the other gallery employees love to guess who will buy what, and tonight's no different. They even have a betting pool. Louise is in the lead, judging the clientele. She says, "*Reed.*" My eyes dart around the gallery, looking for my son, but then I realize she's referring to the photograph. She laughs, which makes me uncomfortable. "He's been there for ten minutes, but he's not in the market for real art. Just stopping by after a spaghetti dinner next door."

I get up and start to browse around the expansive room. The lights are bright on the photographs but dimmed in the rest of the gallery. While talking with patrons and doing an interview for *Art Times New York*, I have found that the pace has been fast, but I've had pockets of moments to myself. I couldn't have designed a better evening.

A large group leaves, and it feels like the place is clearing out. I check my watch. It's almost nine o'clock, so there's only a short time left. I shake hands with a man who fell in love with one I named *Rat*. I thought I was being so ironic since it's a cat I caught on film climbing out of the gutter. He got the concept and bought it.

Standing there, ten feet behind a man who makes my breathing deepen, I stare at the back of his head.

The shoulders.

The height.

The build.

The hair.

If it were another time and place, another life altogether, I'd swear I was staring at the man I once thought I'd be with forever . . . as he stares at the face of our son.

I take another sip of wine, but the taste never really did much for me. It's a nice crutch at the moment. I walk closer, close enough that when the wind sneaks through the front door, I find myself closing my eyes and remembering him.

"If you don't talk to him," Kathy whispers in my ear, startling me out of my memories, "I will. Sweet baby Jesus, I will."

I laugh softly, covering my mouth with my hand. Hip bumping her to send her back to the desk, I mouth, "He's all mine."

"You go get him, girl."

"Shh." I laugh again, a little louder.

He shifts but doesn't turn back. I take a deep breath, another sip for courage, and then walk toward *him*. It's a name I don't say anymore, but it lies on the tip of my tongue, so desperate to taste it again.

I'm not sure if I even want it to be him. I'm not dressed for the occasion of running into my ex-boyfriend, so I don't know if I'll be relieved if it's not. What nonsense am I talking about? *It's not him.* Don't be ridiculous. How would he be at my gallery opening in the middle of the city? What are the odds of that?

The film.

The party.

The coffee shop.

Considering our history, I'm not sure it would be that far-fetched to run into *him*. But this isn't Atterton. *It's New York City.*

Just in case, I stand close behind and put *him* to the test. "Didn't mean to sneak up on you."

His head drops forward as if he needs a moment. Because of me? Or? Turning his head to the side, he doesn't look back, but replies, "Sometimes life does that."

I find myself soaking this in—the hope, the coincidence, and the good memories we once made. "When you least expect it." I stand next to him, not daring to look into the green eyes I still have memorized. Despite trying to remember his face during the downfall like I promised, I never could get over seeing him lying next to me, looking at me like I was his whole world. Maybe I was for a short time.

He was mine.

Now my world is vastly different.

We both slowly turn, and when I lay my eyes on *him* again, I feel my heart beating for the first time in years. "Hi," I say, feeling it's only right since I'm the host tonight.

"Hi." His voice is still so familiar but with an older tone running through it. He must be twenty-eight based on the month, so maybe life has deepened it.

"What brings you into the gallery?"

He looks behind him, and says, "The restaurant next door."

"Woot!" I hear Louise and the slap of a high-five as she scores another off him.

Chuckling, he says, "They're happy."

"Yeah." All the rehearsed scripts I had written, practiced, and stored just in case this day ever came are forgotten, some of the anger as well. Is that what time does? Dulls the edges? *We can only be so lucky.*

I'm not disappointed in his answer, but would I feel better if he had looked me up?

Glancing at the photo, he turns back to me. "These are incredible."

That's when I realize which piece he's been standing in front of for the past ten minutes. My heart starts pounding for different reasons. "Thank you." The words come rushed as panic sets in. "Did you see the Atterton collection?"

"No. I was drawn to this one when I walked in." He moves closer. "Those eyes . . ." Looking back at me, he adds, "Those are your eyes."

I take two steps back, hoping he follows. The placard with the name *REED* printed on it is just one peek away. "It's over here," I say, ignoring the comment.

"Yes, I'd like to see the collection," he responds as if the question is still fresh in the air.

Unlike the rest of my collection, the four photos hang in a quad. "They just make more sense together than apart."

"Some things are meant to be."

I hadn't allowed myself the investment in him, purposely avoiding doing a once-over. But when his eyes are on the art, I give myself the luxury. Dress pants and a white shirt that was probably crisper at the start of the day. Black tie to match the pants. He looks very handsome and ever the businessman . . . attorney like he wanted to be? My nerves get the better of me. "It's weird standing here with you again. Not that we've ever stood together in this gallery, or in any gallery for that matter, but you know what I mean."

He slides his fingers through his hair—*some habits never die*—and he chuckles. I didn't realize how much I'd missed the sound until hearing it again. "I do," he replies with a playful elbow nudge. "And I have to agree."

It's been six years, but there's so much that's different about him, not an ounce of arrogance rolling off him. And his green eyes, like emeralds the first time I saw them, don't hold the same intensity they once did. I met a troubled boy willing to burn down the world for me. I don't know what he's been through, but the vibrancy of the green has settled into the aftermath.

He shifts, pulling his attention from the walls and putting it on me. "It's been a long fucking time, Story Salenger with an E."

A sadness permeates the air between us. For me, it's that I know our time is coming to a close. Whether this is good for me remains to be seen, but here in the now, I'm loving every second. "It sure has, Cooper Haywood."

"Tell me if I'm out of line, but—"

"You ready to go, Cooper?"

Her slender fingers lie over his upper arm, the red nails matching a red flag in a bullfight. Her body *almost* presses to him as if she had to stop herself. The blonde in the heels with sky-high legs and the A-line skirt to show them off sucks the breath from my chest.

His date? Girlfriend? Wife? *Oh, shit.* I look at her hand and then to his, but no rings are wrapped around the finger that counts. As I die inside, everything moves in slow motion. His gaze falls to the floor before reality returns and time speeds back up. He says, "This is the photographer I was telling you about."

Her blue eyes light up like she's meeting a celebrity. "You're very talented. Cooper saw the exhibit and insisted we stop. We didn't even know it was yours until we saw the name on the wall. Incredible work. I, especially, love . . ." She points. "The empty bottle beside the bed."

That bottle from the after the first time Cooper and I had sex, the first time I'd been with anyone, the first time I fell in love. So many firsts are wrapped up in that photo. *So many are wrapped up in him.*

I'm not sure at what point I tuned her out, but I stare at Cooper like he just broke my heart again. "If you'll excuse—"

"The glove. The bottle. The bed. And the rain outside the coffee shop." The words shoot from his tongue as if he's had them locked and loaded for years.

"You remember?"

"How could I forget? I still have the originals you gave me."

I laugh, a little embarrassed now. "I can't believe you held on to those."

She says, "I'm Heather, by the way. Cooper told me you went to college together?"

My gaze travels from her to him. "Story," I reply, shaking her hand. "Yeah, we're old college chums." The three of us stand there awkwardly with the laughter dying between us. That's my cue to leave. "Thanks for stopping by. It was great to see you."

With our eyes on each other, the intensity returns, piercing me in ways that I haven't felt in years, fixing me to the spot. He asks, "Heather, do you mind giving us a minute?"

"No problem. I'll just wait outside." To me, she says, "It was a real pleasure to meet you."

"Thank you for coming."

As soon as she walks away, he says, "I work with Heather. Nothing more."

"I almost expected her to be Camille," I snap back.

He shoves his hands in his pockets and shakes his head. "No."

Despite how honest he appears, my guard is still up. "I have no right to say anything, even if you were dating, so don't explain for my benefit."

"I want to." Moving into my personal space, he doesn't make apologies. He stakes a claim. "We once said the universe brought us together."

"I don't have room in my life to believe in such frivolous notions anymore." I want to tell him I have a son to protect at all costs. I can't let the innocence I once had put us in jeopardy. "Everything is cause and effect. We both know that all too well."

"Okay. You held an opening, and I showed up. Cause and effect. We can call it whatever we want, but have coffee with me?"

Taken back, I stare at him like he's a lunatic off the street. My hands fly up in front of me. "Slow down. I'm seeing you for the first time in years, and you want to have coffee?" I stab my chest. "With me?"

"With you, I do." His eagerness is slightly contagious, but I temper myself.

"Like you didn't give up on us? Like you fought for me?" My thoughts run wild, not quite comprehending how we got from shouting on a street in Atterton six years ago to standing here together cordially as though none of that happened. "I don't think that's a good idea."

"Maybe a drink, if that suits you better?"

"It's not the liquid, Cooper. It's the history." I'm not sure I'm strong enough to revisit that part of my life. Shifting, I need distance and air to breathe as if he's sucking it right out of me. I remember how much we consumed each other. I remember because when we went our separate ways, there was nothing left of me. I spent days, weeks, months, and years putting myself back together piece by broken piece.

I can't go through that again with him.

"I want to buy one of your pieces." I almost ask which one, but I don't need to. I already know the answer before he says, "*Reed.*"

And that's the reason I agree. "I'm free for coffee."

"Excellent." His smile is just as charming as it always was, the age only making him more handsome. *Damn him.*

35

Cooper

"Dr. Haywood?"

"Hm?" I scan the list of symptoms and am glad I don't see anything popping out at me. Growth and weight are tracking—

"Dr. Haywood?" I look up from the chart. With a purple stethoscope around her neck and dipping into the pocket of her white jacket, Heather is waiting in front of me as if I've missed the question. "What is it, Dr. Lazarus?"

She adjusts the tortoise-framed glasses with fake lenses on her nose. She once told me that she started wearing them in medical school to distract from her attractiveness. She started getting more respect after that. It wasn't a confession to brag but more a frustration that she had to do it at all. I imagine it would be quite maddening. She's a bright doctor, and for that alone, she's always had my respect. "I was saying I had a lovely time last night."

"The food was good." The food was fuel at best since it had very little flavor. At Heather's suggestion, we tried the restaurant. I was working late and hadn't eaten, and we had work to discuss. *Two birds. One stone.*

When we arrived, it crossed my mind that maybe I'd been set up. The lights were too low, and the piped music playing in the background didn't give a sense that we were in Italy but more of a themed tourist trap. We got the opportunity to discuss the new schedules, but other than that, the only thing that redeemed the night was the gallery next door.

We've become friends over the past two years . . . Well, not friends who hang out, but it's pleasant to see her at work when our paths cross. Though last night was probably a mistake. It will probably be best if we keep our meals relegated to the break room or cafeteria downstairs.

"I appreciate you going after my date canceled."

New information. "No worries. I have to eat."

"Me, too." She laughs but catches herself, the wave of her hand and small shake is giving me different vibes than usual. I'm getting the distinct impression she's suggesting we make a move toward an after-hours relationship. Leaning in, she whispers, "If I'm way off base, Cooper, please tell me."

Lowering the medical chart, I'm at a loss for words, which is something I'm not used to. I've had a few relations, but the ship portion of that sailed with Story a long time ago.

It's not you, it's me feels too cliché, even if it fits the situation. "I'm not in a place to date." Maybe too blunt, but these days, I have no room for much else. When she starts fidgeting with the stethoscope, guilt comes over me.

I don't owe her an explanation or details of why I don't put myself out there anymore, how I watched the woman I love walk away in the middle of a spring storm, or that I spent years fighting my parents in court. That food has no flavor because I miss eating ramen in bed with Story, or how I never minded driving the extra three miles in Atterton to get her favorite chicken sandwich because I selfishly liked the additional time with her.

I don't share my sins of setting Troy Hogan up to take a fall just so I could shoot my shot with his girl. Or the worst of them all, driving fifty in a thirty and slamming into the back of a pickup truck that would set off a chain of events leading to the murder of Story's mother.

No, I'll keep that inside, not buried but right on the surface of any joy I might find. She thought her picker was broken before we met, but I'm the bad guy Story Salenger never saw coming. I'm not fit to be with anyone else, not wanting to inflict that pain on another.

As colleagues, I respect Heather enough to say, "I know it's hard to put yourself out there, and I do appreciate you taking the temperature of where things stand between us. I've not dated in a long time, not since . . ." I won't say her name for fear of jinxing it. "To be completely up front, Heather, I wasn't honest before. I'm actually meeting someone who I'm interested in for coffee, so I don't think that would be fair to either of you if I accepted your offer."

Empathy shapes her smile. "I think that's the nicest *no* I've ever received. Thank you for your honesty, Dr. Haywood." She takes the chart from the hook next door, and says, "And for the record, I'm rooting for you."

So am I. I open the door and see the worried mom pacing and her daughter standing on the exam table. Giving the little girl a helping hand, I ask, "Who's this little punkin?"

IT FEELS stalkerish to stare at Story without her knowledge.

I do it anyway.

Expecting to see a girl in flannel pajamas or workout pants that were never used for working out and an Atterton sweatshirt, it takes my mind a second to replace the image with the woman before me. A fitted white shirt with big sleeves that end above her elbows, fitted dark jeans that don't hit her crossed ankles, and red shoes with no heel.

Other than at my parents' parties, I've never seen her that dressed up.

Her hair is similar to how I remember—on the darker brown side with highlights from the sun with fewer flyaways and long lashes that draw your eyes to hers. She looks younger than her years and probably still gets carded. It's those lips, the natural color that I loved turning pink and then a deep rose color from kissing, that have my heart aching in my chest.

She's not mine, but I'm starting to wonder if she ever was. Maybe I was just lucky enough to have her touch my life for a short time. Maybe the universe always intended her to find love elsewhere. It wouldn't surprise me. There's no wiping my slate clean.

I can't help but think I need to drink her in, the sight of her the anti-venom I need to get used to seeing her again and in proximity. Running into her . . . if that's what we can call it since I was standing in the middle of her exhibit on Thursday night, was a shock to my system, a volt of energy reviving parts of me that I thought had died along with our relationship.

I'll be sitting across from her for as long as a cup of coffee takes to drink. I swear to fucking God, this is about to be the slowest cup of coffee in history.

I move in, making sure she sees me. The effort is not

needed since her eyes find me the moment I come around the large topiary in the garden seating of the restaurant she chose. "And here I showed up early so I wouldn't keep you waiting."

She stands, her hands grabbing onto my arms to lean in and greet me before I think she realizes it. Holding her, I flex my fingers around her forearms. Story laughs. "Sorry," she says, starting to pull away. "I'm used to New York greetings."

"Yeah, me too." Her skin is soft under my fingertips, that jolt sending a shock to my heart again. I don't want to let go. *Please don't let go, Story.* "We still can."

"I don't think that's wise." *She's probably right.* Her hands release me, and she sits down.

I'm about to scoot her chair in, but she does it first. The gentleman is not a role I often play these days since I don't date. But she's setting her boundaries before we've taken the first sip.

Sitting across from her, I notice that her cup is already half-empty. *Fuck.* That gives me four, maybe five sips before she's going to be leaving me. A server comes with menus and a smile. She and Story have spent time together, judging by the relaxed smiles they exchanged. "May I get you something to drink, sir?" the server asks when she turns to me.

"What's the largest coffee you have?"

"We have ten, twelve, or sixteen."

"Sixteen, please."

"We also have a special on mimosas and Bloody Marys for brunch."

Story says, "A spicy Bloody Mary and another top off on the water, please." She looks at me as if we're a tag team.

"And a glass of water."

Tapping the menus she set on the table, the server adds, "Take a look, and I'll be back shortly with your drink order."

"Thank you." I think I just scored more time with that order alone.

"I'm starved," Story says, her eyes barely seen above the menu. I'm not upset that she wants to eat. The menu is tipped forward, and she leans in. "Remember how we used to eat a whole meal for two for under two dollars?" Her smile is radiant, the memories as she looks at me the only light shining in her eyes. Waggling the menu, she shakes her head. "Now, we can't even get a side of toast for under four dollars."

I confess, "I still eat cup of noodles sometimes."

"So do I. Easy to make and just hits the spot sometimes."

I don't want to look away from her, from her eyes with the golden centers to the green pastures of her irises. They're still a unique coloring. It's the eyes in the photo titled *REED* that drew me into the gallery. Reed with her eye color and my hair . . . "Guess some things never change."

"Not much," she adds with her gaze back on the menu. She shrugs. "But I guess some things do."

The remark feels pointed, though she doesn't follow it up. Should I? Should I push for more details that she doesn't owe?

The server delivers the drinks, and we place our order. I added five sides to make this brunch last for hours. As soon as we're alone again, Story asks, "You must be starving as well?"

"Famished."

She takes a long pull of her cocktail. "Should we get the small talk out of the way before getting down to business?"

I'll take whatever I can get with her if it means more time. "Sure. Do we start with our résumés or the weather, in what part of the city we live or what we like to do in our free time?"

Her giggle is light, but it's authentic. "You're right. We never really were ones for petty conversations."

"They're not petty. They're just not us."

"No," she says, spinning the cocktail glass by the base. "No, we're more jump right into the deep end kind of people."

I don't tell her that's not me anymore. Lessons learned the hard way made me reevaluate everything, including my approach to life. Given a second chance made me more cautious. I should have treated our relationship with more care back then. Maybe I wouldn't be sitting across from her like strangers trying to find something to talk about now.

She adds, "Or were," reading my mind. Maybe life has thrown her curveballs that landed wrong as well. Taking another sip, she pushes it away like it's all she intends to drink. She never was one much for alcohol. I'm not either anymore. "What did you want to talk about, Cooper?" Her tongue dips out and glides as if she wants to lick every bit of my name from her lips.

I didn't get the chance to take her in the way I would have liked the other night like I do now. She's so fucking beautiful that it's hard to think clearly in her presence, much less protect myself.

Is that what I need to do? Protect myself from the one person I never needed to?

How do I talk about the photograph? What do I say? It pulled me in off the street before I saw the name of the artist. But I knew, seeing something more in the eyes that made me walk into that gallery.

Passing her film quote test with flying colors was easy. It makes me curious how she could ever think I'd forget something that only the two of us shared. *Never.* Not one second of us is forgotten. I often travel back in my memories just to feel us, to feel anything again, to see her smile, and have her laughter ring in my ears.

I drink water, using the time to get reacquainted with reality again. "We had a bad ending." Not sure what else to say.

"Sometimes, that's all we get." That doesn't sound like the Story I used to know. *Has life treated her harshly or just me?* Her gaze travels across the garden away from mine. She's hiding her real feelings, which isn't something she did before. But accepting the fact that she's not that same girl and I'm a long way from the same guy is near impossible right now.

This may take a few times seeing each other to keep my thoughts with her in the present, to us in the now instead of reliving the memories. We'll never be those people again. So is this the closure that will allow me to move on, to change the direction of my life for good?

I'll hate it. Roaming this world without her, pretending that the best thing I ever had I lost, kissing another woman in the morning like someone could replace the woman across from me now. The void I thought this meeting could fill grows wider instead.

The food delivery offers breathing room, and when I catch my breath coming harder, I know I'm not alone. She takes a bite.

I pick up my fork and knife, and say, "Let's talk about Reed."

She practically spews her food and starts hacking. Grabbing her throat, she continues coughing until she drinks some water. *That tells me all I need to know.*

Having it confirmed is not what I expected today.

I put off my feelings, not wanting to interject hope or disappointment or . . . whatever else I'm supposed to be feeling into this. She hasn't said the words, but I feel the truth between us. From the fear in her eyes, she does, too.

Still trying to catch her breath, she exhales a shaky breath. "It's a . . ." She takes a breath in, then drinks more water. "It's one of my most talked about creations."

Narrowing my eyes, I study how her eyes can't meet mine and the words as curated as her collection. I set my utensils down and sit back in the chair, thinking we're going to be here a while. "I'm not mad, Story."

"Mad?" I never understood how someone who'd been through such a tragedy had managed to hold on to her innocence. Not sexually, but the purity of who she was without being tainted by the events. She still does that very well, even if she knows exactly what I'm talking about.

"I don't blame you for what you did."

Staring at me from across the table, she's rattled by my words. She sets the glass down before the water tips over the edge. "What did I do?"

The server returns to deliver napkins and check on us. "We're fine," I reply, my eyes never leaving Story's. When she leaves, I add, "I'm fairly certain you remember my name."

"Cooper." Tears threaten her eyes. She looks down to dab the napkin at the corners.

"Cooper . . ." I leave it there for her to fill out the rest.

Looking back up, she says, "Cooper Haywood."

"Cooper *Reed* Haywood." I grin, not because I take pleasure in upsetting her, but it hits me as hard as it does her. *I have a son.*

36

Story

I feel sick.

Panic rises like bile up my throat, and I wrap my arm over my stomach, hoping to hold in the contents.

Now I regret not easing into this conversation with the small talk we hate so much. *Is it too late?* "The weather has really warmed up today." I use my napkin to fan myself though the shade has kept me cool.

Cooper shifts in his seat and then rests his elbows on either side of the plate. Grasping his hands together, he bounces his chin to them a few times. I wasn't expecting to see him at the gallery, dressed fairly ordinary in jeans and a white button-up shirt as if he wanted to blend in.

That's not how he looks today. The clothes are nice, similar even—darker jeans, a black button-up—but it's his hair—enough gel to keep the waves tamed, but not so much that his hair doesn't look incredibly soft. Eyes that it's a shame are hidden behind sunglasses when he arrived are hitting me with their full vibrancy now. That jaw that could cut ice has the lightest covering of scruff as if he's chosen to take the day off from shaving. Are Sundays his days to relax, or did he go for a run this morning? Is the six-pack I once dragged a tongue over hidden under button numbers two, three, and four?

Anger rolls through me. How can I find an ounce of attraction to a man who caused such devastation? I hate myself more for laying that back at his feet. Have I learned nothing? I need to hold on to the anger. Forgiveness could lead to opening the door to him, and once a Haywood is allowed entrance to your life, they destroy the whole thing.

"I think we're past the weather. Let's circle back to Reed and how the child in the photo shares *your* eyes and *my* name."

He sees through me, something he always did. I could try to beat around the bush to buy time or even eat brunch like this isn't going to always go back to my son. I pick up my fork to distract one of us, though I'm not sure which one.

"Hey," he says, breaking through my frenzied thoughts. Lowering his hands to his lap, he sits forward. "Talk to me."

"I can explain."

"I know you can, Story." He sits back again, settling in for more than a casual chat over coffee. "I want to hear everything. You don't have to hold back with me."

He's too calm, too in control of his emotions when it feels like our next storm is brewing inside me. Did he already know? I can't read his mood, his expression, or even his tone like I used to. Is he happy about this news or upset? Is he trying to set me up to take me to court, or is he being sincere?

Who am I kidding?

I can't hide any longer—hide in plain sight, living my life, as I've done for the past six years.

Reed looks just like him, but with my hazel eyes. I won't be able to lie. Regret fills me as my heart starts beating erratically. I should have never entered the photo into the collection. It's not even for sale. It's just near and dear to my heart for obvious reasons.

I'll take him. I'll take him somewhere far away if I'm threatened.

I need to protect my son. If Cooper knows, he could try to take him from me. He'll win because I withheld the information. No judge will believe the girl from the wrong side of the tracks versus a name synonymous with prestige in this city. Cooper has more money than the devil. I can't fight against that. My good intentions will never win against the evil of Haywood money.

Panicking again, I feel my hands begin to shake. Before I have time to tuck them under the table, he reaches over and covers one. "I meant what I said. I don't blame you for what you did." I hadn't noticed how the panic had subsided or how my hands calmed under his. I didn't notice until he sat back again. "I'm not mad. I'm . . ." Now he struggles to find the words like I do.

He dips his gaze to the napkin in his lap. If I were to take a photo of him, I'd name it *Defeated Man*.

The past doesn't weigh me down so much when I realize how much of the burden he's been carrying. Two minutes ago, I almost went to the bathroom and left, ready to disappear until my son . . . *our* son turned eighteen. But when Cooper looks up, he has tears in his eyes, muting the brighter green into a soothing sage, though I find no comfort in the downfall of Cooper Haywood. He is a victim of his circumstances.

The same as I am.

He says, "You saved him, which is something no one did for me."

My heart pangs in my chest, every heartstring that once connected me to this man reattaches. I can't let my guard down.

"Story . . ." The reverence in his voice is heard as if it's the lifeline he's clinging to. Is that what he thinks I can do? Save him by sacrificing my son to the Haywood family tree? "Tell me the truth, Story."

There's no anger in his words, nothing but pain defacing his features. I hate how weak I feel. My mom buried us in her lies. I would never want to encumber Reed the same way. I'm not sure what to say, so I stick to silence and try to navigate through the conversation.

Cooper turns his attention to his coffee and takes a drink. When he lowers it again, he says, "I have no contact with my family."

"I don't know what to say to that." I twist the cloth napkin in my lap. "I'm sorry or good for you?"

An easy chuckle breaks through the heaviness, freeing his lips to smile. "The latter probably works best. I sued them."

Oh. "I didn't expect you to say that. That must have been very difficult to go through."

"To go through, yes. To do," he says, shaking his head. "Not at all. I should have done it sooner. It might have saved us." His gaze drops with his chin. When he peeks back up, I can see he's embarrassed—something I never saw on him when we were dating. A light pink even appearing on the apples of his cheeks.

If he ever wanted to charm a woman, that would do it. Humble sincerity is very attractive on him.

"I meant . . ." He laughs again, knowing there's not really a way to row this boat backward. With a smile still in place, he sighs. "I meant what I said. If I'd done it sooner, we might still be together. I say this knowing that doesn't change what happened to your mother."

Shifting in my discomfort, I say, "I'm not in a place to revisit that part of our past. Not yet."

Yet? Dammit. Why'd I say that like there will be more opportunities? I can't put my life or Reed's in jeopardy by allowing a man who could potentially steal my heart again back in. No, I can't have that because I don't know where this is going, but it's not ending with us back together or becoming besties. "We're having brunch, Cooper. That's all."

He nods once. "I understand."

Then I start to think that maybe this was all planned. Hiding in plain sight under my real name wasn't hiding at all. I could have always been easily found if someone was looking. This could be a ruse to break me down and get me to trust him again. "If forgiveness is what you're seeking or you're in a program where you contact—"

"I'm not. I know forgiveness isn't possible." There's no life in his eyes, but I've seen a glimmer of it a few times, always when he smiles.

He's made no move to threaten me, said nothing to set off alarms. Neither my own safety nor Reed's has felt like it's on the line. I'm sensitive to certain topics, but that's to be expected. I'm not sure that he's as awful as I've imagined him to be for the past six years. I need to suss out the situation before giving him the potential ammo he needs to use against me.

The facts are right in front of us.

1. *He knows Reed is his son.*
2. *He knows how to find me.*

3. *The universe is definitely conspiring against me.*

I ASK, "Why did you sue your parents?"

"Because I was seventeen when they forced me to sign everything over to them as guardians. I had no representation, and I was a minor. There was nothing legal about the proceeding. But as an attorney, my father knew that," he answers without hesitation. "I had trust funds that were rightfully mine that they illegally changed the age in which I could access. They even buried them in a Swiss bank account that gave them the oversight to use the money how they saw fit. It was a fucking nightmare."

"You sued them for money?" Even I hear the judgment in the flatness of my voice.

"I did. Maybe you would have done things differently, taken a higher road. You were always more noble than me. I used the only tool I had to hurt them and to end the manipulations. Money."

Raising my hands, I swing them across an imaginary marquee. "I would have thought this would be headline news. Your family is so well-known."

He takes another sip of coffee. Each minute that passes seems to put us both more at ease. And with that ease, I see *him* again, the man I loved so fiercely that I would have forgiven him for what happened if he'd only fought for me. "The last thing my parents want is a scandal. I got what's rightfully mine, but they still retain their fortune."

I grow more in awe of him with each addition to the story. Not because he went to their level, but because he didn't. He just beat them at their own game. They can afford the best lawyers in the world, but he won. "And you won? Amazing."

"I won everything I fought for if I signed an NDA and didn't tell anyone."

I tilt my head and lean forward, relishing this news. I take a bite of my food and then take a sip of my watered-down Bloody Mary. "Can I ask you something personal?"

He picks up his fork and knife and starts in on the scrambled eggs I know are cold. "Of course."

Leaning in again, I check our surroundings for spies and eavesdroppers. Since the coast is clear, I whisper, "How good did that revenge taste?"

He swallows his food and then leans in, mimicking me. "Delicious."

Grinning, I sit back. "God, I wish I could have been there. And when I say there, I mean a fly on the wall when they'd lost it all, including you. They thought money and love were the same thing."

"Still do."

Because the tension has mellowed, I start eating again. "I'm not usually supportive of hurting others, but your parents . . ." I bite my tongue. He may have sued them, but does anyone really want to hear that their parents are monsters? That brings me back to what he said earlier.

"I don't blame you . . . I'm not mad . . . You saved him, something no one did for me."

Maybe he's telling the truth. Maybe I can trust him.

I didn't have a father in my life, so I never knew what I was missing, but Calliope kept my hands full anyway. I have the hindsight to look back and pick the moments I love to remember. I'm still shuffling through the ones I want to forget. But my Reed, my sweet son, deserves the world . . . *And his dad.*

Only if Cooper has really cut off contact with his family. I search his eyes for something that will expose the lie, but I only find the same raw honesty he used to have when he'd tell me he loved me.

I should think this over and not make any rash decisions. But my soul is still drawn to him, my heart recalling how good we once were together. We didn't break us apart. We lost faith and let others intervene.

Legally, he's risking everything by sharing this information with me. I'm confused why he would fight for years to win if he's willing to risk it all if I open my mouth to the press. Left with only one question, I ask, "If you had to sign a nondisclosure agreement to get the money, why did you tell me?"

"It's all I have to give as a guarantee that you can trust me."

37

Cooper

Story has been troubling her bottom lip for the past three minutes. I've kept track of the time.

On the one hand, I appreciate how protective she is of her, *of our*, son. I honestly could have never asked for a better mother for my kids. On the other hand, she holds all the cards; everything has been laid on the table. All she has to do is make a phone call to a reporter or post the settlement details online. Tell a friend who likes to gossip, or use it against me to keep our son, my son, from me.

I understand the time she's taking to weigh the options. Every second kills an ounce of hope I was admittedly, stupidly, holding on to inside.

"You once promised me," she says, "that you would never hurt me."

"I remember." I remember breaking that promise every day of my life. How could I have known what I did as a teenager would come back to haunt me? She'll never forgive me for that, but I don't forgive myself either.

"I left my door unlocked for you. The other side of the bed remained empty until the day I moved out. I can't watch *Breakfast at Tiffany's* on Christmas anymore because instead of my mom, I think of you."

"It's a sad movie anyway."

She scoffs in laughter as tears spring to her eyes. "You once said we're all a little sad, but some of us are better at hiding it than others. I didn't really understand what you meant back then. I do now."

"I'm sorry for stealing your sunshine, Story."

"It's still here behind the clouds."

The server shows up and starts clearing the plates. "Anything else?"

"I'm good," I reply, sitting back to give her space but keeping my eyes on the woman across from me as this meal starts wrapping up. Still watching and waiting for her to open all the way up. "Story?"

She pauses, glancing at the server, but when she looks at me again, she says, "I think I'm good."

"Yeah?"

"Mm-hmm." There's a certainty to her tone and the confident nod of her head that has me feeling the progress we've made. I just hope we can hold on to it.

When the server sets the bill down, I reach for my wallet and hand my card over just before she leaves the table. "I'd like to get this."

Story says, "Thank you."

"You're welcome."

An awkwardness is quick to invade the empty table between us, but then she says, "Cooper? I've been afraid to ask you something." She shrugs. "Many things, actually, but we don't have time for that."

"I have the time."

She smiles, one filled with that sunshine we mentioned. "Unfortunately, I don't." She taps her watch. "Not today." *Another day?*

My back straightens to attention because she genuinely looks disappointed. I just don't think I can push her into another meeting. It's her call what happens next. Again, she holds all the cards because I willingly took the risk and gave them freely. I wouldn't have done that for anyone else.

Knowing she has other places to be today, our time feels rushed, so I ask, "What was it that you wanted to ask me? You can ask me anything."

She takes a sip of her water, then leans in conspiratorially. "You don't owe me the answer, Cooper." I love hearing her say my name without hate embodied in it. "But I don't see a ring or even an indentation where one used to be. You said you're not dating Heather, but did you marry Camille?"

"Camille?" I practically pull a muscle in my neck from jerking back. I start laughing from the mere suggestion. "Camille Arden?"

Story is not amused.

My jaw drops. "You're serious?"

"Of course, I'm serious." Waving her hand in front of her, she adds, "Clearly, you didn't by that reaction, but she told me she would and that you would never marry someone like me."

Shaking my head in disbelief, I drop my jaw even further. "She said I wouldn't marry someone clever, beautiful, kind with the biggest heart, thoughtful, and intelligent, someone who is willing to put in the work whether it comes to a job, school, or a relationship? I'm confused what kind of person she'd think I'd marry if I wouldn't want those attributes?"

She tries to restrain her grin, but one side rises and then

the other. Pink spreads across her cheeks right before she says, "You always were a charmer."

"If I could charm you, Story Salenger, I would, but I have a feeling you're resistant to anything to do with a Haywood."

"Except one." The quietest of gasps is heard as she sucks in a breath that she's now holding. With her pretty hazel eyes wide with worry, she says, "I, um—" She gets to her feet and grabs her purse, but it slips from her hands from hurrying.

Story's always made my heart beat erratically, but this time, it's a race against time. I stand, but not wanting to make a scene, I whisper, "Tell me, Story. Please."

Her gaze is darting around as her eyes fill with tears. "Not here," she says, passing me and rushing toward the exit.

The server comes over and sets my card down again. "Sorry, I got pulled into the kitchen."

I scribble my name and copy the cost of the meals for the tip. Dashing through the inside of the restaurant, I don't see her. I run outside and frantically look both ways. But there's no fucking sign of her. "Fuck."

People waiting in line for the restaurant move farther away from me. When a mother covers her child's ears with her hands and puts herself between us, I huff. "Sorry."

Scrubbing my hands over my face, I take a deep breath and then exhale just as slowly.

"Cooper?"

I turn around.

Story's standing there, not ten feet from me. I close the gap, keeping two between us.

The tears that were in her eyes earlier aren't there now. The fear I heard in her voice is nowhere to be found. Instead, I'm greeted with a soft smile and a peek into her soul. I missed seeing her look at me like this, like we have a lifetime ahead of us.

She says, "I think you should meet your son."

Story

"Slow down," Lila yells to Jake. When he stops ahead, she redirects her attention to me. "You're going to need to back up, Story. How the hell does Cooper Haywood know he is Reed's sperm donor?"

I nod toward Reed on the other side of me, and whisper, "Don't call him that."

"Wow, you're already defending him? That must have been a damn good brunch last week."

I stop, my hand tightening on Reed's. "What's wrong? Why are you so angry?"

With her eyes on her own son, she whispers, "He wasn't here to pick up the pieces." When Jake starts walking back toward us, she looks at me. "I was. It wasn't pretty. In fact, it was damn messy."

Reed says, "She says damn a lot, Mommy."

"I know. Don't you say it, though. Okay, buddy?"

He nods, so I turn back to Lila, giving her scolding wide eyes before we start walking again. She sighs, but then continues, "Look, Story, his last name gives him access to money and lawyers that you won't be able to compete with. If Cooper wants this kid, or worse, his parents want a second chance, you'll lose him."

"Do you not think all of this has been running like a loop inside my head? I slept on his floor last night just to be near him and spent half the night staring at this perfect human who's kind and smart—"

"Just like the woman who raised him."

Hooking arms with her, I pull her close. "I appreciate that." Jake takes Reed's hand. "No more than five feet ahead, guys," I remind them of our rule. "I trust him, Lila. I may be wrong, and if I am, I'll pay the ultimate price. But he told me things that give me faith that he's being honest."

"Like what?"

We round the corner, and the boys take off running. They know once there are no streets between us and the park, they're good to go.

Navigating between what's in the NDA and what else he told me is more difficult when put on the spot. That's what sold me. He put his heart and fortune on the line for me, entrusting me with that information. He might be the greatest liar who ever lived, but I don't think so. I think he's being truthful.

I reply, "He's no longer in contact with his parents."

"For how long?"

"It sounded like years, and he made it clear that there would never be a reunion."

Releasing each other, we cross the park, walking in the grass to the playscape. "That's a step in the right direction."

Reed knows he's not allowed on the big climbing structure until I get here but leave it to him to want to impress Jake. I hurry to spot him, but like any five-year-old, he feels invincible. "No, Mommy. I got it."

"Okay, but hold on with both hands." Standing off to the side, like barely off, I pretend not to be guarding this kid with my life. When I see Jake walking across the top, I already know what's coming next.

Lila stands a few feet away with her phone in her hand. "So does the dude still have money or what?"

This is when it gets tricky. From what it sounds like, he has a fortune from the lawsuit, but I have no idea what he has otherwise. I hate lying, but that is not information I feel I can share, even with my best friend. "I'm not sure."

"He's late," she says, holding up her phone as if this proves he's a terrible human.

"A minute late is okay, Lila."

"What does he do for a living?"

"I don't know," I blurt. "I don't know much of anything other than, yes, it was a damn good brunch, but not because of the food."

"Why then?"

"Because when I lowered my walls and really listened to him, I heard the man I fell in love with. I saw the man I thought I'd be with forever sitting across from me." I cover my eyes to hide the tears threatening to fall, but they do anyway. "And more than one time during that meal, I imagined what it would be like if we were there as a couple instead of whatever we were now."

"What was it like?" This time, it's not Lila asking the question.

My lids fly open to see Cooper standing nearby. I could hide in shame, but what's the point. "You're really the last person I wanted to hear me say that."

"I understand, but now that it's out there, what was it like?"

Already exasperated by my out-of-control emotions around him, I ask, "What was what like?"

"What was it like being together again? Being in love like we never had an end?"

Lila says, "I think I'll go find a park bench and raise

some hell in a mom's group online chat." Rolling her eyes, she laughs. "They're so easy to rile up." She starts walking toward a bench but stops and turns back. "It's good to see you again, Cooper."

"You too, Lila. Hey, is that Jake up there?"

"Sure is. A twenty-year-old trapped in an eleven-year-old's body."

He says, "Funny how that never changes. Kids always want to grow up too fast, and parents want to keep them little forever."

"Sounds like you've been doing your research."

Seeing how easy it is for them to fall back into the rhyme of a friendship has me jealous. And if she thinks I'm not going to give her a hard time after she got mad at me for inviting him back into my life . . . *well, it shall be entertaining.*

"Something like that," he replies, looking over my shoulder.

I already know what he's staring at, *or whom*, but I follow his gaze anyway. For a few seconds, we stand there in silence, watching Reed, who's showing off for Jake and always wanting my attention—good or bad. He just likes me to watch him play. I'm tired from work some days, and others, I've not had a decent night's sleep. I have what my mom used to call "adult problems" from bills to not enough hours in the day. But Sundays are always Reed's and my play day.

As for the only other man in my life that has ever mattered, guilt settles in, and I walk over to him. "How are you doing?"

"Trying not to—" An exhale catches him as emotions seem to build. He runs his hand through his hair and then squats down, trying to breathe through it.

An overwhelming wave of regret for keeping them apart

rips through me, crashing into my heart. It doesn't matter what he said at brunch because there's no way he can't hate me. But I can't make this about me. *Not now.* I will fight for my son always, but right now, this is about Cooper and Reed, not me. I move closer, unsure if he even wants me to. I do it anyway and then reach over to gently rub his back.

It's been so long since we've touched this way other than an accident or habit like at brunch. The muscles are still hard through the cotton of the shirt, but it's not that making my heart kick up a beat. It's the connection between us, the bond that never left.

His eyes close, and his mouth opens. I pull my hand back, not sure if I'm making him feel better or worse, but when he stands, he looks at me. "Please don't stop."

Now my breath is taken, but I nod my head and reach behind him to rub his shoulder blades and higher. Cooper's hand covers mine, and he says, "Reed's amazing."

I smile, filled with pride, my eyes meeting Cooper's, and say, "He is, like his parents."

And then the sound of my son's scream pulls me away just before he hits the ground.

38

Story

"You're a doctor?"

"Yes," Cooper replies, then adds,"in residency," as if that changes the fact that Cooper Haywood is a doctor. *Not an attorney like his father.*

That probably shouldn't make me as happy as it does, but I'm only human, and I love that he broke the mold to follow his own goals. No parent would ever be disappointed with their kid becoming a doctor, yet knowing the Haywoods, they probably were.

Since my butt is going numb from these uncomfortable chairs, I tuck my leg under me, which has me angling more his way. "Nothing against lawyers, but I'm glad you're a doctor. Why didn't you tell me?"

"It didn't come up." He glances toward me out of the corner of his eyes. The hospital waiting room is sterile and the ugliest shade of green, the opposite of Cooper's eyes.

Swerving his hand in front of him, he says, "We always

take the scenic route in a conversation. Figured we'd get there eventually."

"That's a valid point, but now you're the father of my child, so I should probably know these things." I smile at him and raise an eyebrow playfully. "Don't you think?"

"I do think, Story." I receive his full attention, but I don't get a smile in return. "But I've *always* been the father of your child. Not only *now,* like I'm stepping in when it's convenient for me. I would have been there all along if I'd had the choice."

Taken aback by how upset he is, I realize I didn't even catch that I had said the word now. "I'm sorry. I don't know why I said that other than you're here right now, literally right here, and you weren't before."

I keep checking for any sign of the doctor or a nurse who can tell us how it's going. Worrying about my baby breaking his arm has me on edge, but now I have Cooper to worry about. It's a lot to manage when I'm only used to the two of us.

"I get it, but it was sort of a twist-of-the-knife comment since I had no choice."

I stare at him, trying to understand where the pain's coming from—my comment or something deeper. I can't control what's happening with Reed, so I try to alleviate the other pain. "It was a slip of the tongue, but I see how that could be hurtful. Again, I'm sorry." Uncomfortable in the conversation, I put my feet back on the ground, sit forward, and rub my temples. "The last thing I want to do is add stress to this already stressful situation." I glance at him again. "And I don't want to hurt you because there's a bigger picture that we're in the middle of as well. It's a lot."

Too antsy to stay seated, I stand to pace the waiting room of the ER.

"It is a lot. And I appreciate the apology, but you don't owe it to me. I know you didn't mean anything by it." He's so patient, so understanding. I don't get it. Not that he wasn't with me, but he used to be filled with an angst simmering just under the surface. But maybe having his parents out of his life has given him the peace he always desired.

"Cooper, we should talk about this and what it means."

"I agree." It seems the day's wearing on him as it is me. His lids hang a little lower, and his hair is over his forehead. He's rolled up the sleeves on his forearms and kicked his long legs out in front of him.

I keep pacing, my mind bouncing between the surgery to reset Reed's arm and the man who's showing up to be a part of Reed's life. I stop in front of him, and say, "I don't regret telling you about him, but there's going to be a learning curve where we figure out how to maneuver in this new relationship."

"I want to be a part of his life."

And there it is. It was never about seeing or meeting Reed. It was about building a father-son connection, a relationship between just the two of them. "I'm not naïve to believe it was ever intended to be less, but this is happening very fast, Cooper." I sit back in the chair I'd abandoned and lean on the arm. "I've been a single mom since before he was born. Every doctor's appointment, taking care of myself when some days were damn hard, eating healthy for him while also looking for a job after graduation. Other than Lila and Jake, *and they've been a godsend*, I was alone."

With both of us resting on the arm of the chair between us, his fingers lift over mine. "You're an amazing person, Story. I can't imagine how difficult it was caring for yourself and the baby when you felt alone."

"I didn't *feel* alone. I *was* alone. But don't get me wrong. I was pregnant, but I was also devastated that you were gone."

His fingers leave mine, making me wonder if it's a punishment for making him feel bad or because he's struggling through this like I am. Cooper rests forward with his elbows on his knees. Turning to look me in the eyes, he says, "You didn't love me anymore."

Though his voice is resolved like this is old news finally sinking in, it's a harsh allegation to put out. A shiver runs up my spine as my pulse starts racing. "Why would you say that? Is that what you believed?"

"I had no choice in what to believe. You walked away and left me."

The mere accusation is offensive, but that argument is blurrier in my memories. So much was happening. I had the papers to process, the rain and something happened to my umbrella. Cooper passed out in that car and then was hungover. I sit up and look around the waiting room. Others have cleared out over the past few hours, including Lila and Jake, but we're here together. Shouldn't that mean more than our hurt feelings?

Holding two fingers to my temple, I say, "I don't remember everything from that day, but I know I never said goodbye."

"Telling me I broke you is the same thing."

The words are sharp and cut deep. The pain in his voice from that day is fresh. I grip the chair as my heart shatters on the cold linoleum—for him and for me, for the misunderstandings that complicated our past and the events that ruined our future. I whisper, "It wasn't the same thing for me."

This isn't a conversation I ever thought I'd be having, especially not while waiting for doctors to put my child's broken arm back together. When his head lowers into his hands, I don't hesitate to reach over and rub his back again to comfort him. Not only for him. *For me.* The simple act of bonding with him makes me feel better as well.

It's not hurried, and he doesn't move away, but he looks at me again, and through the exchange comes a different kind of understanding—acceptance.

He's not the bad guy.

And I'm not the hero.

We're caught somewhere between the two.

I glance over when the doors down the hall slide open, my stress peaking. "What's taking so long?" I ask in frustration.

"He'll be in recovery before he's moved into a room."

I turn to him. It's not his words that calm me, but his voice. A smile, feeble at best, is all I can currently manage, "As a doctor, don't you have privileges?" I shift again, my back now aching.

Leaning back again, he crosses an ankle over the opposite knee. "What kind of privileges would those be?"

Rolling my wrist, I say, "You know, for information and access. Stuff like that."

His gaze travels past me to the nurses' station before he pushes to his feet. "This isn't my hospital, but it's worth a try."

"Thank you," I say, punching the air in encouragement. If he can get any information, it would be better than what we have now.

He's up there too long, leaning on the high counter as if two long-lost friends have run into each other. And the nurse is a little too into it. I roll my eyes, but he catches me as he returns. Smirking, he asks, "What's that about?"

"Nothing. Any update?"

"There were no complications, and he's recovering just fine."

An audible sigh of relief escapes me. "That's good news." I don't know why I reach for his hand, but ours slip together so easy, and I squeeze. "Thank you."

"You're welcome." He squeezes mine right back, and we sit there holding hands until a nurse finally comes out looking for us . . . looking for me.

"Mrs. Salenger?" My eyes dart to Cooper and then to the nurse.

I stand. "It's *Ms*."

The nurse continues, "Everything went well. The doctor is finishing with another emergency that came in. Come on back. I'll take you to Reed's room where she'll talk to you in there."

We start walking, but then I stop and look back.

As if she can read my mind, the nurse says, "I'm sorry, we can only have one visitor at a time since it's after dinner."

Cooper gives me a reassuring nod. I soak it in, remembering how I always felt safe and cared for with him around. "Thank you," I mouth, turn back, and keep walking, not sure if I'll see him again tonight.

AFTER GOING over everything with the doctor and hearing the care instructions for when I take him home, I check on Reed, covering him with the blanket and making sure water is ready on the side table for when he wakes up. The sound of my son's heartbeat through the monitor gives me comfort, knowing it's strong and steady. I eventually sit on the vinyl loveseat, not sure if it will be an hour or three before he wakes.

With time flowing as slow as molasses, I get up, too unsettled to sit for long, cross my arms over my chest, and stare out the cracked open blinds to a view of air-conditioning units and a busy street just beyond. The door clicks behind me, and I look.

I'm not at all disappointed to see Cooper—quite the opposite—but I am confused. "They only said one visitor. How did you get in?"

"I walked," he says with a smile. My mind fills in the *ba dum bump*. I roll my eyes and grin, but he's already busy checking the equipment and reading vital signs. He ducks back out and grabs the chart from outside the door. Apparently, everything looks as it should because he appears satisfied when he returns it to the hook.

I find relief seeing the same on his face. It's nice to have a doctor in the family. . . *Reed's family*. I mentally make a note feeling a little sad that a separation between my family and Reed's can be made.

"I also used my doctor privileges." Seeing his smirk is a welcome reprieve from the heavy strain of today. When he moves to sit beside the bed, his smirk falls into a gentle smile.

I remember that look, the one that made me feel cherished and loved. I move to the opposite side of the bed, and before the moment gets too heavy, I whisper, "I knew you had superpowers."

I'm given a glimpse of a smile when Cooper glances up at me. His eyes return to Reed, and he sweeps his hair to the side. I'd never noticed that my son had the same cowlick as Cooper until I see them together now.

He's my son through and through, but I feel like an intruder, so I step back and give Cooper time alone with him. Sitting on the loveseat, I'm sure the emotional drain is from the day, but for some reason, my chest feels heavier, the heart clench stronger watching Cooper with his son.

He stays, taking everything in about him that he can. I'm sure he's spotted the little wave of freckles across his nose that he gets from me. And the minutest bumps on the bridge of his nose that he gets from Cooper. He has my hazel eyes, but those enviable lashes aren't mine. Reed's hand is small compared to Cooper's, but one day, it will be the same or larger than his dad's.

When Cooper comes to sit next to me, he's smiling—small but genuine. "I can't believe I have a child. He's just . . . everything. So perfect."

"He is." I clasp my hands together on my lap.

A shyness comes over him, and he tilts his head down, but he doesn't look away. "So are you. You're amazing, Story."

"He's the best and brings out the best in me." Tilting my head to tap his shoulder, I laugh. "And sometimes the worst. I'm not perfect. But for him, I try to be everything he needs."

His arm comes around me suddenly, and he pulls me into an embrace. It's shocking, and my emotions go crazy, unsure how to react. But the longer I'm here, the more I let the heavy emotional load I've been carrying for years emerge.

Tucked into his arms, I feel safe again. The tears come fast and unexpectedly, but it feels good to set myself free. Reed's going to be okay. I can finally release some of the worries I've been holding so tightly to today and maybe others I've held on to for too long.

When I tilt my head to find his eyes, they're already set on me. My breathing shallows as little things I loved so much with him come back. Forehead kisses and strong arms wrapped around me. Spending hours in bed after the sun set talking about everything and nothing. I still can't eat strawberry yogurt without remembering how he cared for me when I was sick. My smile grows through the tears, thinking about when we met and the day turning into night and how we were forever for a short time.

The bigger things like the hotel on Christmas and that the camera he gave me was the one I relied on to help to get me through life once he was gone. And although I have a different camera now, that one sits on the same desk I kept like his first note to me once did. I have files upon files of my photography from back then, all because he saw more in my talent than I did.

And for someone who never thought himself worthy, he makes it so hard not to fall in love with him. I rest my head against him, savoring this moment I've been gifted once more. Just in case it's the last time.

"Although you felt you had to protect Reed by leaving me, you saved him. They would have dug their claws in, so I don't blame you for not telling me or wanting better for him than what I received."

Sitting back, I'm in awe of him. "I appreciate that you recognize the position I was in and that you're not holding that grudge between us. I also need you to know that it was the hardest decision I've ever made. But your mother . . ." I shudder, remembering how inferior she made me feel. "She treated me so horribly."

"I know I can't make it better, but know that I'm sorry. I'm sorry for ever putting you in their path."

"Once she threatened to have me arrested . . ." I wrap my arms around my belly. "She didn't know I was pregnant, but I couldn't risk the baby to see you. She made me choose. I was so close to you, but I couldn't take the risk."

His brow twists and pinches together in the middle. "What are you talking about?"

"When I came to tell you I was pregnant." Judging by his expression, he doesn't register what I'm saying. "I drove to the Haywood house. You didn't come see me, so I went searching for you instead."

The vinyl squeaks under him when he sits back and scratches the back of his neck. "When was that exactly?"

"I don't know the date. I think Saturday or Sunday. After our big fight. When I found out about your involvement—"

"The fight in the rain?" He deflates, his expression falling with his shoulders. "You drove from Atterton to tell me you were pregnant?"

"I did, but your mother wouldn't let me see you."

Leaning forward, he takes my hand. It's a bold move, but the dormant butterflies in my stomach are awakened as he holds it again. "I need you to listen to me, Story."

"Okay, but you're scaring me."

His hold on me tightens. "I don't mean to. I just . . . Wow. I . . ." He looks up at the ceiling and then takes a deep breath. When he turns back to me, he says, "I was never told you came by."

"I'm not surprised." I can't help but inject my own commentary when it involves his parents.

"My phone was stolen, and I didn't get a replacement for a while. You were going to tell me about the baby?"

"Of course. I never said goodbye." I caress his cheek, trying to calm the frenzy in his eyes. "I knew that no matter what was said or happened prior, you deserved to know about our child."

Water glistens in his eyes. "You tried to tell me."

He's not asking the question, but it lies in the greens of his eyes. "Yes. I drove to Haywood and made it halfway up the stairs before she told me I had to leave or I'd be arrested. I wouldn't have put it past her to call the police on me."

A mixture of sadness and anger weaves through his striking features. "Neither would I." When he turns to me again, joy is populating his irises. "But you tried. You fucking tried for me."

I nod as his joy catches fire inside me.

A darkness rolls in, tamping the joy he'd found. He says, "The fight outside your apartment . . . when you left, I went looking for your ex."

It takes me a moment to piece together that time. "Troy?"

"We had a long-standing feud way before he met you." Directing his gaze to our clasped hands, he continues, "I didn't want to die. I just no longer wanted to feel."

Fear unnerves me as I try to riddle through what that means. "Cooper, what did you do?"

"I didn't have you, and I didn't care about anything else, much less myself. I didn't fight back because I didn't matter."

I find his eyes, returning him from the distant memory he was losing himself in. "You always matter to me." The words come easy and flow from my tongue. Not past but present tense.

Reed stirs, and I'm on my feet. It's a false alarm as his breathing evens again, and he stays asleep. With my little guy sleeping comfortably, I stand at the window and stare out again. Cooper looks up from the loveseat. "Until today, I never knew you tried to tell me."

Leaning against the wall, using it to hold me up from the life that's brought me down, I ask, "You threw yourself to the wolves because you didn't think I cared."

"I spent months bitter that I had survived while recuperating. Bitter I didn't have you in my life."

It's a gut punch of information. "It's frustrating because our lives could have been so different."

He stands behind me and rubs my arms. "I could have been a dad this whole time." He leans in and whispers, "I could have been with you all these years." Those are the words that will haunt me—*what could have been.*

Does it matter now? We can't change the past. Does an opportunity lie in the future?

Exhaustion sets in. My mind is too tired to keep going tonight. "I need to rest, Cooper." I sit down, needing time to process the tragedy that we were so in love and lost it all because of the lies involved. I lean my head on the back cushion, my eyes still locked with his.

He says, "Get some rest." And then I close my eyes.

My eyelids feel like they have a stack of quarters weighing down on each of them, but I force them open anyway. I yawn, not realizing I'd fallen asleep. A quick glance at the bed tells me Reed is still sleeping. Rest means healing, so I'm not upset, though I am a little anxious.

Cooper's next to Reed as if he can't stop hovering. I imagine he would have done the same with Reed in his crib, if given the opportunity. It breaks my heart to know that he'll never get the chance.

When he sees I'm awake, he comes to sit next to me. Keeping his voice low, he says, "I'm thinking this might not be the time and place for me to meet him. He'll be waking up just out of surgery and probably scared to be in a hospital bed. That will be a lot for him at his age to take in. I don't want to add to any anxiety." The emotions that over-whelmed him at the park return, and his voice cracks. "The focus needs to be on him healing, not on me."

My heart aches again for him and for Reed for having to miss another opportunity that he's not even aware of yet. I know that all Cooper wants is to meet his son, and the damn universe is still conspiring against us. Not sure what to say, I sigh. "I'm sorry."

"No, don't be. It's not your fault."

"We'll set something up for next weekend when he's home, settled, and I can make sure he's not in any pain."

"I think it's best." He stands, and I don't know why I do, but I stand as well. Tucking his hands in his pockets, he says, "I guess I should go before he wakes."

I walk him to the door like we're at the end of a first date. The thought gives me pause, and I scold my heart and head for confusing the signs. I bite my bottom lip and tug on it to remind myself that this is not a date and there will be no kiss.

But when I look up at him, he's watching my mouth like he wouldn't be upset if it was pressed to his right about now. It's not, though, and I need to force distance between us before I cave in. "Thank you for being here."

"Of course. We have each other's numbers now, so call or text me if you need anything, anything at all."

"I have a question."

He stays, suddenly not eager to leave. "What is that?"

"What kind of doctor are you?" I get that a dentist is a highly trained and skilled physician, but I'm going to be really disappointed if that's what kind of doctor Cooper Haywood is.

And there's that smirk . . . *please don't be a gynecologist either.*

"I'm a pediatrician."

And just like that, I'm swooning for this man again.

When he walks out, I'm left with a stupid grin that stays way past its invitation. I go to the bed to check on Reed again. If I could crawl in without hurting him, I'd let him snuggle up to me like we do on Sunday morning.

He'll be excited about the cast, feeling very big boy that he's part of the broken bone club. With him sound asleep, though, I settle back on the vinyl loveseat and close my eyes to sneak in a few winks before he wakes.

My phone buzzes with a text shortly after. Cooper: *Despite the broken bone and hospital visit, it was amazing to see him, and it was really good to spend time with you again.*

I smile, holding my phone to my chest and letting this little bliss I've found get the best of me since there are no witnesses.

Cooper: *Too much too soon?*

Giggling, I text him back: *Not too much.* I pause and take a breath before adding: *Not soon enough.*

39

Cooper

One Week Later . . .

ME: *I'm fucking nervous.*

Story: *Don't be. You're meeting him today as Mommy's friend.*

What the hell am I supposed to say to that?

"Mommy's friend?" I grumble. It's sad that our kid will never know just how amazing his mommy and I were together, how we used to laugh until our cheeks hurt and never needed alcohol or drugs because we were so high on each other. It's too bad he'll never see how we loved so hard and were willing to risk it all for each other until we couldn't any longer.

I thought being Story's ex was bad. Now, I'm relegated to Mommy's friend. That's worse by all standards. That's me not even making it up to bat, much less first base or hitting a home run.

Mommy's friend. *Fuck.*

Reed is the priority, so I guess I'll take what I can get when it comes to Story. I toss my phone to the bed and finish getting dressed.

Story: *Seriously, don't be worried. I know this is weird, but we'll get through it together. Let's try to have fun.*

Yeah . . . *fun.*

What if he doesn't like me, or we don't click? I'm envious of parents who get the benefit of that instant bond built from the get-go instead of having to be introduced.

I pull on a dark gray T-shirt and some jeans. I'm not sure what's been planned other than Lila's hosting a barbecue at her place to keep things "light." That also means Reed has Jake to play with if things go south. Story didn't say that, but I could tell she was covering her bases just in case.

Since I have a few stops to make, I head out to hop on the subway.

I grew up running around the city and the five boroughs, but a lot has changed in the past ten years. I don't even recognize this Brooklyn neighborhood. With my hands full, I ring the bell of the restored brownstone and wait.

I wasn't nervous when I met Story or when I took the MCAT. I wasn't nervous about suing my parents or pursuing a career as a doctor.

Meeting my kid for the first time? Now, I'm fucking nervous.

The door opens, but some guy is standing inside. Something is vaguely familiar about him that I can't quite put my finger on.

"Hey," he says as if he had to muster the greeting. "I'm Lou."

Lou? Lou . . . "Oh Lou! Whoa, man, you're a blast from

the past." And now I'm nervous again. Is Story dating Lou? *Motherfu*—

"Cooper, come on in," Lila says, swinging the door open wider. "Why are you guys just standing here?" She reaches forward and takes the bag from me. "You've got your hands full. You know it's just a casual get-together, right? You didn't have to bring all this."

"I wanted to."

"Well, I'm not going to say no to all the cheeses one could ever want. Lou's lactose intolerant," she says, thumbing over her shoulder at him.

"Sorry, man," I say.

"It's okay." He shrugs. "I'm used to it."

Lila summons me inside. "Looks like a whole charcuterie in this bag. The rest of us can polish it off."

I step inside, but before I go any farther, I stop to shake Lou's hand. "It's good to see you again."

"I'll be honest, I didn't think it would be nice to see you again, but I've been hearing good things. So I'll just leave the past in the past where it belongs."

"I appreciate that, Lou."

As I walk toward the back of the house, the sound of the boys outside screaming and having fun drifts through an open back door. I look out the window to see Reed running around with a blue cast on his arm. Lou points at the TV with a game competing for noise, and asks, "You okay with the game on?"

"Sure. I'm not much of a sports guy these days. Not enough time to enjoy it."

"I hear ya. My software company sold last year to a firm in Silicon Valley. After I finish overseeing the transition, I'm taking Jake on a stadium tour next summer. Twenty stadiums in thirty days. It's all mapped out."

"Congratulations." I nod, trying to decipher the relationship here. "That's cool."

I look around, but Story's not to be found. Unloading the bag and display board, Lila whispers, "She wanted to do a little touch-up."

"Ah." Maybe she's a little nervous, too. I set the flowers and bottle of wine down, and Lila laughs. "What is it?"

She shakes her head and gives me a wink. "You'll see. Nice rosé by the way."

"I didn't know what to bring. And what will I see?"

"Wait until Story comes downstairs." She shifts things around on the counter to make more room. "You brought too much, Cooper, but thank you. It's appreciated." She comes around and adds, "I didn't approve of her bringing you into her life or Reed's." *Not a great start, I think.* I'll wait for my final judgment to see where she's going with it. "But when I saw you, and particularly when I saw you with Story . . . It's good to see you again." She hugs me.

I wasn't sure where that was headed, but I hug her back. "It's good to see you, too."

With her head near my ear, she whispers, "Hurt her again, and I'll kill you." Leaning back with a warm smile, she pats my shoulder. "Capisce?"

Story is lucky to have her in her corner. "Understood."

"Good."

When she steps into the backyard, Lou says, "She's harmless, but I'm not."

It's hard to imagine Lou getting in a fight, but what do I know anymore? "All right." This must be the *fun* Story spoke about.

"Beers in the fridge; the bar's over there." He starts laughing and then joins Lila in the back.

"How do I look?"

I turn to see Story coming down the stairs—her long hair held high in a ponytail on the crown of her head, fitted jeans, and little white sneakers. Her makeup is light, but she never needed that anyway. "Incredible."

"Oh." She looks up when she hits the landing. "Cooper, I didn't know you were here."

"Only for a few minutes."

We both spot it at the same time. Pointing at each other's tees, we start laughing. She plucks hers away from her chest. "I guess being around you made me sentimental."

With our matching Atterton University T-shirts on, I say, "Great minds think alike."

"And go to the same college."

"That too." As the laughter simmers, I say, "Thank you for having me over."

"Yeah, I'm glad you were available since it's so last minute. I just wanted to make sure Reed was in a good place because I know he's going to be busy running around all day."

Glancing out back again, I tuck my hands in my pockets. "Looks like he's doing well."

She looks up from the island and smiles when she sees him. "He has a lot of pent-up energy from sitting around all week."

"I bet." I rock back on my heels. "I'll let you lead."

Her smile is so natural like her beauty that it's almost too much for me to take in, knowing she's not mine to kiss. "Thank you." She grabs a bottle of water. "I'm having water. What can I get you?"

"Same."

When she reaches for another, she sees the flowers. I jump over and pick them up. "I brought these for you. Not sure why, but they reminded me of you." It was a stab in the dark, so I hope she likes them.

"That was very sweet, Cooper." She takes the bouquet and holds them to her nose. "Thank you. Peonies are my favorite. I'll put them in water when Lila comes in." After setting them down, she walks to the back door, and asks, "Ready to meet Reed?"

Despite my nerves, the only answer for me is, "Yes."

Story holds her hand out for me and waits at the door. I didn't expect the added perk, but I'll happily accept it. Carrying our bottles in one hand and holding each other with our formerly free hand, we walk outside together as a united front.

Lila and Lou are sitting at the outdoor table on the patio while the boys still run around in the yard. When we walk down the steps and onto the grass, Lila calls Jake to come help her. I think that's the signal for Story because she releases me and calls out to our son. "Reed, come here. I want you to meet someone."

The boys look annoyed that their game of chase must end, but both do as they're told and head to their respective parents.

Full of sass with the hand of his broken arm anchored on his hip, I've seen that before somewhere. I glance at Story and grin.

"Mommy, I'm it, and I don't want to be it anymore."

"Sorry," she says, "that's how the game is played. You either play by the rules, or you don't."

"I can make my own rules."

"Yes, you can do that as well. Hey, buddy, I wanted to introduce you to a friend of mine. Remember how I mentioned Cooper would be coming by today?"

"I member." He's not quite smiling at me and a lot suspicious. I work with kids every day, but you have to learn their angle, what they like to play, or what they're into. But somehow, I already feel like I'm failing when it comes to my own kid.

I kneel to talk one-on-one with him and hold out my hand. "Cooper Haywood, it's very nice to meet you."

Reed takes my hand and looks me right in the eyes. "Nice to meet you." He glances at Story for approval.

She rubs his head and nods. "You did good."

Feeling pleased with himself, he says, "Are you staying for burgers, Cooper?"

I might be setting myself up, but I sure hope not. "Would you like me to?"

When he nods, it's so tempting to hug him, to tell him you're mine, kid, and I'm yours. We're stuck together now. But that will have to wait for a few more meetings.

Over the past hour, this has gone better than I imagined. He's not only receptive to me being here with his mom and him, but he has come over to talk to me several times on his own. I've just taken a sip of water when he sits down in a chair next to me, and says, "I saw you at the park last week before I broke my arm."

"I saw you, too. Great climbing prior to the accident."

"Yeah, we all slip. We all fall sometimes," he says, sipping from a juice box. "That's what my mom says." His cheeks are red from running, and the hairline of his forehead is soaking wet. I don't remember ever having the freedom to just be a kid. Story's giving that gift to him. Looking at me, he asks, "Why were you crying, Cooper?"

I chuckle. The kid hits hard with that callout. "I wasn't crying. I got dirt in my eyes." A little fib won't hurt, especially when it's to protect him.

His eyes go wide, but he rolls them like his hazel-eyed mom. "Jake threw dirt in my eyes once. I didn't cry."

Hard crowd to please. I laugh, but then nudge him with my elbow. "Guess you're a tough guy, Reed."

"Yup," he says as if it's a fact. Then he looks at me again. "What are you?" The question comes unexpectedly, and I'm at a loss for an answer. I glance over at Story, not sure what I am anymore.

"Mommy's friend."

"Oh, I thought you were her boyfriend."

I could be, but I'll keep that to myself. "What made you think that?"

"I heard her tell Aunt Lila that she loves you."

This time, my eyes go wide. "Loves or loved?'

Under the slurp of the last dregs of juice, he shrugs his little shoulders and then hops up. "I don't know."

Me either.

But I wish I did.

Cooper

Story was right. *This was fun.*

More fun than I've had in a long time.

I even got invited to play a game of tag, but when Reed tripped over a tree root, it was game over. Story said she was glad there was a doctor around. She may not have said she was glad *I* was around, but I'm taking the liberty to interpret it that way.

After a patchwork of Spongebob bandages and Scotch tape on the elbow of his cast, which was dirty but didn't show any signs of damage, Reed was mighty impressed with my skills.

I wish there were more hours to this day. I don't think it's sunk in that Reed is my kid. Mine. Half my blood. Half my legacy. The good I've been feeling sours thinking about my family tree. Watching Story and how great a mom she is to him is the only hope he's been given.

My need to meet him, to know my offspring, was based on an instinctual level like any parent wants with their kids, overriding my common sense. Maybe I should keep my distance. I should take today and hold on to it to let him live to his full potential—happy, healthy, successful in terms that he defines. Maybe it's my genes that will fuck him up if I'm in his life, like they're activated by my presence.

It's something I definitely need to take under consideration. Can her environment overrule my heredity?

I talked Story and Reed into lying under the clear skies and stars once the sun set and the sky went dark. Lila threw a blanket out the door before we had time to ask. I'm thinking we have an audience. *At least it's one rooting in our favor.*

As soon as the three of us are lying on the blanket, reality hits. Story and I may not be together, but we'll always be connected by the little guy between us. We'll always be a family. I point up and say, "Do you see the man in the moon?"

Reed giggles and shakes his head. "How'd he get up there? In a rocket?"

Story tickles his ribs, sending him to full-on fits of laughter. I shouldn't be, but I feel a little twinge of jealousy that they can be so close, and I can't. Not yet, at least.

She is laughing so hard when he tickles her right back. She settles him beside her again. Grabbing his feet, he's rocking back and forth, his feet pushing off her and then me. My little family.

Story says, "Dr. Haywood . . ." It's the first time she's called me that, and we share a knowing exchange over Reed's head.

"Yes, Ms. Salenger?"

"I'm worried about my son. He seems to be unable to lie still. Do you mind taking a look?"

I sit up, and say, "Mr. Salenger?"

"Yes, Doc?" Reed says in a mimicking voice. This kid is too much.

"Pulse." He touches his wrist. I take his fingers and touch them to his wrist. "If you press two fingers right here, you can find your pulse. Press a little harder but not too much."

His eyes go wide. "I can feel my heart beating in my wrist, Mommy."

"That's a cool trick, Dr. Haywood."

I grin at the ridiculousness. "Who needs medical school when you have Spongebob bandages and can find your pulse in your wrist?"

Story says, "Don't downplay it. It's really impressive."

"Well, my professional opinion is that Reed has a case of the wiggles."

"How do we treat it?" she asks, tickling his ribs.

"Homework?"

"Oh no," she says, acting very serious for effect. "That definitely makes it worse."

Reed is waving his arms in the air like a helicopter propeller. "Mommy is good with math. Me too. Twelve plus twelve is twenty-four."

"It is. Very good." I look back and forth between Reed and Story, happy to listen to either of them all day and night. "Tell me about your mommy and math."

Even in the dark, I can tell when she gets embarrassed. "It's no big deal. I don't save lives, but I can save you lots of money on your taxes or even make money for you on investments."

"That is impressive."

She props herself up on her elbow, facing us. "I turned down a promotion last month. I was pretty proud of the offer, though."

I follow her lead and lie sideways, my head weighted on my elbow. "Why'd you turn it down?"

"It would require me to be at the office for longer hours. My time with Reed is more important, and I still like to sneak in my photography."

Reed turns to me and smiles as if he's surprised to still find me here. Did he already forget or—"When you have your next playdate with Mommy, can I come?"

I glance at Story over his head. It's the slightest of nods, but there was no hesitation. "Sure, buddy. What should we do?"

"The zoo."

"The zoo?" I ask, astonished by how fast he answered. "What's your favorite animal?"

His claws come out, and he scrunches his face. "The tigers. Roar!"

I jump, pretending to be startled. "Dude, you scared me."

"Mom jumps. Jake says grownups fake that stuff to placate little kids like me. What does placate mean?"

This took a turn.

Story's arm flies into the air, and she points. "Is that a shooting star?" Lying back down, she slips her arm under Reed's head, and she holds him, rubbing his shoulder. "Those stars move fast."

Story says, "I don't think I've ever laid outside and stared up at the stars before."

I let that sink in. She basically raised herself but look how amazing she's doing with him. "It's rare to be able to see stars with all the buildings and lights in the city. This neighborhood is nice that it's not been torn down and replaced with condos."

Reed asks, "What's a condo?"

Softly laughing, Story says, "A tall building of apartments."

She stretches her arm out to me, and I take her hand. We lie there together for a while, me wishing this would last forever, again.

She looks at me over Reed's head, and whispers, "Today was a great day."

The woman knows how to be charming. "The best," I reply.

Glancing down at the sleeping five-year-old, she shifts just a little and then smiles at me. "Want to help me out?"

I get up and scoop him into my arms. "Where are we going?"

"Third floor. Think you can handle it?" She winks.

Shifting his weight, I maneuver his head onto my shoulder before I reach the patio. Through the window, I see the game's still on with Lila, Lou, and Jake sitting on the couch together watching it, and though I'm still not sure what the relationship is between Lou and Lila, I know Lou's not here for Story.

She stops just before going inside. She straightens Reed's shirt, but I have a feeling something else is on her mind than how this kid is dressed before bed. Looking up at me, she says, "He's so big in my arms yet so small in yours."

I'm not sure what's happening, but her eyes start to glisten. "I'm so sorry for keeping him from you."

I could hold a world of anger inside for missing so many milestones that I keep track of for other families in my line of work. But that would only leave us both feeling empty. "We made the best decisions at the time. There's no going back, babe—*Story*," I correct myself. "So let's just try to stay in the present and move forward."

She nods and leads me upstairs. By the time I reach the

third floor, I'm huffing, and I'm a runner who works out. "How do you carry him up here?"

"Very slowly and with lots of breaks." She laughs. "He needs to use the bathroom before he gets in bed, or he could have an accident."

I'm capable as a doctor and a man to teach this kid to use the bathroom, but I set his feet on the ground because I don't want to make any assumption that will have her pulling back.

When they're done, he climbs into the bottom bunk bed, and she tucks him in. After a kiss to Story, he holds his arms out for me. I kneel and lean over into the cave of his bed. When he wraps his arms around my neck, I drop my head to the pillow beside him. I rub his arm, wishing I could hug back, but he's tucked snug as a bug, and I don't want to mess with Story's routine.

His hair smells like a mixture of the outdoors and cotton candy. Something on his fingers is definitely sticky against my neck. He hugs me like he wants to choke me to death, and I wouldn't change anything about him. I love him. "Good night, Reed."

"Good night, Cooper." It guts me just a little to hear that name instead of another. But I'll take what I can get to be in his life.

41

Cooper

"When can we schedule our next playdate?" I ask, sending her a little wink as we stand awkwardly on the front stoop. "I haven't been to the zoo since I was little. Patrice would take me with her kids at least once a year."

"Patrice," she says, the name coming out as a happy memory. "She was lovely. How is she?"

I take a step down, then lean against the railing. I could spend all night out here talking with her, catching up and reminiscing. "Good. I don't see her much, but since she no longer works for my family, I spent last Christmas with her family."

A soft smile comes, and I'm beginning to detect a devious side to Story. I approve when it comes to my family. Story says, "I could see how much she cared about you. She'll love Reed."

"She would." The thought of introducing Reed as my son to people in my life isn't something I'd given myself permission to dream about. There aren't many, but Patrice is one of them, if not at the top of the list. Anytime her family was going on an adventure—the beach, the zoo, Coney Island—she'd add me to her brood. She's the only saving grace I had as a kid until I became too difficult to handle as a teen. "Maybe we can take him together to meet her?"

"That'd be nice."

It's not a date on the calendar, but I'll take the positive reaction. Some things take time, and I'm not sure Story and I should rush any changes in Reed's life. I'm not looking for an upheaval, but more of a slow adjustment where it's normal for me to be around. And then one day, maybe that name change.

Rocking back on her heels, she asks, "So, the zoo?" She nudges me with her elbow. "I bet you're excited about that." The sarcasm is duly noted.

Sliding my hands into my front pockets, I look at Story. Us in our matching alma mater T-shirts, both a little older, but God, she's still so beautiful. I think life has been harder on us, making us detour when we would have preferred a straight shot. But slowly and steadily, I'm starting to think we're getting back on the same track. At least, I hope we are. "Everything with the two of you is exciting to me."

She looks at me, strands of hair escaping from her pony-tail and the streetlamp shining in her eyes. Tilting her head, she asks, "What?" with a modicum of shyness creeping in. "What are you looking at, Cooper?"

I want to kiss her. I want to hold her in my arms again, knowing it's not just because of some tragedy that forced us together. I want to go to bed with her, even if we didn't have sex, just for one more chance to wake up with her in my arms and watch the sunrise in her eyes. I remember so much about that morning in May six years ago—brushing our teeth together and kissing in the shower until the water ran cold, coffee and donuts from the gas station as I filled the tank before we headed to Haywood for my graduation party. How she loved me. I could see it in her eyes. I felt it in her touch. My soul knew I'd never survive without hers wrapped around it.

I never got the warning that it was the last time we'd do those things, we'd love that hard, or we'd be us.

I want what we used to have so badly I could shout, but only on one condition. Reed would still be a part of the package. "I just like looking at you, babe."

She blushes, tucking her hair behind her ear, not caring that I slipped in the name at the end like it's another time, another opportunity for us.

The front door opens, and we startle apart like we were busted doing something we shouldn't. Lila looks at us and shakes her head. "We're going to bed," she announces, then points at me. "You're going to make sure this one . . ." She nods to Story. "Gets home safely."

Story checks her watch. "What do you mean, you're going to bed? It's eight o'clock."

"Jake's already reading, Reed's asleep, and yeah, Lou and I are heading upstairs. But us going to bed doesn't mean you have to." She waggles her eyebrows. "Take this as an opportunity to go out and have some fun." She shrugs. "Or stay in, just not here." She tosses Story her purse. "I'll get Reed to school in the morning. Have fun, you two."

Story's mouth is hanging open when the door shuts. Two bolts and what sounds like a chain are slid into place. "I'm thinking she means it," I say.

Stomping down the steps, she says, "She definitely means it." When she reaches the sidewalk, Story turns to look back up at me. "Well? You heard the lady. We don't have to go home, but we can't stay here. Are you coming, Dr. Haywood?"

I jog down the steps. "Abso-fucking-lutely." Stopping next to her, I ask, "Where are we going?"

———

STORY WOULDN'T LET me enter her duplex, conveniently located around the corner from Lila, but she left the door open for me to peek in. The space feels big with the height of the ceilings and the walls painted white. Shelves of colorful books are tucked between two large windows. On the opposite side is a wall of eclectically framed photos I imagine she took, breaking up the gallery feel. Toys litter one side of the living room, and cups left on the table bring the most human element to the space.

For every inch of white, there's an equal section of color. She runs down the stairs, her lips glossed and the wild strands tamed by the elastic. She didn't change clothes, but I catch a whiff of her floral scent when she dashes out and turns to lock the door. "Snoop," she says with a smile she's struggling to restrain.

Leaning against the railing, I chuckle. "I don't know what you're hiding in there. You have great taste."

"Thanks, but I'm hiding the mess." The street is quiet. Other than the occasional car passing by, I've only seen a family going for a stroll. It makes me happy that Reed lives somewhere he can see blue skies instead of only skyscrapers. That patches of grass exist nearby, even if they're small, rather than needing to head five blocks or more to a park.

Still embarrassed, she goes on, "Between my schedule and Reed's, I'm not as neat as I used to be. I would have cleaned up *if* I were expecting guests."

I don't like the sound of that. Does she have guests over? I'll have to revisit this. "I liked the way it looked. Mine is . . . lifeless in comparison." Ready for that visit, I say, "Maybe I can come over sometime and help put together the puzzle on the floor?"

Tucking her key into her bag, she nods. "Reed would love that. Just let me know your schedule. I'm sure you work crazy hours."

"Yeah, it's busy, but we've just set our new schedules for the next six months and hired two new doctors, so I won't be working eighty hours a week anymore."

"Don't burn yourself out," she says, her voice dipping in concern. It's not just the worry I hear. I detect it in her eyes when she passes me.

"I could come by when I'm on call. It would be just as easy being here as at my place to take calls."

We start down the steps, and she asks, "I just realized I have no idea where you live. I bet you live in a fancy tower in Manhattan." I do, but I'm having flashes of college come back—a conversation of the building I lived in then versus how cozy her little studio walkup was. Glancing back at her front door, I find not much has changed in our styles. We've just grown up.

"It's a nice building."

She only takes a few steps down the sidewalk before stopping. "Doorman?"

"Yes. His name is Frank."

"That's a good solid name. Is Frank a solid guy?"

Chuckling, I reply, "Yes, Frank is good people." That makes her smile for some reason. It doesn't matter what either of us achieves or earns or our successes. She's always making sure others are treated right. *She should be protected at all costs.*

Rolling her hand on an outstretched arm, she sing-songs, "We're here."

I look behind her at the empty sidewalk and the row of homes and back to her front door. "Where?"

She nods her head to the left and then clicks a button. We both stand on the edge of the single-car driveway watching the garage door roll up. It only takes a few feet to expose the contents inside. "Holy shit!" I run my hands into my hair and squat down before it. "You kept my car!"

"Shh." She laughs. "You're going to disturb the neighbors." Pulling the key from her back pocket, she dangles it off the tip of her finger. "As for keeping it, I really had no choice. It was either sell it on the illegal market, return it to your parents, which I just decided that was not going to happen, or keep it since I didn't have the title or any documentation. Want to take it for a spin?"

I snatch the key from her. "Shit yeah. Get in."

"Well, I kind of can't until you pull it out of the garage. Tight space and all."

"Wait right there." I take a slow, appreciative approach. "Look at you, girl," I whisper, dragging my fingertips over the hood. I rest my cheek against the cool metal. "I missed you."

"You're ridiculous, Cooper. You know that, right?"

"I have no shame in my Jaguar-loving game." I slide into the driver's seat and start the engine. "That purr," I say, rubbing her dash. She's in mint condition. I look through the windshield at the woman standing with her hand on her hip and teasingly tapping her foot. She jokes about not selling it, but this could have brought in six figures even with depreciation. She deals with finances, so I know she understands the value. I prefer to think she kept it in great condition for me, or even for Reed, which is the same thing.

Basically, my baby took care of both my babies.

MAYBE HOPE HASN'T FLOWN out the window, and there's a second chance for us.

I chuckle as she sticks out her leg and pops her thumb in the air. As soon as I pull out of the garage, Story's opening the car door before I can put it in park and open it for her myself. She buckles in and asks, "We have all night. Where are we going?"

"I have an early shift."

"I have an early meeting."

The excitement fizzles. "We're not kids anymore."

Laughter escaping, she says, "We're also not old enough to say we're not kids anymore."

Chuckling, I shift into gear. "You're right. Hungry?"

"Depends. What are the options?"

"Gas station dog and a thirty-two ouncer?"

She leans back in her seat, angling her head toward me. "Thought you'd never ask."

I didn't mention the gas station was in Jersey, but Story didn't mind. We talked about our work and lives, our favorite parks to walk, how she ate a Danish in front of Tiffany's on 5th Avenue like Audrey Hepburn, and our Christmas spent in the hotel.

And then we rode in the car, neither of us needing to fill the silence between us.

Until I do because I'm feeling every second of this time with her, and it feels amazing. "I missed this," I say, keeping my voice befitting the hour as we drive back to her place just before midnight.

Her head rolls left. She looks tired. "Driving your car?"

"No." I glance over at her again, starting to struggle myself.

I lose her attention as she turns forward, her gaze lengthening through the windshield. "Me too."

Trapped in a car is probably not the best time to bring up certain topics, but I'm tired and don't want to play games with her. "Reed told me he thought I was your boyfriend because he overheard you say you love me."

Her mouth opens, and her finger rises, then it closes, and she lowers her finger. She finally huffs. "I did say that, Cooper. I was telling Lila that I was so in love with you, referring to, you know . . ." Her voice goes quiet. "Back in college. He must have overheard only part of it. I shouldn't have said anything at all. It's probably confusing to him."

"He didn't seem confused. He didn't seem to mind at all."

"He's five and doesn't understand how life works."

Gripping the steering wheel, I say, "I do, and I was so in love with you."

There's no great moment shared or anything to mark this as a memory. I'm not sure if she's pretending she didn't hear me when her window slides down, or if she's at a loss for words. "It mattered then, not so much now." But I hear the disappointment in her tone and see the sadness in her eyes.

"We don't have to be left in the past just because it's been that way."

Her head is already shaking before I get the words out. "I can't risk being hurt."

"Everything's a risk. Being in this car right now is a risk, but you're still sitting here with the wind blowing on you. You're tasting the freedom of escaping the city—"

"But I did that in the safety of the vehicle with a seat belt keeping me secure."

Reaching over, I take her hand and hold it on the console. "Can't you see? You did that in the safety of us because we were secure."

"We were breakable, which is why we broke." She breaks our hold and rests her hand on her lap.

"I'm not accepting that bullshit anymore."

Offense widens her eyes, and her mouth drops open. "You're not accepting what?"

"We got a raw deal, Story, the short end of the fucking stick when it came to our relationship." I pull up to a red light and stop. Looking at her, I say, "We deserved better. We deserve a second chance."

"A second chance?" At least she didn't scoff, but less shock and more happiness would have been preferable. The light turns green, but I sit there, refusing to take my eyes off her.

Her eyes volley between mine and the light like she's watching a tennis match. "Cooper, go."

"No."

She glances over her shoulder, but with no other car behind us to pressure me to go, she knows we're staying. "What do you want me to say? You want me to say, come on back, Cooper, all is in the past?"

"Can't you? Will you never forgive me?"

"It's not about forgiveness. Honestly." Her shoulders lose momentum and fall as she sighs. "I already forgave you because there's nothing to forgive."

A rush of confusion rolls through me as I try to reconcile the words so they make sense. "What are you saying?"

She's hesitant, but then her hand returns to mine. "I'm saying that nothing you did led to my mom's death." She wipes at the tears I didn't notice had filled her eyes. "He would have killed her anyway."

"But—"

"If I blamed you, I'd have to blame myself for wearing those shorts. You see how none of it makes sense. Me wearing shorts doesn't make someone kill another person." She takes her hand away again, and I let her, though I want to hold tight until we get through this. "You hitting his truck or him getting a ticket doesn't force his hand and make him do what he did."

"He was going to do it anyway."

Her gaze falls to her lap, and her fingers fidget together. "Don't you see, Cooper? We could have worked this out back then." When her eyes find mine, I see the devastation of what could have been. "We could have still been together and fought through this."

I check the rearview mirror again. The only cars are beside us. Finally, the universe is on our side. "I can't change the decisions I made or how you were treated behind my back. We were both abandoned in a sense, but if I could, if I could go back and change everything, I would for a second chance."

"Not everything."

"Not Reed." I grin just thinking about him. And then she smiles too. I take a heavy breath in the lighter moment, but it's only a momentary reprieve. "There are so many regrets weighing us down that the only remedy is to be open to the possibility."

The light turns red, but this time, a car is waiting behind us. *Fuck.* I say, "Tell me I'm not the only one who feels something still between us? That I'm not alone thinking this might not be such a bad idea?"

Looking out the window, she bites on her lower lip and shakes her head. "We don't make sense. We never did, Cooper. It wasn't a lack of love that tore us apart."

"It was a lack of trust." The light turns green, and I drive this time.

Silence is a copilot as we drive the rest of the way. It's not the comfortable silence we usually sit in. This one was full of tension and unresolved feelings being exchanged. I can only imagine the thoughts going through her head. She must hate me.

I back into the driveway, and she gets out before I return the car to the garage.

Story isn't flashy. She's not the bragging type either. She's true to herself and honest with everyone else. I see the look on her face, the wall that's gone up around her as I trek up the driveway to the sidewalk, and I fucking hate that I'm the cause of it being there. As soon as I reach her, I hold up the keys. "Thanks."

"Keep them. They were always yours." *I'm discovering we were always each other's*, even when we weren't.

We stare at each other, neither making a rushed move to get away. It's tempting to pocket the keys and come take her and Reed for a ride sometime, but I give them back to her. "It's your car. I'll make sure to get you the paperwork, so everything is legal and on the up-and-up." When she doesn't take them, I add, "You never did answer my question."

The garage door begins to roll down, catching my attention. When I turn back, she's heading for the front steps. I would have walked her to the door anyway, but I also don't want Lila kicking my ass. She finally stops midway, and says, "I don't have the luxury to make a misstep."

"And that's what I'd be? A misstep?"

The hold on her bag tightens, and she elevates her chin just enough to notice. "You're Reed's father, Cooper, and that's more important than what I feel."

"So you do feel something for me?"

"I'd be lying if I said otherwise."

I'll take that. I'll take that door opening, and one day, she might open it all the way. I nod, feeling we made progress in a good direction. "It was a good day."

She grins. "The best."

I start down the steps, pulling my phone out to call a cab. A car drives by, and I look up at her. She's opening the door but stops and turns back. When our eyes meet again, she asks, "Want to come in?"

42

Story

I don't know what I'm doing, but it doesn't feel wrong. *It never did with Cooper.*

He doesn't run up the steps. Instead, he takes each one with purpose. My heart skips a beat when he reaches me, my eyes dipping closed as if we're about to kiss.

Gah! I wish he'd kiss me again.

On the head.

The cheek.

My neck.

The lips. I'm not picky. I just want one more kiss to tide me over. But I know one more will never be enough. *Not with him.* He could kiss me day and night, and it would only make the craving stronger.

I open my eyes.

He says, "Didn't mean to sneak up on you."

"Sometimes life does that."

"When you—*oh, fuck it*." He cups my face, and his lips crash into mine.

Our mouths are together, the spark ignited into a flame. I grab the front of his shirt to bring him closer, pushing up on my toes as adrenaline surges through my body. His arms wrap around me, and I'm lifted, carried backward through the open door. Our lips locked as our tongues meet like old lovers.

The door is kicked closed, and he adjusts me in his arms, holding me by the ass. My legs go around him as I cling to his neck.

Caught in the cross path of the entry, the living room, and upstairs, he shifts. I can tell he's unsure where to go, but my back hits the wall, and he says, "God, I've missed you."

My lips are left tingling, but that's when I see him, like I'm seeing him for the first time—that same look in his eyes when he came into the coffee shop needing Wi-Fi. I see it now. It was never about the connection to the outside world. He saw me, and I saw him, and after that, it was only ever about us.

I kiss him again because he makes me feel greedy. I kiss him again because I don't need to forgive him. He was always forgiven. I kiss him because he didn't choose the contract or Camille. He chose me, and when we couldn't be together, he chose to be alone.

"You waited," I say, it finally dawning on me. "You waited for me." As his eyes search mine, I hug him so tight that he'll never forget this feeling. Nothing can come between us, not unless we invite it. I will never let that happen again. "You didn't know, but your heart and soul did."

"I didn't let anyone in because there was no room for them. Only you. Only ever you, babe." His breath is warm against my neck, and when I look back, I see the truth. It's always been there. I just wasn't looking.

Now I see it so clearly in the emeralds of his eyes. I kiss

him again, and he turns me around. "Where are we going?" he asks, repeating the same question he asked me in the car.

"Depends."

"On?"

I kiss the corner of his mouth, struggling to keep from smothering him with kisses. "How fast or slow we're taking this." *Please say fast...*

Leaning back to catch my eyes, he asks, "Since when did we ever take things slow?"

"Upstairs. Now." He dashes up the stairs as if I weigh nothing and stops on the landing, looking left and then right. I say, "Left."

When he rushes over, I reach behind me and open the door, worry filling me as I wonder what he'll think of my room. He kisses me again as he carries me inside, finding the bed quickly by the light of the small lamp. Setting me down, he comes with me. He slides between my legs, creating a delicious pressure between us.

If he's not careful, I'm going to ravage this man. He's all over me, and for a moment, I lie there and let him, soaking in the feel of my heart racing again, his lips leaving a wet trail and the air breezing over it, my body reacting to his.

"You okay?" he asks with his mouth pressed to my neck.

"I'm so good. So, so good." I wrap my legs around him and urge him a little higher.

He's good at catching the unsubtle hint and moves up until we're face-to-face. Hovering over me, he chuckles. It's the purest sound accompanied by the easiest smile. I had enjoyed the others since seeing him in the gallery, but this one is different. This one is for me and full of possibility.

Dipping down to kiss my lips, he softens his smile, but his eyes are just as bright. "We're doing this, aren't we?"

"Yes, we're most definitely doing it."

Chuckling, he says, "I meant, giving us a chance, but I'm the fucking luckiest guy if I get to make love to you."

Our lips come together again, and we start moving, our limbs tangling as much as our tongues. I feel him everywhere and not there fast enough. I tug at his shirt while he tugs on mine. But somehow, I get twisted and stuck with it over my head. "A little help here."

His hands drag along my sides as he whispers against the fabric, "We could do a little sensory play, Story."

I don't care how badly my arms ache as I hold them in the air like this, his words are pointed right toward my vagina, and I'm all for it. My breathing deepens, and I feel his hot breath on my breasts with only a bra between us. I'm so damn glad I wore the sexy black lace one.

Lowering my arms to his shoulders, he kisses across my collarbone, disappears, and then yanks the shirt off by the hem. "I decided I like looking at you too much."

I'm sure my hair is a mess, and when I touch my lips, they're already swelling. The little makeup I put on is gone, and though I'm a little heavier compared to my college days, Cooper Haywood looks at me like I'm the most beautiful woman in the world.

I'm going to make him feel so good for that.

"Jeans?" I ask, eagerly. "Or too fast?"

Rolling to his back, he starts yanking his down. "My vote is off." By the time we both are free from the confines of the denim, I'm already climbing on top of him. Leaning forward, I plant my hands on either side of his head. "I'm so damn happy."

The tips of his fingers glide along the length of my arms. He lifts on his elbows and kisses my chin and then my lips. "I love you, Story. I *still* love you."

The rush of our bodies coming together for the first time

calms, and the air turns. I left the lamp on earlier, and now I'm glad. I wouldn't want to miss his expression for anything. The confession makes me swoon, but the love I see written in the anguish as he waits for me to respond does me in once and for all. "I love you, too. I never stopped."

This time when we kiss, we scramble to get naked as well. It's not until he's positioned over me and at my entrance that he stops. "I'm not prepared."

"You don't have a condom?" I ask, panting through my words. My body, a traitor, is squirming against him already to feel him deep inside.

"No. Not on me."

I moan gratuitously and leverage his shoulders to satisfy the craving. "Oh, fuck it." I roll my eyes just before sinking onto his erection, the back of my head shoving into the pillow, and I close my eyes. But when he doesn't move, my eyes fly open again. I can read the question before he has to say it. "I'm on the pill."

"Okay," he says with a smile playing on his lips. "That's good."

"It is good, but I need you to move, babe. Please."

"Yeah. On it. *On you.* In you. Yeah. I'm just going to shut up now." His hips start to thrust, sending delectable chills through me. It's been so long since I've felt this wanton for sex. The blame lies squarely on Cooper's shoulders.

I smile, embracing the fullness, the tingling sensation as my body stretches for his and acclimates. This sense of wholeness that I haven't felt since him fills my body and soul.

It's all so much, so fast, and too slow, harder and with not enough built-in breathers as we fumble through the sheets and each other. I ride him, getting drunk on his expression as he savors every inch of my exposed body on top of him.

I drown in each thrust that hits deeper, so much that I let my moans fill our ears as our skin becomes slick with need and desire. We make love, fuck, and everything in between. We laugh together. We love together. We come, and we recover together.

Lying naked on top of the covers, I turn my head, my body too depleted to make the effort. And then a swell of happiness surges through my veins at the sight of Cooper lying on his side of the bed again.

His eyes are closed as if sleep is about to drag him from me, but then his hand finds mine, and our fingers entwine, like our hearts. He faces me and says, "I can't believe you're in my life again."

"When you least expect it."

"Best day ever."

I slide over and drape myself all over him because I have Cooper back in my life, and I will never let him go again. I kiss his chest. "The best."

He wraps around me and rolls me to my back with him draped over me. "Who cares about early shifts or meetings?" A kiss connects us together and deepens, our bodies coming together again.

We're slower this time, the frenzy still smoldering inside but kissing, studying, touching every nook and cranny, ebb and flow of each other's bodies. Making out and making love.

Sleep just about tackles us in bed after our breathing evens, and the heaviness subsides when he says, "You used my line."

I laugh though it's not the words but the giddiness I feel that's bubbled up. "Which one?"

"Fuck it."

I laugh even harder. "It fit. Although it's kind of your thing, you're not the only one who gets to say fuck around here." I caress his cheek just before snuggling into my favorite spot against his side. With his arm around me, he kisses the top of my head.

"Speaking of *around here*, do you want to talk about your room? "

"Oh." I cringe. "That."

He pops up on his hands and takes a leisurely scan around the room. Glancing back at me, he says, "It's like going back in time."

"Guess I blew it. You found out I'm a total weirdo."

"I already knew you were a weirdo, but that's okay. I'm a weirdo, too." Shaking his head, he says, "I'm also feeling very twenty-two again. Your bed is even in the same spot as it was in the apartment."

"It's a new bed, though."

"I'm thinking that's all that is new. The room's flipped but the same. The same desk is under the window with your camera on top. The dresser is probably still full of old flannel pajamas." He flips the covers off and walks to the desk, tapping twice. I know what he's doing. When he looks back at me, he says, "You kept it. You kept my note." He then looks at the room again. "You kept everything."

"I couldn't bring myself to get rid of it. The memories we created there . . . we created Reed." I lie back, trying not to feel awkward. I had my reasons, and they were enough for me through the years. Stacking my hands behind my head, I say, "I had you when I lived there."

Coming back to bed, he slides in next to me. "I wish I'd had the same, but nothing at my apartment was you and me. We were a studio walkup just off campus." He brings me into an embrace, and he kisses the soft spot under my ear. "Free from everything that held us back before, we get to be whoever we want together."

"As long as we're together, that's all I need."

When he lies back, something comes over him, and he scrubs a hand over his face. "I told you I love you. Like I just blurted it out there. That could have gone sideways so fucking fast."

I take his hand from hiding his face and kiss each knuckle and then his palm. "Being sideways with you isn't so bad." Sitting up enough to kiss his lips, I add, "I love you, Cooper Haywood."

His hand moves against my cheek as he stares into my eyes. Then he lifts, and our mouths come together. "I love you, Story Salenger. I'll be the best Mommy's friend you've ever had."

I burst out laughing. "That should be easy. I never had another."

"You always were too good for me."

"I'd say I'm just right, and we're perfect together."

I snuggle back, relishing the quiet moments as much as the laughter. But soon, my eyelids are too heavy to keep open. Listening to Cooper's steady heartbeat, I give in.

I DON'T MEAN to stare but seeing Cooper drink coffee across from me has my heart floating on cloud nine. It's so unexpected yet feels so right.

Setting the mug down in the sink, he rinses it like the knight in shining armor he is, and says, "I need to get going, or I'll be late." Coming around the peninsula, he holds my hips, swaying them gently. He always was a hip man. "When can I see you again?"

We've had a Sunday pattern going on for weeks. "I was thinking next Sunday is too far away."

"If I had my way, it would be tonight, but I understand your schedule is very different from mine." Embracing me, he asks, "What works best for you and Reed?"

"You being in our lives." My words have him leaning back to find my eyes. "What about we make Mondays puzzle and pizza night?"

His smile could light up the pre-dawn sky. "Sounds like something I'd like to do with you guys."

"Good. Maybe we just start from there and let things happen naturally."

Kissing my forehead, he pulls back. "Music to my ears."

I walk him to the door. He kisses me once more before jumping down the five steps onto the sidewalk. My heart stops like it does every time my son tries to do that. Rolling my eyes, I cup the side of my mouth. "You're worse than Reed."

"Cooper!"

Oh, shit.

Reed comes running down the sidewalk with Lila and Jake close behind.

He runs into Cooper's arms and hugs him. This time, when Cooper hugs him like he'll never let go, my heart stops for different reasons. When he buries his head against Reed's neck, I cry . . . like a baby.

Lila comes up the steps and hugs me. "Must have been a good night if you're smiling while you're crying about it."

"It was the best," I say, sniffling through my words.

"Hey, Mom?"

I turn back to see them together, looking more like

father and son than I've seen. I wipe back my tears. "What is it, buddy?"

"If Cooper had a sleepover, why wasn't I invited?"

My finger goes in the air, and I'm about to answer before realizing I'm not sure I should say that. *Um.* You'd think I'd be used to the tough questions by now, but my mind goes blank.

Then Cooper says, "I just brought your mom coffee this morning."

"Ew," Reed replies, completely disinterested now. Wriggling in Cooper's arms, Reed is set back down. He runs up the steps. "I need my backpack."

Lila says, "Seems like you and Cooper need to wrap things up a little earlier next time." Leaning in, she asks, "Is there going to be a next time?" My friend is blunt to put things nicely, but she's also fiercely loyal and the best friend I could ever ask for.

"We had sex and said I love you. Not in that order."

"Um . . . huh?" Her gaze pivots to Cooper, who gives us a little wave. Then a huge smile rises on her face. "Don't you guys ever take your time?"

Reed hugs my middle and then runs between us. "Hey Cooper, want to walk to school with me?"

"Abso-fu—Absolutely, buddy." When Cooper looks back at me, I tap my watch. I thought he was about to be late.

He shrugs. "See you later."

Three words that beat goodbye any day.

I lean against the doorframe and watch them together—Reed bouncing in all his energy, Cooper carrying his backpack, both having a great discussion that, apparently, involves big arm gestures—until they turn the corner.

This is a very good day.

43

Story

Three Months Later . . .

Everyday life.

It wasn't a series of great events that happened. *Just life.*

Nothing out of the ordinary to make a more interesting story to tell at parties. *"He walked into the coffee shop needing Wi-Fi . . ."*

His version starts a little differently. *"I saw her across the party with some other guy."*

"Not for long," I'm quick to add.

"No." He always smirks at that part. *"Not for long."*

Cooper and I eased into a routine that became the pattern of our days and nights. Weekdays and weekends. Sometimes, we went out, but mostly, we stayed in and spent time with Reed.

Maybe when so much trauma happens at the start of adulthood, you naturally crave the opposite. Excitement

these days is found in different ways, calmer and more
peaceful.

"Mom."

I look up to see Cooper and Reed staring at me. Reed
says, "It's your turn."

Ah. The game. I spin the wheel on the board, then move
my car six spots. "Triplets? I don't think so. I'm going to spin
again."

"You can't." Reed is giggling. "That's a lot of kids."

I start laughing. "Yeah, I can't imagine that many kids."

Cooper says, "I can. I can imagine it."

Left speechless with my mouth hanging open, I widen
my eyes. *Well, shit.* Does he want more kids? Do I? He makes
it sound easy, but there's so much to be considered before
adding to our family. Guess it's something to start thinking
about.

"I'll finish my residency next year, and I can apply in
Brooklyn for a full-time position, either at one of the hospi-
tals or in private practice."

I'm still staring at him, trying to process how he has all
the answers as if he's already thought this through.

With Reed here, it's not something I want to have an
open discussion about before we can talk one-on-one. "I
think that's a conversation for another day."

"You told me you'd give me a brother or sister if you
could." I side-eye the kid. He has no clue how to hold our
cards close to his chest.

Cooper sits back and crosses his arms over his chest,
raising an eyebrow in challenge. "It's your move, babe," he
says.

Challenge accepted. "Reed, I said that because you
asked for one for your fourth birthday, and I couldn't give
you a sibling."

His head jerks to Cooper. "But Cooper's here now. I'll ask again for my next birthday."

Rapidly blinking with my mouth open again, I'm not sure what he is inferring about Cooper being here now to make a baby happen, and it's definitely not a conversation I want to have over a game of Life and bowls of Cocoa Pebbles.

I shoot Cooper a hard glare, which makes him laugh.

He sits forward again, resting his elbows on the table. "Don't worry, I can have that conversation with him," says the pediatrician. *Thank God.*

I turn to Reed. "You have Jake. You're basically brothers."

"Yeah, but when he turned twelve a few weeks ago, he told me to scram." He plonks his arms on the table and sticks out his bottom lip.

"I'm sorry, bud." I rub his arm, hoping to soothe the hurt feelings.

But this whole thing is a lot to think about. "I'm not opposed to the idea. I just need to think about it. Can we back burner this conversation just for a little while?"

Reed and Cooper exchange a look before they start laughing. It's the high-five that clues me in and gives them away.

These two are peas in a pod. I stand no chance. "I was just set up, wasn't I?" Reed's still giggling but gets up from the table. Although he's up a little later than usual, I say, "We're not finished with the game. Where are you going?"

"Gotta go, Mom. Cooper got a new tiger book. *Roar.* He promised to read to me before bed. If I don't go now, you'll say lights out before we can."

Because I'm such the meanie mom. I'm thinking I just moved from the good cop to the bad cop in this relationship.

"Is this just a guy thing, or are moms invited, too?"

Cooper replies, "Moms are always invited," just as Reed says, "It's a Cooper and Reed thing."

Reaching across the table, Cooper covers my hand with his. "You're always invited. I'm still just the novelty dad."

"No, you're more than that, and I wouldn't have it any other way."

When Reed runs upstairs, well-aware that we don't get to read our books until we brush our teeth and get in our pajamas, Cooper takes his car from the board game. Removing the little peg in the driver's seat, he puts it in my car next to me....*and my four kids.*

"Open your hand," he says. When I do, he places the car on my palm and wraps my hand around it. "It feels like we've lived a lifetime, but we're only twenty-eight. Is it such a far-fetched idea to want to expand our family?"

"You just got Reed in your life, and now you want more kids?"

"I want all the kids I can have with you, but I only want more if you do. That kid upstairs is more than I could have ever asked for." He kisses my head and says, "You know you're welcome to read the book with us."

"No, it's fine. I've been fortunate to have more than five years. I'm okay with you and him making up for lost time."

He nods and then grins. "I'll see you upstairs."

"See you upstairs."

Little moments that make up the most important times in our lives are what matter, and I've been given a second chance. I wouldn't trade this for a fancy penthouse or mansion on thirty acres. The only thing that bears the legacy that tried to suffocate Cooper is his last name. He's been given a fresh start and deserves it.

I put away the game but pocket the little car. When I turn the lights and lock the house for the night, I grab two glasses of water, then head upstairs. It's good to be prepared after a heavy workout. I wink but then realize, like a fool, I'm winking for myself.

When I reach the landing, I'm unlatching the gate when I overhear Cooper say, "You're turning six soon. What do you want for your birthday?"

"I want a fast car like Mom's in the garage."

I laugh to myself. The silence from the bedroom, though, tells me everything going on in Cooper's head. I'm not sure how hard Cooper is biting his tongue, but I bet it's painful. I stay long enough to hear Cooper reply, "Yeah, Mom's car is amazing. I think you're a little young for one like that, but maybe you'll get the car when you're older."

"Promise?"

"I promise, but we'll have to talk Mom into it."

"You can. All I get is brush your teeth, live a good life, do your homework, and I love yous." I'm still grinning like a loon. If that's the worst the kid's got, I'm doing a pretty damn good job. "But if *you* ask her, she'll listen."

"Why do you say that?"

"Because she gets all gooey when you talk to her." Reed sounds so annoyed.

Cooper chuckles, but then says, "I get kind of gooey myself . . . wait. Never mind. Come on. Lights out."

I hurry to set the glasses in the bedroom and then make it sound like I'm coming up the stairs and stomp across the hall. Peeking in, I knock on the open door. "May I enter?"

When Reed looks at me, his little smile, that's looking more like Cooper's every day, hits me in the feels. "I'm ready, Mom."

I cross the room. "Mom? Now I'm just Mom? What happened to Mommy?"

His shoulders bounce from the bed. "I'm almost six."

"Yes, you are. Can I be Mommy until then?" I tickle his ribs.

"Yes. Yes," he says, wriggling.

I lean down and kiss his cheek. Looking at him, I tap his nose, and say, "I love you."

"I love you, too, Mommy."

I'm mush in this kid's hands. I walk to the door and let Cooper say his good night. It's more involved with a secret handshake that I'm not privy to, and I think there are two bops on the head followed by a bro-hug, as Reed calls it. Cooper has definitely made up for lost time.

I hear Reed's door closing as I slip off my pants and pull on a pair of sleep shorts. Cooper enters our room and closes the door with the added click of the lock. He stayed that first night and just kind of never left. We made it official when he sold his condo in Manhattan last month. "How much did you hear?"

"All of it." I smirk. "How bad a hit did your pride take over the car?"

Chuckling, he starts undressing. "The car is yours. The paperwork has been filed for the change in ownership."

I still don't understand why this was important to him. Doesn't he understand that a car will never replace the man? But there's no use arguing when it's already a done deal. Anyway, we've moved into the stage of what's mine is his and what's his is mine, so it doesn't matter.

He's so good to me, but more importantly, he's amazing with Reed. I smile. "I know your job makes you an expert, but being a dad comes natural to you, Cooper."

He looks up after setting his clothes on a chair. "Yeah, you think so?"

"I couldn't have asked for a better father for my child, *or future children*."

We stand across the room, suddenly still with our eyes fixed on each other. I didn't realize the gravity of my words until after I said them. It wasn't planned. Only how I feel.

"Do you mean that?"

"I do." Our voices are just whispers between us, but the emotions are felt loud and clear. Even with only a lamp on, I can see the light reflected in his eyes just before he drops his head and wipes across his face.

When he looks up, he says, "I didn't even think I wanted kids. All I saw were people who hated the burden until I went to Patrice's house. I saw the difference and changed after that. I knew if I had a child, it would be like that. They'd know that they're the center of my universe." He walks over and says, "Along with my wife."

"What about girlfriend?"

"You're more to me than that word can ever describe." Bringing my hand to his mouth, he kisses it. "I love you, babe."

"I love you, too." He returns to collect his wallet from his pants pocket and sets it on the desk.

I fold down the blankets so the bed is ready when we are, then sit on the end of the mattress. "We never talked about our relationship with Reed. He might not understand what we are to each other or how he fits into that picture."

"He knows."

"How?"

"Because we've shown him, Story." He sits next to me, our hands always coming together like a magnet to steel. "The other stuff is, it's just words kids his age don't really understand. They're commonly used labels, but they don't know what they mean until you show them. We're doing that every day."

I lean my head on his shoulder. "He's learning love by example."

"He had a great head start because of you."

Although Reed has taken to Cooper, I've struggled with when we should tell him he's his father. Cooper hasn't asked and would never put any pressure on me to rush things, but I know he wants that despite the labeling of our relationship conversation.

I'm Mom. *It's a label I'm most proud of.*

He's Dad. *It's time Reed knows.*

When I lift my head, I say, "You've never asked me why I named him Reed."

Cooper's gaze falls to our clasped hands, and he turns them over. If it were free, he'd be running it through his hair. I just know it, so I hold him tighter. He looks up and asks, "Why?"

"So you'd always be a part of him." His gulp is hard as he swallows down my words. I add, "But that was before I realized he'd be your twin."

Laughter chokes from his throat, and he smiles. "It's kind of hard to miss the resemblance, huh?"

"Yeah, cutest kid ever. I think we should tell Reed you're his dad."

Cooper freezes. Literally doesn't move a muscle as he stares at me.

"Are you okay, Cooper?"

He blinks first and then seems to come to life—a shake of the head, his shoulders rounding, and a scrub of his face all happen before his eyes return to mine. "Fine." His grin grows like a weed in sunshine. "I'm great." There's no hand running through his hair or shoving his hands in his pockets . . . not that he has pockets in his boxer briefs.

He's great, and I believe him.

"Story?" he whispers. My breath halts in my throat. Maybe I assumed too soon. "Thank you for having Reed, for raising him, even without me. Thank you for being Mom and loving him enough for the both of us."

Now I'm choked up, the lump making the act of swallowing a little harder.

He wraps his arms around me and kisses my cheek. "I have him only because of you. Thank you."

"And I only have him because of you. What do you say we tell him soon?"

"I'd really like that."

Sitting back, he lets his fingers trail along my scar. "No matter how many years we have ahead or how many are in our past, you will always be the best part of this life for me."

It's my turn to tear up. This man, he thinks I saved him, but he'll never understand how he saved me. We make no sense on paper or to others, but to us, we do and isn't that what's important?

As for the scar he's tracing, the red has faded, and it isn't as angry anymore. *Neither is he.* Though both of us have so much that we could be if we had held on to it—his parents, the years we lost, my mom's death, *her life*.

I used to dream of having the scar lasered and once considered getting a tattoo to blend it away. But it's a reminder of not only my mom but how far I've come. It's a piece of my history that I now consider my art. Reed thinks it's the coolest, and Cooper kisses it and tells me it reminds him of the stem of a peony. I'm good with that.

Using the years to think about my mom, she had a lot of struggles in her life. But I try to remember that she chose to keep me. After that, she raised me the best she could. And at the end of her life, she fought for me. I don't think I ever fully gave her the credit she deserved. I said it, but now I know it. Calliope taught me some hard lessons, but the one that stands out the most is to live life on my own terms. I'll teach my son the same. She was one of a kind, and mine.

Cooper and I climb under the covers on our respective sides of the bed. His scars are on the inside and a little harder to reach. I think Reed and I are doing a good job, though. Cooper's right. He's more than the label of my boyfriend, Mommy's friend, or Reed's buddy. But as he said, there's an unspoken understanding between the three of us. We know what we are to each other, and that's all that matters.

I sink into the bed next to him, my body tired from the day, but my mind is going full speed. "Cooper?" I ask, peeking over at him. "Why didn't we just get married back then? It would have ended any opportunity for that contract."

"That's true. It would have taken away any ammunition they had to make me get married." His eyes meet mine. "But would you have married me? Would you have said yes?"

"To put an end to that nightmare. Yes, I would have."

"And otherwise?"

I don't have to think about it because I already know the answer. "Yes."

He rolls to his side to face me. "What about now?"

I roll to my side to face him, already grinning. "Are you asking?"

"I could be. Depends on your answer." He smirks, but I get the bonus wink as well. "I was planning to do it this weekend."

Screw the butterflies, my happiness bursts like fireworks in my chest. "Don't you think three months is a little fast."

He leans forward and kisses me. "Since when did we ever take anything slow?"

Angling onto my back, I invite him over. He moves quickly, settling between my legs and cups my cheeks. I caress his, and say, "The answer is yes."

We seal it with a kiss . . . and then I score an orgasm before he slides back up my body ready for the main event. Feeling light as air, I ask, "Do you want to play doctor tonight?"

"I'm not really into that role play."

"What are you into, Cooper Haywood?"

"Financial analysts with a passion for photography."

I burst out laughing before I remember I need to keep it down. "That's oddly specific." I play coy because it's fun with him and blink my eyelashes.

"Well, how about this?" He kisses the base of my neck and then says, "My real kink—I'm really into Story Salenger."

"An engagement that involves sex—"

"Great sex," he interjects.

"Valid point. An engagement that involves great sex is not really a story we can tell our grandkids or kids of any sort. It's rated R for eighteen plus, but even if our kids are older teens, this is not—"

"Hey," he says, then kisses me. Left breathless and wanting more, he says, "You're not just great sex to me. You're also the love of my life. That's our story, and I'm sticking to it."

I kiss him just as our bodies align to come together again, and then whisper, "I'm that good, huh?"

Chuckling, he says, "Best I ever had."

44

Story

Sunday ...

"Five feet," I remind my Tigger of a kid. He's so excited he's practically bouncing like his favorite fictional character. Reed is leading us straight to the tigers. He knows the path from the entrance of the Bronx Zoo to the exhibit.

I keep him close for safety but give the five-year-old enough freedom to feel he's pushing boundaries. Cooper and I usually hold hands, but overly crowded places, like the zoo on Sundays, have us prepared to dart.

Shifting the backpack he's wearing with our day's supply of necessities, he glances at me. "How are you feeling?"

My amazing man. He's worried about me right now? "I'm good."

His arm comes around my shoulders, and he squeezes me close to kiss my head. "It's going to be a change. I don't think a big one, but a change from one parent to having two.

I know you're okay with that, but more so that you're ready for it."

"I'm ready." I hate losing the contact when he lunges forward right before a family comes between us and our kid. Already the protective dad, always has been with Reed, and protective of me in other ways.

Cooper doesn't need to work, but he shares with others what he does for us—cares for us and our needs. I saw it when he first met Reed and the way he kneeled to give our son eye contact and to speak on his level, to listen to him and let our son's imagination soar.

I caught a glimpse of that on graduation day when Cooper and Jake walked ahead of Lila and me. Jake was around Reed's age now and totally looked up to this amazing man who talked to him with respect, but also listened to him. I see Cooper treat Reed the same.

And although it was a fleeting time in our lives, Cooper braved a storm and floods to get medicine for me. He took care of me when I was basically a stranger. Well, a stranger who he'd just slept with, but he could have left. He came back. He came back to take care of me. I have doubt that he'll spend his life caring for his family.

I catch up to them ahead at the exhibit. We didn't discuss who would say what or rehearse it, so I'm not surprised that Cooper is waiting for me to take the lead. I wait for my little monkey to climb onto the ledge of the viewing window and then point at the smaller tigers lounging in the sun. "Which one is the mommy?"

"That one," Reed says, pointing.

I had no plan, but this seems like one that works for him. "Why that one?"

"Because the smaller one is only five feet away."

Cooper and I exchange a knowing smile when he kneels

on the other side of Reed. I ask, "And which one is the daddy tiger?"

He looks between the ones we see but doesn't answer. I don't know why I feel a knot in my stomach, but it's growing bigger every second.

Reed turns to eye Cooper and then he touches the faint lines on the side of his right eye. Turning back to the tigers, he points at one I hadn't noticed before. The large animal sits regally on top of a rock overseeing his pride. That's our Cooper, the king of our hearts, protector of all things Salenger. He says, "That one because he has stripes like Cooper."

I avoid looking at Cooper altogether because he'll only make me cry. Struggling to keep my voice from shaking when my emotions take over, I take a deep breath and rub his back. "Hey buddy, I wanted to tell you something important."

"What?" Reed looks at me and then at Cooper. He promptly sits on Cooper's knee like its sole purpose is to be a seat for him.

Looking more at home than ever, I know this is it. Some might be sad, but I'm about to give him something that I used to wish I had. I say, "Cooper's your dad."

Reed stretches his arms over his shoulders and starts touching Cooper's face. Cooper pretends to bite his fingers. Giggling, Reed says, "Okay."

"Yes, it is okay, but I want you to really listen and understand." With his eyes looking into mine, I smile. "You know how you grew like a weed in my belly?"

"Mmhm."

I pause, realizing I don't want to talk about how Cooper planted the seed. That's a whole other conversation that I'll leave for the professional. "Actually, don't think about weeds. Think about blood. We share blood—"

"Ew."

Saving me, Cooper says, "You and your Mommy are related. What she's saying is that we're also related."

"You and Mommy?"

"No . . ." His head wobbles. "Yes, but different from you and me. We come from the same family, like how you come from Mommy."

"You, me, and Mommy are a family."

Cooper grins. "Yes, we are. I'm your dad."

Reed looks at me like he's bored, and he's definitely antsy. "Will you do Dad Duty at school?"

"What's Dad Duty?" Cooper asks.

Feeling a huge sense of relief to get that secret released, I reply, "Dad Duty is when the dads volunteer at the school. It's a shift once a month during lunch. You play four square or a game of basketball. You just spend time with all the kids."

"Mom comes, but I got laughed at last time."

"You fill in at Dad Duty?" Cooper asks, already smiling.

"A lot of the fathers in the community can't take off work. Since I always pulled double duty anyway, I wanted to be there for the kids. And I have a really good free throw. The kids are impressed when I nail it."

"Oh, yeah?" He laughs. "You'll have to show me sometime." He lifts Reed and angles him his way. "I'll be at Dad Duty every month, but what do you think about me being on Dad duty every day in your life?"

"All the time?"

"All the time."

"Forever?"

"Forever."

"Can I call you Dad?"

That's the punch in the heart neither of us saw coming. The tears escape before I can stop them. Cooper isn't faring much better, but his tears never leave his eyes. He says, "I'd really like that." He wraps his arms around him, and they hug so tight that I think I'm going to need the Jaws of Life to separate them.

"Do I get to be a Haywood, too?"

Cooper taps his nose. "You always were, but if you want to add that into your name, maybe somewhere in the middle, we can ask Mom."

I ask, "We don't have to make a decision today, but do you like Reed Haywood Salenger or Reed Salenger Haywood?"

"I don't know." He shrugs. It's a lot to figure out in one day, but no matter what he decides, Cooper's right. He's always been a part of both of us.

Popping off Cooper's knee, Reed holds his hand out. When Cooper takes hold, Reed looks up and asks, "Can we get cotton candy, Daddy?"

Oh lordy, this kid. He knows how to work a situation to his advantage. I'm not sure if he gets that from Cooper or me, but I have a feeling we're in trouble when he becomes a teen.

"Absolutely."

Six Months Later

"You have a buyer," Kathy whispers, pointing across the room. "Blond hair. Rich. Willing to spend her husband's fortune to get back at him for having a mistress."

My eyebrows shoot up. "That's a lot of information. How do you know?"

She nods twice toward Louise. "She's the mistress."

I gasp, covering my mouth.

Kathy shrugs. "She also wants to build her art collection of up-and-comers."

"I'm an up-and-comer." I laugh at my joke, but when the gallery owner doesn't, I ask, "Which photo is she interested in?"

"*COOPER*." She shrugs again. "Guess she likes looking at your husband. A revenge purchase I can back. He's also a gorgeous man."

"But *COOPER* and *REED* aren't for sale. It even says it on the placard."

"I don't know what to tell you. Rich people think everything's for sale. I've already told them so. Maybe figure out a price and throw it out to see if she bites."

Hmpf. Not sure I like putting a price on my husband. I toss around numbers in my head as I cross the gallery, but nothing sticks. It feels dirty, like something his parents would do, *and did*.

The woman is dressed in designer clothes from head to toe. I can tell by the crazy mixture of patterns. Her thin legs dip from the knee-length skirt, and she's in platform red heels. It's a look I could never pull off but go her! "Hi, I heard you were interested in—"

"Cooper. Yes, very interested. How'd you get his picture?"

"I took it." I stand beside her, staring at the matching pair of photographs—Reed and Cooper—peas in a pod and my little family. But her voice triggers bad memories of pearls in the grass. I look at her. *Fuck.*

Camille looks the same, maybe a little tired, but it's after seven o'clock. Maybe she had a long day . . . or maybe her life decisions are catching up with her, and the fillers aren't strong enough to fight against the evil polluting her pores. I wince, hating that I just sank to that level of depravity.

She rotates as if her neck doesn't twist to the side. I rub the side of mine as she looks me over disapprovingly.

I could tug at my silk tank to straighten it or try to pull my jeans over the little muffin top I've developed, but why? Because she doesn't approve? Camille Arden doesn't matter to me. The people in those photos do.

She says, "You look familiar to me. Have we met?"

"A long time ago. I'm sure nothing you'd remember."

Crossing her arms in front of her chest, she says, "What's your name?" I point at the black letters on the wall. She hums and then adds, "Story Salenger? Nope, nothing."

"Maybe you'll recognize my married name? Mrs. Cooper Haywood." I imagined that feeling a lot better when it played out in my head, it being a more you reap what you sow sort of moment.

Camille doesn't huff and storm off. She just looks at me and then asks, "And that's your son? Cooper Reed?"

"Yes. It's our son."

Looking back at the photos, she covers her stomach with her arm.

I touch her arm. "Are you okay?"

"No. I went to see my husband at the office earlier." Her eyes water. "He told me he wants a divorce because he and his mistress are having a baby."

My head whips around to see Louise laughing and touching her belly, celebrating the news. When I turn back to Camille, I say, "I'm sorry to hear that."

"I went to see him to tell him that *I'm* pregnant."

Oh. My heart sinks for her. Tears spring to her eyes, and

she's quick to dig a pair of large black Chanel sunglasses out of her bag. She puts them on and says, "I don't know why I'm telling you this. I made your life miserable." Her arms go wide. "You win. You won, Story. You got everything I ever wanted, and I got what I deserved."

Other patrons look our way.

I lower my voice and try to see her eyes through the dark shades. "I was a single mom for years." Her lips part in surprise as she stares. I continue, "So I understand what that's like. I'm well-acqainted with the fear that comes along with it." I dig a card out of my pocket. "If you'd like to grab a cup of coffee and talk about it, give me a call."

With the card between her fingers, she asks, "Why would you do that for me?"

I shrug, not sure myself, quite honestly. "You just seem like you might need a friend."

"I have friends. Lots of friends," she says defensively.

"Okay. Use it or don't. Either way, you have my number."

She looks around with offense disfiguring her face, but then pockets my number in her purse. She looks awkwardly around the gallery, and then says, "You're a very good photographer."

"Thank you. Cooper's not for sale," I say, my husband or the photo, to make sure I'm clear.

She laughs lightly. "He never was." Walking toward my Closet Collection—shoes, bags, candy wrappers, and diet drugs—she says, "I really like these and would like to buy them."

"Really? Do you want to know the price?"

"No. Whatever it is, double it." She hands me a black credit card. "But can we ring them up before my husband cuts me off?"

"Absolutely."

"THAT'S WILD," Cooper says, spooning ice cream into his mouth.

"I thought so, too."

"I don't understand how you can be so nice to people who literally plotted for your demise."

"Two reasons, I'd never want to be so lost in life that I'd wish that kind of ill will on another person. Secondly, everyone deserves a second chance." Holding my finger up, I add, "Except your parents. They can rot in hell."

He chuckles and then presses his cold, sticky lips to mine. I purr. "Delicious."

"Just like you." I thought he was leading that somewhere, like into the bedroom, but nope, he finishes the ice cream and sets the bowl down, and says, "Did I ever tell you about this girl named Eliza from back in college?"

I put my hands up. "Stop. We're not going to do this. If you slept with her or anything else, I'm not interested in that part of your past."

"Can't I just confess?"

"No." I tap his chin. "Just let it go. It doesn't matter anymore."

"Are you sure?"

Since he sounds like he really wants to get this off his chest, I ask, "Are *you* sure?"

"She's been in the rearview for a long time." He lies back on the couch, and I settle down next to him.

"Then that's the answer." Lifting up again, I say, "You're not going to believe this. Camille bought four of my photos."

He strokes my hair back and tucks some behind my ear. "That's incredible."

"They were revenge purchases, but she still bought them for forty thousand dollars."

"Holy shit."

"That's what I said," I say, my voice pitching.

Since we're struggling to get comfortable, he's the one now sitting up. "What's a revenge purchase?"

"She paid for them on a credit card to get back at her husband. But she did say how much she liked them."

He pulls me onto his lap. "Of course she liked them. They're amazing. How about we go out this week and celebrate? I'll even let you buy me dinner since you're the money bucks."

"Says the millionaire." I tease him, but I haven't done so bad myself. Some of my investments have really paid off over the years. I even bought my house outright.

"Eh. A little higher than that."

I slow blink at him, which drives him nuts. That, and my golf clap. "Multimillionaire?" I should have started here since I already knew the basics. He's Haywood legacy, after all.

"A little more than that."

"Jesus, Cooper, if you say billionaire . . ."

"I didn't have to. You did."

"Billionaire?" I can't process having that amount of money. My clients can, and some do, but it's like Monopoly money to them. Me? Yeah . . . I'm blank about what someone does with that much to spend frivolously. "Don't you think a wife should know these things? Especially when your wife is a financial analyst." I might give him a hard time, but out of all the investments I've made, he's the one who's worth the most to me.

"You said you didn't want to talk about money before the wedding."

"Because I thought, *as I stated then*, you were crazy for not wanting a prenuptial agreement."

He kisses my shoulder. "If I can trust you with my life, Story, I can trust you with my money. Anyway, that's why I'm telling you."

"You're lucky I married you for your big . . . *heart*, ya charmer." We finally settle in to watch the movie, one we saw years ago in a theater together before we knew each other, and with our son sleeping upstairs. "I love you, Cooper."

"I love you, Story."

EPILOGUE

Cooper

Four Months Later ...

MONEY COULDN'T FILL the void my family left behind. The lawsuit couldn't heal the damage done.

Putting a ring on the love of my life came close. Finding out I have a son and getting to be in his life is right up there as well. Sitting on a bench in Central Park watching Patrice spend time with them both? Sounds cliché, but it's priceless.

Story runs back and plops down on the bench next to me. "I'm too tired to run today."

"You've been putting in too many hours." I hate sounding like *that* guy, but she's been running herself into the ground for the past four months.

"Between trying to figure out my next collection to taking over clients for a co-worker who left last week without warning, Reed's new tuba ambitions, and being a doctor's wife, I'm wiped."

I wrap my arms around her shoulders and let her rest against me. "Not to add to your load, but I've been thinking about our wedding."

"What about it?" she asks, turning to face me.

"It was just down at the courthouse, which is great with me, but I don't want you to have any regrets. Do you want something bigger?"

"I didn't marry you for anyone else. I married you because I love you. Anyway, we had everyone we loved there. It was a small group, but a mighty supportive one." Lila and Lou, Patrice, Jake, and my best man, Reed. It's a tight-knit group. "But because we got married so fast, we never did get a honeymoon. I wouldn't mind a fancy trip." She slides over and plants herself on my lap. "What do you think about that?"

I still feel bad I couldn't take one after the vows, but I couldn't get the time off. Now, I'll do anything, including quit if I'm forced to, to give her this trip. Rubbing her hip, I ask, "Where do you want to go?"

"Wherever you are."

"Charmer. I'm right here with you. I always will be."

She smiles, tipping her head back in the sunshine.

I've fucked up more times than I can keep track of and set my world on fire just to watch it burn. But it was Story, this magnificent woman, who showed me how beautiful life can be, and always believed in me, even when times were tough.

What a wonderful life she's given me.

"What about the Maldives?"

Her hazel eyes with bright gold centers find mine. "Too long of a flight."

"The Bahamas?"

Tightening her arms around my neck, she says, "*Oooh*, I can get on board with that."

"I'll make the arrangements. You don't have to do a thing."

She waggles her eyebrows. "Now you're talking my language."

"We need to talk," we both say at the same time, our heads jerking back in response. Once the shock wears off, we laugh. She says, "You go first."

Shit. I've been nervous about this for a long time, not sure how she's going to take the news. It's probably best if I just rip the bandage right off. "My parents added an amendment into the settlement."

Her body tenses. It always does if either of those subjects comes up. She sighs with a roll of her eyes. "Can you tell me?"

"I'll tell you anything. Nothing will ever keep me from sharing with you." I gulp despite that being absolutely true. "But you might want to brace yourself."

"*Oh, good grief.*" Her hands fist behind my neck, the tension from anticipation straining her expression. "I'm not prepared, so just say it, Cooper."

Rip the bandage off. "I was granted my trust funds and a large portion of the Haywood wealth that would have come to me eventually." She nods. Swallowing becomes harder for me. I hope she doesn't freak out and sees it as a good thing. "But the rest remained under their names. It's substantial."

"Okay."

"When they pass, it won't come to me."

I see the moment it dawns on her, reaching her eyes as they widen. "Don't say it."

"Do you really not want me to say it, or do you want me to say it slowly and let it ease into the atmosphere?"

A heavy sigh is released, and so am I when her hands

return to her lap. "Does it have to do with Reed?"

I nod. "He'll inherit everything else."

"Which is?" she asks.

"The penthouse in the city, Haywood House in the town of Haywood, two generations of collected wealth in various properties and assets as well as whatever they have left in their bank accounts."

"Jesus, Cooper." She rubs her forehead. "No one needs that kind of wealth, much less a kid. Look what it did to you."

I reposition her on my lap. "Look, Story. Money isn't evil. It's just . . . money. Some people are bad. You know that first-hand. Some are awful. I know that well. But we can continue teaching him the values you've already instilled, and we have the opportunity to take our money and do good in the world."

The tightness in her lips eases, and a smile, although small, appears. "Valid point. We could do a lot of good with our money collectively."

"See? All good things."

She digs in her pocket before wrapping her arms around me again. "Question. They don't know about Reed, do they?"

"No. The amendment states any of my offspring."

She grins mischievously. "Well, that leads me to what I wanted to talk to you about."

"Do I need to brace myself?" I joke, holding her by the hips.

"I don't think so, but we do need to think about a larger house. Close your eyes and open your hand."

The stress of moving seems like the last thing she'd want to add to her plate. I close my eyes, then open my hand.

Something is placed on my hand before she closes my fingers around it. "You can look now."

When I unwrap my fingers, a little car with a family of four pegs sits in the palm of my hand. I look into her eyes, not wanting to jump to conclusions, though I already am in the best of ways. Please let this be true.

She says, "Don't get too excited. It's not triplets."

"You're pregnant?" I ask, a smile cracking my cheeks wide open.

"I am." She caresses my face. "Are you ready to be a daddy again?"

"Abso-fucking-lutely." Tilting her down, I kiss her until we're both breathless and left laughing in pure happiness. This is what life is about.

I remember everything about the woman in my arms from when I first saw her across the party. Dark-brown hair, those eyes that stole my soul. Sunset tights. A smile that could compete with her halo. And feel fucking lucky that I was arrogant enough to twist the fates and take a chance. We didn't work out then, but she's all mine now.

"I love you, husband."

I kiss her and whisper against her lips, "I love you, wife."

"Daddy?" Reed calls me.

Because of them, and a new little one on the way, I'm the luckiest guy in the world. "Yeah, buddy?"

"Come see the ducks."

Story hops off my lap and waits for me to stand. Our hands come together, and we start walking in the direction of our son. He's waving frantically for us to hurry, but sometimes, it's good to take things slow. I lean down and kiss her on the head. "Thank you."

"For what?"

"Everything."

Smiling up at me, she says, "This is a good day."

"The best."

This is the *Story* of my life, told in two chapters—*before and after*—we met. We might have started in a storm, but it's only blue skies ahead.

YOU MIGHT ALSO ENJOY

<u>Recommendations</u> - Three books I think you'll enjoy reading after Best I Ever Had, in addition to We Were Once. All are stand-alones that will grab your heart and carry it through the story.

READ FOR FREE IN KINDLE UNLIMITED

Everest - I let her slip through my fingers once. I won't make that mistake twice. Secrets broke us apart. Can a second chance bring us back together?

READ NOW

Missing Grace - You will be on the edge of your seat with your heart on the line as two soul mates fight for the future stolen from them.

READ NOW

Never Got Over You - When once time isn't enough comes a sweep you off your feet second chance romance. Free in Kindle Unlimited.

READ NOW

WE WERE ONCE

Published in the United States of America
ISBN: 978-1-940071-94-7

PROLOGUE

I've never died before, but I recognize the feeling.

CHAPTER 1

Chloe Fox

"Promise me you'll protect Frankie with your life, Chloe."

Glancing sideways, I find it hard to take this seriously. "Um . . ."

My mom hugs Frankie to her chest like the son she never had. "You'll give him a good home, feed him, and nurture him?"

I think this is taking it a little too far. "It's a plant, Mom, not a human."

"It's not just a plant. It's a bonsai tree. They're fickle creatures—"

"Technically, it's not a creature. It's a miniature tree."

"Creature or not, promise me you'll take care of it, Chloe. This isn't just a plant. This little guy can provide harmony and calm to your place."

"Mom, I got it." I attempt to pry the potted plant from her, but when she resists, I ask, "Do you want to keep Frankie? He'd love New York City. You can take him to

Central Park or a show on Broadway. A quick trip to MoMA or the Statue of Liberty—"

"Very funny." She shoves him toward me. "Take him. I bought him for you."

"We can set up a visitation schedule if you'd like?"

That earns me an eye roll that's punctuated with laughter. "You might think I'm being dramatic, but I can already tell this is what your apartment is missing. I wish you'd let me decorate it more. So, mock me if you must, but that little guy is going to bring balance to your life."

"It's a lot of pressure to put on a plant, don't you think?"

"Little tree," she corrects stubbornly as if I've insulted the thing. Crossing her arms over her chest, she raises a perfectly shaped eyebrow. "You want to be a doctor, Chloe. Treat it like a patient. Water, attention, and care. The basics."

Holding the plant in front of me, I admire the pretty curve to the trunk and branches. It's easy to see why my mom picked this one. "I'll try not to kill it like the plant you gave me last year." I set the plastic pot down on top of a stack of textbooks on the coffee table. "But you have to admit that I gave that ivy a great send-off."

"You did. Right down the trash shoot." She laughs again, but I hear the sadness trickling in.

"Why are you getting upset?"

The green of my mom's eyes matches the rich color of the leaves when she cries, just like mine. "I think the bonsai has had enough water for one day. Don't you think?" I ask teasingly to hide how much I hate the impending goodbye.

She laughs, caressing my cheek. The support she's always shown me is felt in her touch. "I've had the best time with you over the past few weeks. I'm going to miss you, honey."

Leaning into it, I say, "If everything goes to plan, I'll be in the city next year, and we can see each other all the time."

"You've worked hard. Now it's time to enjoy your senior year." Her departure pending, we embrace.

"I enjoy working hard, and my grades still matter this year if I want to get into med school."

A sympathetic smile creases her lips when she steps back. "I'm sorry you feel you have to be perfect all the time or that you feel medical school is the only option for you. It's not. You can do—"

"It's what *I* want." This subject was the final blow to her marriage to my dad. They disagreed about a lot, but my schooling and future were the sticking points. I don't want to relive it.

Moving to the couch, she fluffs a pillow, but I have a feeling it's only out of habit. "Seeking perfection is the easiest way to find disappointment." She eyes the pillow, satisfaction never reaching her eyes. Standing back, she swings her gaze my way. "Happiness is a much nobler mission."

After she divorced my father, she put it into practice. After leaving Newport for Manhattan two years ago, she's happier than ever. "I know you have big plans, Chloe, but you're only young once. Go out with Ruby. Have fun. Kiss boys. You're allowed to do what you want instead of what others want for you. You're allowed to be you."

Be me? The words strike me oddly. "Who am I?"

"Ah, sweet girl, whoever you want to be. New experiences will allow you to see yourself through a new lens."

I sit on the couch, blocking her view of the pillow she just fixed. "Is that why you left Newport?"

"Yes, I wanted to discover me again. In Manhattan, I'm not Norman's wife or the chair of the preservation society.

I'm not running an eight-thousand-square-foot house or hosting garden parties. In New York, I get to be Cat Fox and Chloe's mother. Those are my favorite roles I've ever had."

Working with my father might have been great for my résumé, but back home, I'll always be compared to the great Norman Fox. I'll live in his shadow if I return to Rhode Island and won't ever stand on my own accomplishments. So I understand what she means a little too well. She seems to think she was saved. *Is it too late for me?*

"Do you know who you are?"

"I'm learning every day. All I'm saying is life is happening all around you. Look up from the books every now and then."

Turning around, she takes one last glance around the apartment. "You need a pop of color in here. I can send sofa pillows."

I get what she's saying. She's the queen of décor and has strong opinions regarding my life. She'd love to not only throw some pillows on my couch but also put a man in my life.

She never understood that good grades are much more rewarding than spending time with boys who want nothing more than a one-night stand. "Don't send pillows," I say, grinning.

A sly grin rolls across her face. "You can snuggle with them, or a guy—"

"You want me to date." I sigh. "I get it."

"College guys aren't the same as high school boys." She takes her purse from the couch and situates it on her shoulder as she moves to the door.

I roll my eyes. "Could have fooled me."

"You just haven't met someone who makes your heart flutter."

"You're such a romantic."

Kissing my cheek, she opens the door, and says, "Take care of yourself, honey. I love you."

"Love you, too." I close the door and rest against the back of it, exhaling. After two months of working at my father's clinic and then staying with her in the city for the past two weeks, I'd almost forgotten what it was like to have time to myself and silence. Pure, unadulterated—

Knock. Knock.

I jump, startled from the banging against my back. Spinning around, I squint to look through the peephole, and my chin jerks back.

A guy holding a bag outside my door says, "Food delivery."

"I didn't order food," I say, palms pressed to the door as I spy on him.

A smirk plays on his lips. Yup, he flat-out stares into the peephole with a smug grin on his face. Plucking the receipt from the bag, he adds, "Chloe?" The e is drawn out in his dulcet tone as if it's possible to make such a common name sound special. He managed it.

I unlock the deadbolt but leave the chain in place. When I open the door, I peek out, keeping my body and weight against it for safety.

Met with brown eyes that catch the setting sun streaming in from the window in the hall, there's no hiding the amusement shining in them. "Hi," he says, his gaze dipping to my mouth and back up. "Chloe?"

"I'm Chloe, but as I said, I didn't order food."

He glances toward the stairs, the tension in his shoulders dropping before his eyes return to mine. "I have the right address, the correct apartment, and name. I'm pretty sure it's for you." He holds it out after a casual shrug. "Anyway, it's getting cold, and it's chicken and dumplings, my mom's specialty that she only makes on Sundays. Trust me, it's better hot, though I've had it cold, and it was still good."

He makes a solid argument. All the information is correct. I shift, my guard dropping. I'm still curious, though. "Your mom made it?"

Thumbing over his shoulder as though the restaurant is behind him, he replies, "Only on Sundays. Me and T cook the rest of the time."

"Who's T?"

"The other cook." He turns the bag around. Patty's Diner is printed on the white paper. Then he points at his worn shirt, the logo barely visible from all the washings.

"And Patty is your mother?"

He swivels the bag around and nods. "Patty is my mom."

My stomach growls from the sound of the bag crinkling in his hands, reminding me that I haven't eaten in hours, and chicken and dumplings sounds amazing. Only "culinary cuisine," as my dad would call it, was acceptable when I was growing up. Comfort food didn't qualify because anything with gravy instead of some kind of reduction was a no-no.

Grinning, he pushes the bag closer. "As much as I'd love to stay here all night and chat about the mystery of this delivery, I have other food getting cold down in the car. You're hungry. Take the bag and enjoy." He says it like we're friends, and I'm starting to think we've spent enough time together to consider it.

I unchain the door and open it to take the bag from him. Holding up a finger, I ask, "Do you mind waiting? I'll get you a tip."

As if he won the war, two dimples appear as his grin grows. The cockiness reflected in his eyes doesn't take away from the fact that he's more handsome than I initially gave him credit for.

Handsome is a dime a dozen in Newport. Good genes passed down long before the Golden Age run in the prestigious family trees of Rhode Island. So good-looking guys don't do much beyond catch my eye.

He says, "I can wait." I pull my purse from the hook near the door and dig out my wallet. He fills the doorway, snooping over my shoulder. "Where are you running to?"

Huh? I look up, confused by the question. "Nowhere."

Following his line of sight, I realize what he's referring to just as he says, "The treadmill. That's the point. You never get anywhere."

"It's good exercise."

"Yeah," he says, his tone tipping toward judgmental. "You're just running in a circle. Stuck in place."

"I'm not trying to go anywhere. I'm—"

"Sure, you are."

When I answered the door, I wasn't expecting to have my life scrutinized under a microscope. "Why do I feel like you're speaking in metaphors?"

"I don't know. Why *do* you feel like I'm speaking in metaphors?" His tongue is slick and his wit dry, which is something I can appreciate, even when it's at my expense.

Handing him a ten, I say, "Hopefully, this covers the therapy."

He chuckles. "I'm always happy to dole out free advice, but I'll take the ten. Thanks." Still looking around, the detective moves his attention elsewhere. "Nice bonsai."

"Thanks. My mom gave me Frankie."

"Frankie?"

I tuck my wallet back in my purse and return it to the hook. "The little tree?"

Eyeing the plant, I can tell he wants to get a closer look by how he's inching in. He says, "Bonsais aren't miniature trees. They're just pruned to be that way. It's actually an art form."

"You seem to know a lot more about it than I do," I reply, stepping sideways to cut off his path. "Are you a plant guy?"

"I like to know all kinds of things about plants. Mainly the ones we eat. I wouldn't suggest sautéing Frankie, though."

"Why would I sauté Frankie?" I catch his deadpan expression. "Ah. You're making a joke. Gotcha." I laugh under my breath. "You're referring to food."

"Yeah."

I take the door in hand as a not so subtle hint. "I should get back to . . ." I just end it before the lie leaves my lips. I have no plans but to study, and that sounds boring even to me. "Thanks again." I'm surprised, though, when he doesn't move. "Don't let me keep you from those other deliveries." *Hint. Hint. Hint.*

He remains inches from me, and I look up when he says, "Thanks for the tip."

"You're welcome."

Shoving the money in his pocket, he rocks back on his heels. "Hope you enjoy the food."

Pulling the door with me as he passes, I remain with it pressed to my backside. "I'm sure I will."

"Anytime." I barely glimpse his grin before he turns abruptly to leave. Then he stops just shy of maneuvering down the stairs and looks back. "You need balance in your life."

Shock bolts my eyes wide open, and my mouth drops open as offense takes over. Standing in my discomfort, I consider closing the door and ending this conversation. But

I step forward instead, leaning halfway out. "Maybe you need balance."

Through a chuckle, he replies, "The bonsai. You said your mom gave you the plant. She thinks you need balance in your life. Mine gave me calm. Mom knows best. That's all I'm saying."

Pulling the door, I take a step back, glancing at him one last time. "Thanks, professor," I remark.

"Have a good life, Chloe." His laughter bounces off the walls of the hallway.

I shut the door, bolting the lock and attaching the chain, not needing the last word. "I will," I say to myself. After a quick peek out of the peephole again to verify he left, I set the bag next to the stack of books and take a second look at the plant. "By the way he was looking at you, I thought he was going to plant-nap you, Frankie." He sure was all up in this little guy's business.

Must be a biology major.

I begin to unpack the bag, trying to ignore how his presence and the faint scent of his cologne still linger but notice how it feels a few degrees warmer. "I wouldn't blame him," I tell Frankie. "You're a beautiful specimen."

Getting up, I lower the thermostat before trying to figure out who sent the food. With perfect timing, my phone begins buzzing across the coffee table. I race back to catch a text from my best friend: *If you hear from me in ten minutes, call me right back.*

Quick to respond, I type: *Another bad date?*

Ruby Darrow, the heiress to the Darrow Enterprises, and I have been close since we roomed together freshman year. I can't wait for her to move into her apartment next door. Her return message reads: *I'm not sure. If you hear from me, then yes. Yes, it is.*

Me: *I'm on standby.*

Ruby: *Because you're the best.*

I take my duties as her friend very seriously, so I set the phone down next to the bag and pop open the plasticware. When my phone buzzes again, I'm fully prepared to make the call, but this time it's not Ruby.

Mom: *I had food delivered for you. Did you get it? Chicken and dumplings. I'm in the mood for comfort food and thought you might be, too.*

I wish I would have known ten minutes ago. Eyeing the bag, I smile. I can't argue with her choice of dish, but I'm just not sure if the pain in the ass delivery was worth the trouble.

Even a baseball cap flipped backward didn't hinder his appearance because, apparently, I just discovered I have a type. Small-town hero with a side of arrogance. *Jesus.* This is Connecticut, not Texas.

Despite his appearance, I wasn't impressed. Dating cute guys has not worked out well for me in the past. The local bad boy doesn't fit into my plans or help with my "balance" as he points out I evidently need.

So rude.

I balance just fine. School. Trying to think of more, I get frustrated. I'm at Yale for one reason and one reason only—to get into the medical school of my choice—and to do that, I need to keep my brain in the game. The school game, not the dating game. "What does he know anyway, Frankie?"

Returning my mom's text, I type: *Got it. Thank you.*

Mom: *Promise me you'll live a little, or a lot, if you're so inclined.*

She's become a wild woman in the past two years. I'm happy for her, but that doesn't mean I have to change my ways to fit her new outlook on life.

As I look around my new apartment, the cleanliness brings a sense of calm to me. After living in my parents' homes over the summer, it feels good to be back at school and on my own again.

Me: *That's a lot of promises. First, caring for Frankie, and now for my own well-being.* I laugh at my joke, but I know she'll misinterpret it, so I'm quick to add: *Kidding. I will. Love you.*

Mom: *Hope so. Live fearlessly, dear daughter. Love you.*

Feeling like I dodged another lecture on "you're only young once," I smile like a kid on Christmas when I find a chocolate chip cookie in the bag. With just one bite of the food, I close my eyes, savoring the flavor. "Patty sure knows how to cook."

I click on a trivia game show and spend the time kicking the other contestants' butts as I eat.

Soon, I'm stuffed but feeling antsy about the dough sitting at the bottom of my stomach, so I get up and slip my sneakers on before hopping on the treadmill. I warm up for a mile with that bag and the red logo staring back at me, so I pick up the pace until I'm sprinting. "I'm not trying to go anywhere. It's good exercise," I grumble, still bothered by what the delivery guy said. A bleacher seat therapist is the last thing I need.

I start into a jog and then a faster speed, though my gaze keeps gravitating toward the bag and the red printing on the front—Patty's Diner. The food might have been delicious, but I can't make a habit out of eating food that heavy or I won't be able to wear the new clothes my mom and I just spent two weeks shopping for.

I barely make four miles before my tired muscles start to ache. I'm not surprised after a day of moving, but I still wished I could have hit five. I hit the stop button and give in to the exhaustion.

I take a shower and change into my pajamas before going through my nightly routine—brushing teeth, checking locks, turning out the lights, and getting a glass of water. I only take a few sips before I see Frankie in the living room all alone. My mom's guilt was well-placed. I dump water in the pot and bring it with me into the bedroom. "Don't get too comfortable. You're not staying here."

Returning to the living room to grab my study guide for the MCAT, I hurry back to bed and climb under the covers. But after a while, I set the guide aside, behavioral sciences not able to hold my attention against my mom's parting words.

Classes. Study. Rest. Routines are good. They're the backbone of success. I click off the lamp, not needing my mom's words—*live fearlessly*—filling my head. Those thoughts are only a distraction to my grand plan. *Like that delivery guy.*

We Were Once is now available in ebook, paperback, and audiobook.

ALSO BY S.L. SCOTT

To keep up to date with her writing and more, visit her website:
www.slscottauthor.com

To receive the scoop about all of her publishing adventures, free
books, giveaways, steals and more:

CLICK HERE

Join S.L.'s Facebook group here: S.L. Scott Books

Read the Bestselling Book that's been called **"The Most Romantic
Book Ever"** by readers and have them raving. We Were Once is
now available and FREE in Kindle Unlimited.

We Were Once

Audiobooks on Audible - CLICK HERE

Complementary to Best I Ever Had

We Were Once

Missing Grace

Everest

Until I Met You

New York Love Stories (Stand-Alones)

Never Got Over You

The One I Want

Crazy in Love

Head Over Feels

Hard to Resist Series (Stand-Alones)

The Resistance

The Reckoning

The Redemption

The Revolution

The Rebellion

The Crow Brothers (Stand-Alones)

Spark

Tulsa

Rivers

Ridge

The Crow Brothers Box Set

DARE - A Rock Star Hero (Stand-Alone)

The Everest Brothers (Stand-Alones)

Everest - Ethan Everest

Bad Reputation - Hutton Everest

Force of Nature - Bennett Everest

The Everest Brothers Box Set

The Kingwood Series

SAVAGE

SAVIOR

SACRED

FINDING SOLACE - Stand-Alone

The Kingwood Series Box Set

THANK YOU

You are amazing.

Thank you for trusting me with your time, for allowing me to hold your hand along these emotional journeys, and for opening your heart to my books. I can only do this because of you. Thank you! XO, Suzie

To my team (Adriana, Andrea, Danielle R.., Dani S., Elizabeth B., Erin S., Jenny S., Kristen, Letitia, Michele),

I am so grateful for your kindness, speed, support, encouragement, and patience. I only got to the end because of you being a part of this crazy ride. I love you and cherish you endlessly,

Suzie

Love always to my world - my family <3

FOLLOW ME

To keep up to date with her writing and more, visit S.L. Scott's website: **www.slscottauthor.com**

To receive the newsletter about all of her publishing adventures, free books, giveaways, steals and more:

https://geni.us/intheknow

Follow me on TikTok: https://geni.us/SLTikTok
Follow on IG: https://geni.us/IGSLS
Follow on Bookbub: https://geni.us/SLScottBB